P9-CDB-624

The Death Ship of Dartmouth

Also by Michael Jecks

The Last Templar
The Merchant's Partner
A Moorland Hanging
The Crediton Killings
The Abbot's Gibbet
The Leper's Return
Squire Throwleigh's Heir
Belladonna at Belstone
The Traitor of St Giles
The Boy-Bishop's Glovemaker
The Tournament of Blood
The Sticklepath Strangler
The Devil's Acolyte
The Mad Monk of Gidleigh
The Templar's Penance
The Outlaws of Ennor
The Tolls of Death
The Chapel of Bones
The Butcher of St Peter's
A Friar's Bloodfeud

The Death Ship of Dartmouth

Michael Jecks

headline

First published in Great Britain in 2006
by HEADLINE BOOK PUBLISHING

An imprint of Headline Book Publishing

1

Cataloguing in Publication Data is available from the British Library

ISBN 0 7553 2301 7

Typeset in Times by Avon DataSet Ltd,
Bidford-on-Avon, Warwickshire

Printed and bound in Great Britain by
Clays Ltd, St Ives plc

Headline's policy is to use papers that are natural, renewable and recyclable
products and made from wood grown in sustainable forests. The logging and
manufacturing processes are expected to conform to the environmental
regulations of the country of origin.

HEADLINE BOOK PUBLISHING
A division of Hodder Headline
338 Euston Road
London NW1 3BH

www.headline.co.uk
www.hodderheadline.com

This book is for Webb and Welk.

Good friends for more years than
I can remember.

Cast of Characters

Sir Baldwin de Furnshill	The Keeper of the King's Peace, Sir Baldwin is known as a committed seeker after the truth.
Simon Puttock	A stannary bailiff, Puttock has been a friend of Baldwin's for eight years, since 1316. Recently he was promoted to act as the Keeper of the Port (see *Glossary*) of Dartmouth's representative in the town.
Rob	A teenaged youth who has been taken on by Simon as his servant while he lives in Dartmouth.
Stephen	The latest in a line of clerks to Simon.
Sir Andrew de Limpsfield	A man-at-arms in the service of Lord Hugh Despenser.
Sir Richard de Welles	Coroner to the King, from Lifton in Devon.
John Hawley	One of the four major merchants and shipowners in the town.
Peter Strete	Clerk to John Hawley.
Paul Pyckard	The second of the leading merchants of the town, Pyckard is suffering from a terminal illness.
Adam	Loyal and devoted to Pyckard, his master, Adam is an excellent captain and leader of men.
Gilbert	One of Pyckard's best shipmasters, Gil is a well-known and respected captain.

Moses	Pyckard's closest and most trusted servant, who is like a son to him.
Danny	Moses's younger brother, Danny chose to serve their master by joining his fleet and became a good sailor.
Philip Kena	The third local merchant, Kena is eager to advance himself.
Hilary Beauley	The fourth of the leading merchants, Beauley is the youngest and most ambitious.
Hamo	Cooper to the ships in Dartmouth's haven.
Hamund Chugge	A confessed murderer, Chugge has decided to abjure the realm (see *Glossary*).
Ivo le Bel	Although a sergeant and upholder of the law, Ivo is not known either for his courage or his intelligence.
Odo	Vincent's closest companion, he is a good sailor, albeit a harsh leader.
Henry Pyket	Known in Dartmouth as one of the best shipbuilders and wrights.
Vincent	Despite his brutality, Vincent is nevertheless respected for his courage and seamanship.
Alred Paviour	A notable professional, Alred is a roadmaker, or paver.
Bill	Bill has worked with Alred for many years.
Law	The youngest of the trio, Law is apprenticed to Alred.
Cynegils	An old sailor fallen on hard times.
Emma	Cynegil's daughter.
Sieur Pierre de Caen	A French knight who has recently been living in the Queen's household.
Bishop Walter II	Baldwin's friend, Walter Stapledon, Bishop of Exeter.

Glossary

Abjurer — A man who was accused of a felony could agree to 'abjure the realm'. He would be taken from his sanctuary and led to the gate or stile of the local churchyard, and there made to swear an oath to leave the country. If he deviated from the instruction given by the Coroner, any man could behead him on sight.

Alaunt — Large, tenacious hunting dog: a cross between a mastiff and a greyhound.

Cog — The basic ship of the medieval English merchant navy, the cog was clinker-built i.e. having a hull constructed with overlapping planks. A strong vessel, it could have castles added fore and aft, when required for war.

Futtock — A large framing timber that doesn't reach as high as the **sheer** or as low as the keel.

Halyard — The main rope used to raise and lower the **yard**.

Hulk — Conjecturally from the Greek *holkas* – a towed ship or merchantman. The hulk had no keel. Instead, the **strakes** met at the **sheer** at the prow and the stern. The hull was uniquely curved as a result.

Keeper of the Port — In 1319 the Abbot of Tavistock was made Warden of the Devon Stannaries and Keeper of the Port of Dartmouth for ten years. He had a lease of all revenues for an annual fee

	of £100. This meant that the Abbot could take all customs from Dartmouth. A good 'farm' indeed!
Ratlines	Horizontal ropes set to create a ladder up to the **yards**.
Sheer, sheerline	Of a hull, the upper section.
Sheet	With square-sailed ships, this was the rope that led to the bottom corners of the sail. Loosening or tightening this rope would change the angle of the sail to the wind.
Strake	Each long plank that ran horizontally along the hull, from stem to stern. Usually these overlapped the strake below.
Thwart	A plank on which a rower could sit.
Wale	A thicker **strake** than others. When guns were introduced, this led to the stronger strakes being termed 'gunwales'.
Yard	A wooden spar slung from a mast and used for suspending a sail.

Author's Note

This novel is partly based around the terrible Affair of the Silken purses, in which the Queen of England, Isabella, saw gifts which she had embroidered herself and given to her sisters-in-law, being flaunted on the belts of three knights. In an age of Courtly Love, giving little tokens to a knight was hardly unknown, but to the Queen it must have seemed inappropriate, to say the least, for her brothers' wives to give away her gifts.

Such treatment must have rankled. And so she went to her father, the King of France, and told him. I wonder whether she realised how catastrophic the results of this act would be? It led to the death of one sister-in-law, life-imprisonment for another, and it almost certainly caused the early death of her beloved father.

Many times I have been asked whether I use the internet much for research. This book is a prime example of why the internet is of no use whatsoever to a serious researcher, other than as a guide as to where to look for further information.

When looking into the matter of the silk purses, I first consulted my own collection of books, then went to the web to see what I could glean from there. It was wonderful. I found lots of reports of the 'Case of the Tour de Nesle' as the matter became known. However, no one account was the same. I do not propose to go into the variations available on the web, but suffice it to say that I have so far come up with *five* different estimates of Isabella's birthday. The problem with the web is, you can never tell whether the research is genuine or whether it was compiled during an hour's tedium by an acne-ridden youth from Idaho.

The great advantage of a book written by one such as Doherty, Weir or Mortimer (see my list at the end of this *Author's Note*) is that the publisher will have checked the credentials of the writer; the latter will have gone to great lengths to validate any conclusions he or she has reached; the editors will have gone through their material in detail, and copy editors and others will have added their own five penn'orth. This is why I have more faith in words written on paper than material on computer.

What I also rely on, to a greater or lesser degree, is my own gut-feel based on two decades of research. Usually I can make a good estimate of what might have happened in the past, and on the occasions when I've not been able to confirm facts, it has astonished me how regularly I have been proved right subsequently.

Of course, the problem for an historian is that many of the original histories were themselves written decades or even centuries after the events; we are relying on the words of chroniclers like Froissart and hoping he had good sources. Froissart was probably born about 1337, and didn't get to England until about 1361, so he certainly did not write about Isabella from the perspective of a first-hand witness.

This book is set almost entirely in the beautiful Devon port of Dartmouth. At the time of this story, Dartmouth consisted of three different areas: Tunstal up on the hill; Hardness down at the river's edge but north of the mill pool; Clifton, south of the mill pool. The southernmost part of Dartmouth, which is still known as Southtown (a name first recorded in 1328), was a separate administrative district in 1324, a part of the neighbouring manor of Stoke Fleming, and was only brought into Dartmouth's borough officially in 1463. I'm afraid I've let Baldwin and Simon play fast and loose with the borough boundaries in this book, because the alternative would have been to have a novel that was even longer than this one turned out to be!

Dartmouth has always been a very important part of Britain's history. It had a marvellous deep-water harbour that was first used for the Second Crusade in 1147 and the Third Crusade in 1190. There was space for hundreds of ships, and it became a popular naval port because it was relatively easily defended as well as being superbly well sheltered.

As the years passed, Dartmouth grew in importance. It depended originally on cloth exports from Totnes, but with the acquisition of large parts of south-western France by Henry II's marriage to Eleanor of Aquitaine, the city expanded with the wine trade.

One of Dartmouth's most famous sons is John Hawley. However, the keen-eyed reader will wonder how it was that he could have so stimulated Chaucer during a meeting in (probably) 1373 or so that Chaucer wrote about The Shipman in his *Canterbury Tales*, based on a man who was already a reasonable age in 1324. Well, the John Hawley of Chaucer's time was the son of *another* John Hawley. It seems clear to me that the Hawleys were simply following that good old tradition of re-using a perfectly adequate Christian name. 'If "John" worked for father and grandfather, it'll do for the lad' seems to have been the attitude. I have no idea whether the John Hawley who so impressed Chaucer had a grandfather also called John, but it is not an unreasonable assumption.

The two books I would recommend for anyone seeking a little more information about Dartmouth, if you can find them, are W.G. Hoskyns's mammoth tome *Devon*, published by Devon Books in 1954 and updated regularly since. The other book is *Dartmouth* by Percy Russell, published by BT Batsford Ltd in 1950.

In the course of my search for accurate information about Isabella, her husband Edward II, and the appalling Despensers, I have acquired a goodly library. To any reader, I can heartily recommend the following titles, in no particular order. Alison Weir's marvellous *Isabella – She-Wolf of France, Queen of England* (Jonathan Cape, 2005); Charles Hopkinson and Martin Speight's *The Mortimers – Lords of the March* (Logaston Press, 2002); *Edward II* by Mary Saaler (Rubicon Press, 1997); the excellent *The Greatest Traitor, The Life of Sir Roger Mortimer, 1st Earl of March, Ruler of England 1327–1330* by Ian Mortimer (Jonathan Cape, 2003); Harold F. Hutchinson's *Edward II – The Pliant King* (Eyre & Spottiswode, 1971); Paul Doherty's *Isabella and the Strange Death of Edward II*

(Constable, 2003); not forgetting Michael Prestwich's *The Three Edwards – War and State in England, 1272–1377* (Weidenfeld & Nicolson, 1980) and R. Perry's *Edward the Second – Suddenly, at Berkeley* (Ivy House, 1988) – and last but certainly not least, Georges Duby's *France in the Middle Ages 987–1460* (Blackwell, 1991).

A final thought: as always, any errors or omissions are my own responsibility . . .

. . . or the fault of the teenager from Idaho. May his acne never fade if he has led me astray!

Michael Jecks
North Dartmoor
October 2005

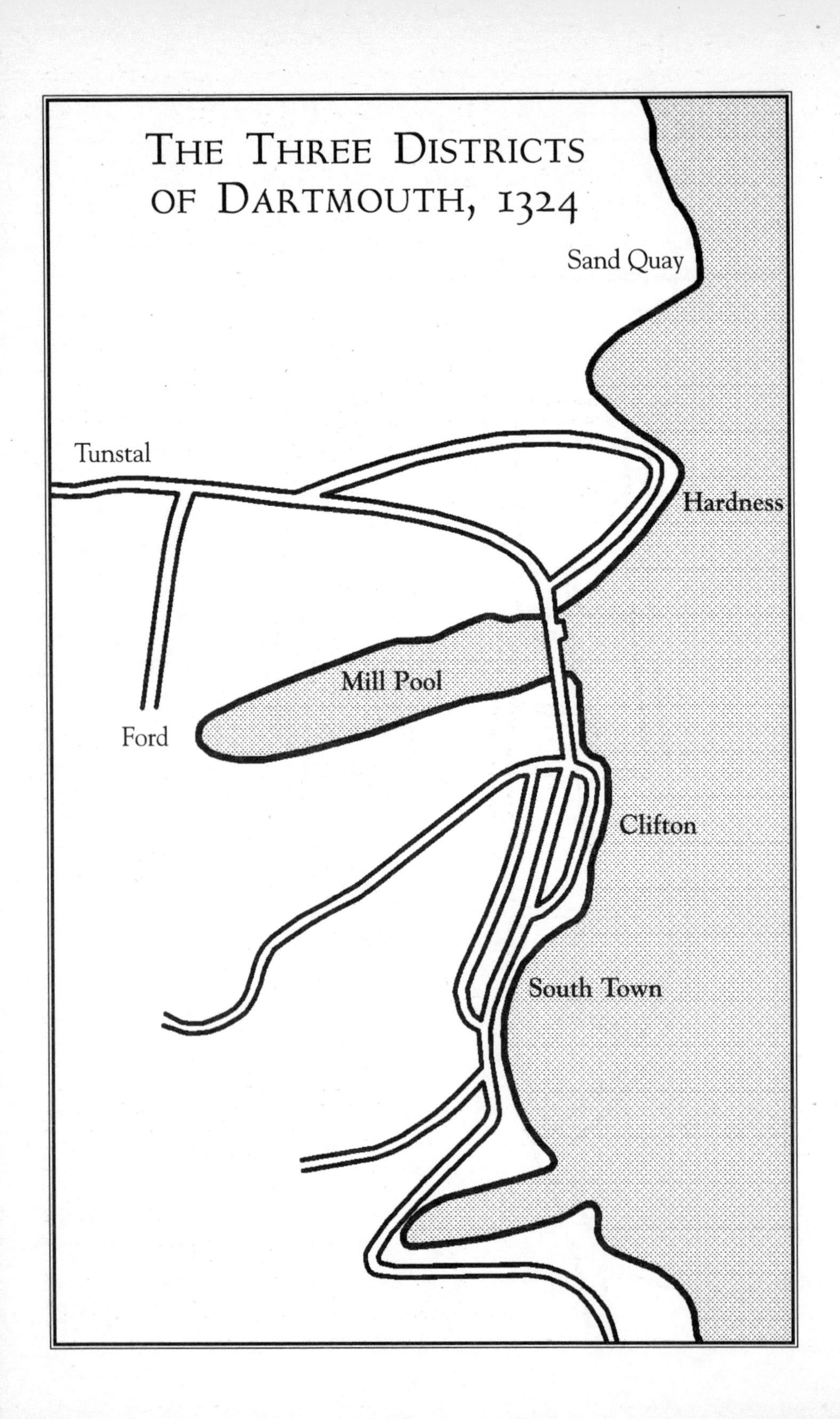
THE THREE DISTRICTS OF DARTMOUTH, 1324
Sand Quay
Tunstal
Hardness
Mill Pool
Ford
Clifton
South Town

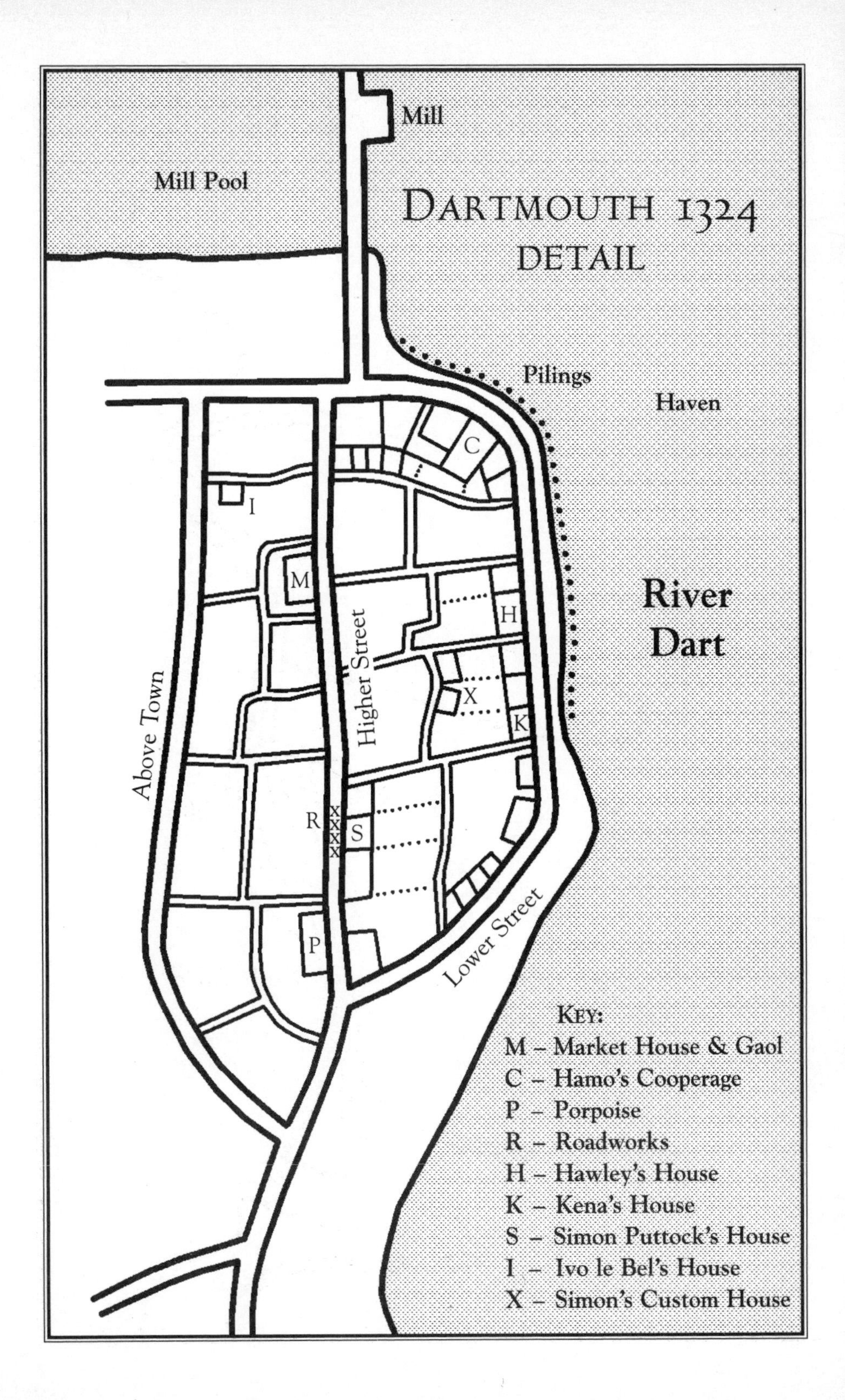
Mill
Mill Pool
DARTMOUTH 1324
DETAIL
Pilings
Haven
River
Dart
C
I
M
H
X
K
Higher Street
Above Town
R
S
P
Lower Street
KEY:
M – Market House & Gaol
C – Hamo's Cooperage
P – Porpoise
R – Roadworks
H – Hawley's House
K – Kena's House
S – Simon Puttock's House
I – Ivo le Bel's House
X – Simon's Custom House

Prologue

Late summer 1309, off the Breton Coast.

Danny would remember that night for the rest of his days.

He was heartily sick as the wind came up and a powerful gale started blowing from the south-south-west. Only a boy, he had been put on this ship after his father had died. He was an orphan, along with his older brother Moses. Their mother had been gone these last three years, and their father went down a month ago when his little fishing boat was caught in a storm.

There was a crack, and he felt the ship heel over. The shock was enough to stir him from his bleak mood.

This was an older ship. The decking was loose board to give quick access to the hold beneath, and the open deck was where the crew slept, under heavy canvas awnings, hoping that the weather and spray would not persecute them too much. From all Danny had experienced so far, that was a forlorn hope. At the rear of the ship was a castle, underneath which was the solitary cabin where the ship's master would normally sleep.

Even though he was so young and on his first voyage, Danny could tell that the ship was suffering greatly. The mast was groaning, the canvas taut and straining, while all the sheets hummed with the wind. At the top of the mast, the great flag snapped and curled like a whip with every change in wind-direction. It was reassuring that the older hands like Vincent and Odo were not overly troubled. Or if they were, they didn't show it.

The men ran to the ratlines, clambering aloft and spreading out over the yards, and when Odo gave the order, they began hauling the sail up, in an attempt to tie it off and stop the hectic wind from ravaging it.

That was when they had the first disaster of the long night. Even as Danny stood, trembling with weakness and nausea, there was a scream, and one of the younger sailors slipped from his position near the mast itself.

The seamen depended on their horny feet maintaining a firm footing on the rope that ran under the yard, bellies hooked over the top as they hauled up the sail. This lad was one of the new young members of the crew; his feet were less hardened, and his foot slipped. As the ship swayed beneath him, he lost his balance and fell. One hand clutching wildly at a rope as he toppled, at last he grasped it. But it was a near-vertical sheet, and as he plummeted to the deck the palm of his hand was rasped away, leaving a smear of blood all down the hemp. There was a scream, followed by a crunch like a lettuce being hit by a mallet. Then, silence.

If the lad hadn't died, perhaps the men could have reefed the sail, but as they stared in horror, it was too late and disaster struck them all. The sail flapped loose and then tore in half. In moments, the two halves were shredding, and now a tattered medley of flags were curling overhead. Long strips detached themselves and flew off ahead, chased by the wind that drove the ship on – and that was when Danny knew he must soon die. He scarcely noticed the door opening to the master's cabin. He was staring at the boy's body as it flopped about on deck with the ship's roll; in that corpse, he saw himself.

Without a home, or any family apart from Moses, who was nine, the seven year old would have starved, were it not for the charity of the Church and the kindness of his benefactor. Master Paul Pyckard had sometimes used his father as crew on his ships, and when he heard of the two boys' plight, he had his men seek them out. Before long, Adam, the sailor with the enormous beard, had tracked him down and taken him in, and the lad had been thankful for the offer of a warm cot for the night. To his delight, there was a fire in the morning, and bread and dripping to eat, washed down with as much ale as he could hold. At the time, still weak after the years of famine, and without food for almost three days, other than scraps from the church, young Danny had scoffed so much, he had promptly brought it all back up, but from that day he began to recover. Now, a month later, he was still weakly, and feeling alone and vulnerable but so much better than before.

Adam had become his closest friend. Reliable, always cheerful, he was Pyckard's most trusted lieutenant, and just as it was only natural that Danny should pay his way by serving on Pyckard's ships, it was as natural that he should want to serve with Adam. Moses had been taken in to live with Master Pyckard, and was settling in happily, learning the work of a servant.

Usually Adam would not have been on this craft, an older cog of some twenty tuns called the *Saint Rumon*, but she was strong enough, else Master Pyckard would never have let his most valued possession, his beautiful French wife, travel in her.

Madam Amandine was as sweet as a sister to Danny. He could admire her beauty, with the juvenile appreciation that noted perfection of form without lust. Amandine was slender and pale-skinned, with a slight peach tone to her cheeks. Her eyes were set wide apart under a high, intelligent brow, and her oval face was regular and unmarked with signs of pox or scurvy, so rare in these years of starvation. She was kind and gentle, and Danny worshipped her, as did the other men on board; she was respectful and attentive even with the lowliest sailors. And when, as now, she suffered from the dreadful consequences of a not-strong belly and vomited, the crew fought to take her little tidbits which were 'guaranteed to settle her gut' as the men all believed. It had taken some persuasion from Adam to make them leave the poor woman in peace after their ministrations began to make her feel even worse.

Rather than leaning over the sheer with him, she remained in her cabin with a bowl. Even over the wind, he could hear her wretchedly moaning. He joined in, spewing and retching as the ship lurched and rolled, men up at the yard attempting to replace the sail, until it grew clear that they could achieve nothing. It seemed to last the whole night. And then there was another, greater shuddering and wrenching, and men began to scream. Danny could hear the panic in their voices, and in the naked terror in the men's eyes, he saw death. They would drown. *He* would drown.

He had no fear. His father too had been killed in a storm. It was the way for a man to die when he spent his life at sea. No, Danny had no fear, but he did think regretfully of the life he would lose, just as he was beginning it with Master Pyckard.

There was another slamming shock and the ship seemed to settle.

'She's on the rocks, boys!'

Over the monstrous howling of the wind, Danny could hear a new noise. No, not hear: he could *feel* it through the soles of his feet. It was the crackle and shriek of a dying vessel as the water poured in through joints and seams, forcing timbers apart. He clung to a set of oaken planks that suddenly reared up from the loose decking, and lay on them as the ship began to break. Adam was at his side, a hand on his shoulder, peering at him with concern, and then he saw men running from the mast to the sides, desperate men who couldn't swim and who had nothing to cling to. Adam raced to the master's cabin, but as he went, Danny saw the door burst wide, and then the wall of the cabin fell away; he saw the green sea thundering through it, sweeping table, benches, pots and cots from inside. And in among it all was Amandine, with blood on her hands and legs as the timbers of the dying *Saint Rumon* flew about her.

And then a giant wave tossed him overboard, and all he knew was the searing pain of saltwater in his lungs and a roaring sound in his ears.

Chapter One

Devon, September 1324

Her tears stayed with him all the long night after he left her, but there was nothing he could do to dry them. Not now. Probably not ever.

Sieur Pierre de Caen would have taken her with him. He *longed* to. But she would have none of it. She was a woman of honour, and the shame of fleeing the realm with him would have been too much, even if the alternative would cost her life. It was a price worth paying, she said.

No! He had tried to reason with her, to show that she was mad to think of staying, and he toyed with the other possibility, of capturing her with hired men, and taking her away by force . . . but that would have made her hate him, and he couldn't bear the thought of her reproach.

Escape would have been so much easier from London. He could have joined a ship to leave for France, if there were any vessels from his homeland in port. If not, he had money enough to bribe his way on a small craft . . . But he wasn't in London. He had been with her in the household at Taunton when they had heard the news.

A man had to protect himself, and sometimes, just sometimes, he had to protect those who were dearest to him by leaving them. That was the truth, and he was glad he had chosen to flee. With luck, she would be safe, and he could take news of the King's actions – or Despenser's, if the truth be told – with him back to France.

There was a rasping sound behind him, and his heart began to pound. All the long journey here, he had feared betrayal and pursuit. He dared not turn, because to do that would prove to any hunter that the suspicions about their quarry were right. No one could see his face and doubt that he was guilty.

Had he been in London, this journey would have been so much easier and safer, for a man in the Queen's favour could still, just, gain immunity from the devils who obeyed the King's advisors, an immunity that was entirely lacking at a distant town like Taunton. There were too many places in the countryside where a man could be waylaid, with no one the wiser as to his name or title, let alone his position as a noble knight from the Queen's own household. Isabella had little authority in the land now.

There was another noise from behind him – the clatter of a heavy boot slipping over cobbles – and he smiled to himself grimly. It had taken him so long to lose the men he was sure would be following, he hadn't thought that others could catch up with him again so speedily, but everyone was so fearful of upsetting the King or his favourites that mouths could be opened without bribes. The mere threat of the King's displeasure was enough to make any peasant confess to what he had seen: a rider clad in dark blue and scarlet, riding a powerful black stallion.

So instead of making for the nearer coast, up to Bristol as they'd have expected, he'd thought it wiser to escape to the south, to Dartmouth.

At the time it had made perfect sense. Better by far to hurry south and seek a quiet little port which had reliable sailings. Dartmouth was not among the largest, where the King's officers would have too much control and interest in foreigners, but nor was it the smallest, where any stranger would stand out. He had been here before, and knew that the port had a deep haven from which ships could always sail with ease.

It was the delay in Exeter which had given him the problem. While he walked the streets of the old walled city, prayed on the hard stone floor of the Cathedral, or rested in a tavern near the Close, someone had seen him and sold the news of his arrival. Since Exeter, he had been sure that his steps were dogged. Well, it was no surprise. The King was convinced that Pierre was his sworn enemy. All because Pierre had fallen in love.

The shame of it! To know that he had won the heart of a nobleman's wife, a man to whom he owed his livelihood and fortune, that was appalling. There was no more contemptible crime than petty treason, but now he was guilty of it in his heart. And as soon as the opportunity provided itself, they were guilty of it in fact.

He hurried along the darkened street, then down a side alley, and thence back up to Lower Street and to a second alley. This he bolted down at full speed, hoping against hope to rush the man from behind. He would have managed it, too, if some lazy householder hadn't left a pile of trash lying in the middle of the alley. He saw it at the last moment and tried to leap it, but his foot caught, and he was sent sprawling. The noise wakened a dog, and he heard it barking furiously. Footsteps hurried towards his alley, and he made a swift decision to go on, racing at full pelt back up to the top road.

At the alley's entrance, he stood panting, his sword already in his hand as he cautiously set his shoulder to the wall and peered round, but there was nothing.

The silence was broken by rumbustious singing, and he saw a group of tattily dressed sailors half shuffling, half rolling in that curious manner they had when on firm land. They were all plainly more than a little drunk, from the songs they were singing and, as they passed him, Pierre was assailed by a gust of warm, ale-sodden breath. He thrust the sword back in its scabbard and slipped in behind them, trying to copy their gait. As they passed by the entrance to an inn, he left them and walked inside.

It was a poor enough place, with the thin scattering of reeds on the floor barely covering the packed earth. In the middle sat a smoking fire, with a trivet set over it, while at the farther end of the room were five barrels of ale.

Pierre made his way to the host, who stood with a thick apron over his enormous gut, and asked for a pint of ale. While he fingered a few pennies, he enquired whether there was a room available.

These Englishmen were pigs! In France, a man of quality might assume that if an innkeeper had no single room adequate that was free, a lesser fellow would be evicted. Here, he was told, and the man kept a straight face while he said it, there was only one room with two large beds, and all the clients could use them. However much Pierre fiddled with his cash, increasing the sum eventually to a shilling, the response was the same. It was unnerving to find a man like this innkeeper prepared to challenge a knight's instruction. Heaven forfend that such arrogance could come to the French peasantry!

It was surely a reflection of the trouble between France and England. A war made for bad manners.

He had hoped for a quiet room alone, but if that was impossible, he had other options. He agreed loudly to the room, paid up the full sum and then wandered to a table, his ale in his hand, and waited.

Three men soon entered one after the other. The first, clad in faded green tunic and worn hosen, with a knife hanging from a cord about his neck, was so plainly a sailor, from his horny hands to the weather-beaten face and grizzled beard, that Pierre could disregard him instantly as a spy. A paid assassin, perhaps, but not a spy. The second looked more the part: he was oddly clad in a good red jack over a fine woollen tunic, with a hood sitting far back on his head to show an eye with a devilish squint. Short and hunched, he looked desperate and dangerous, but as Pierre eyed him covertly, the newcomer roared sociably in welcome at a group of men near the bar and was soon engaged in raucous conversation.

The third seemed unlikely to be a spy. He wore a thick leather apron like a joiner or mason, and Pierre heard several men mutter something that sounded like 'paviour'. He strode past Pierre without a glance in his direction, to a table at which two others sat, one older, one apparently an apprentice.

Pierre was beginning to wonder whether he *had* been followed at all, for here it was at least thirty miles from Exeter alone, and surely he would have noticed someone on his trail . . . when a fourth man appeared in the doorway. He was an older fellow, and well used to rough living from the look of his shabby hosen and jack.

'Ho, Cynegils, are you coming in?' the host called over. 'You want an ale?'

It was plain enough that the man was a local, and a regular here at this inn, but although he nodded and grunted at the landlord, he remained on the threshold studying the room. When his eyes fell on Pierre, the Frenchman saw the flash of recognition in them, and knew he was dead meat.

With a poor display of casualness, Cynegils left the room and disappeared, strolling back in a few minutes later with a nonchalance that would not have deceived a blind beggar. He went to the bar with the host and sat down facing Pierre.

If Pierre had entertained any doubts about the man, the way the host peered at the newcomer was enough to dispel them.

'What you up to, Cyn?' he asked suspiciously.

'Nothing. Just get on and serve me, will you?'

There was a hurried discussion, and the landlord shot a confused glance at Pierre, but seeing the Frenchman's fixed stare, he hurriedly moved away to draw a jug of ale for Cynegils.

Pierre gave an elaborate yawn, stretched, and drained his pot. Rising, he made his way to the rear door which gave out to the sleeping chamber, so he understood. He stumbled slightly, like a man unused to strong ale, and shut the door before darting along the passageway and out into the inn's garden. There was an overwhelming stench of piss there, but at the moment Pierre cared nothing for that. He stepped behind the door, waiting.

Soon enough, he heard the door from the hall open quietly, and the sound of steps making their way down the passage, where they stopped.

Pierre debated whether to launch himself in through the door and tackle the man, but decided that if he did so, the fellow might scream to warn his companions, and they would be sure to come to their friend's defence. This Cynegils was known here. No, better that he wait here until the man had checked the bedchamber, and then hurried out to the garden to see how Pierre had made good his escape. Except he wasn't going to escape. He would hide here, catch the man and learn who had sent him.

But then suddenly there was a sharp knocking sound, then a rush of feet, and Pierre had to move away in alarm, as two men came barrelling out, a third held between them. The two looked at Pierre. It was the apron-clad workman and his older companion.

The apron-clad man looked Pierre up and down, then hawked and spat. 'This one was going to knock you on the head, I reckon.'

'You stopped him?' There was some doubt in Pierre's mind. These men had apparently helped him, but perhaps they were good at feigning. There had been a third at their table, he reminded himself. Where was *he*? Fetching the man who had paid this Cynegils?

'You want him or not?' the older man demanded. 'Personally I couldn't give a—'

'Calm down, Bill. He's just been close to having a blade through his back, and he's probably wondering about us. That's fine.' The man with the apron was eyeing Pierre with a knowing expression.

'Friends, I owe you my thanks.'

'Someone's watching for you,' the man said speculatively. 'I'd reckon you should find somewhere safer to stay the night.'

'I know one man,' Pierre said. 'But I don't know where he lives.'

The other nodded his head towards the back of the garden. 'If I was you, I'd be out of here now. There's a big gap in the wall, over there. The landlord's been trying to persuade me to get it fixed for him on the cheap. You can slip out there easy enough.'

Pierre needed no urging. He ran to the bottom of the garden and found the tumbled section, just as the man had said. Vaulting over it in an instant, he stood debating with himself, fear making him pant, and then he set off quickly but quietly round to the front of the inn again.

Further up the road, he noticed a paviour's trestles set up. The roadway was being repaved, he guessed, and that was his last thought as the blade settled on his back just behind his kidney.

Chapter Two

The appearance of the cog as she sailed into Dartmouth's harbour was so peculiar that the men found their eyes drawn away from the corpse at their feet. Even Hamo, who was no sailor, found himself distracted and turned to stare into the haven with all the others.

'Christ Jesus and all His saints,' he murmured.

Everyone had seen ships which had been knocked about in foul weather, but from the look of her, this was no simple disaster of wind and wave. Some other fate had overcome her, and Hamo had an idea he knew what it was. The timbers looked more black than pitch alone could have made them; the rigging, even to the cooper's untutored eye, was odd, as though it was all freshly replaced, and that in a hurry, while the mast was much too short.

In front of the cog was the *Christopher*, John Hawley's ship, and the sight of it made Hamo's lips twist into a grin. Yes, if Hawley had seen a rich prize like this, he would do his best to rescue her, in the hope of being able to keep her. Never a man to turn his nose up at a profit, was John Hawley.

'Wake up, you churls!' bawled Ivo le Bel, the local sergeant. 'Let's get this over with. Hamo, I know you want to get down there and sell some barrels, but that can wait, by God's pain! Sweet mother of Christ, look at his head!'

Hamo glanced back at the corpse just as Ivo le Bel clambered out of the hole. The sight made him swallow hard to keep his breakfast down. At his side, the scruffy stranger with his leather apron was making a fuss.

'What's he doing here in the road?' he whined. 'I just don't . . . Ach, if a man *has* to fall and kill himself, why should he wander up the road until he finds my hole and falls into that? Aren't there enough damned wells around here to fall into?'

Ivo le Bel shot him a look. 'Shut up, Paviour. There's nothing to be done about this, least of all whining. We'll have to get the Coroner here as soon as possible.'

'Good. Is there one in this borough?'

'Here?' Ivo gave a loud chuckle. 'No, we'll have to send for one. We're not big enough to justify our own down here.'

'Oh, no! I've got to get cracking with my work, or I'll be late. This is going to take days!'

Ivo shrugged. 'You can do what you want, man. It's no affair of mine. But if you try to move this body, I'll tell the Coroner *and* the Sheriff. There's no getting away from it. This poor fellow fell into your hole last night and brained himself on the rocks.'

Hamo the cooper peered down again. The trench here was quite deep, it was true. Alred, the paver, was here with his apprentice and labourer to mend several stretches of roadway that had begun to fall apart in the last few years; the burgesses were sick of the complaints from people saying that their carts couldn't travel up here any more. A sum had been agreed, and this Alred Paviour contacted. The man had travelled all the way down from Exeter. If anyone could mend the roads hereabouts, it was a professional like this Alred.

However, it had to be admitted, he *had* left the road here in a state last night. The street was in constant use, and yet he'd lifted a large area and left only one wooden trestle at each side to stop people from falling in during the hours of darkness. That was plain foolish, when there were so many taverns along this stretch. Look – the Porpoise was only a matter of yards away!

His eyes went back to the strange ship in the harbour. He saw the enormous splash as the anchor dropped into the water, even as a rowing boat started off from the shore. It headed for the *Christopher*, at the same time as a boat was launched from John Hawley's cog. Hamo could hear shouting, for noise always travelled clearly over the water here, but his ears could not discern any words. The little boats rocked on the gentle swell, men discussing the damaged cog, no doubt, and then the *Christopher*'s rowing boat lurched forward to the shore, while the second began a leisurely perambulation of the strange ship.

'It's not *my* fault,' the paver was grumbling on. 'The fool should have seen the barrier.'

'What barrier?' Ivo demanded.

'I had trestles and timber set up to stop anyone falling in – I'm not stupid!'

Ivo glanced about them. 'There's only the one trestle, so far as I can see. Where's the rest of the stuff, if you were so careful to put it all up? Because if you can't produce it, the Coroner's going to assume that you are lying, and that you put this man's life in danger.'

'Someone must have stolen them!'

'Really? I wonder if the Coroner's going to believe that. If no one else saw them, you'll be fined heavily.'

'I saw them, Sergeant.'

Ivo snapped his head around, but Hamo was already grinning to himself. He recognised that voice.

'Ah. Morning, Bailiff,' Ivo said warily.

The *Saint John* was sound at the waterline and below. That much was clear enough. The flames hadn't caught hold completely.

Henry Pyket was a good shipwright, and he had experience of rescuing cogs which had been badly damaged either in battle or foul weather. First, and most important, was to view the exterior and see whether the vessel was still seaworthy. His concern was to have her beached quickly for safety if necessary, but if she was not too badly damaged, and he could have her looked over at leisure, then so much the better. He was busy with other work to complete just now.

Henry was the first shipwright on the scene, by good fortune. As soon as the ship had started up the river towards the haven, one of his carpenters had called him to look at her, and he had realised that there could be money in a job with this one. He'd shouted for a rowing boat and two men and was leaving the jetty even as Hawley's cog, the *Christopher*, dropped anchor.

Hawley was in his own boat and on his way to meet Henry in a few moments. As soon as they were within hailing, Hawley gave a shout and his four oarsmen lifted their oars and drifted. The nearer man glanced over his shoulder to gauge the distance, and then let his oar drop to push Henry's boat gently away before they could collide.

'We found this cog floating without a crew,' Hawley called. 'Can you give her a good look-over? I don't want the cargo lost.'

'At once.'

If there was any risk of her sinking, Henry needed to get the ship out of the water as soon as possible so the cargo could be saved. On a cog this size, there could be enough to make a good profit for all involved in the salvage.

From this initial glimpse, he reckoned that she was safe enough. The smell of burned pitch and scorched wood was very strong, though, and he wrinkled his nose as well as his brow as he rubbed his chin reflectively. 'Take us nearer.'

As the oarsmen heaved, Henry opened his jack. The breeze was cool, fresh off the sea, but the sun was blazing down on them from between the clouds, and he was feeling hot. He pulled off his cowl and scratched at his thin, lank hair, idly pushing his head into his cowl again as they slowly encircled the ship and he could see her from every angle, until he snapped an order, and they rowed in to the ship's sides. There, he studied the strakes closely, peering at the caulking, reaching out and feeling for himself how well she was coping. When he nodded to himself, he heard a snigger from behind him.

'You concentrate on your oars, Jankin.'

'She's riding low. Must have a good cargo aboard,' Jankin said, ignoring him.

'Perhaps.' Henry couldn't be bothered to argue with his son today. Better that he should concentrate on the cog herself.

A small ship, this. But then few ships in this part of England were large. There were none of the great vessels which a man could see down south in Castile or even over in Yarmouth on the east coast. Some there were at least 200 tuns, using the standard measure. All ships were assessed in terms of how many standard Gascon 'tuns' they could carry. Each of the enormous wine barrels weighed somewhere in the region of a ton, and they provided a handy measure against which to assess ships.

From the look of her, this ship would hold twenty or so tuns. Master Hawley's ships were all about forty tuns, like the *Christopher* here, but Master Pyckard, another local merchant and shipowner, liked smaller ones that could navigate the smaller ports, saying that they could hurry over the seas, empty themselves speedily, and return. He had three of them, the *Saint John*, the *Saint Simon*, and the *Saint Denis*. There had been one more, the *Saint Rumon*, but she had sunk some fifteen years ago, when there had been a sudden squall.

Poor old Paul – he had lost his treasure, his beautiful young wife Amandine, in that freak storm. Never been the same again since, really.

'Master Hawley did say she was carrying a lot,' Jankin persisted. 'Look how low she is in the water, Father.'

The young man's voice held that hint of greed familiar to all those who eked a living at the coast. While they lived in fear of the sea, they depended upon it too, and although sometimes it could rise up and destroy them, at other times it would bring them a generous harvest. A single shipwreck could supply enough to maintain an entire community for months. Here, safe in the haven, they rarely found wrecks from the sea, but when a good seaman like John Hawley captured a prize, the effects would ripple through the town.

'I heard him. Let's just make sure she's safe first,' Henry said, eyeing the sheer above his head and shaking his head. It made no sense that a man would attack a ship, kill the crew, and then leave the valuable craft with all her cargo aboard. What kind of a fool would do that?

Henry Pyket was a heavy-set man of almost forty, with a great pot-belly, his tanned face square and kindly, with oddly gentle eyes. Few men in charge of a good-sized shipbuilding business were known for their generosity and charity, but Henry had always been different.

Taking a grappling iron, he swung it contemplatively in his right hand, the one which was missing two fingers, before hurling it aloft.

It snagged, and he tugged, but it came free and rattled over the decking, from the sound of it, until he saw the top spike appear over the sheer. Then it gripped as he put his weight on the rope, and he nodded to the oarsmen as he stepped forward, and hauled himself upwards, his legs walking him up the strakes to the sheerline.

Once there, he clambered over with the ease and skill of a sailor, standing on the blackened decking and gazing about him.

'Begin at the bottom,' he muttered to himself. That was the rule which his master had always stressed when he was still an apprentice, and he was strongly reminded of it now. Then, he and his master had been surveying a French hulk, and although they did not know it at the time, the hull was sorely stressed and damaged. From above, it looked fine: the line of the decking was straight enough, the mast stood firm in her rigging, and she rode high enough in the water, but when they went into the hold and saw the water slopping about, they understood that the strakes were dangerously loosened, and that they must either stabilise the leaks or evacuate her quickly.

This one was riding smoothly enough, just rising gently on the swell, and he felt hopeful that they would not have to do too much to keep her cargo secure. He walked to the coaming before the hold, and glanced over the edge. Barrels and bales moved about, and he could hear the sloshing of water, but there was no great invasion, so far as he could see. It was only the very bottom that was truly wet. Still, best to be sure.

There was a ladder, and he gripped it firmly, looking around. All about him up here was blackened. Much of the decking would need to be ripped up and replaced. He wasn't sure if the damaged mast would survive a strong blast. Best replace that too, just in case. In the prow lay a filthy mess of blackened canvas, and thin wisps floated about every so often as the wind caught them: burned sails. There were metal rivets and shreds of leather about the place, too. It was almost as though . . . but that would make no sense.

Reluctantly, for Pyket was never happy on ladders – give him a strong hempen cable for preference, he swung himself over the coaming, and let himself down into the dark depths.

Here he was shin-deep in cold seawater. As he stood there, sniffing, listening, he could feel the movement of the ship through his bare feet. The creaking and groaning of moving strakes was deafening, and the steady lapping of water in the bilge and at her sides was magnified until it sounded as though waves were hammering at her. More troubling were the five barrels which had been dislodged from their moorings and now floated about, threatening to crush him if he was careless. The great bales were massive; he felt sure from the smell that they were full of cloth. An experienced seaman could recognise the odour of different cargoes without difficulty.

It was not that smell that made him scowl, though. No, it was the overwhelming stench of oil. And the atmosphere of terror that even to his stolid mind seemed to pervade the vessel.

Bailiff Simon Puttock smiled, and Ivo le Bel quailed.

The Bailiff was a tall man with calm grey eyes in a slightly pale face. In the past, when he had been Bailiff to the Stannaries of Dartmoor, he had been responsible for maintaining the King's Peace over the wild lands, and he had travelled widely, his features burned to the colour of old oak. Since he had been promoted to this new position at Dartmouth, he had been forced to remain indoors more often, which he deplored. For him, far better that he should be able to wander the open moors, free of concerns and God-damned figures. He couldn't return yet, though. Not for a while.

For all that Simon would prefer to be at home in Lydford, there was something attractive about the noises of this busy, industrial port. The slow, steady creaking of timbers as ships rolled from side to side, the trickle and slap of small waves, the howl of the wind on a cold evening when a man was already in a warm house by his fire, all were welcome. The assault on the nostrils was less so, though. There was a permanent stench of fish from the salting yards where they were gutted, spread and dried, and it was not enhanced by the odour of rotting flesh where the fishguts lay in the middens, to be dug over by the great seagulls. Tar and seaweed, hemp and coal smoke, all smothered the town like an unwholesome blanket, and at the same time there was the perpetual din of the smiths, carpenters, shipwrights and others, all of whom seemed to delight in as much clattering and crashing of metal and wood as possible.

'Sir Bailiff, I hadn't seen you there.'

'I'm no knight, Ivo – you know that. Why are you in charge? Did you find the body?'

'This is my tithing, Bailiff. I am responsible to the Coroner when he arrives.'

'Fine. What happened?'

'This fellow says he put up boards to protect people, but the victim still fell in. He must have struck his head – look.'

Simon winced at the sight. The man's head was a mess: he had fallen forwards, clearly, and his left temple was a bloody, blackened wound.

'As I said, I watched the paver here put up his warnings. Some thieving bastard must have stolen them, leading to this accident.'

The man lay in the hole with his head at a curious angle, his legs twisted together. The left arm was under his body, while the right was flung out into the middle of the hole. His head was resting near the wall, the wound right by a rock which had been smeared with his gore.

Simon asked, 'Does anyone know him?'

There was a ripple as all shook their heads.

'Ivo, have you sent for the Coroner?'

'I was about to.'

'Hurry, then,' Simon said, and he set off for the pie shop down near his chamber, where his clerk would be waiting for him.

As he crossed the street, he saw old Will the gaoler – a tatty, degenerate-looking man with a paunch like a bishop and a threadbare white beard – walking up to the gaol in the market square. There was no one there so far as Simon remembered, but Will was a dedicated man. The gaoler was generally amiable, and called 'old Widecombe Will' because he had been the youngest son of a farmer from that little vill. Bored with prodding cattle to pull the plough, he had preferred to run away to sea. At least, that was his tale.

It was not entirely true. He *had* been a farmer's boy, although the legitimacy of his birth left a little to be desired. Also, rather than leaving his home from boredom, there was the matter of Millicent, the maid from the neighbouring hamlet, who had grown suddenly large with child. Still, in essence he had not lied. Now the father of six other (legal) children, and four grandchildren, he had a certain position in the town, and he was immensely proud of it. And part of his responsibilities for this year was the maintenance of the simple gaol.

The Bailiff sighed. Another day of numbers and reports lay ahead. Oh well. He knew he must remain patient. Before long, with fortune, he would be able to go back to Lydford. To his home, his beautiful wife Meg and their children. They would be missing him, as he missed them. He was needed there.

At the door to the pie shop, he hesitated, recalling that body in the hole. There were some details that looked out of place. Surely . . . but no. The fool of a sergeant must have moved him; there was nothing to worry about. Yet the scene stuck in his head, even as he entered and chose a good beef pie.

Henry splashed through the water, running his hands over the strakes. There was no apparent leaking, and as he passed down the hull, he began to relax. All about him was the constant noise of running water, trickling, dripping, slopping about, but that was the normal sound of a working ship. The important thing was, he could see no holes or broken strakes, and by the time he had reached the stern, and had stumbled only once over a rib, he was feeling much happier. The second side of the ship appeared to be as safe, but he was nothing if not assiduous.

It was as he stepped over the rib, planting his foot carefully down in the water, that he felt something brush against him. He screamed shrilly as he took in the sight of the corpse under the water, with its gaping mouth, pale, dead eyes and the hand that moved gently as though beckoning Henry to join him in death.

Chapter Three

By the time Simon had entered his little counting-house, his latest clerk was already sitting at the trestle table, an anxious frown marring his brow as he added figures from a row of tally-sticks. Seeing Simon, he looked up and his mouth moved into a smile of welcome which somehow didn't touch his eyes.

'Bailiff – oh, right. Good. We've a lot to get through today. There's a new ship come in.'

'The burned one?' Simon asked, crossing the room. At the far side there was a broad window which was shuttered most of the winter, but now in the late-summer was more often opened. He pulled up the heavy bar and set it on the floor, then pushed the shutters wide on their hinges. 'It is one of the few advantages of this job, you know, that I have this marvellous view. And you, Stephen, persist in closing the shutters at every opportunity!'

Stephen, a thin young man of two-and-twenty, smiled nervously. 'I feel the chill so much, Master Bailiff, and—'

'Chill? Look out there at the sun,' Simon scoffed. 'It's a beautiful day, perfect weather. You could ride across the whole forest of Dartmoor to South Zeal market and back today.'

'As you wish, sir,' Stephen said. 'Yet the open window will let in every gust and gale, and it blows my parchments all about the place.'

'Use a stone to weight them down, then,' Simon said unsympathetically, leaning against the window's frame and listening. The hammering was continual down here, near some of the shipbuilders. At first he. had hated the din, longing for the peace and tranquillity of the moors, but now he had grown accustomed to it, and when the men stopped working in the evening, he rather missed it.

Stephen, he saw, was hunched a little more at his work. It was unkind of Simon to insist on having the shutter open, he knew, but he couldn't help it. He needed the air. It was just a shame that no clerk seemed able to cope with it.

His experience of clerks was not extensive, and less than positive, but he was gaining an insight into them and their work.

The first, Andrew, had been a whining pest; the next had been a weedy, frail man, little better than a boy, really, who'd been sent back when his coughing had grown so insistent that Simon could not concentrate. He secretly believed the lad was faking illness to shirk his work, but the abbot had assured him that the fellow had been sent away to recuperate as soon as he returned because he was ravaged with a fever; the third had been wealthy, and clearly a great deal more fit. He had been sent back to Tavistock when Simon encountered him in a tavern's bedroom with two women.

This Stephen was more pleasant than any of the others. Less cocky (in both meanings of the word) than his immediate predecessor, he managed to look ascetic, while still reserving some spirit. Simon's occasional irritable outbursts could reduce a weaker man to tears in a moment, but Stephen would listen, and if there was a rational cause to the explosion, would sometimes offer useful advice. If there was no good reason, however, he would just sit back with a puzzled expression that was somehow amused and condescending at the same time. At first this had made Simon ashamed, then it infuriated him, and now, after some weeks, it actually soothed him.

The fact was, there were many frustrations to this job. As well as Simon's anger at being removed from the job he knew and loved, he missed his family. Especially after the return of his old servant, Hugh. And now, of course, he wanted to be nearer home and Tavistock since the death of his patron, Abbot Robert.

Abbot Robert. There was a man who would be sorely missed. Simon had all but idolised him. To those who knew him, he was a powerful force for good. For those who did not, it was hard to know where to start to describe him: kind, generous, worldly, and a man of business like no other Simon had ever met. He had taken on

Tavistock Abbey when it was in a terrible state, and had been forced to borrow heavily to keep the institution afloat. That was many years ago, forty-odd, and in the time since, he had built Tavistock up to become one of the most effective and wealthiest convents in the whole of Devon and Cornwall. Simon had respected him hugely . . . and loved him. Abbot Robert had replaced the father who had died some years ago, and Simon felt the loss sorely.

Without a spiritual and businesslike head, the abbey was marking time, and all could feel it. Stephen here was in a similar position to Simon. Both knew full well that their position would be discussed at the highest level, as soon as the new abbot was confirmed in his post, but neither could influence the outcome. It left a man feeling peculiarly isolated.

If Stephen was not wearing the cloth, Simon could easily believe that his slender frame, large blue eyes and fair hair could be a sore temptation to many of the women about the town. From what he had seen of other clerks, not even the cloth itself would protect them from womanly ways. Not that Stephen's predecessor had needed much tempting . . .

Ach! It was no good. There was too much on his mind to keep him concentrating on his work.

'The ship, master,' Stephen prompted him now. 'She was found on the sea some miles out, just over the horizon.'

'Yes – and?'

It wasn't only his work, either. He had his daughter Edith to worry about, and her impending marriage, long-threatened and now imminent. Well, she was old enough, and her young man, Peter, was bright enough. Simon had persuaded her not to marry, though, until Peter had completed his apprenticeship to Master Harold, the merchant. Better not to have the expense and worry of a woman to support when he wasn't his own man yet. Except that now Peter had succeeded in winning his position, Simon was still anxious. For some reason he could not accept that his little girl was old enough to be wed. Well, he would have to grow accustomed to the thought, and that was an end to it!

'She is fully loaded,' the clerk went on, 'but there's no one alive on board.'

'What do you mean? She must have had a crew of ten or more!'

'Eleven, Bailiff.' Stephen shook his head a little, and then tilted it. 'Let me send for the master of the ship that found her.'

Master Hilary Beauley called an order, gripping the nearest shroud as he peered ahead. He shouted again, and felt the ship begin to slow. Until now she had been racing ahead while he kept his eyes on the far distance, but now he was near enough, and he bellowed a third command down to the men at the halyards and up on the sail itself. Soon the great sail was rising as the men reefed it in, clutching great handfuls and hauling it up until only a tiny fraction of the canvas was catching the wind. The ship slowed in her majestic progress, and he could feel her begin to level out.

'Get my boat ready!' he bawled down.

This delay would hold up all those in the convoy. His was the first ship to return, but just behind him, he knew, were the others. The law said all ships were to travel in convoy, to protect them from raiders, but this particular convoy had not started out that way.

Pyckard's ship had been first to leave the port. His little vessel had careered away, and it was only when it was already gone that the others realised what a march he had stolen on them. Beauley had set off immediately with his own ship, with Hawley, so he felt sure, a short way after him. From that moment, time was critical. If Pyckard's ship reached France a long time before they did, Pyckard's merchants could make their own prices, and when the others arrived, their own cargoes would be less attractive.

Hawley had one of the fastest and best ships available, and since the concept of the convoy was already rent asunder, it was every man for himself. Each master knew that. Beauley could make good speed, but he must be overtaken by Hawley in the end.

So when Pyckard had gone, he quickly followed, desperate to beat his competitors. If he was to make his profit, he would have to be as quick and seamanlike as he ever had been.

'Boat's away!'

Beauley swung down and stepped lightly across the decking. He sprang up to the wale, the thickest strake at the top of the ship's side, and let himself down the ladder into the boat. 'Haul away!'

Sitting here in the rear of the boat, he felt a thrill of anticipation, which was only dulled by the lousy oar-strokes of the man in front of him. 'Stop trying to look through the back of your head, man,' he snapped. 'I'll tell you when to ship oars.'

Alred Paviour kicked at a pebble and glowered down at the body. This was one job he should have refused. A simple hole in the road, and a few other repairs, and he'd thought he couldn't possibly lose; they were offering a fixed contract and it had seemed too good to turn down. But he'd always had a thing about sailors, and this damn town was absolutely full of them: great horny-handed, hairy-arsed, swearing sailors reeking of fish and seaweed and other things he'd prefer not to guess at.

'You might as well go to the tavern, master. There's no point waiting here.'

Glaring at the watchman standing guard over his hole, Alred swore softly. 'You know how much this is costing me?'

Aye. And every time he entered the tavern alone, it went quiet. People didn't like strangers down here, and when you saw that almost all the men in the taverns were sailors, who'd be willing to cut your throat as soon as look at you, you realised that this was a very dangerous place. Never trust a matelot, that was the paver's rule.

The watchman was sympathetic. 'Nothing you can do about it. The Coroner's been sent for. If you're lucky, he'll be only a couple of days.'

'Even if he is, he'll need a day to arrange his inquest,' Alred grumbled. 'I've seen them in Exeter. Bloody fools take a good time over their inquests, and all the while poor workers suffer.'

'We don't take so long here,' the watchman said with a chuckle. 'This isn't some borough in the middle of a city where they can bugger about for days. We've got work to be getting on with down here. You wait and see.'

Alred nodded bitterly. A man of middle height, with grizzled hair and beard, his eyes were more used to laughter, but today there was nothing to laugh about. He glanced down at the corpse, shaking his head. This fellow must have been a lover, a son, a father, perhaps . . . and now all he had become was sport for others to gawp at.

There were plenty who kept coming to take a look. Two youngsters, a boy and girl of ten or so, were standing up at the edge of the hole even now, their mother or nurse with them, all three peering down, wide-eyed, at the dead man. Well, it was best that everyone who could might see him, so that someone could identify him when the Coroner arrived.

Turning, he made his way to the Porpoise further down Higher Street. It was a small alehouse of the sort he would normally avoid in Exeter, but here . . . where else would a body go? Blasted place was hopeless. In Exeter, there were attractions all the time: you could watch the baiting, see a duel, or go and watch the jugglers and fools at the market square. Ah, how he missed Exeter.

The alehouse did have one advantage, though: it was cheap. He walked in, stooping under the low lintel, and looked about him for the others.

'That bloke said the Coroner should be here in two days, and he may be quick to come to a conclusion,' he said when he had joined them.

Bill and Law were his helpers. Bill was a taller man, his eyes a pale blue, his features wrinkled from laughter and sunburned in a round face. Law was darker, with steady brown eyes set in a narrow face, and he was much shorter. Only sixteen, he had been apprenticed to Alred for two years now, and was bright and quick, if not strong enough yet to do much of the heavier work.

'Two days? What do we do now, then?' Law asked.

'Wait until we hear, I suppose. We can't go and do anything until we're allowed. Oh, God's ballocks! What a mess! Why did we ever come here to this miserable midden?'

Law shrugged. His real name was Lawrence, but Bill and Alred had agreed early on that the shortarse didn't justify so long a name. Now he leaned forward eagerly. 'See that girl over there? She's been making eyes at me for the last while. Reckon she fancies me!'

'Law, she'd be more likely to fancy a hog,' Alred sighed. 'Your face looks like you've been rolled in a bed of nettles.'

'It's not that bad!' Law protested, a hand going to his volcanic chin.

'Don't be too hard on the lad,' Bill said. 'It might just be that she's got lousy eyesight.' He burst out laughing.

'There are many eye me up, I'll have you know,' Law said sulkily.

'They're desperate in a town like this,' Alred chuckled, then sighed. 'What are we going to do for money if we get held up? Christ's pain! what made me take this job in the first place?'

Bill smiled, showing his uneven teeth. 'Because you said we'd clean up in a little place like this. You said we'd charge them through the nose for everything they needed done and we'd live the high life when we got home again. You said the locals down here never saw anyone from the real world and had less sense than a peasant from—'

'Yes, yes! All right!' Alred said hastily, aware of all the eyes in the place going to him and his friends. Bill's voice was penetrating. 'But in the meantime we're losing money. That road has to be repaved, and I agreed a fixed price for the job. If we're held up, we won't make a penny profit.'

'You agreed a price for the job?' Law burst out. 'You always taught me that a fixed price was daft, that you'd never know if something was going to go wrong, and that you always need to be flexible in case of problems.'

'Yes, well – this proves I was right, doesn't it?' Alred snapped, adding nastily, 'And it was you supposed to put up the barriers, wasn't it?'

'I did! You know I did!'

'They weren't there this morning, were they? How do I know you put them up right? If it was that easy for some thieving scrote to nick them, you can't have fixed them in place all that well, can you?' He sank his face in his cup of ale.

'It's not my fault all this happened, as you well know!'

Alred grimaced, then: 'No, it isn't.'

Law grinned. 'Come on, Alred. What are we?'

'Don't. Just don't say it.'

'What are we, eh, Bill?'

'We're paviours, Law. We keep people moving.'

'What are we, Alred?'

'Yes, yes, yes. We're bleeding paviours. But that isn't going to help us when . . .'

'Hey! Is the paver in here?' It was Stephen, the clerk.

Alred closed his eyes and screwed up his face. 'See?' he hissed. 'And now I'm going to go and get stuffed for finding a stiff. I hope you're pleased with your work, lad! *Yes* – I'm here.'

'Come with me. The Port Reeve wants a word with you.'

Hamo the cooper was at his bench outside when he heard the boat returning to the shore. It scraped along the piles of empty clam and oyster shells that shingled the beach, and the men inside jumped out, hauling her up the slope to lie out of the water. Hamo watched idly as Jankin took the great stone anchor and thrust the rope from the boat through the hole bored in it, and then Hamo returned to his work, shaving a stave to fit a broken barrel. Much of his work involved mending damaged vessels. He didn't know what he'd do if sailors were more careful!

'Come on, Henry, let's be getting you out of there,' a man called.

Hamo noticed that Henry Pyket was still seated on the thwart, his face in his hands.

'Come on, Dad, eh?'

Jankin was a steady fellow, sound and as hard as oak in a fight, and Hamo was oddly affected to see how he went to the older man and placed an arm about his neck comfortingly.

'Hey, Jankin, you want some help there, boy?' he shouted.

'We're fine, I think, Master Hamo,' Jankin responded, but he didn't sound it.

'Let's help him out of there, eh?' Hamo went over and said gently, 'Henry, have you hurt yourself, man? Hit your head on a beam?'

'We've all seen them, haven't we,' Henry said dully. 'You've seen your share of dead men, I daresay, Hamo?'

'We all have, aye. There isn't the year we don't see enough washed up on the beaches.'

'But have you ever been touched by one?' Henry gave a shudder of horror. 'He was in there, he was, poor Danny, and a-wavin' like he was asking me to join him. It turned my stomach, it did!'

'Danny? What was *he* doing in there?' Hamo asked, bewildered.

'He's dead, Hamo. Murdered, like all the others.'

'God's teeth, you mean that's the *Saint John*?'

'There's no one on board, I swear. Only Danny down in the hold, and he's dead. All the other men have gone,' Henry said with another shiver. 'The ship's cursed, Hamo. It must be. Sweet Jesus! It's like the devil came up and took 'em all. Took 'em all down into the sea with him.'

Chapter Four

Simon was sitting in his favourite chair when John Hawley entered. 'Master Hawley, good day. You have a rich prize, I see.'

'Has your man told you about it?'

Hawley was a bluff, sturdy character. His eyes were as grey as Simon's, but in Hawley's there was a glint of steel. He had a reputation for fearlessness in the face of the elements, which was a good trait for a ship's master, but there was another aspect: utter ruthlessness to those who stood in his path. It was rumoured that during the recent crisis in relations between King Edward II and the French King Charles IV over that place – Saint Sardos or somewhere; Simon wasn't sure exactly, but the two nations had gone to war over it, wherever it was – Hawley had made himself some good profits by taking a privateer's papers and capturing all the ships he could. There were many. Those which were owned by the King's allies were supposed to have been freed and their crew unmolested, but there were strong suggestions that this Hawley, with his 'Devil take you' attitude and the quizzically raised eyebrow, had occasionally forgotten that rule.

He was shorter than Simon by a half head at least, and his shoulders weren't so broad, but for all that Simon would not have liked him for an enemy. He wore his short sword with the easiness that only professional masters of defence could emulate: it was a part of him, whether sheathed like this, or gripped in his hard, leathery fist.

Crossing the floor to Simon, Hawley held out a hand, and Simon stood to take it. Both nodded, each respectful of the other, if wary. They were aware that their objectives and ambitions were entirely different.

Respect was easy with a man like this. There were men of the sea whom Simon had known who knew nothing of ships and coasts, men who depended on their navigators and crew to keep the ship safe. They were invariably slothful, drunken fools, in Simon's mind. Not so Hawley. He had been living aboard ships since he was a lad, and as the years passed, he had grown knowledgeable of all the coasts, if the stories were true, all the way down to the Portuguese king's lands. Simon could imagine him being entirely uncompromising in the face of cowardice or incompetence. He was a determined man, as bold and daring as any knight, but less constricted by the code of ethics which so many knights claimed to espouse.

Not that many lived their lives constrained by them, if Simon was to be honest.

For the rest, Hawley was rich, as demonstrated by his crimson velvet cote-hardie, and the softness of his linen beneath. If salt had marred his hosen, they were still made of good, thick wool, and his shoes were of the best Cordovan leather. It made Simon feel tatty in his old robe from last year. Since the death of the abbot, he had not felt it was the right time to ask for the annual replacement that was the perquisite of his position.

'I saw it for myself,' he replied now. 'It was burned?'

'Aye. All above decks quite badly, although below there's little damage. There's a stench of oil all about it, but I think much didn't catch, by fortune.'

'Do you know whose ship she was?'

'She has the lines of the cog *Saint John*, one of Paul Pyckard's ships, but I can't be sure without looking through her more carefully.'

'You mean your men didn't?' Simon asked with a slight smile. He wouldn't call the man a liar, but it seemed unnatural for such a bold seafarer not to have looked.

Hawley stared at him blankly, not returning the smile. 'We were sailing from here to Bordeaux as part of the fleet.'

Simon nodded. The haven was more empty than usual, because recently all the shipmasters had been ordered to sail in groups for their own protection. Since the opening of hostilities once again with the French, it was necessary to protect ships from the depredations of French privateers.

'It's a journey we've made often enough, Bailiff, with a hold filled with wool and tin amongst other things. Lots of produce to sell, and we should have made a goodly profit. Then, last night, when we'd only made a day's journey, we saw the gleam of fire in the distance as the light faded. I ordered the sails to be reefed and sailed for her, wondering what had happened, whether this was a random act of piracy – you know what those French are like.'

'Yes.' Simon did. They were exactly the same as the man in front of him.

'When we got closer, there was no sign of another ship. All we knew was, this cog was ablaze. So the first thing we did was stop the fire. I reckon what happened was, they soaked her sails in oil and put a torch to them, thinking the whole ship would go up in flames in an instant, but it takes a bit more than that to put paid to an old ship like her. It's like burning stone, when the timbers are so well weathered. As her attackers sailed away, though, they'd have seen roaring flames, and maybe thought she was gone.

'It took a long effort, hurling water from all the buckets we could grab,' he went on. 'We put paid to the worst of it by dropping a sail over the side, lifting it on the windlass, and aiming it filled with water over the worst of the fire. Then it was a case of climbing over there and putting out all the smaller ones.'

'It can't have been a pleasant sight.'

'A ship in such a state is never pretty.'

Simon allowed a fixity in his stare. 'I meant the people.'

'There were none.'

'What?' Simon asked, unsure whether he had heard aright.

'That's correct, Bailiff. There was no one aboard. There's already talk about her being a death ship, that the devil's taken her crew.'

Sir Baldwin de Furnshill was sitting on his throne-like seat in the hall of Exeter's Rougemont castle listening to the cases before the court of gaol delivery, at which the felons would be delivered from the gaol either to freedom or death, and was delighted when the last case had been heard and justice passed down.

It was the hardest part of his function as Keeper of the King's Peace, this listening to the miserable churls who passed in front of him. They were invariably fools, or brutal outlaws who should preferably have been throttled at birth, rather than being left alive to harm others. One in particular, a devil with one eye and a ferocious scar through his empty socket, spat when he heard the sentence of death, and swore he'd see the justices in hell.

Baldwin knew the case intimately. The man had stolen from a miller near Tiverton, killing the poor man in front of his family, then raping the mother and a daughter, before stabbing them both. The mother died, the daughter still lingered – although Baldwin was sure that her broken heart would never heal and she must die within a year and a day. And why had it happened? Because this man had taken offence at an innocent comment passed by the father. He was a foul creature, and the sooner he was dead the better. Others, though, did *not* deserve their punishment.

With that thought in mind, Baldwin scarcely noticed the man calling to him until he had almost walked into him.

'Sir Baldwin? The bishop would like to speak with you.'

'Oh? I shall come with you, then,' Baldwin told the young cleric in black garb. 'It's only a short walk.'

'He is not at the palace just now, Sir Baldwin, but at his manor at Bishop's Clyst. He begs that you will join him there.'

Baldwin winced. It was late already, and he had hoped to be finished in time to ride homewards to see his wife and Richalda, his daughter. Lady Jeanne was six or seven months into her pregnancy, and he was attempting to spend as much time as possible at her side while they waited for the day when their latest child might be born. 'Very well,' he said reluctantly.

'I have already asked the grooms to prepare your horse, Sir Baldwin. I hope that wasn't presumptuous.'

It was. Baldwin gave him a long, steady look. 'I suppose not. No, it was sensible, if we are to go and visit my lord Bishop. Do you know whether it is a matter of business or simply for conversation that he wishes to see me?'

'It is not a matter of pleasure, I fear.'

Baldwin nodded and grunted, marching to the inner ward.

Exeter's castle was important as the administrative centre of the city, still, but from up here, gazing about him, Baldwin could see that the defences were falling into decay. The towers had been roofless for forty years or more, and the dereliction was becoming noticeable. Three of the towers had begun to collapse a few years ago, and now were little better than shells. If the city was held under siege again, as it had been so often before, the place could not withstand a single strike from a modern trebuchet.

It was a sobering thought. He swung up onto his horse, contemplating the walls and small piles of rubble from collapsed masonry. Two hundred years before, this had been strong enough to hold out for months when King Stephen besieged it. Now it wouldn't last five minutes. Even the immense ditch and curtain wall were useless, the one filled, the other crumbling. And no one would do anything about it. It was that which made him most bitter. This was an important castle, deserving of a little money to bring it up to standard, but no one would pay. It was so short-sighted, especially in these difficult times.

Putting it from his mind, he clapped spurs to his mount's flanks and clattered over the old drawbridge.

It was not far to the bishop's manor. The two men left by the east gate, then took the Heavitree road south-east, passing by the gallows on the way. Baldwin averted his eyes from the bodies hanging there.

By the time they had reached the new bridge to Clyst St Mary, Baldwin was looking forward to refreshment. It was only a few minutes' ride to the bishop's little manor, and soon they were rattling the boards of the drawbridge that spanned the small moat. Ahead was the hall itself, while left was the chapel. Baldwin had only been here a few times, but he knew it well enough. The stables were on the right, and he dropped from his horse, giving orders to the cleric to have the beast rubbed down carefully before he was fed, and strode off to the entrance to the hall.

'Sir Baldwin, I am glad to see you.'

The bishop was a tall man, slim in build, and with a face that Baldwin privately felt had seen too much deviousness. Bishop Walter had spent too many years involved in the politics at the heart of the realm, supporting those who had sought originally to curb the King's worst excesses, first by imposing rules on him, a course of action that was doomed to failure as soon as the King felt himself powerful enough to break with those who tried to enforce the rules; and more recently as the King's ally. He had been responsible for the realm's finances as the Lord High Treasurer, and even now Baldwin knew he was a trusted confidant.

That, Baldwin found difficult to comprehend. To be an ally of Edward's was to be an ally of the Despensers, father and son, both called Hugh, and Baldwin could not forgive any man who sought to aid them. Little better than licensed thieves, they were felons who could extort, steal, arrest, torture and murder anyone without fear of restraint. Yet the younger was the King's closest friend and – so it was rumoured – his lover.

In all the years Baldwin had known him, he had held the bishop in the highest respect. He was an old-fashioned cleric, perhaps, but Baldwin had thought him honourable and compassionate. There was nothing in his dealings with the man that had led him to alter his opinions. Yet now the good bishop was supporting the King and the Despensers.

'My lord Bishop, I am glad to see you looking so well,' Baldwin said.

Stapledon held out his hand for Baldwin to kiss his ring. 'Don't be sarcastic with me, old friend. I'm sixty-three years old now and – by God! – I feel every one of them. *Wine!*'

Baldwin smiled casually, and was surprised when the bishop did not reciprocate. His face was pale and unsettled. He wouldn't meet Baldwin's eye directly, and that was most unlike him. It persuaded Baldwin not to speak openly about any political affair. As matters stood, any who spoke against the Despensers were likely to find their homes raided, their wives raped and tortured, children slain, and all that they prized ruined. He would not put his wife and children at risk even at the cost of alienating an old friend like Stapledon.

'I am tired, Baldwin. Trying to keep the peace between the King and his wife Isabella is like trying to mould water. You can make it take shape, but as soon as you remove your hand, all falls away! The latest plan on Despenser's side is to make all the barons and lords swear an oath to him, saying they'll live or die with him . . .' Stapledon grew silent as the door opened and his old bottler entered with a tray on which were set out jugs and goblets. The bishop waved his hand and the man left after putting the tray on the table.

'What would you do?' Baldwin asked.

Stapledon eyed him, then picked up a parchment and peered at it short-sightedly. With a grimace, he reached into his robe and took out his spectacles, which he opened and held to his eyes. 'I would have peace in the kingdom – first and foremost between that unhappy pair, the King and his Queen. The old King should have realised when he made them marry that sealing a pact with France was sure to lead to sadness. How could any man expect his son to find happiness with a Frenchwoman? We know what happened to her sisters-in-law. That was enough to kill her father.'

'You speak of the affair of the silk purses? Yes, as I recall, she was the instrument of their downfall,' Baldwin noted.

'True enough,' Stapledon agreed heavily. 'I have seen her accounts, and she took ten torch-bearers with her to the French king to tell him that night. I think she was shocked by the result, though. All her sisters-in-law imprisoned, one dying so soon afterwards. And the men – to be killed like that . . .'

'I have heard some of the story,' Baldwin said, 'but it was during a period when I was exercised with other matters. Perhaps you know more?'

Stapledon took a gloomy sip of his wine. 'It was in 1313. I was with her and the King. Isabella had travelled to France with her husband to try to heal the rift that had opened between the two kings. You remember all that? Edward was passing over gifts to Piers Gaveston, his . . . friend.'

Baldwin smiled at his diplomatic pause. Rumours of the King's affection for the man had been heard by the meanest peasants. To hint at such an affair could cost a man more than money, though, and there was never any way to tell whether a servant could be listening. Baldwin could not help glancing at the door as he motioned to the bishop to continue.

'At the time, the French king was concerned because Queen Isabella had not received any lands as dower, her finances were dependent upon King Edward, and she actually had to stay with him the whole time, without the money to create her own household. It was ridiculous. Anyway, her father showed his displeasure in no uncertain terms, and began to intrigue behind our king's back. He hinted that Gaveston was an enemy of France and himself, and to say that any man who supported Gaveston was likewise an enemy.'

Baldwin gave a low whistle. 'I had not heard that.'

'It is why Gaveston's death was such a relief to so many of us,' Stapledon admitted. He poured wine for himself, holding up the jug for Baldwin, but the latter declined. 'When Gaveston was slain, it healed much of the rift between Edward and the French. Then, of course, Edward the king's son was born. So in May 1313 we went to Paris.

'King Philippe was delighted. He was to meet his grandson for the first time, and his court celebrated our visit with feasting and dancing. While there, the Queen's brothers were knighted, and she gave them gifts, as well as presents for their wives: three silken purses, one each to Blanche, Marguerite and Jeanne, the three wives of her royal brothers.'

He lapsed, shaking his head grimly, but Baldwin did not interrupt his thoughts. Patiently he waited for the bishop to continue.

'Such innocuous little trinkets they seemed. Even such as they can cause disaster, though. A year later Queen Isabella returned to France to continue negotiations with her father on behalf of her husband, and noticed that the purses were now being worn at the belts of three other knights.

'She was suspicious at once, and went to tell her father that same evening. I mentioned the torch-bearers? I wasn't with her on that trip, but I heard all about it. Dear God!

'The king was enraged. He felt, rightly, that this brought shame and dishonour on his house and his line. His sons, the princes, had been cuckolded in the most flagrant way. Their wives had engaged in lewd feasting and dancing, emulating the debauched whores of Gomorrah in their pride and lust for pleasure. The king immediately had them all followed, and learned that they met their lovers, the d'Aunai brothers, in the Tour de Nesle, a palace nearby . . .'

'I know it,' Baldwin said shortly. He hated to think of the events that had led to the slaughter of two young men.

The bishop noticed his manner and continued more gently, 'Two of the women confessed immediately. The third denied adultery, but she was to be punished anyway, for not telling the king or her husband what the other two were up to.'

'What became of the women?' Baldwin asked.

'The sisters-in-law were all condemned. Blanche and Marguerite were sent to the Château-Gaillard in penitential dress, wearing rough hair clothing that would sear their flesh. Marguerite did not survive the first winter in that harsh environment. She froze to death in one of the upper chambers. Jeanne was held in the milder castle at Dourdan for a while, and eventually the Parlement released her after declaring that she was innocent of adultery. Blanche remained at Château-Gaillard: I presume she is still there. Her marriage has been declared null by the Pope, so she is merely a woman of no honour – a poor slut with no man to protect her.'

'I was in France in that year,' Baldwin said quietly. 'I recall the men being executed.'

'The two knights could hope for no pity. They had polluted the loins of the women who would become Queens; they had desecrated the lineage of the court. It showed how the *fleur de lis* had been undermined by frivolity and lewdness. They were hanged, I think?'

Baldwin shook his head, his face grim at the memory. 'No. The king wanted an example to be made. One of the guilty men escaped as soon as he heard of the accusations and fled to England; his brother was less swift to run and was captured. But running away to the very place where his accuser was herself the Queen was foolish in the extreme. He was taken and returned to France.

'They were brought to the execution grounds of Montfaucon, and there Gautier and his brother Philippe d'Aunai were bound to wheels. Over time their limbs were broken with iron bars; then their testicles and tarses were hacked off and thrown to the dogs. Only when they had suffered in anguish for a long while were their heads struck off and their bodies clamped in gibbets to be hung on display for the mockery of the populace, as proof that no man could contaminate the royal family with impunity.'

'I heard that the shame hastened King Philippe's end,' the bishop said sadly. 'He was dead before the end of the year.'

Baldwin's jaw clenched. 'I think it was more likely that God had chosen to call him to His throne. When the Grand Master of the Knights Templar, Jacques de Molay, was murdered on King Philippe's orders, it's said de Molay demanded that the king should stand before God to defend himself for destroying God's crusading army.'

'You believe that?'

The memory of the injustice made Baldwin continue, even though his usual caution should have advised him to be more circumspect. 'I believe with my entire heart and soul that Philippe was evil. Any man who could commit such a crime against a holy and religious Order deserves no less. He killed the Templars, and suffered for it.'

'I do wonder, though . . . the punishment for his misdeed was truly dreadful,' Stapledon mused. 'To think that a man's line could be so devastated. Perhaps it was God's vengeance, as you say. Certainly none of his sons have been blessed so far, have they? After King Philippe IV died, his son Louis X survived him by only two years. Philippe V became King in 1316 but died in 1322, and the last brother, Charles, has been on the throne now for two years. I do not know how healthy he is, but there is no heir as yet, I believe?'

Baldwin shook his head. He was still remembering that appalling year in which the d'Aunai brothers and so many others had died. He had no sympathy for Philippe.

In 1314 Sir Baldwin had been forced to come to terms with the destruction of his ancient and honourable Order, the Knights Templar. His comrades had been arrested on Friday, 13 October 1307, while he and some of his friends had been out of their preceptory, and as a result he had escaped the torturers, the indignity and shame. Yet he *had* been scarred, he told himself, eyeing his hand. It did not quiver or shake, but only because of an enormous effort of will.

'So, Sir Baldwin, I must ask you for a favour, if you would be so kind.'

There was something in his tone that brought Baldwin to attention instantly. 'What is that, my lord Bishop? If I can serve you, you know I would be glad to,' he said, but he was warned by the bishop's reticence that this was no ordinary request.

Chapter Five

It was late that night when Simon returned to his little chambers and sat before his fire with a bowl of hot soup and hunk of bread. He didn't bother to go to his table, but sipped straight from his bowl as he contemplated all he had learned that day.

Originally he had taken a larger house in Dartmouth, but that was when he had hoped that his wife Meg might join him here. Since hearing of the death of Abbot Robert, it seemed clear enough to him that he would not be staying here for long. The good abbot had been his enthusiastic patron, and with him gone, it was likely that the new abbot would seek to install his own friend or loyal servant. Simon had quickly decided to take a smaller place.

It was comfortable enough, though. Situated in the upper of the two streets, a short distance from the Porpoise, a rowdy tavern, he had a fair-sized front room, a smaller kitchen and parlour behind, and a pleasant solar chamber above the front room for his bed. Outside there was a simple privy in his garden. For a man living alone, it was fine.

There was a squeak and rattle from a loose sign further up the road, and although the noise normally didn't affect him, today it grated on his ear as though there was an invisible connection between his head and the rusty metal. When he heard a cat screech, he shot from his seat, spilling soup over his lap, making him curse loudly. He was not the only man in Clifton or Hardness who felt the same anxiety that night, he knew.

It was always hard when his friend Baldwin heard of some little precaution he took: Baldwin had a hard-nosed manner about all sensible safeguards, calling them 'superstitious nonsense' or somesuch, but Simon didn't care. As far as he was concerned, it was proof of Baldwin's foolishness. Simon wasn't superstitious, anyway. He simply didn't believe in taking risks.

There was something about that great ship lying in the haven, blackened and charred . . . as though it had been sent to hell, and only returned when the devil had taken her crew. Poor fellows. Stephen had said there were eleven of them, too. All with wives and children, no doubt. All who would now struggle to make a living.

There were some men who fully deserved such a fate, no doubt, but Simon could not help but wonder at the wholesale nature of this destruction. It was a proof of the danger that all men lived with at all times, and a warning to make sure that they shrived themselves when they could, so that their souls might leave them with full confidence. No man knew the moment of his death, and these poor sailors were a prime example of that fact. If only they had been to church before they sailed, and had given Confession full honestly. Perhaps one or two did. Maybe they were already up in heaven. Simon heard a fox call, and closed his eyes, only to open them wide at a scratching behind his wall. No, it was a rat or something. Nothing else.

Christ's ballocks, but he must calm himself. The whole town was the same. Everyone was jumpy and fretful. No surprise, really, when a man considered how sailors depended so much on their instincts. To learn that some eleven men had been lost, one of them found dead in the hold, but the others gone as though they had never existed, that was terrifying. There would be many families tonight who would have no sleep.

One of them was Widecombe Will's. Simon had seen Will later in the afternoon, when people began to realise whose ship it was. Will was with one of his daughters: Annie. She saw the ship and shrieked with horror. Her man Ed had been one of the crew. Simon recalled him – a game lad, brawny and powerful. Now Annie was on her knees, throwing dust from the road in all directions as she squealed and groaned.

'You don't know it's the *Saint John*,' Will was saying.

'You think I don't recognise my Ed's ship? He was only going to be out for a couple of days, and now look at it! Everyone knows it's his ship! My Ed! My Ed! He's gone!'

The ship was one of Paul Pyckard's. There was little doubt of that, as soon as they'd been able to take Pyckard's clerk and servant, Moses, to the ship and had checked the cargo against the manifest which recorded all the goods loaded. She was clearly the *Saint John*, and if they needed further proof, the sight of Danny's corpse was enough.

Although Simon felt squeamish at the sight of all dead bodies, it was those who had died from fire and water that most repelled him. Today, seeing that poor, whitened face, the flesh cold and soft as a fish's, Simon could have turned and thrown up. It was bad enough to be on a ship, without the added churning in his belly caused by the dead sailor.

'Who is he?' he'd demanded as the nausea began to fade slightly.

'I think his name was Danny. He came from Hardness,' Hawley said dispassionately. He stood with his legs set firmly on the deck as though his boots were nailed to it, unconcerned by the rolling or the body. 'Leaves a widow and three children, if I'm right.'

Henry Pyket had been brought back from the shore, and was sitting shivering on a coil of ropes. 'I didn't bring him up here until I was told to, Bailiff. I don't want to be fined for moving him when it wasn't my fault.'

'Shut up!' Hawley grated. 'The Bailiff has better things to do than worry about your hurt feelings.'

'It's not a problem, Master Shipwright,' Simon comforted him. 'If the Coroner tries to be difficult, tell him to speak to me. You couldn't have left the corpse down there in the hold. There was no point in that. Better that we took him out and brought him up here.'

'Then it's on your head,' Hawley noted with satisfaction.

'I'll support your decision,' Simon said sharply. He turned to the shipwright. 'He was under the water, you said?'

'I stepped on his arm, poor devil. He was there, under the surface, with a bale of wool on top of him.'

'From the look of him, he was stabbed first,' Simon said, looking reluctantly at the corpse.

'Makes me wonder whether there's any more down there,' Hawley said speculatively. 'Perhaps the rest of the crew are there as well?'

'Yes, Master Hawley? You think there could be more, eh?'

This was from a heavy-set man with an enormous paunch, who staggered up the ladder to the deck and stood there, puffing a little as he gazed about him. Behind him came another man, taller, and more wiry.

Simon shrugged. 'It's possible, Master Kena. Good day, and good day to you, Master Beauley.'

The two were well known to the Bailiff. The portly Master Philip Kena, clad in a thick fur-trimmed cotte with a hood that had an extravagant liripipe and gorget in bright blue, was a close competitor to Master Hawley. He had twinkling eyes of grey-blue that were often wreathed in wrinkles as he laughed uproariously at some joke or other, but Simon disliked and mistrusted him. He was too sure of his own position and importance, and Simon sensed that he would be a dangerous enemy.

The slimmer man, Master Hilary Beauley, was a lesser merchant of the town, who lived still in Hardness, north of the mill, where more of the poorer people had their dwellings. His colouring was in stark contrast with Master Kena's, for where the latter was pale with some colour, like an apple which has been left out in the sun over the autumn, Beauley was as dark as a moor, with skin the colour of an oak apple. His dark eyes were everywhere at once, as though he was always looking for a new customer or supplier.

'Who could have done this?' Beauley wondered now, gazing about him.

Hawley shrugged. 'French privateers. Maybe the men of Lyme? They've always hated us. When they see our ships, they often try to board and fight.'

'They're a weird lot in Lyme,' Kena said.

'Cut your throat as soon as look at you, if they know you're from Devon,' Hawley nodded.

'The men from Lyme? What's the matter with them?' Simon asked.

'They reckon they own the oceans, that's what,' Kena explained.

'It was fifty years ago they last had a pitched battle, wasn't it?' Hawley said.

'Aye, before my time,' Kena agreed. 'They had a great fight that day. But we won it.'

Simon had never heard of a fight that the pugnacious Dartmouth, Clifton and Hardness men had lost – not from here in the towns, anyway. 'And that's all? Because of a fight before any of us were born, you say that they must have taken this ship?'

'No. Last time they took a ship and plundered it, that was two years backalong,' Hawley said.

'You just said it was fifty-odd years ago.'

'That was when there was a battle between us and the men from Lyme. If you're talking about simple piracy against a Devon ship, that's different. The bastards joined with some sailors from Weymouth or somewhere, took the ship, stole the cargo, killed the crew, and scuttled her. God rot them!'

Sitting in his little chamber later, Simon recalled the expression on Hawley's face as he spoke those words. Here was a man who was more than happy to repay a debt. Especially a debt of blood, visiting vengeance on the men who had caused him grief.

It was an attitude much in evidence about the town. As he'd left the ship, returning with relief to terra firma after giving permission for the cargo to be brought ashore, Simon had noticed others muttering as they looked at the vessel moored close to the harbour. Their eyes were full of anger and resentment, and many was the time he heard the words 'Lyme bastards'.

Many years ago, an arrogant squire at Oakhampton Castle had said to Simon that the locals here in Devon were as patient and calm as the cattle they herded. 'They can't be roused by anything,' he had drawled.

Simon had replied, 'If you want to rouse a Devon man, insult his woman, or his child, or his dog, or his cattle. But before you do, make sure you have some men with you.'

'Ach, they aren't capable of anger. They're bovine, I tell you. It's all the oats they eat. Ha ha! If you eat cattle feed all the time, it's no surprise you end up that way.'

'Before you say that to one, you'd best have your sword ready,' Simon said with a cold rage. He was a Devon man himself, born here and raised here.

'A sword? More likely a stick to prod them.'

Simon stood, and in a moment the man was lying sprawled flat on his back. 'How did you . . .?'

'If you want to insult those who spend their whole lives wrestling cattle to the ground so they can be branded, you should learn to take a fall,' Simon had said coldly, and walked from the room followed by cheering and loud applause from all the Devon men in the room. All the same, he was glad that the squire didn't leap up and draw a weapon. He had publicly shamed the man, after all. Perhaps it was the presence of Hugh, Simon's ever-truculent servant, who stood gripping his thick staff ostentatiously, that was enough to put the squire off the experiment.

Yes, a Devon man roused was a fearful thing.

'Definitely the men from Lyme, I'd say,' Hawley had said again, and Kena murmured assent while Beauley nodded sagely.

It had struck Simon that these three men were the main competitors of the ship's owner, Paul Pyckard. He looked about them again, and then asked, 'Tell me, masters, where were all your ships when this happened? Master Hawley, yours was at sea, I believe. Master Kena?'

'I hope you don't mean to accuse me of trying to steal this ship, Bailiff,' Kena said with wide-eyed shock.

'Or me,' Beauley said with an intimidating calmness. Like that sudden quiet before a thunderstorm. 'I would be most unhappy to think you accused me of being a pirate.'

'So all your ships were at sea, is that what you are saying?' Simon asked. He knew that all had been away. It was Stephen who recorded the movements of shipping and told him each morning which ships were at anchor, which had sailed.

Kena spoke with an oleaginous smile. 'It is the law, Bailiff. We are supposed to be using numbers to protect our craft. We have to sail in convoys.'

'But not this vessel?' Simon asked.

Beauley was sharp-toned. 'The captain, whoever he was, sought to beat us to the French coast, rot his bowels! His ship was smaller, but he wanted to get there quickly and sell at the highest price, buy the best wines cheaply, and return. He would have done, too.'

Simon said no more, but as he left the ship and clambered down the rope ladder to the little boat that would row him back to shore, he was deep in thought.

He did not truly think that any of Pyckard's competitors could have done this. The men of Lyme – yes, possibly – but this lot? No.

'Who could have done that to her, then?' he wondered aloud. And shivered as the devil intruded into his thoughts again. Only the devil would have taken the men and left ship and cargo.

Master Kena could not sleep. His wife was tired and he found it impossible to remain in his bed while he felt so wide awake. She was too young for him to spoil her sleep. Bless her, she would have been glad to sit with him and talk, had he asked her to, but that wasn't fair. She was less than half his age, and she deserved a full night's rest now that she had paid the marriage debt earlier in the evening.

Rather than disturb her, he rose from his bed, pulled on his gipon and a fur-lined cloak over the top, and wrapped himself in its thick folds before going to the door and cautiously stepping down the stairs to the room beneath. Here was the comfortable little chamber where he and his wife would sit of an evening, and although the fire was long dead, there was some residual heat about the hearth. He drew up a stool and sat before it, his face feeling the vague warmth.

There was no doubt that business would be affected by the disaster of Paul Pyckard's ship. All eleven crew gone – it was a terrible shock to the town. Many people of Dartmouth had stated that they felt sure the devil had taken the men, but Kena himself believed that if the devil intended to take any man, he would have taken some of the others from the town. There was plenty of choice for his eternal fires, truth be told.

Still, if superstitious shipmen refused to sail, men like Kena would suffer. This could not be permitted to continue. It was a matter of urgency that those responsible for the crime should be discovered as soon as possible.

It was bad enough that business was already suffering because of the squabbling between the English and French kings. When rulers fell out, it was lesser beings who suffered, and just now, all merchants in England were watching the sword-rattling with growing alarm. The new policy of sailing in convoy meant that most ships were safe enough, but it also meant that a man had trouble finding crew. The sailors were all spoken for, and unless a master chose to offer bribes to tempt matelots away – as Kena himself had done – he might have to sail with a skeleton crew.

That was why Pyckard had been forced to take on strangers, which was always bad luck. Unknown crew members could well prove untrustworthy when attacked, after all. They had nothing to tie themselves to a ship or a master but his money, and where was the trust in that? Kena himself had bought off four or five of his men, so Pyckard's ships were definitely undermanned. Kena's poaching of the sailors was but one source of the enmity between him and Pyckard.

Pyckard had been unlucky with his ship, but soon all the local merchants would suffer similar losses if this war proceeded. Hawley seemed a bright lad, much like his father John Hawley before him. Both had a nose for a contract and a bargain, and both would happily spit in the eye of the devil himself if it meant more profit for them. They had the ships and men, too. They could easily afford to run greater risks than others. Then there was young Beauley. He had two ships he could call his own, and his attire and demeanour were looking richer every year. Like Hawley, he would draw a sword and yell defiance rather than give up his craft or his cargo. Beneath the skin, all ambitious merchants were but a breath away from felony. Certainly he himself would kill any man who got in his way.

As had Pyckard that once . . .

All merchants would dispute now and again. There were so many issues on which they were in competition: the best victualling spot; the best mooring; the best merchants in Britanny who would provide the most profit. The rewards went to the man who could demand and take what he wanted. When other merchants wanted the same resources, fights were inevitable.

The fight with Pyckard had been bitter and long-standing. Paul Pyckard and he had started in the trade early in the King's reign, back in 1307. At the time, Pyckard had been a forceful young merchant – but so had Kena. Pyckard had shipped a great cargo of cloth from Totnes, beating Kena to the best of the merchandise at the local market, and Kena was convinced that it was because he had paid a bribe to someone there.

That was fair business. All the merchants did it, and the fines which were imposed when a man was found to have acted illegally were so negligible compared to the money to be made that all merchants looked on the fines as nothing more than minor business expenses to be taken into account during trading.

Yet it had infuriated Kena to be bested. The only remaining stock which he could purchase had been rough 'dozens' – a thicker, less desirable cloth, and therefore not so profitable. All the while as his men stored the stuff in the hold, he had wondered how he might win his own back on Pyckard, but to no avail. Then, some months later, he met with a King's Purveyor, who was seeking transport of cargoes to King Edward's French possessions; Kena saw the potential immediately. He kept the deal close to his chest, preventing any others from hearing of it, and made a good killing. And then, because that early trade still rankled, he mentioned his suspicions about Pyckard's trading to the man.

As luck would have it, the Purveyor had only a short while before he tried to buy some cloth for the King's household, only to discover that there was little to be had. Now he researched that market day and some others, and heard that much more cloth had been sent to market than had eventually been sold. It was a simple case of forestalling.

Pyckard was meeting the dealers outside the town, offering a good sum for the whole lot, and then reselling it in the market when it opened, for a good profit. However, he was keeping back a large proportion of the goods to sell in France, where the profit would be even greater.

The fine imposed after the Purveyor's report had hurt Pyckard, although it had made Kena laugh. The next time Pyckard saw him in the market, he turned his back on Kena, and would have nothing more to do with him from that moment.

That was fine by Philip. He had no wish to be friendly with Pyckard, especially not after the way his men had behaved. One day he had let his wife out alone, and Pyckard's men had . . . well, enough. Kena had one ambition: to be the most powerful merchant in Dartmouth. To achieve that, he would stop at nothing.

Especially if it could hurt Pyckard and his men.

Chapter Six

Baldwin had slept in a guest room at the manor. Usually in an older house everyone would sleep together, but Stapledon had invested quite a sum already in ensuring that this little estate was as comfortable as possible, and there were several small chambers for guests up in the roof area. For once, while sleeping away from his home and his wife, Baldwin fell asleep almost as soon as his head hit his pillow.

The bishop had been born in Devon – in Holsworthy, if Baldwin recalled correctly – and it was a source of astonishment to the knight that this kindly, generous man could have sought to become embroiled in politics at so high a level. Bishop, Lord High Treasurer to the King, an expert in administration as well as consummate ambassador and negotiator, Stapledon had been at the heart of the nation's political life for fifteen or sixteen years now, and the effect was all too plain on his features. The last months had been unkind to him.

Ever since Baldwin had first met the bishop, Walter had been involved in the government of the country. Stapledon was driven by a desire to do good: his creation of a school at Ashburton, his founding of Stapledon College in Oxford, his constant round of visitations in his diocese, all pointed to a man who took his duty of care seriously, to help the people whose souls he must serve. It was that aspect of his nature that appealed to Baldwin.

Now Baldwin dressed slowly in the cool morning. From the open shutter he could see over trees, which sparkled and gleamed in the sun as the drops of dew caught the light. It was a scene of perfect beauty and it made him beam with contentment.

Then his face hardened. The previous evening, the discussion about the dreadful affair of the silk purses, followed by the memory of the destruction of his Order, had lent a deadly edge to his enjoyment. It felt almost as though the bishop was reminding him of the frailty of men, and the vague idea that he was warning Baldwin would not leave the knight as he pulled his shirt on over his head, tugged on his crimson tunic and cote-hardie, and buckled on his small riding sword.

Entering the hall, he found it full of the first servants. They were eating four to a mess, while the second servants waited on them. Soon the first would all leave, and then the second would break their fast. Up on the dais at the far end of the hall, the bishop sat in his great chair, a careworn cleric in black garb with no decoration but his ring and the crucifix about his neck, and did not touch the bread or meats that were spread before him. He looked up as Baldwin entered.

Baldwin had often felt that directness was the easiest approach when he was in doubt, so he marched to the top table and bowed. 'Sir, last evening you started to tell me that you wanted me to go to Dartmouth for you, but you did not wish to discuss the matter in any great detail.'

'I grew distracted by the matter of the silken purses,' Stapledon admitted. His eyes met Baldwin's briefly, then scanned the room behind the knight. 'I am too old, I fear. All these years in the service of the King have addled what brains I once possessed. Ha! You can argue if you wish, Sir Knight, but I know the truth. I wasted your time.'

That was a relief. Baldwin had begun to wonder whether this favour which the bishop wanted to ask would involve him in politicking. He had no desire to have any part in the disputes between the King and his Queen, nor between Edward and any of his subjects who had grown disillusioned with his reign – and God alone knew, there were enough of *them*. Ever since the last bloody war, in which he captured his own cousin, Thomas of Lancaster, and had him put to death, people had become more and more fearful. Edward's men had rampaged up and down the kingdom, hunting out all those whom he accused of being traitors allied with Thomas, taking them, lords, barons and knights, and slaying them in their own cities, hanging their rotting carcases from gibbets at the city gates. It was unheard of for an English monarch to dare to behave so brutally to his own people.

More recently, matters had sunk to a new low. The Despenser family, father and son, had taken to stealing all they coveted. As matters stood, Baldwin was sure that the younger Despenser was the wealthiest man in the land after the King himself. Those who stood in his path died.

'Let us go for a walk,' the bishop said, standing abruptly. 'We can eat a little later, if you do not object?'

Casting an eye over the men eating at their trestle tables, many with their gaze upon him and the bishop, Baldwin nodded. The bishop signalled to a cleric at the corner of the room, and a fur-trimmed cloak was brought for him, together with a soft felt hat. While the weather was so clement, Baldwin refused the offer of another cloak and hat.

'This matter is very important,' the bishop said as they crossed the court, 'and I did not wish to speak more of it in front of all my household.'

'Does it involve the King or the Queen?' Baldwin asked outright.

'Gracious God! What on earth made you ask that?' the bishop said, stopping dead in his tracks.

'Bishop, I am not a fool. If you are about to tell me that the Queen has taken a lover and given him a silken purse, I would refuse to help you,' Baldwin said lightly.

The bishop attempted a laugh. 'The idea!'

'I am serious, though. I would be disinclined to help if it means I grow involved in politics,' Baldwin said as they marched over the drawbridge and stood staring at the distant smoke and haze of Exeter. 'I have a wife and daughter to consider.'

'I can understand that,' Stapledon said heavily. 'My concern is that if you don't, the land could again be engaged in war.'

'What on earth makes you say that?'

'You have to understand the problems,' Stapledon sighed. 'Very well . . . It is all because of Lord Hugh Despenser. Hugh and the King are very close, you understand. It makes the Queen feel left out. There are messages between Edward and the French court every few days, and they are growing less diplomatic each time.' He began to walk again, his head down. 'Despenser has no love of the French. You remember when he was exiled?'

'Yes. It was when the Lords Marcher took Despenser's castles and marched on London. They forced the King to exile him and his father.'

'Yes. Young Despenser took a ship and began to attack any who sailed in the Channel; he captured the cargoes and killed the crews.'

'There was a Genoese ship, I think?' Baldwin recalled vaguely.

'Despenser attacked it in the Channel, yes. He slew the entire crew, and then stole the ship and cargo – five thousand gold pounds. And in all that time, the French would not allow him to use their ports. Ever since then, he has hated them – perhaps all the more so because they have allowed his enemy, Lord Mortimer, to take sanctuary there. Mortimer is still there, of course, somewhere. That has coloured the King's attitude to the French as well. So all the while, Queen Isabella is growing more and more alienated from her husband. If she loved him once, it must be terribly hard for her to continue to feel any affection for him now. He looks on her as his enemy, as a spy in his own home. How could a woman of intelligence and spirit accept that for any time? I've heard rumours that the King might even take away her lands again, and force her to depend upon his charity. Is it any wonder that she seeks protection from another?'

'And who might that be?'

Stapledon hesitated. 'Her brother Charles is the King of France, and he is a great warrior. He has not been beaten in many years. We can make no dent in his great hosts. When he wishes, he overruns Edward's lands in France and steals them from us.'

'Again – what do you want me to do?'

'In court I have grown to know the Queen well. She has some friends whom she trusts above all others. One of them is a good, noble lady, a woman with an estimable husband. She is honourable . . .'

'Yes, yes, yes, she is good and honourable,' Baldwin said a trifle testily.

'I am sorry. This whole affair has thrown me into a turmoil. Well, this lady has done nothing to put herself into bad odour, but a knight fell in love with her. He thought she would be an easy conquest, I fear, and when she resisted him, he used force to violate her. And now he has left our Queen's household to flee the land.'

'I see.'

'It would be marvellous news if he had left the country. I know that the Queen was distressed to hear that one of her countrymen – you see, to make matters worse, he was one of her kinsmen – could behave in such a way with a lady in her household. She would be glad to know that this wretch had fled.'

'Could there be any doubt? Except I see in your eyes that there is more, Bishop, is there not? Why do you not merely capture this Frenchman and hold him?'

Stapledon winced and looked away again. Baldwin could see his attention was concentrated on the great fish pond that lay a matter of a hundred yards away. There was a thin mist lying over the water and wraithlike tendrils spread from it to the grass. 'I have heard conversations . . .'

'Whose conversations? Come, Bishop! If you wish me to do your bidding, at the least you could ensure that I am fully aware of the problems and dangers!'

Stapledon cast him a dark look. 'It was young Despenser. He was discussing the Queen's finances with the King when I walked past the room. She no longer exercises patronage, Baldwin, and she lives away from the King at all times.'

'Why?' Baldwin wondered.

'This is entirely for your ears, you understand?' Stapledon hissed. He held Baldwin's eyes until the knight nodded. 'Very well, then. The King is displeased with her because although all the nobles have been asked to swear an oath to Hugh Despenser, to "live and die" with him, she has refused to make the same commitment. Hugh Despenser is convinced that she intends to harm him. Now he has suggested that since her brother, the King of France, has raised the question of Gascony again . . .'

'What question? He has taken it back and made a truce with us.' Baldwin's tone was carefully neutral. Last year, at St Sardos in the Agenais, part of King Edward II's territory, the French had begun to build a fortified town. Edward's Gascon subjects had attacked, killing a French sergeant, and Edward had prevaricated over sending those guilty into the French king's territory for punishment. As a result the French took Gascony and declared the territory forfeit. Edward responded by sending a host to retake his lands.

But his captain was Edmund, Earl of Kent. He upset the Gascons by extorting money from them, and then took and raped a girl he desired. He lost a battle against the French and agreed a ludicrous truce that left the French holding most of the Duchy.

All because a French sergeant was killed.

'King Charles is demanding that our king should go to him in Paris and do homage for the Dukedom.' The bishop looked mournful.

'There should be no difficulty, surely? The French king would promise safe passage.'

Bishop Stapledon glanced at him. 'Perhaps he would. And would he then apologise if Mortimer appeared in council with him? Mortimer escaped from the Tower and fled to France, so they say. It would humiliate the King if he arrived there to find his enemy waiting. Or would he murmur his gravest commiserations after a vassal of Thomas of Lancaster had sprung forward and stabbed our King to death, or poisoned him? You know the French – they are a wily, cunning people. Anything that would make our King suffer shame or pain would be to them only a cause for celebration. And the French king has already written to say that in his realm, Despenser will be as welcome as Mortimer in this. He insults the King's favoured adviser!'

Baldwin said nothing. His own views on Despenser were too virulent for expression.

'So this man must leave the country – *safely*. Then I can tell the Queen that her lady-in-waiting is safe from the Frenchman's depredations, and we do not antagonise the French king further. I would like you to find him if you can, and let me know where he is.'

'I see,' Baldwin said.

Stapledon sighed. 'He passed through Exeter two days ago. I had a man follow him, and he has sent to me to say that the fellow is now in Dartmouth. Since then, nothing. My man has disappeared.'

The Bishop stared at the ground for a long while, and then in a quiet voice he said, 'Baldwin, my friend, I would consider it a great favour if you would do this for me. The lad who followed him was my brother Richard's son. If some evil has befallen him, I do not know how I shall tell my brother. There is no one else I can send on this very private mission.'

There was a long pause. Baldwin had always done all in his power to avoid becoming embroiled in the murky world of politics, but he was reminded that this kind bishop had been a good friend to him over the years – and it was not truly a political matter. What Stapledon really desired was to find his nephew, not the Frenchman.

'Sir Baldwin,' the bishop went on, 'if he is harmed, my brother will be heartbroken. Bernard is his pride and his life.'

'I shall go, naturally, my lord,' Baldwin said. 'Though I do not know that there can be a happy conclusion to the business. If I learn that this Frenchman has harmed your nephew, I reserve the right to track him down and execute justice. It is my duty, Frenchman or no.'

'You are an excellent man, Sir Baldwin. A man of honour!'

'I do not know that,' Baldwin without a smile. 'The Queen's lady – she is recovered?'

'I do not know whether she will. It was a violent attack. But we should do nothing about it – that is vital! The man must escape so we don't further exacerbate the problems over Gascony. And the rape itself must remain secret. It would bring terrible shame to the Queen and her King, were it thought that one of her household could rape an Englishwoman and escape. Imagine how the realm would respond to that!'

Baldwin shook his head. Both as a father and as a loving husband, he felt he would prefer to destroy this Frenchman for his actions, no matter what the consequences.

'Perhaps you should become an advisor to the King,' the bishop went on. 'You should go to Parliament.'

Baldwin shuddered. 'I hope I shall always do my duty, but God forbid that I should be forced to such a pass! I shall seek the Frenchman for you, and I shall be happy to learn where your nephew is. Tell me, what does this Bernard look like?'

That morning, Simon had woken with a feeling that all was not well. He lay back in his bed and rubbed his eyes blearily. From the open window came the fresh smell of damp soil, and he was sure that it had rained overnight. He listened to the rattle and bump of carts, and hoofs clattering on the cobbled street, and above all, the steady thrumming of ropes in the wind. It was a sound that was all-pervasive here, with so many ships lying in the haven, and Simon was almost accustomed to it now.

The sun was still low in the sky, so at least he had not overslept. Scratching at a bite under his armpit, he wondered vaguely what it could be that seemed so strange to him. It was only when he gazed about and saw there was no smoke, that he realised his fire was not yet lighted, and he growled angrily.

Without a doubt, he was the unluckiest man in the world, to have been plagued with such a pathetic, god-forsaken churl as young Rob.

When he had first arrived, he had known that he must take on a servant, and it had seemed a good idea to get a fellow who was young and quick to learn. Rob he had found by the simple expedient of asking the woman next door if she knew of anyone. She had been happy to recommend the son of her own maid, and soon Rob arrived.

Scruffy the boy was certainly, but also sharp-eyed with a weaselly face, like a small ferret forever seeking the next rabbit. He was clad in a simple tunic, a leather jerkin and cowl, and bare-footed like so many who lived near the ships. Boots cost money, and when the sailors disdained such wastefulness, many of their children had to learn to do without too.

Simon had never heard of a husband to his neighbour's maid, and he suspected that Rob was one of those lads who was born as a result of a ship coming to the haven for a brief stay. They said that many sailors had women in every port – the truth was, many had children too.

Rob was about as conscientious as any lad would be. He was lazy, slow to rise in the morning, always hungry and feeding himself from Simon's larder, and invariably not near when he was needed. Like now. He was still in his bed with his mother, no doubt. Simon was tempted to march in there right now and tell the good-for-nothing fool that he was no longer needed, but that would entail searching for another brat. God's ballocks, he didn't need that!

Rising from his bed, Simon padded about the room. He poured water from a bucket into a bowl and rinsed his face as best he could, cleaning under his armpits and round his neck. His chin was badly stubbled – he'd have to go to the barber again. It was an annoyance, having to shave every couple of days to keep looking presentable. Still, every man had that problem. He dried himself on his shirt, then pulled it over his head. His tunic went over that, and he sat back on his bed to pull on his hosen, first his left leg, binding the laces that held it up, then the right. A cote-hardie over the top, and he was ready for the day. The fire was stone cold, and he kicked at the ashes of the night before with a brief anger before storming out.

In the street, he took a deep breath. There was a mist in the air, and its cool freshness reached down into his breast and set a tingle deep in his lungs. It made him feel like a reborn man and, smiling, he turned to his neighbour's door and banged on it briskly. He recognised this door from halfway down the road, the hinges squeaked so badly. Why they didn't put some grease on the hinges, he didn't know. Today was no different.

'When Rob's awake, could you tell him that if he's this late again, he'll be without a master?' he said with a cold politeness to Rob's mother, and marched down to the pie shop with a spring in his step.

A large jug of morning ale and a pie, and the morning would surely start to improve.

It was only as he sank his face into a foaming beaker of ale that the conversation of the day before returned to him, and his eyes became more introspective.

The last thing Dartmouth needed was a new squabble with an old enemy.

Why should the Lyme men have attacked that ship? Surely it was more likely French pirates?

Or a local ship with a gripe against Pyckard and his men? he wondered. Merchants were always bickering among themselves. Perhaps he should speak to Pyckard, just out of interest. See what *he* had to say about it.

Chapter Seven

Alred woke at almost the same time as Simon, but his head was so full of loose pieces of iron that they rattled with every movement. He opened an eye experimentally, then snapped it shut in a hurry. There was nothing worth looking at that way, and if he attempted to turn over, he ran the risk of his head falling off.

God's teeth, but his head hurt. There was nothing quite so bad as a head like this first thing in the morning, he told himself. Then he reflected he was a liar as the gripes from his belly kicked in. Urgh! He knew he should have eaten something before going and drinking so much. He said it to himself every damned time. It wasn't too much to remember, was it? Except by the time he realised it was a problem, he'd always just woken up with a belly that felt like this . . . He hurried to his feet, hitched up his belt, gave a pained hiccup and fled outside to the open air.

Odd how fresh air makes a man feel better most mornings when he's been taking a little too much. It was that way now. He had felt ready to throw up in there, but now, with the smell of the sea in his nostrils . . . Yes, he was much better already. No need to be— Oh God!

After he had wiped his mouth and the first rough clenching of his belly muscles had subsided, he leaned with one arm on the doorframe, puffing out his cheeks. 'I'm too old for this shite,' he gasped.

'What's wrong, Dad?'

'Law, I'm not your father, so don't be so bleeding disrespectful.'

'What's the matter then, Al?'

'Cheeky b— Just don't ask. All I can say is, when you get to my age, *if* you get to my age, take things easier. There's no point killing yourself every other night.'

'You hung over again?'

'There are times I really hate you, Law. You know that?'

'You are my master still,' Law said. 'Suppose you could try to thrash me? It might make you feel better.'

Alred snarled, 'If you're going to talk rubbish, boy, go and fetch me a morning whet. Sweet Christ, but my mouth tastes like a rat crawled in and used it as a privy!'

'You're sure you can cope with more ale?'

'Piss off!' And as the lad laughed and went on his way, Alred said to Bill, 'I really hate that kid sometimes!'

Bill was still sprawled on his blanket. He sat up now and yawned. 'Law acting the fool again?' he asked as he scratched and then stretched luxuriously.

'You can have no idea.'

'He's your apprentice, Al. You ought to teach him respect.'

'Oh, go swyve a mule,' Alred said weakly. 'You wouldn't say that if you were in this body.'

'Haha! That's why I feel safe to take the piss today.'

Alred wandered to a large log and sat down, belching and releasing a gust of foul-smelling wind.

'Ach, don't fart as well,' Bill complained. 'It's bad enough in here already.'

'I know. Next time I'll demand a better storeroom.'

'It's got straw, so it's warm enough, I suppose. What we really need is a nice cuddly woman in here to keep us busy, though.'

'You can get one of them in any of the taverns in Lower Street, I daresay,' Alred said absently. He burped again, and shivered. Why did he feel as though there was an icy chill in the place? Yet he was sweating like a hog in sunshine. There was no sense to it, but he got like it every time he drank too much.

'I don't think we can afford any of them!' Bill said, sinking back on his makeshift bed.

Leaving him there, Alred went to the door again and peered out.

The street here had a good view over the haven most mornings, although today it was obscured by a low mist that lay over all the water. It was a curious sight, a white, rolling smoke that poured in up the river from the sea. Projecting from the nothingness beneath was a forest of mastheads. It was very odd.

He made his unsteady way the few yards over to the pit. All his sand and gravel was still there, and the pile of cobbles ready to be inserted and rammed home to create the new surface. And there, in the hole, was the dead man still, waiting for the Coroner's visit. A thin crowd of gawpers stood at the end of the hole, peering down at the corpse.

Alred walked to the edge and gazed with them. It was strange to be looking down at the hole like this. Usually he would be in there mending the roadway, and he'd have a different view of people. He'd recognise some from the sight of a chin or nostrils seen from beneath. Women he would view from a more interesting perspective than most men would ever gain.

There were several who stood and stared today. Some urchins, a few tranters and tatterdemalion scroungers, and one man who must have been a sailor from the way he rolled as he walked, a big man with a square face and a chin that had only very recently been shaved. He looked the sort of man who was capable with his hands, strong and self-reliant. The fellow was familiar, but as so often, seeing him from an equal footing, as it were, Alred couldn't place him.

'Morning, master,' the watchman said. He was sitting on the step of a building nearby, his staff resting in his crossed arms, legs bent so that he had to peer over his knees to talk to Alred. 'You sleep well?'

There was more than a hint of jealousy in his tone. Alred gave a slight grimace. 'Sleep? In that little workshop? No, friend. There's no comfort on a solid floor like that, and if there were, the worry about finishing all this in time to get on to my next job would stop me being able to enjoy myself.'

'Strange. I would have thought the constant snoring would have kept you awake rather than the cold or worry,' the guard said drily. He yawned. 'Some of us have been fighting the damned pigs away all night.'

It was the same everywhere, as Alred knew too well. Any family would have a hog or two – they were a staple. And it was easier to let them feed themselves by rooting about in the kennel or among the other piles of rubbish that lay about in the roads. 'No town in the country can keep the streets safe from pigs,' he said.

'You're right there. There were three last night, one after the other, all trying to get to this poor devil's corpse. I know them, mind.'

'How?'

'Oh, we mark them. If a pig's found wandering and is being a nuisance, we cut off its tail and charge the owner to get it back. That's the first time. If we find it again, we kill it, and he can have the body if he pays a fine – four pennies, one per foot. We'll have to do more soon, though. The damned things are making a mess of the place.'

Alred said nothing. This area was a mess anyway. He allowed his gaze to move up the street, from the corpse here in the working, past the large dungheap from the stable further down the hill, to the pile of broken timbers and trash from a house whose outbuildings had collapsed, past the kennel full of human excrement, and on.

The watchman got the message. He muttered sourly, 'Let's just hope the Coroner gets here sooner rather than later. We all need to get back to normal.'

'That poor bugger won't, though, will he?' Alred commented, jerking his chin at the body in the hole.

'No. Wonder where he came from?'

'He's not a local man?'

'Him?' the watchman chuckled. 'He's about as local as you are, man. I've never seen him before. Christ Himself may know where he's from, but I don't.'

* * *

Simon arrived in his rooms to find Stephen already frowning at a set of records.

'I cannot make these numbers add up, Bailiff.'

'I never can either,' Simon said lightly. 'Stephen, I am going to visit Paul Pyckard. Do you know where he lives?'

'He's not far from Hawley's house on Lower Street. Three doors south, I think. Why?'

'I want to speak to him – see if anything was actually stolen from his vessel. Pirates normally try to steal everything they can. But not to take it, slaughter all the crew and even try to burn it . . . that makes no sense at all.'

'No.' He was still a moment. 'Have you heard what people are saying?'

'Let me guess: the devil came and took the evil bastards because the master had insulted a nun on his last voyage?'

'He did?' Stephen said, wide-eyed.

'No. What can you tell me about Pyckard?'

'I haven't been here as long as you, Bailiff. You know him better than I.'

'You will have heard more gossip than I,' Simon said knowingly. It was always the case that while merchants might detest each other, their clerks would still deal with each other, discussing the antics of their masters as a source of joint amusement.

'He's not been well for some weeks. I know that much. He was married, but his wife died in a storm at sea on one of his ships, these fifteen years since. He was distraught when that happened, I heard. They were devoted.'

'Yes. I heard that too,' Simon said. 'What of the ship?'

'The *Saint John* replaced one he lost years ago, I think. Someone told me that that cog, the *Saint Rumon*, was his first; he bought it from the proceeds of importing spices and cloths. Now he's got three ships.'

'Very good. See if you can learn anything more.'

'I will do what I can, Bailiff.'

'I won't be long,' Simon said next, making for the door. 'I

merely want to see if I can understand this. It seems most . . . curious.'

He repeated that word to himself as he strode up the street towards the house Stephen had indicated. The mist was burning away as he walked and he could see some of the nearer ships beginning to show themselves, the great hulls looming through the bright fog like ghosts. There was a strange effect on his eyes. He'd noticed it before when there had been a mist in from the sea, but never so clearly as now: as he stood on the shore, he could almost imagine he was being drawn out into the clutching tendrils of fog, to be swallowed by the ships.

Superstition! he told himself. Now, in the daylight, he felt much bolder. There were more important things to worry about today!

Alred was soon back with the others. They were chatting in lively fashion as he appeared in the doorway.

'Ho ho, here's the master!' Law cackled. 'Been sick yet?'

'Be silent, boy. Sweet Jesus's pains, you'd drive a man to drink, you would. Did you ever pour me that drink.'

'Have a hair of the dog that bit you,' Bill said more sympathetically. 'Come on, Al. It's not as though you can't hold it. Fetch yourself a beer. What are we?'

Law laughed again. 'We're paviours!'

'I can't hear you, Al.'

'Bleeding paviours.'

'Still can't hear you!'

'We're bleeding paviours, you deaf son of a goat!' Alred said, and despite himself he grinned as he said it, marching to the small barrel they'd bought earlier in the week and pouring a measure into a drinking horn he'd stolen from the tavern. He took the drink to the doorway and peered out. Soon the ale began to seep into his belly and bowels, and he did feel better. He smiled at Bill as he clapped him on the back and walked out to buy some pies.

But as Bill left, Alred frowned again. That square face in the crowd kept returning to his thoughts. He only wished he could figure out why.

The house was a pleasing building, clearly recently built, with a solid oaken frame and well-limed cob filling the gaps. Simon knocked on a door that had been limed as well, and waited.

It took a little time for the door to open and a nervous-looking man peered out at him. 'Yes?'

'I want to talk to Master Pyckard.'

'I don't know that he's ready to see people yet. He . . .'

'Tell him the Bailiff of the abbey is here – the Representative of the Keeper of the Port. I need to speak to him now,' Simon said roughly.

The face took on a still more anxious appearance, then the man slipped away, the door closing quietly behind him, a bar or bolt sliding into place to lock it, leaving Simon fuming in the street. Then there was the sound of slowly marching feet, and the rattle of the lock, and the door opened.

'Bailiff? We've met.'

Paul Pyckard was a man of a little less than Simon's height, with a face that was oddly skull-like. The cheekbones stood so prominently that in the shadow of the doorway it was hard to believe that there was any flesh covering them. His eyes were bright and hard, compelling as a snake's, and when his mouth opened, his grey teeth matched the colour of his skin. Clad in a heavy robe with fur trimming, it was hard to imagine he felt the cold in this weather, but Simon wondered if that was because he was truly unwell.

'Master Pyckard, I am sorry about your ship, but I wondered if you could help me. I want to know all I can about it.'

'You'd best come inside,' Pyckard said, and stood back from the door, shuffling like a very old man.

As Simon entered, he sensed a coldness that was nothing to do with the house. It was as though Pyckard himself was exuding a chilly atmosphere.

This was not the man he remembered. Last time they had met was only a matter of three weeks ago, and then Pyckard had seemed fit and well. He'd had the broad shoulders, hearty manner and bronzed skin of a natural sailor. His bluff character was in keeping, too. Simon had always thought that seamen were so used to risking their lives that they made the most of every moment on shore.

'You see a difference in me?' Pyckard asked as he led the way down the passage.

'I confess, I was surprised to see how you have changed, master.'

'It began some weeks ago. At first it was just a bit of a pain in my belly, and I grew short of breath.' As if to confirm his point, he wheezed and coughed wretchedly. 'No, I need no help, I thank you. After a little while, the pain began to grow. Ach, and now it's with me the whole time. I cannot concentrate at all.'

'You've seen a physician?'

Pyckard threw him a look that combined contempt and annoyance. 'I am not so poor that I would seek to save money at the cost of my life, Bailiff.' He continued on his way, leading Simon into a large parlour at the rear of the house, where he walked painfully to a large chair, sinking into it gratefully.

'Sir?'

'Yes. You want a drink?' Pyckard asked.

The servant who had opened the door so nervously stood by the buttery at the far side of the room. Simon asked for ale, and Pyckard a quart of wine, and the man disappeared. At least Simon could now comprehend his trepidation. The whole household must be in fear of the thought of the death of the master.

While he waited for the drinks to arrive, Simon studied the room. It was obvious that Pyckard had enjoyed a successful life. His walls were covered in rich hangings, one a set of three hunting scenes that gleamed and glimmered in the light. His hearth was paved with bricks, while the rest of his floor had been tiled, the cost of which Simon could only wonder at. High overhead there was a louvre arrangement which was opened and closed by pulling on a rope. A sideboard with three shelves displaying highly polished pewter tableware added to the sense of opulence in the room.

The man himself was clearly unaware of it all. He sat uncomfortably, wincing every so often, shifting in his seat, grunting and sighing. His fingers rapped on the arm of his great chair as though in time to some internal music. When the drinks appeared, he grabbed for his jug, almost spilling the wine down his breast, and poured a large gobletful, all but draining it at the first draught.

'Master Pyckard, it's plain that you aren't feeling well. Would you prefer me to come back later?'

'That, Bailiff, could be a waste of your time if you tried it,' Pyckard said with a twist of his lips that was intended to show humour. 'I may not be here for much longer.'

'This pain abates somewhat through the day?'

'There are stupefactives which my physician has given me, but they work less and less well. No, there is no cure and no means of preventing the pain. I've confessed, and that took a weight off my soul, which helps a little.' He looked past Simon's shoulder to the tall window beyond. 'There is some peace from that.'

'Something you did in the past?' Simon wondered.

'Something that's none of your affair, Master Bailiff!' Pyckard snapped, but not rudely. He squirmed in his seat again. 'So ask away. It's what you're here for!'

'It's your ship – the cog *Saint John*. I'd heard that there was nothing taken from her. Is that right?'

'So far as I know, yes. I haven't been to inspect her myself, of course. I don't think I could walk so far. Christ alive! It is hard enough for me to walk to my door and back. Only two days ago I could walk about the town – but now? Nothing!'

'Does it not trouble you that the ship was taken and her cargo left aboard? That to me seems most strange.'

'There are many strange things in life, Bailiff. The *Saint John* was one of my older vessels, so perhaps these pirates decided she wasn't worth the capture once they'd taken her.'

Simon tried to keep the disbelief from his voice. 'You are suggesting that mariners would take her, and then leave her to burn, still with a valuable cargo on board, because they thought she was too old and not worth their time? Surely they'd have seen that from the outset? If the craft was not worthy of capture, they would have left her.'

'You are not a man of the sea, are you, Bailiff? Let me explain. The ship was perfectly well worth taking from the point of view of the cargo, but she herself was – *is* – old. Perhaps they saw the second ship arriving and knew there was no time to move all the cargo from the *John* to their own ship. And the *John* is a slow beast. Seeing a faster ship appear over the horizon, they may simply have sought to destroy evidence of their crime. It could have worked, were Hawley and his men less fast and seamanlike.'

Simon fiddled with the long tongue of his belt, which dangled over his thigh. 'Master Hawley caught the ship and put out the fire in a very efficient manner.'

'He's a good man, Hawley.'

'It was fortunate that he appeared at that moment.'

'Yes. But it was on the main route we both use.'

Simon nodded. 'Do you have any idea who could have attacked her?'

'On the open sea? Are you joking? It could be any one of a hundred hundred men. There are pirates from all over Normandy, the Breton lands . . . they come here and pick off what they can all the time. They've stopped their raids on the shore now, but our ships are always at risk. Then there are the men from our own coast. If a ship from a Cinque Port saw a ship in danger, it might wonder whether it was worth taking her and stealing the cargo rather than helping her to port.'

'What of the men of Lyme?'

Pyckard shrugged. 'It's possible, I suppose. Yes. They have had arguments with us for many years now. It's only two years since the last fight. Probably about time one of us was caught by them.'

'Is it so normal for you to fear the people from other towns?' Simon asked. He *was* still very new to the ways of the sea, he reminded himself.

'Those daft buggers from Lyme have no comprehension of the

rules of the sea or of land. Well, what can you expect from a bunch of peasants from Dorset, when all's said and done.'

'But why should they pick on your ship?'

'I think it all began when some Dartmouth men found some rich fishing fields. When the men from Lyme heard about it, they barged in and tried to take the fishing from them.'

'I see,' Simon said. This was one of those disputes that had started in the mists of history, and which was kept alive by a number of unscrupulous folk who saw benefit in being able to steal from others who had worked for their rewards. 'And the last fight was two years ago?'

'About that. They helped the men of Weymouth and Portland when those thieving churls robbed a Plymouth cog. They took the ship, killed the men aboard, stole all the goods and scuttled her.'

'Is it normal for them to sink an enemy's ship?'

'What else do you do with it if the thing's clearly recognisable? Better to burn and sink her than leave her as evidence of your crime.'

Simon was tempted to ask whether Pyckard himself had engaged in such actions, but somehow this did not feel like the right time. The man was looking weaker and weaker, and his hand, as he reached for his wine, trembled like one who had the ague. If, as he had said, he had already confessed to his own crimes, what was the point in Simon's asking too? He wasn't going to be around for much longer, for good or ill.

'There was nothing on the ship that would have tempted a man to rob it?' he tried.

Pyckard's hand stilled, as though he was concentrating with a massive effort. Then the goblet rose to his mouth, and he slurped at it thirstily, as if it was an elixir that could save him. 'The cargo was all there – I've already said. There was nothing too valuable, anyway. The more expensive items I'd saved to be sent on my next sailing.'

'And the crew were all dead. No one remained?'

He sighed and sat back again. 'Apparently so.'

'How many crewmen were there?'

'Eleven all told, I think. The master and ten more. Yes, eleven.'

'What can you tell me about them? Who were they?'

'Oh, the master was Adam. I regret losing him, for he was my best man. He's been with me for years. I trusted him with my life, and many times he has repaid my trust. Then there were Odo and Vincent, two men I've also known since they were young. They were rough and ready types, but sound in the ways of the sea. They were brought up to it from childhood, so it's no surprise. They certainly knew how to sail, but they were bastards on board . . . *and* on land!'

'Why do you say that?'

Pyckard stared at him and, for a moment, Simon thought there was genuine hatred in his eyes. 'They would drink and fight, or even try to rape women in the town. I will not miss them, the churls! But there are others who deserve to be mourned: like young Danny from Hardness. He was an orphan I took in some years ago, along with his brother Moses, when his father died at sea. He always wanted to follow his father . . .' his gaze turned inward sorrowfully, 'and I suppose he has had his wish, poor Danny. There were others – three brothers from Exmouth I've used for many years . . . Why do you need to know?'

'What of the others? That's only half of them.'

With asperity, Pyckard spat, 'There were men from Hardness, and some few from farther afield! Strangers, all of 'em. That black-hearted piece of hog's dung Kena bought up four or five of my men just as the ship was sailing. I had to find new crew in a hurry, damn him! Who are they? I don't know. I'll see them in hell soon, so I'll ask them then! Right – what more do you want to know? I've told you most of them. The rest are dead, so their names hardly matter, do they?' The merchant settled back and closed his eyes, drawing several deep breaths. 'I am sorry, but this slow death is exasperating! A dagger in the throat would be preferable to this drawn-out torture.'

'I am sorry, Master Pyckard. I am just trying to understand what could have happened. So you can think of no reason why the ship should have been attacked?'

'Wrong, Bailiff,' Pyckard said, but his voice was weary rather than bitter. 'I can think of many. There are lots of people who might like to ruin me by destroying my ships and livelihood. Kena hates me, and he likes to thwart me. Perhaps *he* had *his* men take my ship – and then the cowardly sot saw a sail on the horizon and ran away before he was caught. You take your pick, Master Bailiff.'

Chapter Eight

Hilary Beauley swung himself from the ratline over the sheer and onto the rope ladder, letting himself down into his boat. 'Cast off,' he ordered.

The little vessel lurched under the strong pull of the two oarsmen, and he was soon on the beach at Hardness. Here he sprang from the craft onto the shingle and set off homewards.

His house was less impressive than those of Kena or Pyckard, let alone Hawley, but he was happy that he was making enough money. Soon he would have another ship, and then he could begin to expand his contacts, start to import more valuable goods, take tin and cloth further afield, bring back spices and dyestuffs. The things that made a man wealthy.

Others he had grown up with had taken to business of different forms. For him, though, the only thing that mattered was the quick route to riches. He had studied merchants when he was young, and as soon as he could save, he had invested in a mercantile venture to Portugal. The wines brought back had not been so successful as the Gascon ones, but he had hopes that if the French remained in Gascony, as they threatened, the value of foreign wines would naturally increase. Until the Portuguese realised that, he could make a lot of cash. And it was easier than following the convoys. Damn that – in convoy every man was under the eye of his competitors. No one liked that.

His ship was almost ready. He'd looked to its fittings with care, and now, with a sudden injection of money, he had enough to order the new ship as well. Plans were being drawn up with the shipwrights, and when they were ready, he'd be able to order it.

The new one would be a bigger ship, a cog of forty or fifty tuns.

The threat of war with France was worrying, of course. Like all the other merchants, he depended on the money which trade with Gascony brought in, and even if he kept his Portuguese interests going, there was always the danger of fresh piracy. The Bretons were very competent sailors and their fast boats could be a significant hazard to a merchant vessel. The fate of the *Saint John* would soon be forgotten. That was nothing: if the Bretons caught a ship, it'd be wholesale slaughter for the crew and the theft of everything on board. The money which one cog like her would bring to a small French fishing community could not be ignored.

As soon as war was declared, all the town's ships would be pressed into the King's service, too. Usually Edward would pay quite well, by the tun, but there was no saying how long it would take before the money would start to come in. Even if Beauley lived, it could be months or years before the King made good the debt. And by then, the ship could be sunk or stolen. War was a fickle master.

No, best look to making money while he could and try to avoid being pressed into the King's host. Perhaps he could ensure that his competitors were called into service rather than him. After all, other men had larger ships for transporting horses and men, while if smaller landing ships were needed, his was rather too large. The dangers of bringing an army over the water were well enough known to all. With any luck, his vessel should fall between the two stools. Especially if he was careful to make clear that the others in town had better craft for raiding as well.

The others would do the same to him if they had a chance. And he was shrewd enough to know that this was exactly what they would attempt: a brief talk with a government procurer, perhaps with a bribe as well because the devils were venal to a man. Well, if that was what the likes of Hawley, Pyckard and Kena would try, so would he.

Hawley, Pyckard and Kena . . . Pyckard would soon be no threat; he was dying, and anyway, since the loss of his wife in that squall in 1309, he had been a weaker man than the others. They were still fighting to be the most important merchant in town; while he had given up. Oddly, he had developed more of an interest in the future since his imminent death had become so obvious. A man didn't need an oracle to foretell his end. It would be very soon now.

Yes. Now all Hilary had to worry about were the other two: Hawley and Kena.

Hawley had been first on the scene when the *Saint John* was discovered, he reminded himself, and Kena wanted more than anything to be able to damage Hawley. Perhaps there was some leeway for Beauley in that. He could set the two of them against each other. And anyone with a brain must see that Hawley was the most likely killer of the crew of the *Saint John*. He had got there first. Perhaps he didn't rob anything because he knew other ships were near, including Beauley's own. The thieving old goat would scarcely have been able to keep his hands from the cargo else.

Perhaps he ought to visit Kena.

Baldwin had been offered a place on a ship to make his journey, but he rejected that in favour of a ride. The roads were appalling from Exeter down to Dartmouth, but the weather had not been too bad in the last few weeks and he hoped that the tracks would be dry at least. With luck it would take only a day and a half. He asked the bishop to send a messenger to his wife Jeanne explaining his delay and reassuring her that he would be home again as soon as possible, and then ordered that his horse be saddled and prepared. After packing his few belongings into a satchel, he walked down into the hall to take his leave of the bishop.

'You are ready, Sir Baldwin?'

The knight nodded, sitting and drinking a little watered wine as the bishop finished surveying some papers and then passed them to a clerk to deal with. He looked at Baldwin. 'I have already taken Mass for my servants. Would you care to join me at my chapel? I should like to pray for your success and safety.'

Nothing loath, Baldwin followed the bishop into his private chapel, and the two men washed their hands together before kneeling.

It was a proof of the bishop's kindliness, Baldwin felt, that he should have asked Baldwin here to join him. It was rare that he would ask someone to kneel with him. In fact, in all the years Baldwin had known him – eight now – he had never before been asked to pray with Bishop Stapledon. He felt honoured.

That feeling stayed with him all the way from Bishop's Clyst to Exeter itself, and out the other side as he went over the great spans of the bridge, trying to ignore the foul stench from the tanners' yards at Exe Island. He was still aware of the warmth of the bishop's farewell as he rode along the well-beaten trail that led through the bustling town of Newton Abbot and on to the little village of Ipplepen in the early afternoon. He had covered a good many miles, perhaps seven leagues, and his horse was glad of the rest as he asked the keeper at the priory's gate whether he might stop a short while and partake of their hospitality. Fortunately the priory had only that morning racked off a fresh ale, and he was offered a bench to sit at, bread, cheese and ale. The Augustinian monks who lived there were known for their generosity, and after a good quart and a half of their strong ale, Baldwin was determined to excuse himself and continue on his way, for else he must lose the afternoon's travelling. He was keen to complete his mission, both so that he could return homewards, and also so that he might reassure the bishop that nothing untoward had happened to his nephew.

'Ridiculous, anyway,' he muttered to himself as he checked the girth and pulled a face. This horse was always keen to avoid too tight a strap, and all too often a lazy groom would fail to tighten it properly. Feeling the horse's head turn towards him, Baldwin met his gaze sternly, then suddenly jabbed a thumb up into the beast's belly. As he neighed angrily, Baldwin tugged the girth hard and managed to buckle it two holes tighter than before. 'Don't be so froward,' he grunted as he clambered up and began to make his way beneath the priory's gatehouse.

The warm glow which he had felt began to fade almost as soon as he left Ipplepen. The hospitality there had been of the best – but only after Baldwin had made a donation to their funds. It was reasonable that a man like him should be asked to make a contribution, of course, but the change in attitude of their hospitaller had been so plain as soon as he had reached into his purse that Baldwin had felt a little insulted.

And yes, it *was* kind of the bishop to give him the comfort of a prayer with him before sending him off on his journey – a sign of his generous spirit – and yet there was something odd in his expression as he gave Baldwin his farewell. To Baldwin's mind the bishop had looked almost shifty as he said the short prayer for a swift journey and safe arrival. The knight began to wonder at the reasons for the bishop's behaviour, and the only explanations which occurred to him were not comforting.

Simon returned to his place of work and sat for a long time in his chair while Stephen scratched at his parchments. After some while, Stephen rose and offered to buy some wine for them both. 'The weather is a little cool,' he said.

'What, this?' Simon asked, surprised. He had loosened his jack because he felt so warm. 'You have ice in your veins, man.'

'Perhaps,' Stephen said with a dry smile. He forbore to mention that he sat in the full window with the chill gusts blowing through him, while Simon had the benefit of a chair in a draught-free part of the room.

'Pyckard was in a dreadful way,' the bailiff said reflectively. 'I suppose learning that his crew is gone would hurt any man, but he seems to be ruined with this illness too.'

'I had heard he was dying. He has sunk very quickly in the last few days,' Stephen said. 'It's certain sure that he won't last much longer.'

'He spoke of several sailors – the dead man we found, Danny, then two others called Vincent and Odo. There were three from Exmouth, and he mentioned a man called Adam, too, although he seemed to forget him later.'

'I've heard of them,' Stephen said. 'Vincent and Odo are well-known troublemakers. They'd fight and brawl with any. There was even a rumour about them attempting a rape.'

'He said something about that. What of the others? Did you know this Adam?'

'Everyone knew Adam. He was Pyckard's best shipmaster. Adam was the sort of man to whom Pyckard entrusted all his most difficult missions – a strong, capable type, and an excellent sailor. He's the one whom Pyckard will miss most sorely.'

'There must be other sailors as capable?'

'It's not just a matter of competence, Bailiff. Adam was his longest-serving and loyal servant.'

'So if someone wanted to ruin Pyckard, removing this man would have been very effective?' Simon mused.

'Certainly he'll be missed more than Vincent and Odo. They were vicious brutes. Few will mourn their passing.'

'What of this Danny?'

'He was a good lad, I think. Youngish, with a small family over towards Hardness. Moses was his elder brother, and Adam too was related to him somehow, I believe. They were brothers-in-law, maybe? I can tell you this: Adam was a powerful fighter, and if he saw someone hurt Danny, he'd have made the man pay. He looked after Danny from the day Pyckard took him in.'

'He was an orphan, Pyckard said.'

'Yes. His mother had died, then his father lost his life at sea. Pyckard took both the boys in after that, but it was Adam who looked after him really.'

Simon said tentatively: 'I have heard that some sailors . . . they miss their women and can fall prey to . . .'

Stephen laughed aloud. 'If you'd seen Adam, you'd know that was nonsense! No, he was a kindly man, that's all. And he'd been devoted to his master from the early days when Pyckard had nothing.'

Simon sighed heavily. 'Hard to imagine that so many can be taken away so suddenly. It wouldn't be so bad if they'd all died in a gale, I suppose, but to be wiped out by pirates so incompetent that they fail even to steal the cargo, that is astonishingly pointless and wasteful. Poor bastards!'

* * *

John Hawley went up the rope to the ship with the agility of a man who had been a sailor for almost as long as he could walk, climbing hand over hand without pause. Once on deck, he glanced about him at the work going on even as Cynric bellowed that their master was aboard.

'Cynric – what have you found?'

'No more bodies, master. There's some as said they'd prefer not to come here if there were,' Cynric said with a chuckle. In his belt beside his dagger he had a long end of rope with a heavy knob plaited into the end. He tapped it happily. 'They changed their minds, though.'

'Is it obvious whose ship she is?'

Cynric looked at him from the corner of his eye. 'As clear as you could want.'

Hawley nodded expressionlessly. It wasn't any surprise. He'd had no doubt as soon as he'd seen the ship on the horizon, and even after the fire, most men from the town would recognise her outline as the *Saint John*. The cargo had been checked last evening, too, so it had been plain enough. If no one had recognised her, he could have claimed the whole value, perhaps. It would have been a good prize.

'We may be able to claim salvage, of course,' he wondered aloud.

The laws concerning the sea were variable and confusing even to those who lived by them, but if a ship was lost by her master and then her cargo or the ship herself were rescued, her saviour could claim half the value of the ship and her load. Likewise if she was wrecked, a man who found her could claim half. It was the only way to ensure that wreckage which could be of value to the King was reported.

Cynric was eyeing him again from the corner of his eye, and Hawley sighed, 'Come on, then. What is it?'

'You won't like it.'

'Maybe not. What's new?'

'Your clerk. Did you know he's been gaming regularly?'

Hawley shrugged. 'All men gamble every so often. It's like breathing the air, drinking ale or laying a wench.'

'He's been losing a lot.'

'Oh no! Not at the Porpoise?'

There were many establishments in Dartmouth catering for sailors who might have a couple of pennies to spend, but few, if any, had a reputation to match that of the Porpoise. The men there were without any doubt the worst fixers, felons and fiddlers known to any game which aspired to an element of chance. Hawley wrinkled his nose. 'Any idea how much?'

'Pyket reckons he owes them several marks.'

Hawley whistled. 'I didn't know he could afford that kind of misfortune.'

'I don't think he can.'

'I see.' The merchant clapped Cynric on the shoulder, took a last look about the deck then swung over the side again, slipping quickly down the rope and letting himself back into the little boat, which set off immediately for the shore. When it was beached, he sprang out and made his way homewards.

'Wine!' he shouted as he walked in, and went through the front room to the smaller counting-house behind. Here he found his clerk Peter running his pen down a long list of numbers, his face scowling with concentration.

'Ah, master!' he said as soon as he caught sight of Hawley. He continued to the bottom of the page and carefully scrawled a note with his metal scribe on a waxed tablet, before turning to the shipman.

Hawley grinned at him as he sat on his chair at the far wall. He had too many enemies to trust an open door at his back, and preferred always to sit with a wall behind him, any doorways before him, and a strong blade always within reach. 'Come on, then. What's the best of it and what's the worst? Any bad news for me?'

Peter Strete was the least likely-looking clerk Hawley had ever met. Usually they were scrawny, tedious fellows, but this Peter fairly bubbled with good humour: a cheerful man with smiling face, rosy cheeks and bright blue eyes, his manner seemed to show that he saw the best in every one. He was occasionally prone to introspection, becoming a little quiet – usually in the mornings. Hawley now wondered whether those little moods had any connection with his gaming losses?

'Well, master, I doubt you'll regret collecting the *Saint John* in a long month of Sundays. If you succeed in winning her whole value, you'll be taking on a hundred stones of weld, seven barrels of potash, eight hundred iron spurs, three posnets . . . Not a bad result.'

'What's the likelihood that Pyckard can win it back?'

'Depends how keen he is to bother. Any legal argument is likely to last months. We can string it out, too, so he's bound to be dead first. Actually, I doubt he'll bother. It's a good win for no expense, but there's little of real value. The main thing is, the ship herself.'

'Good. There's no one to dispute our claim either, since he has no family left. Right! Do you arrange for the ship to be refitted at our expense, and we'll get the thing back over to Britanny and sell her cargo. If she's still seaworthy, we'll soon know it. My only concern is, she's slow. Perhaps it would be better to have her valued as well, so we can decide whether to sell her off and take the money.'

'We don't want anyone taking her, do we?'

'Like the men at Lyme, you mean?' Hawley said with a cynical lift of his eyebrow. 'I don't think there's any risk of that. Do you?'

'No, sir.' He bowed and walked from the room.

As his servant disappeared into the screens passage, Hawley glanced down at his cash boxes. Strete had no money of his own he reminded himself. All he had was what Hawley gave him. If he was losing money in gambling, he must have found a source of cash.

'Have you robbed me, old friend?' Hawley murmured aloud. 'Because if you have, I swear you'll regret every penny!'

Chapter Nine

The arrival of the Coroner late that afternoon spelled the end of Simon's concentration for the day.

'You Puttock?' he boomed as he walked into Simon's hall, and the Bailiff looked up with irritation from the numbers he and Stephen were so carefully trying to add up.

To Simon, the Roman numerals only made sense when they had been added and the total was already inserted at the bottom of his rolls. Just now, looking at the long list of pounds, shillings and pence, his head was spinning. He could hardly read the difference between one pound and ten on a tally-stick, his eyes were so tired. His response was abrupt.

'I am Simon Puttock, Keeper of this Port. Who are you?'

The man who had entered stood with his legs set widely apart and gazed about him with an apparently approving expression on his face. He was tall, at least six foot one, and had an almost entirely round face, with a thick bush of beard that overhung his chest like a heavy gorget. His eyes were dark brown and shrewd, beneath a broad and tall brow. His face was criss-crossed with wrinkles, making him appear perhaps a little older than he really was, but Simon was sure he had to be at least fifty. His flesh had the toughened look of well-cured leather that only a man who has spent much of his life in the open air would acquire.

'Me?' The stranger's eyes widened in surprise. 'Don't ye know me? I'm Sir Richard de Welles. Coroner.'

His clothing would once have been valuable. A good soft tunic and velvet cote-hardie in red had both faded with the years, and now looked scruffy and over-worn. He had leather bracelets at his wrists, and his leather sword-belt was good quality, but for all that, he reminded Simon of his friend Baldwin. There was another man who rarely took any care over his appearance.

Simon swallowed back his annoyance and stood more civilly. 'Ah, Sir Richard, I am glad to meet you. There is much for you to do.'

'So I heard!' the Coroner said. Simon was sure that the ships on the other side of the estuary could hear every word. 'First, though, I'd appreciate a drink. It's been a long, hard ride to get here today. Where's the best inn in the town? Come on, man. You can show me the way, can't you?'

Simon felt his hackles rise. 'I happen to be very busy. There are figures here which need to be checked.'

The Coroner looked at him, then glanced at Stephen. 'What's *he* supposed to do, then?'

'He is my clerk.'

'So let him clerk. You're the Keeper. You can keep me company! Ha! Come on!'

Somewhat to his surprise, Simon found himself outside his hall and in the street while the Coroner maintained a steady, loud monologue. 'Look at the state of that house there. I remember when it was owned by the richest man in the town. Wouldn't keep me dogs in it now. Looks like someone's been having a piss up all the walls. Ha! Remember this place well enough. Used to have a maid there who'd look after any man who could afford to buy her a gallon of ale. Ha! Trouble was, by the time she was frisky, you'd had enough to melt your tarse. Still had the ability! Oh, Christ's bones in a basket, I remember *that* house. It was where—'

'You seem to know this town remarkably well for one who is so new to it,' Simon observed acidly.

'Well, I'm hardly new, you see. When I was a youngster, I was trained in arms, riding, hunting, drinking and fornication in this very town! Ha! In those days we had more fun, believe you me! We'd fight often enough when the King told us, but there was little of this modern garbage where you're expected to change allegiances depending on who your lord and master thinks might be important at the turn of the moon. We had something called loyalty. HOI!'

The object of his shout was a youth who stood at the street corner up ahead of them. A maid had flinched as she passed him, and it was clear enough that the lad had offered her an insult.

'What?'

Simon vaguely recognised him. He was an apprentice from one of the smiths down near the water's edge.

'What's your name?' asked Sir Richard.

'I'm Humphrey. Why, what's it to you?'

'I'm the Coroner, lad, that's why. If I see you molesting another woman while I'm here, I'll have you arrested and sent to Exeter gaol.'

'I didn't touch her!' the apprentice declared hotly.

By now Simon and the Coroner were level with him, and Simon could sense the fellow's sudden trepidation as the big man leaned down, his jaw jutting. 'I know what I saw, son, and if you touch her again, I'll have you flogged in Exeter. *Clear?*'

The fellow scurried away with an anxious look over his shoulder, and the fact that the Coroner did not move but remained staring at him until he had rounded the next street corner, must have lent wings to his feet.

'Damned little turd! I'm not so old I can't see when a lad sticks his hand down a woman's . . .'

'I didn't see that,' Simon protested.

'You must have done it yourself when you were younger, eh? I know I did. And he thought I wouldn't guess. That's the trouble with these little bratchets today, they think sex started around the end of the famine and no one before that knew anything about it. Well, if the fool thinks he can get one over me, he'll soon learn to regret his impudence, hey?'

'Yes. Of course,' Simon said coldly.

'Cheer yourself, Bailiff. I was in court a little while ago, with a fellow accused of rape, and the justice called the victim to speak. He says "What happened, chit?" "Well," she said, "he was in the lane when I was walking to the cows, and he grabbed me." "Aye," said the justice, "what then?" "He pulled me into the barn." "Aye," says the justice, "what then?" "Well," she said, "he took my hands and he bound them." "Aye," said the justice, "what then?" "He would have tied my legs too, but I thank God I managed to keep them apart and stop him!" Eh? Haha! Good one, eh?'

They had reached the doors of a tavern with a scruffy bush tied over the door, and Sir Richard looked up at it appreciatively. 'This looks a good enough place. Vaguely remember it from when I was a lad. I think I was knocked out in here once during a fight. I'd called a sailor a lily-livered son of a whore, and he took umbrage. Seem to recall seeing a large lump of wood heading my way, and me too drunk to duck. Hurt like hell, too. Still, you live and learn, don't you?'

He led the way in through the low doorway, and Simon, feeling more than a little bemused by the constant monologue, trailed after him with a sense of unreality. The only thought in his mind was, that any man who entered a tavern like this one and insulted the sailors inside was extremely fortunate to live at all. It did not indicate a proper appreciation of life's little dangers.

'Barman, bring a quart of wine for my friend and me!' Sir Richard roared as he walked in, and without looking to see whether his instruction had been heeded, he crossed the floor to a small rough table in the corner. There was a pair of stools at the side, and Sir Richard drew one out for Simon with his foot, before sitting at the other and stretching his legs, his eyes flitting about the room at all the other men.

'A fair selection of the seafaring type,' he said loudly in what Simon was sure he considered was a confidential whisper. 'Plenty of leather, tatty clothing stitched together too often, and strong hearts. Little in the heads, sadly. Always the way with these seafolk. HOI! *Where's our wine?*'

The sudden bellow took Simon by surprise, but still more surprising to him was the appearance of the host, who set down two large jugs on the table and made as though to withdraw.

'Wait!' Sir Richard snapped. He picked up the nearer jug, lifted it to his lips and took a deep draught. Sitting back, he allowed a moment to pass before nodding. 'My host, you have a good wine here. I hope the ship didn't sink so you could win it? Eh? Ha! Oh, don't worry, just my little joke. Bring us some bread and meat. I'm famished. It's a long ride from Lifton. Aren't you drinking, Bailiff?'

Simon had been toying with the jug before him, but just for once, the thought of two pints of heavy wine was unappealing. 'What do you wish from me?'

The Coroner's eyes peered shrewdly at him over the rim of his jug. 'A full explanation of what's been going on here, of course. I may look as if I've lead between my ears, Bailiff, but I want to know who's been turning to piracy and why. I don't like too many corpses in my territory.'

The moment he had left the room, Peter Strete wiped his forehead with his sleeve. There had been a moment then when . . . but it was only his guilt. Hawley couldn't possibly know what he'd been up to. No, if he had the faintest inkling, there would have been sailors in here holding him down while Hawley took a leather strap to his back – and he wouldn't stop until there was no flesh left on him. That was the sort of man Hawley was. The only thing that could make it worse was if Hawley gave the task to his son, also called John. Young John enjoyed seeing people suffer.

Hawley was a bad man to have for an enemy. Taking something from him made a man *de facto* his worst enemy. And Strete had taken much from him in recent times.

Even now, with nothing to fear, he was still shaken every time his master mentioned bad luck, just in case he had uncovered Strete's secret. And the truth was, there was nothing to fear now. The debt was repaid, the hole in the accounts carefully concealed. Even a brilliant clerk going through his rolls would find nothing amiss. In fact, he had covered himself so well as to *add* some money to the purse, so that there was no suspicion of his stealing from his master.

Thank God he had seen Danny in the tavern that day, when those two sailors tried to rape Madam Kena. It was a chance piece of good fortune that had solved his financial problems. When he was drinking to conceal his fear after an unwise evening's gambling, he had overheard a brief snippet. That was all – a quiet, muttered snigger, then a comment about a woman. And from that he had realised how his finances could be brought to an even keel again. And then he had enjoyed two profitable strokes of luck.

Thank God it was over, he told himself, and wiped his brow again.

Alred Paviour was standing at the hole, peering down at the corpse when Simon brought the Coroner to view the dead man.

'Ha! So you are the fool who left an unprotected hole, are you?' the Coroner thundered as he approached.

Alred flinched at the tone as much as the words. 'We did the best we could to block it off, but someone took the trestles away. You know how people can be, when they've had too many pots of ale.'

The Coroner scowled blackly. 'You seek to blame others for your mistake? I dislike that attitude, man!'

'No, I don't mean that, it's just—'

'I see what you mean, Bailiff,' Sir Richard continued, ignoring Alred. 'You! Did you move his body?'

'Me? Why would I?'

'There is little you might do which would make sense to me,' the Coroner answered cheerily. 'So just answer me: did you or anyone else move the body?'

'No! Of course not, Coroner. That would be to break the law.'

Simon tipped his head towards the body. 'You're quite sure no one turned him over to see whether he was still alive? It would be natural, and excusable.'

'Not me, no. Even Ivo left him. Anyway, he was on his back already. What'd be the point of looking at him closer? You can see he's gone. There's nothing there.'

The Coroner nodded, then drew the ends of his mouth down. 'Well, all I can say is, Bailiff, you're clearly right. This was no accident, was it? No, someone must have deliberately killed him and then played silly buggers with the trestles to make it look natural.'

He turned from the works and gazed about him, his hands at his hips. 'Right, we'll hold the inquest in the morning. That will give time enough to gather the jury and also for us to break our fast. Speaking of which, we ought to be thinking about a meal to settle our bellies before bed. Where do you live, Bailiff? You will have space for another small one this night, won't you?'

Philip Kena was in his hall with his young wife when the knock came at his door. He sat back as his servant went to open it, listening carefully to the voices. 'Is that Master Beauley?' he called out.

'Yes, Philip. And how are you today?'

Kena eyed his guest with some surprise. The merchants knew each other, of course, but their connections tended to be professional only. Like many others who had trading businesses, they would often meet at the market hall and talk about their ventures, problems with markets where they were exposed to larger tolls than they had anticipated, or discuss the outrageous costs of some shipwrights, but they tended not to socialise. If Beauley wanted to discuss something, it was clearly a matter which affected them both – and that could only mean the cog which had been attacked.

'Please, be seated,' Kena said, and he whispered to his wife. She stood and curtseyed to the guest, before walking out through the rear door to their solar.

'I am grateful that you can give me a little time, Master Kena,' Beauley said. He took the proffered stool.

'My wife married me late in my life,' Kena said, looking after her fondly as she left the hall. 'I can recommend it, though. You find your household grows more comfortable with a woman in it.'

'I have not had time to seek a woman.' His voice was so cold, it would have frozen seawater.

'Nor did I when I was young like you,' Kena said understandingly. He had seen over forty summers now, while Beauley could only be seven- or eight-and-twenty. It was in part that reason that made him draw attention to his young Millicent. She had married him only three years before, and he had cause to be well satisfied with her. The contract with her father for her hand had been expensive, but not ruinously so, and he had the pleasure of the girl's beauty as well as the comfort of her gentle kindness. She was all that a man could desire from a wife, and her youth excited him more than the raddled old whores whom he had visited before, down at Lower Street. The same ones which poor Beauley must be visiting now, as he told himself.

'These are strange times, master,' Beauley said stiffly. 'The sight of Pyckard's cog was shocking, and the idea that the whole crew was slaughtered out to sea, even more so.'

'Yes, indeed,' Kena said. 'We all expect the sea to be cruel on occasion, but to find that seamen could do such violence on others, that is truly shocking.'

Beauley gave the impression of being ready to leap up like a coiled spring. It was not in his nature, Kena felt, to relax. The moment spent in relaxation was a moment wasted. How different he was from himself!

'I am here because of that. Did the same suspicions occur to you, I wonder?'

'What suspicions?' Kena said, his eyes widening. 'Would you care for a little wine? I have some honeyed larks, too, which are most—'

'No, I thank you. The bodies. Where are they?'

'Ah,' Kena said, and having poured himself more wine, he sat back in his chair with a benevolent smile. 'You have some thoughts on them?'

'If they were thrown overboard, where did they go when Hawley arrived?'

Kena frowned, not understanding.

'Come on, man! We heard that Hawley arrived there soon after the ship was fired. It took him a little time to put out the flames, and the cargo was still there in her hold. People are saying that the pirates must have seen his sails, and rowed away quickly before he could come to grips with them. But if that's true, where are the bodies? If they'd killed the men and thrown them overboard, they'd all have been floating about, wouldn't they? You've seen enough men in the water, just as I have. No, if the bodies were there, Hawley must have seen them.'

'So, what are you saying? That he's lying?' Kena still didn't understand.

'Either the bodies were tied to irons and thrown overboard, or they were carried away in the other ship. Hawley would have no need to lie. If there were dead men in the water, he might as well tell the truth.'

'It's also been suggested that they could have been taken, either to ransom them or to use them as slaves.'

Beauley gave him a steady look. 'And how likely is that? Even if the pirates wanted some of the men, a few would have died rather than be caught, wouldn't they?'

'I don't know who the men were.'

'Didn't you hear? Odo and Vincent were aboard, and Adam. Can you imagine any of them giving in to another ship?'

Kena looked away with a frown on his face. 'You're sure of that?'

'I wouldn't have mentioned it otherwise.'

'At least there's cause for rejoicing in those bastards' deaths! I'll pray for Adam to be sent into Christ's merciful hands, the poor fellow, but for Vincent and Odo, I'll ask for all their sins to be remembered. I hope they burn in hell!'

'I doubt not that your prayers for Vincent and Odo will be heeded. There are enough others in the town would be happy to see them swinging on the gibbet. The point is, though, they were brave fighters. They didn't fear pirates or any others.'

'True enough. So what happened to the men?'

'The bodies must have been carried away. Unless, of course, the men are alive and happy somewhere else. Hiding.'

'*Hiding?*' Kena scoffed. 'You think that Adam could have betrayed his master? Vincent, maybe, but never Adam.'

'Someone could have paid Odo and Vincent. If they had surprise on their side, they could have killed Adam. Danny's body was on the ship . . . If, say, Odo told Adam, and Adam went down to look at him, Odo and Vincent could have overwhelmed even him.'

'True. And that was the sort of work they excelled in, the murderous sons of hogs!'

'If you ask *who* could have paid them, that is easy. What if Hawley offered Adam a job working for him instead of Pyckard – offered him a bribe, may be – and he refused? Hawley can be a most ruthless man.'

'Ruthless enough to remove the whole crew and kill them all?'

'If he rescued some, they may be living anywhere even now,' Beauley smiled cynically. 'Or perhaps Vincent and Odo had another score to settle.'

'Such as?'

'Who can tell? They were guilty of many crimes.'

Kena gritted his teeth. 'You have no need to tell me that! If it were not for some of my own sailors and Adam himself, those sodomites would have raped my wife!'

'Adam?'

'He saw what was happening and went to save her. I rewarded him, and the other men there. But he would not come to join me. I offered him money, but he remained loyal to his master. Perhaps that is it? Odo and Vincent killed him to be avenged for stopping them raping my lady.'

'And then flew from the ship? All I know is, my own men are growing worried that they'll be killed too if they go out.'

'Just killed?'

Beauley gave a humourless grin. 'No. There's also the rumour that the devil took them all. Some of the lads reckon he'll come and take them too. The church is doing better trade than the tavern just now.'

'At least if it was the devil,' Kena snarled, 'he'll have taken the right lads. Odo and Vincent deserved to die after what they did.'

Beauley said nothing, but he was glad to hear that his informant had been right. From what he had heard, Odo had grappled with Mistress Millicent in the street, as though she was a common draggle-tail from an alehouse, before Vincent had tried to pull him and her into a little alley. Only the arrival of Kena's own men had saved her. No wonder the man hated them.

'Well, master,' he said, standing up to take his leave, 'I should be careful about telling people about that. Better if you keep it quiet. After all, if a man is known to hold a grudge against a pair of villeins who attacked his wife, and the villeins suddenly die, people don't bother to look very far for the murderer, do they?'

Chapter Ten

It was almost twilight when Moses slammed the bar across the front door before walking back into the hall and drawing up the shutters.

'Master? Are you all right?' he asked worriedly.

'Fetch me a warmed pot of wine,' Pyckard replied from his chair, and gestured limply with a finger.

It was all Moses could do not to burst into tears. The poor master had been good to all his staff, and his disease had been so sudden, it was hard to believe that this was the same man whom Moses had known and worked for over the last fifteen years. He was so shrivelled, like a leaf in late autumn, sitting huddled in his thickest fur coat and rugs against the chill of death. And at the same time Moses had lost his only other friend. Danny, his younger brother was dead, brutally murdered.

'Master?'

'When I have gone, Moses, there are many who will try to suggest that I owe them money. You must not allow people to take advantage. I leave it to you to carry out my wishes. All my papers and my Will are in my little chest in the counting-room, and the key is here about my neck. You understand me?'

'Yes, of course. I'll do all you ask,' Moses responded dully. He took his master's hand and gripped it, as though he could transfer some of his own life-energy to his master's frail body. He would do anything to keep this kindly man alive.

Pyckard held his gaze. 'I would like you to perform an errand, old friend. Would you do that for me too?'

* * *

On the outskirts of Dartmouth, Hamund Chugge sat down on a rock and pulled at the thongs of his sandal. He rested his staff against his shoulder as he poked a finger between sole and foot until he had found the little pebble, and could hook it out.

It was tempting to stop here and close his eyes, but he couldn't. That would mean death if he was seen, and he wasn't going to let that happen. He would survive this somehow.

The man he had killed had deserved it. He had been a brute! And when he turned up with his piece of paper and smiled at Hamund with that oily grin, Hamund had to wipe it off his face. If he could change the past, well, he would. But he couldn't. So Flok was dead, Hamund was outlawed and must leave the realm, and . . . God knew what would happen to Sarra.

She had suggested going with him, but what would he be able to offer her now he must leave the country? All he had was a possibility of starting afresh in the King's domains over the water, and there was no guarantee that he would succeed in those strange, alien parts. All he could hope for was that his drive for success would help him in his new life, and that one day, if he were able, he could send for her.

'No,' he muttered. There was no bitterness in his voice, just resignation. Better that they should live apart. In time she would forget him, maybe win a better man. There must be plenty of them about, who wouldn't get drunk and murder the man-of-law of the wealthiest and most dangerous man in the country after the King just because he sought to take your living from you.

That any man could legitimately take away another's farm, his lands, his livelihood, and not even offer compensation, that was beyond Hamund. But that was exactly what had happened. The Despenser's man Flok had arrived some months ago, just after Sir John de Loos had died in the brutal fighting against Thomas of Lancaster, the foul traitor who sought to set himself against the King. Sir John was a decent, kindly man, who had given Hamund his freedom some years before, but as soon as he died in the battle, Hamund reckoned Despenser started looking at his lands.

Hugh Despenser was an evil, thieving devil who concealed his insatiable greed behind a mask of boyish charm, so they said. Hamund knew nothing of that. All he knew was that his lands were to be taken from him by this man.

It was one thing for a disloyal subject to see his lands and assets forfeited by the Crown. All those who had raised their swords in support of the Lords Marcher – it was fair enough that they should lose their lands. And the men who supported Earl Thomas, too. They were traitors to the King, so their lands and titles should be seized.

But a land in which those who were devoted to their King and gave their lives for him could see their family and servants deprived of their property and wealth, forced to give up all to the grinning brute who could take them purely because he had the King's ear . . . that was a land where justice held no sway. It was a place in which bullying alone ruled: a bastard realm.

When that oleaginous shite Flok appeared and shoved the parchment at him, pushing him back into the passageway as he demanded to see the lady of the house, Hamund could only gaze uncomprehendingly at the words written so carefully. When Sarra appeared in the doorway, her hair escaping from the coif she had hurriedly pulled on, Flok eyed her like a drunk considering the whores in the stews. Still Hamund had done nothing. He had followed the two into the hall itself, shushing the other servants as they rebelliously eyed the man-of-law while he gazed about him, apparently well satisfied with all he saw.

'This manor is to be forfeit. You, lady, will prepare to leave in two months. At that time I shall return to take over the management of all the demesne.'

'You cannot think to do this, sir!' Sarra had said, her hand at her throat. Hamund could see her despair. She stood tall and elegant in her flowing, green velvet tunic, and Hamund so wished to go to her side and clutch at her hand, but he daren't. Instead he listened with the others as Flok sneeringly waved aside all protestations. Those which appeared to give him the most amusement were the defence that Sir John had been a devoted captain for the King.

'He's no use now, is he? He's dead. So I'm sure that his loyal vassals will loyally support the installation of a new master here; a man who meets more accurately the King's needs.'

There was a certain tone in his voice at that moment, and Hamund understood that it was this Flok who would become master in the hall when Lady Sarra had been thrown out.

Flok had departed a short while later, and the hall was left in stunned silence. There was a moment that seemed to last for an age, and then Lady Sarra moved slowly across the floor, almost as though gliding, until she reached the door behind the dais that led to her solar. Hamund saw her face just once as she walked that gauntlet of shame and ruined pride. She turned to close the door, and as she did so, her eye met his, and he saw a woman destroyed.

Hamund could have remained, of course. If he'd wanted to bow to the man Flok, he could have stayed there and had his daily ration of ale, his food, his annual tunic, and all the other little benefits that made for a good life. But he'd never forget the sight of his lady at that doorway. And he would never forgive himself, were he to leave that poor woman unavenged.

So instead, he had drunk a couple of quarts of ale, sitting near the fire, listening to the muted sobs from the solar, and telling himself that there must be a way to protect and serve his lady. But the more he drank, the more he saw that there was no means of defending her against this kind of attack. All he could do was avenge her and the memory of her husband.

As the light began to fade, he took up his long knife, a memento from the Welsh wars, and a staff, and left the hall. He walked the three miles in the gathering dusk to the vill, and stopped outside the inn. And that night he slew the man who had sought to steal his master's property.

That night Baldwin could have continued on his way, but when he was still a couple of leagues from Dartmouth, he decided that it would be better to take his rest and have a good night's sleep rather than try to complete the entire journey in one day.

He had reached Totnes when he made the decision. The weather was fine, but the sun was already sinking. Baldwin knew that the estuary on which the town of Dartmouth lay was long and winding, and he had no desire to fall into a deep pool in the dark.

The inn he found was a clean-looking long building. Perhaps it was an old place, but the owner had seen to the limewash regularly, and the thatch was only one summer old. Baldwin tied his horse to a ring and entered the stables, and when he saw clean straw and how tidy the stalls were kept, he was content.

Having seen that his horse was well served, he entered the main block and called for a meal. There was a good, thick pottage and some reasonable bread that filled his empty belly, although when he enquired about a room for the night, he found that there was none to be had. His only choice was the main bedchamber, in which five men were to sleep that night, or to remain here in the hall.

In many years of travelling, Baldwin had experienced different inns in several kingdoms, and never had he succeeded in sleeping well in a room with strangers. In preference he decided to remain in the hall. He went out first to see that his horse was well catered for. The grooms had already rubbed and brushed him, and now he was munching contentedly at a fork or two of hay in his manger. Baldwin slapped his shoulder and tickled his ear before leaving. A warrior should always see to the comfort of his mount before all else: it was a rule he had learned early on, and the lesson was ingrained in his soul.

The inn was loud, not raucous but happy, and he knew he would find sleep evasive until some of the patrons had left for their beds. Still, he was warm, full, and tired enough to doze, and he drew a bench to the wall and sat there with his chin on his breast.

In his mind still was the curious behaviour of the bishop. *Guilty*. That was the word Baldwin had been looking for. As though he feared he was sending Baldwin into danger.

The knight considered that for a while. The port of Dartmouth was by no means quiet and safe. No port ever was, of course – but he was going to find out all he might about a man who had raped a lady-in-waiting to the Queen. Such a man should be caught and exiled, rather than simply watched, but Baldwin thought he understood that. There was no need to further antagonise the French king. The countries were already smarting from the last short war.

He only hoped that he was not going to learn that the bishop's nephew was dead. Bernard was a youngish man, Bishop Walter had said, with dark hair, narrow features, prominent upper front teeth, and grey eyes. It should be easy enough to find a man like that, Baldwin told himself, and settled back more comfortably. He would sleep in here tonight, and let the morrow take care of itself.

Simon woke with a head that thumped painfully.

In his life he had woken to hangovers of such variety that he could almost class them. There were those of his youth when, as soon as he had lain in his bed, he had known, by the spinning of the ceiling, that he would feel very poorly unless he was sick before sleep. Then there were the scrumpy mornings, after a bout of cider-drinking, when his blood seemed to have turned to acid, and his head was all but immobilised. After an evening with strong red wines, he felt as though someone had slugged him at the back of the neck with a leather cosh and then there were the days when he had to protect his head from the painful explosions of noise caused by a spider hurtling across a wall.

To this connoisseur of suffering, none of these could stand even a moderate comparison with the state of his head this morning.

'Thought you were never going to wake!' Sir Richard boomed from the corner, and Simon winced: the bellow appeared to make his entire skull vibrate. Reluctantly he opened his eyes and looked about him. For some reason he evidently had not made it to his bed. He was spread out precariously over his long bench, an arm over his breast, the other dangling. It remained asleep as he tried to sit up, racking his brain for a memory of the previous evening.

They had started back at an inn called simply the Bush, drinking some heavy ales brewed by the innkeeper's daughter. After that they had migrated to a powerful red Guyennois wine, and Simon would still have been fine, had the innkeeper not mentioned to Sir Richard that he had some burned wine.

Simon could still taste the stuff. The first sip was foul, like trying to drink a thin, but acrid and oily wine; but the second sip was better, the third not unpleasant, and the fourth was really quite palatable. It was a most peculiar drink, and made Simon feel much bolder, as though he was suddenly capable of feats of courage and endurance.

They had drunk a deal of it.

'Ah! Morning, Bailiff!' Sir Richard stood in the middle of his parlour gazing down at the hearth. 'Did I tell you the one about the man proposing marriage to a young bint? He spoke to her father, and, trying to check her credentials, as it were, said, had she been chaste? "Surely," said her father. "So – she's got no children?" the man said. The father smiled a little at that. "She has had none?" the man repeated, and the father shook his head. "No. Nowt but a very small one, sir!" Eh? Haha! Where's your servant, Bailiff? I can't see him anywhere, and we need to have our breakfast. We can't be late for the two inquests, can we? Where does your fellow sleep? Is he at the back?'

'Next door,' Simon croaked. In the night all moisture from his mouth had fled and now his tongue clacked drily like a board of wood. The Coroner looked as fresh as a bluebell in spring. Simon assumed he had courteously offered the man his bed. Or more likely, Simon had been unable to climb the steep staircase.

'Ah! I'll find the lazy scoundrel. Probably asleep, if I know anything about such lads. He'll be . . .'

Mercifully his voice faded and then disappeared as he marched through the little building, and Simon felt only relief as he heard the door slam. He lay back again and closed his eyes, shivering gently, praying that the Coroner might die on his way and that Simon could sleep until the body was discovered.

'OPEN THIS DOOR!'

Simon's eyes snapped open, giving him the vague feeling that the top of his head was unscrewing. With appalled expectation, he waited. There was a squeaking, which he recognised as the door to his neighbour's house, and then the bellow began again.

‘Tell him that the bailiff and I will be in there to drag the lazy wretch from his bed, Madam, if he isn’t over there and cooking our breakfast in the time it takes me to draw a quart of ale and drink it. And he will get the thrashing he richly deserves if I have to do that.’

Simon felt his belly begin to grind at the thought of his neighbour’s maid’s face. She could stew plums by looking at them, and the effect of the Coroner on her was something he preferred not to think about. Nor the effect of her cold stare on *him* the next time they met.

Baldwin was already on his mount. For once, he had slept well. Last night he had been tired enough after his riding and discussions with the bishop to fall asleep in no time at all, and he woke refreshed and ready for the completion of his journey.

It was a pleasant morning’s ride, following the River Dart down towards the sea. Once, on a journey over the moors towards Huccaby, he had been told that the river he was crossing wandered all the way down to the sea at Dartmouth. He had never sought to verify that, but now, looking at the great estuary, he wondered whether it was true, and if so, how many other tributaries joined that little stream to make such an immense river.

The way was shaded, which was a relief, because even this early the weather was growing hot. He could feel the warmth rising from his horse, and although the land was flat here, he made many halts to let the animal slake his thirst in the river. Before he was more than a few bowshots from the town, though, the road took him up on top of the hills, away from the water itself. This land was ever hilly and criss-crossed with deep ravines that roads avoided. Up on the higher ground again, there was abundant pasture and farming land, although fewer trees.

Before anything else, Baldwin decided he would visit Simon and tell him about his mission on behalf of the bishop. If there was anything odd happening in the town, his old friend the Bailiff would be sure to know about it.

* * *

Simon dressed himself slowly and went out to the privy. After performing his morning's routine in the little hut, he pulled his cloak about him and went to the wall at the bottom of his garden.

This was one of those perfect September mornings, the sort he had always loved on the moors. The weather had broken, and the fierce blast of the sun had abated somewhat. Now the air was fine and clear, the bushes filled with ripe berries. Simon's little plot held some apple trees, brambles and pears, and all were bent with the weight of fruit. He would have to get someone to come and collect it all, for there was no possibility of his idle, good-for-nothing servant managing any such thing.

Good gardeners were always a trial to find. Men liked to boast that they were good at gardening, but in truth it was mostly their women who knew about the plants. The men spent too much time at sea or in taverns to learn much about anything other than tying knots and throwing up, in Simon's rather jaundiced view. He could do with someone out here, though. He looked casually over the wall into the garden beyond the back lane. That was tidier, and as he peered nosily, he could see a maid gathering the last of the year's peas ready for drying.

The lane went nowhere. There was a gate at the southernmost end, but that was kept locked to bar access from draw-latches. However, the attempt at security failed because some while ago the northern gate had been broken. Simon considered it was some poor fellow last winter who was desperate for firewood. No one had mended it in the last year or so, and now all too many people used the lane as a toilet. There was a familiar stench about it now – the sour, musty smell of faeces. He scowled. In the end he'd probably pay someone to come and clear it.

For once the mists had not swept up the river to engulf the town, and the sun could shine down on the newly limewashed buildings, all painted to protect them during the winter weather to come. Standing up here, Simon could see along the line of the shore from Hardness to the north, down to the curve in the river that led to the open sea.

Even up here there was a constant thrumming on the wind, the sound of thousands of taut ropes vibrating and setting masts humming.

'BAILIFF! WHERE ARE YOU?'

At the hoarse bellow, Simon winced, and then reluctantly turned back to his house. He only hoped that the Coroner would soon be finished here in Dartmouth.

Chapter Eleven

Moses threw open the shutters to his master's room and looked back. Master Pyckard was in a dreadful way now, with his parchment-like flesh and grey lips. His skin looked as though it had been covered in a thin layer of wax overnight, and his eyes were dulled, while his breath rattled.

'Master?' Moses asked gently. He edged nearer to the bed, very close to sobbing. When he first came here, it was because his father had been lost at sea. His mother was already dead, and Moses and his younger brother Danny had nowhere else to go. The only childhood memories he had were of this house, because as soon as the parish had announced that they were without parents, Pyckard had come and taken them in.

It had been the luckiest day of Moses's life, and he would never cease praying to God for the soul of this kindly man. Paul Pyckard had rescued him and Danny from a life of poverty, misery and an early death. Both Moses and Pyckard knew it, and both knew the depth of the debt, although neither had ever referred to it. There was no need.

'You have been a good servant, Moses. I am sorry to leave you.'

Moses felt as though his throat would burst under the strain of unshed tears. 'I am glad you're happy, master.'

'I will not live much longer. My affairs are in order.' His face wrenched with a spasm of pain, and he collapsed. 'Ach! God save you from such agony, Moses.'

'Can I fetch you anything?'

'Ale or wine, I don't care which – but hurry!'

Moses scurried to the jug and brought it back. He held Pyckard's favourite goblet to his mouth while the man slurped clumsily.

'Moses, my friend, this is the worst. A man gets used to being able to pick up a drink, stab a slice of meat or wipe his own arse, but the nearer he comes to death, the more he behaves like a muling brat. I feel pathetic. I was once a man with power and authority, damn my eyes!'

'You still are, master. You have many who love you, you have—'

'When I have died, I want a tomb that shows what I am really like. Just a sack of bones, that's all,' Pyckard said without noticing his servant's comment.

Moses bowed his head and wept, both for this man and for those other parents long lost to him and Dan.

'Don't cry on my account, lad,' Pyckard said with some asperity. 'I've not yet gone.'

His tone made Moses grin through his tears.

'I wish I didn't have to leave you alone, lad,' Pyckard said more kindly. 'I know you miss your brother.'

There was no one now. He had lost his mother, father, brother, and now his master. It felt as though the whole of his own life was close to ending. Moses sank his head into his hands.

'Aye, well,' Pyckard coughed. 'I'm the last of my line, so perhaps I shouldn't be sad to hear that one man grieves for me. At least you still have nephews and nieces, eh? Ach, this pain! More wine, please. Thank you!' He rested his head a short while, staring up at the ceiling. 'Moses, look after him. He reminds me of *her*. Will you do that for me?'

Moses said nothing, but he nodded emphatically as the tears coursed down both cheeks. Pyckard lifted his hand and patted the young man's head absently. 'And now, perhaps you should fetch me the priest, old friend. My son.'

'ALL THOSE WHO HAVE BUSINESS HERE, DRAW NEAR!' Sir Richard de Welles bellowed.

He stood at the front of the gathering men, arms crossed over his enormous chest, both arms partly covered by his beard, and eyed the crowd appreciatively. 'My God, Bailiff, they may be seashore peasants, these, but they can dress well. D'you think any of 'em *aren't* pirates?'

Simon burped, all too aware of the acid in his belly grumbling away, and tried to grin. 'I don't know about that, Sir Richard. They are generally law-abiding down here.'

'That's because they refuse to acknowledge any laws they don't approve of,' the Coroner muttered knowledgeably. 'NOW LISTEN TO ME! CAN YOU ALL HEAR ME AT THE BACK?'

Simon closed his eyes and shivered as the roar died away. At that moment it would have taken little to persuade him to pull out his dagger and end the Coroner's life.

The freemen of the town were all present, and Richard and Simon's clerk soon made a selection from all there of the men who would be required for the jury.

'That's better!' Richard said happily. 'I wouldn't want to have to shout all day. Now, do you all swear on the Gospels to answer my questions honestly? Yes? Good. Does any here know this man?'

There was a noticeable silence following the question. The jurors stood shuffling and avoiding each other's looks.

'Are you seriously telling me that a young fellow like this is completely unknown in the town where he's died?' Coroner de Welles demanded. 'You two – come here!'

The lads he had pointed at were a pair of grinning teenagers who had come along to enjoy the spectacle.

'Undress him.'

One of the boys, a slender, dark-haired fellow, looked down at the body, his grin frozen upon his face, while the other stared at the Coroner in shock. 'Us?'

'Get on with it!' Richard de Welles had occasion to use one of his famed scowls. He was proud of them. They invariably succeeded in persuading the reluctant or recalcitrant to obey him, and it worked again now. While the darker of the two slowly climbed down into the hole with his lighter-haired companion, in order to heave the body out of it, the Coroner began talking again.

'Hear me, now! This man was found lying as you see him now. Be careful with him, there, lad. He's suffered enough! You can see his head was resting alongside that large cobble there, as though he had fallen and broken his head on it. Except that would mean he fell in backwards. It's possible he did – that someone pushed him, and he struck his head, say. But I doubt whether he just toppled back into the hole and happened to kill himself. More likely he was attacked and fell in. So that means it may be murder, and someone here in the town knows what happened.'

He glanced down at the two lads in the roadway. 'Haven't you got him out yet?' he snapped.

Simon would have found the sight amusing, were it not for the feelings of cold and heat that chased themselves through his frame. He felt much as an old man would, after sitting too long, his muscles complaining and bones aching. Just now, all he wanted was a rest, with plenty of time to close his eyes. Instead he was getting over-familiar with yet another corpse.

'Bailiff! Come and look at this!' the Coroner called. He was pointing down at the corpse's naked breast. Simon looked. There was no stab wound, but clear on the breast stood a large bruise. Even as he watched, the Coroner reached down and pressed. 'Ha! Yes, someone clobbered him good and hard. The bones are broken. And yes! – if I press the man's skull, the whole side caves in. Look, I'll do it again. Did you all see that? Haha, and there's not much doubt there, is there . . . Oh, mind that. Sorry, didn't expect his juices to squirt like that . . .'

Mercifully, as Simon span on his heel, his attention was taken by the horse trotting along the roadway from Hardness and he heard no more.

'Baldwin! Thank God!' he managed, and then had to leave the inquest to go to the tavern a few doors away, and demand a strong ale urgently while he waited for his friend.'

Hamund Chugge had reached the area above the town as the sun gained its highest point, and he passed through the fertile lands until he came to the bottom of a hill. Here there were some thick woods, and he made his way through them, tramping on stolidly until he reached the top of the hill. Suddenly, the trees stopped and he could see the river laid out below him, and then, as he surveyed the land, he saw the glittering sea.

He could only stand and stare in astonishment. Hamund had never been near the coast, and the largest mass of water he had ever seen was the Taw River as it passed by his old home. It was nothing in comparison to this, though. This, if proof were needed, showed that God's power was absolute. It was daunting to think that before long he would be sailing on that twinkling expanse to a new land. Terrifying.

As the sun scorched the ground about him, he gradually came to his senses again and set off, awed, following the road. It took him down past a little church, St Clement's, and the village of Tunstal, and then down Tunstal hill itself and into the town of Hardness. He made the sign of the cross as he passed by the chapel of St Clarus, and then found himself at the water's edge.

It was tempting to kneel and dip his hands into the water. There was a suck and slap of little waves as he watched, and the boats which had been left beached on the shore were moving and shifting as the tide came in. It was also here that he began to smell the familiar stench of fish. Fishermen were cleaning and gutting their hauls, mending nets, salting and curing their catches, and they stopped and stared at him as he passed by, curiosity and suspicion mingled on their tough, tanned faces.

He could feel their eyes on him all the way as he walked southwards along the shore, gritting his teeth against their condemnation. A man carrying a cross like him, clad in a pilgrim's tunic, with only a staff and a bowl, was marked out as a felon. An Abjuror.

A little way further on was a bridge of solid wood across the creek that fell from the ravine, and he crossed it, staring with fascination at the water-wheel set in the middle. It trundled slowly, making the entire bridge vibrate alarmingly, but what was most peculiar, he thought, was that although the stream must surely have led from the land to the sea, the wheel itself was revolving the other way, turning as though the sea was flowing towards the land. It was a wonderful sight – and rather scary. He peered down at it for a few minutes, but then his courage failed him and he had to stop his feet from taking him pelting across the planks towards the other side and the towns of Clifton and Dartmouth.

Once there, he wandered idly along near the shore wondering where he might go to find a shipman.

There had been nothing concealed about his murder of Flok. There were all too many witnesses. According to them, he had entered the inn with a face filled with malice. Seeing the man at the far side of the room, he marched haphazardly across the floor, plainly much the worse for drink, until he reached Flok and could stand staring at him. The inn was a small place, and had only three stools for clients, but Flok had taken one and two more for the men with him, a man-at-arms, Guy de Bouville, and a clerk. All the villagers who lived and worked about here were standing.

Someone said that Flok had sneeringly asked whether his new servant should return home, he was so incoherent with ale. 'Don't serve him any more,' he had drawled. 'I don't want to have to get the churl carried back!'

'I'm not *your* servant, I'm servant to Lady Sarra,' Hamund enunciated carefully.

'Your master's dead, and I shall be your master soon, man. Now leave this place. You are an embarrassment. You will have to improve your manners if you want to avoid a flogging when I arrive to take the manor.'

'I'm a freeman!'

'You're a drunk – and now you're also servile again, churl. You'll do exactly as you're told!'

It was then that Hamund set his jaw and pulled his knife free. His first blow slashed Flok's hand to the bone; the second stabbed into his shoulder, and caught in the socket, but the third finally ended the man's screaming when he plunged it into his black heart, and Flok fell straight back, his heels rattling on the floor for some minutes.

De Bouville had his hand on his hilt, but he hadn't drawn his sword. He stood before Hamund uncertainly, his eyes going from Flok's corpse to the bloody knife in Hamund's fist. The clerk had left his stool, and was now pressed with his back to the wall behind him as though wishing he could melt into the cob.

Then de Bouville made to unsheath his weapon, but before he could pull it free, Hamund had picked up Flok's drinking horn and hurled it into the man's face, followed by a heavy pottery jug slammed into his skull. He fell instantly.

Hamund walked away slowly, his blade waving from left to right, suddenly drained. Outside, he stood a moment or two in the cooler air, his mind entirely blank. Only when he heard hoofs did he realise his danger. A groom from the inn was leading a rounsey, and he pressed the reins into Hamund's fist, hissing, 'Go! Go!'

He stared at the leather in his hand dully, and then, as the first shouts came from inside, and he heard horns begin to be winded, Hamund shoved his knife back in the sheath, leaped upon the beast, and clapped heels. The horse surged forward, and Hamund covered the distance to the manor in a few minutes, dropping to the ground in the court and hurrying inside.

'My lady, Flok won't evict you,' he panted. 'I have killed him.'

She hadn't believed him. Not at first, anyway. And then the shock came into her eyes, although there was also delight. He was sure he could see that there too; and then the light of joy faded. Both knew he couldn't remain. Despenser would soon come to avenge this slaying.

'You must ride away!' she burst out.

'I can't leave here. Not now,' he said. His mind was too fuddled to think straight. All he could consider was that he had a stolen horse. 'Must get the thing back.'

'You'd worry about a horse when you'll soon be killed for murder?' she urged. 'Go, man. Go with God, but ride!'

She was never so beautiful to him as she was that evening. Her hair awry, hanging loose from her coif, her bright blue eyes dulled with sorrow and reddened with tears, her perfect white skin soft and smooth, the cheeks tinged with colour. He could have worshipped her. 'I can take my fate, mistress.'

'Sweet Mother of God,' she muttered, and then had three of the servants carry him. 'Forget you have done this,' she commanded them as the men took the protesting Hamund across the road, over the field, and quickly up the old roadway to Oakhampton. There they deposited him inside the church, kneeling at the altar.

'This man has killed, Father,' Lady Sarra said to the priest as she slipped coins into his hand. 'Listen to his confession, I beg you, and give him sanctuary.'

It was three days before he saw her again. The Coroner had already visited him and asked whether he would leave the sanctuary and see him to admit to his crimes, but Hamund had refused at that time. He had some days of sanctuary permitted before he need walk into the open. And in those days, he saw much of his mistress Sarra.

At the end of thirty days, he agreed to abjure the realm. The Coroner came with his jury, and before them all, in the churchyard, Hamund swore to leave the land. His route was defined as the road to Dartmouth, and he was instructed to get there as quickly as possible, and to take the first ship that would bear him away. And if there were none on the first day, he would walk into the water in proof of his good faith and desire to adhere to his oath, and he would do likewise on every following day until he found a ship. And if he were ever to return to his native land, any might behead him without fear of punishment.

Guy de Bouville had been there, his swarthy features black with anger. His fingers twitched about his sword hilt as Hamund took his cross and left the churchyard, and Hamund was sure that it was only the group of Lady Sarra's men about him, ringing him, that stopped the other man from pulling out his sword and running Hamund through. De Bouville himself would almost certainly escape punishment – he was from Despenser's household.

No, there had been nothing concealed about his murder of Flok, and he had walked without concealment ever since he had sworn to abjure the realm, obedient to his vow. But now, as he looked over the waters towards the other side of the estuary, he knew that his action would not help Sarra. She had been given warning that her home was forfeit. Despenser wanted it, and what Despenser wanted, he would have. So Hamund had acted in vain.

Perhaps not entirely in vain. He had removed that foul bladder of piss Flok, and that could not be thought to be a bad thing. A man who would go to a widow's hall and tell her to leave her home even in the midst of her misery and mourning, he deserved all that he received.

'You lost, friend?'

It was a thickset sailor who spoke, a man with a face the colour of walnut, clad in old hosen and a much-patched and stained linen shirt. He stood before Hamund, hands on hips, head set to one side as though assessing his value.

'I seek a ship, master.'

'Abjuring, eh?' The man looked him up and down. 'Perhaps I can aid you, then. My master needs more hands for the ship, and there are times a man can't choose his shipmates. Why are you abjuring?' His expression hardened suspiciously. 'Did you rob a man?'

'No! I killed a man who sought to defraud my master's widow.'

'Oh, a murderer, eh? I may be able to help you, then.'

Baldwin met Simon as the jury moved from one body to go and hold inquest on the second, poor Danny's. It had taken a short while to find a good stables and see that his horse was properly rubbed down and fed, before he felt he could leave it and seek his friend. The group of men a short distance from Simon's front door was evidence that there had been something of interest happening, and when Baldwin heard the stentorian tones of the Coroner rising clearly over the normal hubbub of the town, he felt a brief anxiety that he might be too late to serve the bishop.

'Old friend! How are you?' Baldwin asked when he saw Simon. His sympathy was genuine. There were few times he had seen his companion so flushed and feeble-looking. 'Are you all right?'

'Death is attractive just now,' Simon said thickly. 'Don't ask. That Coroner has a belly of steel, I swear. He arrived yesterday to view two bodies, and I feel as though someone has kicked me in the head and . . . you aren't listening, are you?'

'What bodies, Simon?' Baldwin asked.

Simon glanced back at the place where the body had lain. The two young fellows were about to place it on a board to carry it to the churchyard for burial. 'Hey, you two, wait!'

Baldwin and he strode to the board and stared down at the naked corpse lying there.

'What do you think, Baldwin?'

'It matches a description I was given, I fear,' Baldwin said with a frown. He glanced at the two boys listening nearby. 'We need to talk, old friend. Somewhere quiet.'

'And in the meantime, I suppose we ought to speak to the Coroner,' Simon said without enthusiasm. Filled with self-pity, he added, 'He's looking at another corpse. It's a miracle he hasn't a third to look at.'

'A third?'

Simon was in no mood to explain. His belly was a roiling torment, and all he wanted just now was his bed. He led the way to Lower Street in silence, too absorbed in self-pity to consider Baldwin's words further.

Pierre was standing in the shadows when the voice hissed urgently from the open doorway.

'Master? Master Pierre?'

He had drawn his sword before sleeping, and now he moved as quietly as possible across the hayloft, then crouched at the edge, peering down at the entrance. Seeing it was Moses, he waited a short while, carefully staring at the patch of bright sunlight to see if any shadows might betray the presence of other men, before sheathing his sword and climbing down the ladder.

'Moses. You have news of a ship?'

This foreigner was as selfish as any, Moses reckoned inwardly. He was incapable of thinking of anyone but himself, even when the man who had saved his life lay dying in the house nearby. 'Not yet, no.

But I am sure that there will be news before long. First, here's some food. My master asked me to bring you food every day until you can make your way back over the water.'

'He is a good man.'

'Yes.' Moses felt no need to add to the flat statement.

'Have there been men asking for me?'

Moses had no idea what this man might have done. There were enough fellows who had done little or nothing to deserve being chased like foxes for him to feel too worried by that. Still, it rankled with him that this Frenchman did not enquire after the health of Master Pyckard.

'There has been nothing,' he answered carelessly. 'I doubt there's anyone here looking for *you*.'

'There is,' Pierre said with certainty. 'They do not give up, these men. Now, I should see your master and thank him.'

At last, Moses said to himself. Aloud, though, he said, 'He isn't well enough to see anyone, and if you are right and men *are* hunting for you, it'd be a foolish thing to come out in the open and let them see you.'

'You think so? Better to meet them face to face, is what I consider. I prefer to go about as a man, not hide all my life. No, I will come back with you and visit the old man who protects me. If the men are there, I will see them and know whether I am still in danger. If they are not there, then there is no need to hide any more!'

'And what if the men you say are following you, see you entering his house? Perhaps they'll go to Master Pyckard and torture him to learn all he knows about you. Have you thought of that, of the danger you will put *him* in? No. You should stay well away from my master's house.'

'Then I can enter secretly? By the garden, perhaps?'

'*No!* I will not have you in the house. My master is dying! I won't have you upsetting him any further.' Moses's voice broke.

Pierre looked away, staring out through the open doorway. The Frenchman was a good half-head taller than Moses, and he could look down his nose at him with ease, but only a fool would antagonise the servant. He scarcely merited the effort, and even if he did, he was Pierre's lifeline just now. Without him, he would have no food. And he was probably quite right. The best thing to do was to keep hidden, to wait until one of Master Pyckard's ships came free, and then to quietly take his place on board and leave for France.

'Very well. I will do as you suggest. But do you know how long it is likely to be before there is a ship I can join? I cannot stay here forever!'

'There will be one soon. She is being loaded now, and I would hope that in two, maybe three days, she should be ready to sail.'

'That long?'

There was disappointment on his face at having to wait for so long, but Moses didn't greatly care. He deposited the sack of bread, half a fowl and a pot of honey on the floor, and passed Pierre the heavy earthenware jug. 'There are three quarts of ale there. I'll try to bring more when I come here tonight. For now, keep quiet in here. We'll have you back in France as soon as we can.'

Moses glanced about him, then turned and left the place. He would go quickly back to the house and make sure Master Pyckard was comfortable before continuing with any other chores. At the gate which shut off the yard, he hesitated and looked back. In the doorway, so he thought, he could see Pierre standing with the jug still in his hands, watching him. As though he didn't trust even Moses.

The ingratitude of the man! He had turned up late at night, and seemed to expect Master Pyckard to aid him, even though Moses had never seen him nor even heard his name mentioned before. But as soon as the groom from the stable arrived and told Master Pyckard that there was a Frenchie in town hoping to see him, a man by name of Pierre, his master had drawn himself up on his cushions and told Moses to fetch his cloak and gloves. Before long, he had left, and Moses waited for him to return, banished from his master's side.

It would be the last time his master could tell him to leave him alone. Since that evening, Pyckard had sunk quickly. Soon he would be gone, and Moses would be all alone, but for his brother's children.

Moses only hoped that this unkempt stranger wasn't taking

advantage of his master, because if he were, Moses himself would see to it that Master Pyckard won justice, whether he was alive or dead.

Chapter Twelve

The inquest on the second body was much faster. Sir Richard de Welles already had poor Danny stripped and displayed before Simon and Baldwin had reached the quay near Hawley's house. A woman shrieked and wailed with grief nearby, comforted by the man Simon recognised as Pyckard's servant. An assortment of children moaned and wept at her feet. It was enough to make Simon feel a mortifying shame at his reluctance to view this man's body. No matter what Simon felt, he had left a family behind, and men and women who loved him. He deserved to be investigated properly.

'Clearly he has spent some time in the water,' Sir Richard said. He had always disliked examining drowned men. The bodies with their flaccid flesh, white and loose like cheap leather gloves, made even his resilient stomach turn a little. Better to have a man spitted on a lance with his entrails dangling, than a whitened corpse like this.

He prodded the chilled flesh with a reluctant finger. 'Like a slab of fish, eh?' he called unsympathetically to the clerk taking notes. Stephen winced at his lack of tact, but continued writing.

Sir Richard stood upright and glanced about him. Seeing Hamo standing near the jury, and Alred Paviour nearby, he beckoned to them both. 'HOI! Over here, you two. You can help with this fellow.'

These two were older and had experience of corpses. Few who had survived the famine of nine years before were not used to the sight and smell of the dead. Taking the man's arm, they heaved him over and over in front of the jury.

'Right, did you all see those wounds? A clear stab in his breast, with a blade about an inch and a half wide at the hilt. Doesn't go right through him, even though you can see the mark where the cross actually bruised him. Clearly it was thrust in as hard as possible. This man was found on board that ship the *Saint John*, so I'd think he was killed by the pirates and thrown down into the hold where he was partly concealed by the bale.'

'I have a question for you, sir,' a voice called.

Sir Richard turned and surveyed the faces before him. The speaker stood with a youth who must surely be his son, their faces were so alike. 'Who are you, sir?'

'My name is known here, sir. I am the master of the ship which found and rescued the *Saint John*. My name is John Hawley.' He gestured at the body. 'It was my master shipwright who found Danny in the hold.'

Sir Richard glanced over at Henry, who nodded. 'Master Hawley asked me to go and see if there was damage to her under the waterline, and I stumbled over the poor soul in the hold.'

'What of it then, Master Hawley?' Sir Richard rumbled.

'There were other good men aboard her, Sir Richard, some of them from this town, and I'd like to know what happened to *them*.'

'Find the ship that fired your cog, and you'll be part of the way there,' Sir Richard said, but Hawley's words had already started a rebellious murmuring among the jurors.

'It was the men from Lyme did it,' one asserted. 'They're thieving sods at the best of times. They even took a privateer on its way back to port with a good haul, didn't they?'

'They help other ports agin us, too.'

'Not long since they had a battle with us on the high seas.'

Sir Richard held up a hand for silence. 'No more of that! No more, I say! There are no other bodies, and unless you can produce a written authority for me to investigate a suspicious death without a body, I can do nothing. All I can do is hold an inquest on the body that *is* here. Now, does anyone have anything further to say about this body here?'

'There is one thing, Sir Richard,' a smooth voice said from behind him.

'Ah, Sir Baldwin! I trust you are still in God's safe hands?'

'I appear to be remarkably healthy, I thank you,' Sir Baldwin smiled, bowing. 'You know my friend Simon, of course?'

'Yes. We met yesterday,' Sir Richard said.

'You asked whether there were any questions about this corpse. I think there is one thing I should like you to consider,' Baldwin said. He had walked past Sir Richard, leaving Simon at the Coroner's side. Baldwin stood a moment contemplating the corpse, then he motioned to Hamo and Alred to turn the body over.

'I believe that this death was nothing to do with the rest of the ship. It doesn't look like piracy to me.'

The Coroner joined him. 'Why?'

In answer, Baldwin gestured to John Hawley. 'Master Hawley, you are a seaman of experience. Most of you here will know what it is to fight on board a ship. When pirates attack, they will use enormous violence and force to subdue their victims, will they not?'

'That was my question: whenever I have been at war on the sea, the wounds have been ferocious, the attacks bloody. Yet this man has only one accurate stab wound on his breast.'

'Quite so,' Baldwin said. 'I think that this is no victim of the men of Lyme or any other pirates out at sea, Sir Richard. This man Danny was stabbed to death, and then set in the hold to make it appear that he had perished with the rest of the crew.'

It was hard now to remember the happier times. There had been many of them, it was true, but Pierre knew that if he was captured, he would never know happiness of any sort again. His end would be slow and exquisitely painful.

Casting his mind back, he tried to recall when it all started. Surely it was not really ten years ago when he had caught his first glimpse of her? Yes, it must have been: the Year of Our Lord 1314.

In those days, all he had known of her was that she was a slim, tall, and utterly beautiful woman. He didn't think further than that. He was a lowly page and she was a foreign visitor, but there was something about her that called to him, and he could remember now stopping and taking a second look at her as he left the hall to replenish the jug of wine he was carrying. He was a mere servant at her table, and yet when he saw her glance at him, he felt his heart must stop. The thrill of adoration stabbed him with a spark of lightning that was so intense, it hurt.

She could only have been fifteen at the time, and he, still learning the craft of the warrior, was a scant year older – yet their positions were so very different. He knew that there could be no hope of his ever attaining her. She was as impossible to touch as the moon or the stars. Or, rather, the sun, because were he actually to touch her, he would burn in an instant. She was so lovely, so perfectly built and proportioned, no man could be near her and be unaffected.

The second time was the next year, when she was again visiting France, and he had at last begun the great journey. He had risen from page to squire in that time, and now he was gaining a reputation for courage, so when he took his seat at the table, others wished to introduce him to the guests. And so he met her.

That she was so well spoken was no surprise, of course, nor were her delicacy or intellect. Still, there was something else about her that finally sealed his love. It was the luminosity in her eyes. He couldn't describe it any other way: she had a sparkle that made a man warm as soon as her gaze lighted upon him. He felt that look so often, he began to wonder if he had caused offence, and it was only when he saw how she blushed to receive his own adoring looks that he realised his feelings towards her were reciprocated.

Ah! The joy, the splendid delight of knowing that she felt the same towards him . . . and the horror when he at last understood their plight. To remain in proximity, their love unrequited, their whole existences so close and yet never being permitted to share even a brief kiss, let alone a more passionate consummation. Even the memory of their first and last kiss was enough to make his blood course like a galloping stallion through his veins, and when he closed his eyes and imagined what she must appear like in her bed, naked, welcoming . . . it was a torture!

But all torture will end. Sometimes there will be a period of release. Thus it was for them. They had met once by accident, and from that moment they both appreciated the danger they were in. They could not remain in the same household.

Pierre could do nothing that might hurt her. He, who loved her most, could not expose her to the same dangers as those his own family had inflicted on the women in the Tour de Nesle. Instead, he had gone to the mistress of the household, Queen Isabella, and pleaded with her to be released from her service for a while. With a pretty display of regret, she acquiesced, provided that he carry some little messages for her, and so here he was.

At least by travelling to France he would provide the Queen with some sort of service. More importantly, it might save his lady from being discovered as an adulteress with him. That in itself was enough to justify his exile.

Hamund insisted on walking into the sea before he did anything else. His acquaintance told him his name was Gilbert, or Gil, and he was the shipmaster of the cog *Saint Denis*.

'That's her out there.'

'A fine-looking craft,' Hamund said, although in truth he was wondering how such a lumbering great vessel could possibly sail across the vast expanse of water he had seen from Tunstal earlier that day.

'Better than that. She's fleet, she's got a clean keel, and she'll outsail even the worst of the Lyme privateers. Yes, she's a lovely little thing. Are you sure you want to walk into the sea? It's not too warm, you know.'

'I will not fail in my oath,' Hamund said stolidly.

'Walk down here, then. It's a slip for new ships to be launched,' Gil said, indicating the stone roadway that led straight to the water and sank beneath.

Hamund gripped his cross until his knuckles were white, then strode forward into the water. It *was* cold, Gil had not deceived him. He felt a chill tendril float over his ankle, then some flotsam drifted past, and he felt a sudden terror of the water. Quelling the urge to turn and fly from it, he stood a while with his eyes closed, up to his thighs in the sea. The Coroner had told him to do this, and he would do everything as ordered, because otherwise any man could execute him legally. A picture of Guy de Bouville's face came into his mind and he shuddered. It was only when he heard Gil's voice that he opened them again and with relief made his way out.

'Thought you'd fallen asleep in there,' the shipmaster grunted.

'No, no. I was just thinking about a man who wanted to kill me, to avenge his master – the man I killed. If he was to find me doing anything other than climbing aboard the first ship out of here, he'd kill me. I'm sure of that.'

'It is no matter! I am seeking three more men, and won't have some arse murdering you here when I need you on the ship. So! Enough of this meandering, come! We have to get to the taverns before all the men are too drunk.'

Sir Richard sat back and belched after consuming the best of the food Simon's boy had been able to find.

Rob was still smarting. When his mother had been called by the lady of her house to repeat the Coroner's words: 'If that lazy bratchet doesn't get up now, I'll have the steward beat him from his bed!' she had been furious to have her position in the place put at risk, and had kicked him from his palliasse. Then, as soon as he arrived in the Bailiff's house, he had been bellowed at by this huge stranger, who told him to scramble to the pie shop immediately if he didn't want a boot up his arse and to be kicked from one end of Upper Street to the other. When he glanced at the Bailiff for support, all he saw was a look of sheer fury. Simon's eyes were narrowed to slits, and his mouth was a thin line, he was so cross. Rob ran.

He hadn't expected them all back so soon this morning. Usually the Bailiff went out to an alehouse for a drink and took a pie from the shop on his way back to his counting-house. Not today, though. Today these three men had descended just as he was thinking about wandering over to the Blue Dolphin himself. He nodded sulkily when he was commanded to seek out pies and honeyed thrushes, six, as well as a capon. And a loaf, and was there any ale in the house? Or wine? At that point he hurried out before they could think of anything else he might carry.

'Glad that lad's sorted,' the Coroner boomed. 'Seems more inclined to work now. You can't let the idle buggers wander about as if they own the house, Bailiff. Can't imagine how you could have let him get so above himself. Still, he'll be more cautious now. You all right? You look as if you could do with a drink, man.'

'I am fine,' Simon lied. He walked slowly to his chair and settled himself in it, his elbow on his knee, hand supporting his head. It felt appallingly heavy.

Baldwin looked from him to the Coroner, and suddenly understood his friend's malady. He had thought Simon was simply queasy as a result of the sight of the two bodies, knowing the bailiff's horror of corpses.

It was a matter they rarely discussed, but Baldwin himself had seen too many bodies for him to be upset at the sight of another one. He looked upon the dead as mere husks of the people who had once inhabited them. Once the soul had fled, the flesh remained as food for worms. In his youth he had travelled out to Acre in a fit of Christian enthusiasm, seeking to hold back the tide of Saracen hordes which were throwing the Crusaders from the kingdoms of Outremer. He had arrived in Acre as the siege was nearing its end, and he had witnessed the full brutality of war at its worst. He had seen women and children squashed to a splash of crimson by the rocks of the massive catapults; men flung against walls by the enormous bolts of the machines the Arabs fired. They could pass through one thickness of a gate, snatch up a man, and pin him to the stone behind. Yes, Baldwin had seen enough death to last many lifetimes.

When he looked at a body, he did not generally feel grief. The time for that was when the man or woman was still living, and his sympathy or support could save a person from pain. No, when the corpse was in front of him, he was more interested to see what it could tell him about the manner of its death. Some said that when a man died, the last image he saw was imprinted within his eyes, but although Baldwin had peered closely at many dead men over the years, he had only ever seen himself reflected. Yet there was always something to be learned if the man searching was open to clues, no matter how small.

'I am parched!' Sir Richard exclaimed. 'Good God in heaven, you live like a pauper, Bailiff! D'you have no wine in the house fit for a thirsty Coroner?'

Simon gave him a sour look. 'Until last night, yes. Now I fear there is nothing left.'

'Was that all you had?' Sir Richard showed surprise. 'It was such a small—'

'And after the ales and the burned wines, I should have thought there would be no need for more,' Simon said. He felt a little bilious again at the memory.

'Let's hope that idle beggar of yours gets back soon with some vittles, then,' Sir Richard said. 'Ha! Sir Baldwin, did I ever tell you the story of the peasant, the merchant, the knight and the bishop? They were all in a small boat, and the wind built up, and it was clear that they must sink, so the first man, the peasant, said, "I am unimportant. I have done many ill deeds in my life: once I even took my neighbour's sow and knew her carnally, before killing her and curing her. I feel remorse, and I am sure it is my fault God is punishing us for my sin, so I shall jump into the sea to save you, if you all pray for my soul and beg for God's forgiveness," and so saying, he prayed with them, and leaped into the waters. But the weather deteriorated.

'Then the merchant stood up, and he said, "I do not matter. I have made men suffer. When they have owed me money, I have demanded high profits in usurious transactions. I am detested by Christ because I am mercenary and seek to make money from war. But if I jump into the waters, He may relent and let you live, and I may be saved for that one good deed. If you pray for me, I shall go." So saying, he prayed with them, accepted their thanks, and jumped.

'But it did no good. If anything, the weather grew still worse, and the two remaining men stared at each other. It was plain that they must die if both stayed in the boat. Only one could live.

'At last the knight said, "Bishop, you are a good and excellent man. I am only a meagre knight. I have killed and raped across England, and I am known as a felon. But you are a good kindly, honourable man. Would you pray for me?" "My son, for the rest of my life," said the good bishop, and began immediately. When he was done, the knight nodded. "Thank you," quoth he, and threw the bishop overboard! Eh? Haha!'

Simon winced and glanced at Baldwin.

The knight smiled thinly. Sir Richard de Welles's sense of humour was famed. 'What did you conclude about the two bodies, Simon?'

The Bailiff grunted. 'The first was a churl in town for a drink who got seized by a whore's pander, then was killed and robbed. The second died in a sailor's fight and was concealed when the bale fell on him. No mystery with either of them. More concerning is the disappearance of the crew on the cog.'

'The first appears to have been a well-nourished fellow,' Sir Richard commented. 'Probably not a farmer or local peasant. Certainly not a sailor.'

'Why?'

Baldwin responded. 'His hands were soft. They hadn't worked with a plough or with ropes. He was no manual worker. His skin too, was pale. He had a slight reddishness that looked like burning, although that could have been from after his death. Does a dead man get burned by the sun? Anyway, he was clearly a man who spent his life in a quiet environment. He was not well muscled or fit in the normal sense of the word.'

'And he had a stain on his forefinger,' Sir Richard said. 'His right. It was slightly callused. And you saw his brow? A very deep set of frowning-wrinkles. I think it's fair to think that his eyesight was not so good as it once was.'

Simon belched quietly, glancing from one man to the other as they nodded grimly. 'What are you talking about?' he asked tiredly.

'He was a clerk. Probably one who spent much of his time in the cloisters,' Sir Richard said absently. 'The ink on his finger and the frowning point to a man who was used to spending his time with parchment and quill.'

Baldwin nodded. 'Except I should think that he was from the Cathedral Close or a canonical church like Crediton's, rather than a monkish cloister. Monks will pray more often than canons, and his knees were not overly callused.'

'Ah, I missed that,' Sir Richard said. He glanced at the door hopefully. 'Where is that boy?'

'I think you should look for a man who has come into some wealth,' Baldwin said. 'He may have a penner and reeds to sell, too. And a well-made purse, if I guess right.' He knew that the bishop's nephew would have the best quality – and money.

'I shall put some words about. Not that it's really my job to find the murderer. I only seek him as a diversion, as you well know.'

Baldwin smiled. 'Of course.'

'I am interested in this ship's destruction as well, though,' Sir Richard said. 'There is something intriguing about a ship that's had all her crew slaughtered, even if it is some distance away from my responsibility.'

'If murder is committed off the land, you are hardly in a position to investigate it,' Baldwin agreed.

'It would be hard in any case,' Simon said. 'Almost all the ships from the town were at sea that day.'

'This Hawley was first to pick up the ship, though?' Richard noted.

'Yes. But that means little, except I'd be inclined to consider him innocent for that very reason,' Simon said. 'If he'd been there all alone, he'd have taken the cargo, fired the ship, and waited to make sure it sank. He's a cool, collected man. And surely the man who fired the *Saint John* knew little about ships,' he added thoughtfully.

'Why so?' Baldwin asked.

'The men who tried to fire her poured oil about the deck. It made the damage look bad, with charring to the timbers and the sails gone, but really, the ship herself was under no great threat. A sailor would have thrown more oil about the hold, so that the flammable goods in there might catch light.'

'Many men might make that mistake. Couldn't she have caught fire if Hawley was slower to reach her?' Baldwin remarked.

'No. From what I've heard, the oil was nothing like sufficient. You know how it is – if you want a fire to burn, you put tinder over the flame. Here it looks as though oil was spread about the place and set alight, but no tinder or kindling used. Even landlubbers like us wouldn't expect that to work!' Simon grinned.

'Where is that lad?' Sir Richard wondered as Baldwin narrowed his eyes consideringly.

As he spoke, the door opened at last and Rob stomped into the room before standing aside. A paid of apron-clad urchins appeared, holding trays on which were good-sized coffins of pastry. The room began to fill with the succulent aroma of gravy and meats. Rob had the pies set on the table at the side of the room, and then he sent the boys away. 'Capon's finishing cooking, and he'll bring honeyed larks when he's ready,' he said. 'No throstles.'

'The drink?'

'I've got it outside,' Rob said waspishly. He left them and returned a moment or two later, rolling in a small cask. It was one of the ones used locally, made of oaken staves held in place by a binding of hoops shaped from split hazel, each hoop secured by fine strands of elder. He rolled it to the table and attempted to lift it, his face reddening as he strained.

'Good God, boy!' Sir Richard snapped, pushing him aside and grasping the little barrel. He hefted it easily, and placed it on the table. There was a wooden tap; he set it on the bung and drew his dagger, rapping it sharply. The tap slipped in, and he glared at Rob. 'Well? Where are the goblets, boy? Do you expect us to drink from our hands?'

Chapter Thirteen

Hamund was lightheaded after the wine he had been given at the tavern. It was an ill-lit chamber, foul with smoke and sweat, and the men inside were all local folk. When he first appeared in the doorway, the room became subdued, as though all eyes were upon him. It was not so bad as an alehouse in a small vill, where the room would be silenced entirely by a strange face, but it was disconcerting nonetheless. All the faces in there seemed dark, mysterious, and threatening. At a time when not many men went bearded, all in there appeared to be unshaven; hair was worn long, so that it straggled greasily below coifs and caps; and every face was burned to the colour of the oaken barrels by wind and sun.

Gil himself appeared relaxed. He stood with his thumbs in his belt in the middle of the floor, nodding occasionally at a man he knew well, passing his eyes quickly over others. Hamund wondered whether they were men he did not know and thus could not trust. Except he had already taken Hamund while knowing nothing good about him. This reflection made Hamund look more closely at the men who were ignored by Gil, wondering what black history there must be lying on *them*.

'I need three more men for the *Saint Denis*,' Gil said to one small group of men. 'Who here would like a short journey with as much Guyennois wine as you can drink?'

There was a pause, and Hamund saw several men grin and shake their heads, while others stared from darkening brows. One man stood, shifting his heavy leather belt on his belly.

'I could make one more sailing, I reckon.'

'I'm glad there's one fine fellow who enjoys the sailor's life,' Gil said. He ignored two more whose hands were in the air, and first one, then the other, wavered and sank. 'Come on! There must be someone in here who's got some fire in his belly!'

'If you think we're going to sea in a solitary ship while those bastards from Lyme are trying to kill us, you're mad,' a voice called harshly. 'If they could take the whole crew of the *Saint John*, they could take the *Saint Denis* as well. How many more men do you want to see dead?'

'First, Tom, we don't yet know what happened to the *Saint John*,' Gil responded calmly enough. 'Second, even if we knew for certain it was the men of Lyme who took her, that wouldn't change anything, would it? If you allow them to scare you all into remaining in here, cuddling up to each other, you'll have no livelihood to speak of. What'll you do, stick to fishing until the big bullies of Lyme come here to take your fishing as well? Or fight them now, while you've a chance? I've got the *Saint Denis* kitted and fitted, and she's carrying as many men as I can put aboard her. Any who can handle an axe or sword is welcome, and we'll soon put the Lyme men to flight if they try any funny business. Come on, now! Are you all going to give up the sea because of some bandy-legged bastard sons of she-goats from Dorset?'

'Fine words, Gil, but if I was going to sea now, I'd want at least three or four ships with me so that they could protect each other,' the man called Tom said, and immediately others cheered or spoke in approving tones. 'Let the *Saint Denis* wait a few days and we'll come too, along with Master Hawley's ships. Then there'll be enough men to send even the Brittany pirates packing!'

Gil smiled, but Hamund could see he was rattled. His eyes were moving constantly over the men in the room now, gauging the mood. 'So, you're happy to let the Lyme bastards feel that they've won, eh? You'll let them get away with the murder of the crew of the *Saint John*? Even young Danny from Hardness?'

'Better that than adding our names to the list of their victims,' Tom said.

'There's no point opening my master's purse for you lot in here, then,' Gil said, and pulled out a purse from inside his shirt. It rattled with coins. 'That's a shame. Still, I'll have a quart of ale for me, and another for this man here. He's not scared of a few pirates. It'll be good to sail with a man who's got ballocks.'

'Let's hope he doesn't get them cut off, then,' Tom said coldly.

It was soon after their meal that Sir Richard rose, spat and scratched at his thick beard. 'It's time I had a short rest before carrying on,' he said, and yawned hugely. 'Holding inquests and riding about the countryside is exhausting work, d'ye know? I'll to my bed for a nap. Try to keep the noise down while I'm snoozing. I'm a very light sleeper.'

Simon watched him go with eyes that felt sore and rough. 'That man is intolerable!'

'You drank too much last night, then?' Baldwin said with a chuckle.

'It was not my fault!'

'I suppose that cruel Coroner forced you to the floor, sat on your chest and poured the wine into your throat?'

'It was just that he kept on and on drinking. He is quite relentless! If he had two pints, he had to have four. I am amazed that the old devil can function.'

'My friend, Sir Richard de Welles has lived to such a ripe old age because he has the constitution of an ox and a capacity to match. He could consume all the ale in this town and still waken fresh as a rose on a summer's morning.'

There was already a low rumbling. Simon cast his eyes upwards. 'And he snores like a hog.'

This time Baldwin laughed outright. 'Come, Simon, let us go and get some fresh air. That's what you need.'

Simon grunted. Just now what he really wanted above all else was to copy Sir Richard, and even with the loud snoring that was filling his house, he was sure that he would fall asleep as soon as his head hit the pillow. Still, his companion was probably right. If he was to close his eyes for a moment, he would sleep for the rest of the day.

'Very well. After the wine I could do with clearing my head.'

Baldwin privately thought that wine and strong ale was the cause of much that was wrong. As a Knight Templar, he had learned to moderate his drinking, and he had discovered the delights of watered juices pressed from fresh fruits. However, in Britain, most men preferred to drink only good ale or wine. Since returning, he had observed that most fights began and ended with alcohol, and he was sure that if there were no inebriating drinks, the world would be a much more peaceful place.

They left Simon's house up on Higher Street, and turned right, wandering aimlessly, and for the most part speaking little, until they reached the hole in the road where the paver and his team were mending the road surface.

'Good day to you, Alred,' Simon said pleasantly. 'I expect you are glad to be working again?'

'Aye, that we are. We have to complete this stretch and get on to the next town, Bailiff. There's never an end to our task when so many heavy carriages keep rolling by with metal-shod wheels.'

Baldwin observed the other two men with Alred. Bill was spreading gravel evenly over the base of the hole, while Law listened at the hole's edge, where he was supposed to be stacking cobbles. 'You must be glad to see them, as they keep you in business!'

'That I am, Sir Knight. I sometimes think I should pay into a collection for all those who use the heaviest bullock-carts and wagons! They keep us three going nicely.'

'Tell me, Master Paviour,' Baldwin said, smiling easily, 'this body that appeared here – it was clearly some time after you had left the area?'

'Oh, yes. We were finished here just at the time of the ninth hour. You know how it is during the summer, with the greater payments for the working day? Our contract here expects us to work from the ringing of the church bell in the morning to the ringing for the last service.'

Baldwin nodded. All labourers were paid more for the summer months because they were expected to continue working through the hours of daylight. A summer's day was officially separated into twelve daylight hours and twelve hours of darkness, hence the better pay.

'What happened when you finished here? Did you stay nearby?'

'We packed up everything as usual. You can't tell what sort of thieving scrotes you're going to have in a town you haven't been to before, and our tools are our most important belongings.'

'We always pack them carefully,' Law said.

'Who are you?' Baldwin enquired mildly.

'Lawrence, from Crediton, sir. I'm apprenticed to Alred here.'

'Yes, so stop interrupting, lad, before I clout you one for rudeness,' Alred said sharply. 'After we packed up, we went to a tavern for a drink.'

'Which one?' Baldwin asked.

'That one down there,' Alred said, pointing. 'The Porpoise. It's got a good ale in there, and we were thirsty after working hard all day.'

'You set out trestles and boards all round to stop people falling in, my friend says,' Baldwin noted, glancing about him.

'Of course. We couldn't leave the hole and nothing to warn people.'

'I put them up myself, sir,' Law said. 'They tried to say I didn't, but I did.'

'So someone took the trestles away after you left here?'

'Yes. They hid them over there by the building,' Alred said. There was an alley between a house and a large barn nearby. 'Some idiot must have thought it'd be a good laugh to take them and see someone fall in and hurt themselves. Probably a drunken sailor out for some fun.'

'Possibly. Now, you stayed at the tavern for how many drinks?'

'We had a good few,' Law admitted with a grin. 'Master Alred felt rotten the next day, didn't you?'

'So it was late when you walked back past here, and you were very happy?'

'There's no law against that yet, thank the Lord,' Alred said, glaring at his insubordinate apprentice.

'No indeed,' Baldwin agreed. 'But were you so drunk you wouldn't have noticed the trestles being gone?'

Alred opened his mouth, but then he frowned. 'The thing is, the trestle at the other end of the hole was still there. It was only the trestles at the sides and at this end of the hole which were taken. Walking up from the tavern, I remember seeing the trestle near me, and walking round it, but I don't know if the other trestles were here. It could be that someone had already taken them.'

'And if you don't recall *that*, the man could already have been there, dead?'

Law shook his head. 'No chance.'

Baldwin's eyes snapped to him. 'You sound very certain of that. Why?'

'I dunno. I just don't think he could have been.'

'Why, man?'

Law began to regret opening his mouth. Alred had told him to hold his tongue if anyone should come and speak to them about the dead man, but no, he had to speak up and get himself into trouble, didn't he?

Alred tried to rescue him. 'I think he means that we'd be bound to have noticed.'

'Did you? Is that what you meant?'

'Yes.'

'But your master said you were all drunk. You drank lots in the tavern, and when you came back, you saw one trestle only.'

Bill set his spade down and leaned on it. He stared at Alred, then at Law, then looked up at Baldwin. 'What he meant was, there wasn't time for the lad to get back here after we saved him. I don't see there's anything for us to be ashamed about in that.'

Alred turned to him, held his hands up in the air, and let them drop in defeat. 'Fine! You want to tell him all, you go ahead!'

'It's not our fault, Alred. No point getting upset about it,' Bill said. 'Sir, we don't know who the man is who fell into our pit here, but we did see another earlier that evening in the drinking house up there.'

Baldwin listened carefully as Bill told of seeing the stranger at the inn, and of how, when he had gone out the back, as though to find himself a place in the bedchamber, he had been followed by a local man who looked to them nothing better than a footpad. The three pavers had immediately gone after the men, allowing the stranger to move off unmolested.

'This is growing very serious,' Baldwin said with a long face. 'Now, are you completely sure that the man in your pit was not the stranger at the inn?'

'We are that.'

'For one thing,' Alred smiled slyly, 'he had a lovely purse. Red leather, it was, with a draw-string that had a golden tassel. And his clothes were better. Less travel stained.

Hamo was at his workshop at the tip of Smiths' Street, which was how the folk in the town described the northernmost part of Lower Street. The opposite end was commonly called South Town, because over the years as the town grew, it had expanded along the shoreline to the south, since no houses could be built on the steep sides of the hill above.

This was a good place to have his cooperage. From here he could see all along both reaches of the Dart, northwards and south towards the open sea. As soon as a ship returned, he would see it, and although it was not a great help in telling him how many casks he might be able to sell, nor how many to mend, he did at least have warning that his services would soon be required. It was also good that he resided amongst the shipwrights, because they tended to go to him first when they wanted something done.

Hamo yawned. The twin inquests had been tiring, and he was thirsty now after trying to catch up. He had spent the time since working on oak staves, using his spokeshave to trim them all to shape. Now he had one steel ring on the floor, and was carefully setting the staves inside it to gauge their fit. He had a need for one more to space them, and he manipulated the others, trying them for their fit next to each other before he had them positioned well, and only then was he satisfied. Slipping a rope with a loose running knot over the top of the staves to hold them in place, he drew it tight before picking up the last one.

He had a simple jig where he worked: a sawhorse with a pair of pegs at one end. Thrusting the stave's end between these pegs, he sat on the top of the jig then began to work with his spokeshave, drawing the tool towards him and shaving off fine, curling slivers with a smooth action, starting with short strokes near the end of the stave and gradually working further and further up the wood to create a gentle curve from the midpoint down. When he had completed both edges, he set the final stave in the barrel's body and tied that in place too. The fit at the base was perfect. Only then did he reach for the other steel ring and start to set it at the top of the barrel, placing a blunted chisel at the ring and knocking it down with careful taps of his mallet.

It was while he was doing this that he heard a call. Glancing up, he saw a magnificent ship appearing at the mouth of the river. She was a great cog, powerful and elegant, and her sails rippled as the wind changed direction, coming down from the hill.

Hamo gazed at her for a moment or two, his eyes narrowed against the rippling sparks of sunshine on the water. This ship was clearly no ordinary merchantman. She had wealth on display everywhere, from the gold leaf on her prow to the immense silken flag at her mast, and she also had the trappings of war: there was a castle at bow and stern, and plenty of men about her.

Setting his tools aside, he stood watching as the ship travelled majestically up the river, her sails being reefed and anchors dropped as she came level with him. And as she drew to a halt, he saw the painted name: *Gudyer*, just as a little rowing boat was being launched over her side, and observed the laughing fair-haired man who made his way lightly down the rope and into the boat, where two crewmen rowed him ashore.

Hamund was feeling much better as the men began to talk again, ignoring him and Gil in their corner.

'What now, master?' he asked.

'Some will come to drink our ale,' Gil said bitterly, 'and they'll expect good money for the fact that no one else is coming forward. I'm glad I met you this morning. You haven't brought me luck, but at least I have someone with us.'

'What is all this about the men of Lyme?'

Hamund listened, his face growing longer as Gil told him all about the *Saint John*.

'That's it,' Gil finished. 'A crew missing, and the cargo all set to be fired. We were lucky John Hawley and his men arrived when they did.'

At that moment, three men came forward to offer their services, but none appealed to Gil. He tried to tempt others to join him on the ship, but all refused, shrugging their shoulders and not meeting his eye.

Gil gave up after the fourth refusal. 'It's no good. There's no point trying to talk them around if they don't want to do it. We'll just have to make do with fewer men. We should be all right with the number we've got.'

Hamund, having no idea what was required in a ship's complement, felt unable to comment beyond a mild expression of sympathy.

'You can see why even an abjuror will be helpful,' Gil said.

As Hamund nodded, hoping desperately that the master would not change his mind about hiring him, the door opened and two men walked in. Hamund barely glanced at them, but Gil immediately stiffened at his side. 'What does the Bailiff want – and who's that with him?'

Hamund was feeling quite light-headed, but he focused on the two men at the doorway with an effort, and watched as they marched over to the innkeeper.

It was Simon who beckoned the innkeeper to them. 'Saul, this is the Keeper of the King's Peace, Sir Baldwin de Furnshill, and we're here to investigate the death of the man up the road the other day. We've heard that there was a man came in here, and he was followed out back by someone you knew. Tell us what happened.'

'You know Cynegils? I spotted him watching the fellow. Don't know who he was, just some traveller. Like you say, he walked out to the back like he was going to find himself a space to sleep, and Cynegils shoved off smartish through the front door. He came back a little while later, and then sneaked out to the back, where our friend had gone.'

'And then?'

Saul grinned. 'The three pavers saw him, and they reckoned he was up to no good, so they went after him. A few minutes later, back they came, carrying him. Said that Cynegils had unfortunately tripped over and hurt his head. Good for them, I thought. Nasty piece of work, he is. I told them to put him back out in the yard. Anyway, the stranger had it away on his legs. There's a break in my wall out back, and I suppose he bolted over that.'

'What did he look like?'

'French. Good quality clothes, dark blue and scarlet, all in the modern fashion, you know, tight-fitting? He had a weaselly face, all thin with a narrow little nose, and dark eyes with low eyebrows of dark hair. Looked like loads of the Norman sailors who come in here every so often.'

'Have you seen him since?' Simon asked.

'Nope. No sign of him. I reckon he was scared and thought he'd bugger off quick. Why?'

'Didn't it occur to you that Cynegils was not acting on his own?' Simon demanded. 'He was ordered to follow this Frenchman by someone else, I assume, and that other person could have been anyone. And now this fellow's been found dead. Was it the man in here that day?'

'No. I'm sure of that.'

'So perhaps the man who died was the one who ordered Cynegils to follow this Frenchman?' Simon guessed.

Baldwin nodded pensively. 'I should imagine so. I reckon the Frenchman escaped over the rear wall, ran to the front of the building, found this man hanging around for news from Cynegils and knocked him down. The victim would hardly have expected to be attacked by the very man whose death he had planned.'

'There is one other possibility, of course,' Simon considered as the host of the inn brought them a jug of wine and two mazers, then moved off to serve other customers. He leaned closer to Baldwin to prevent eavesdroppers. 'What if the dead man carried something on him that was valuable? Something that was worth more than money?'

'Such as?'

'A ring, say?'

'No. If he had something like that, there would have been a mark on finger or thumb to show where it had lain. This man wore no jewellery.'

'A parchment then – deeds for property? A writ of some sort?'

'Simon, that could be a good guess,' Baldwin said. He felt the need for caution. Here at the inn he felt too exposed with so many men trying to listen in. He lowered his voice. 'There is a tale I should tell you. I was sent here by the bishop to see if I could find his nephew. A Frenchman has left the Queen's household and flees to the sea. Bishop Walter was convinced that he saw the man in Exeter, and told his nephew Bernard to follow the man.'

Simon absorbed the news calmly. 'The Frenchman escaped – and you think that this corpse could be Walter's nephew?'

'The man in your hole in the road? Yes. I fear it. He matches the description I was given.'

'Then we have to seek this Frenchman. He must be the one who ran from Cynegils.'

'I should imagine so,' Baldwin said. 'We must keep our eyes open and tell those who may be able to seek him for us.'

Simon peered at his friend speculatively. 'You said I may have guessed right about letters?'

'It seems odd that this Frenchman should suddenly leave the Queen's household,' Baldwin shrugged. 'Could he not be carrying messages?'

Simon nodded, but his eyes were going about the room now. 'I don't like the look of *him*.'

'Who?'

'That short fellow in pilgrim dress. He looks like an abjurer. Could *he* be our murderer?'

Chapter Fourteen

Hamund was feeling remarkably easy until he saw the two men stare at him. Seeing them walk towards him, he shivered and said beseechingly to Gil, 'Shall we leave now?'

'You!' said a stern voice. 'I am the Representative of the Keeper of this Port. I don't recognise you. Who are you, and why are you here?'

'Sir, I am Hamund Chugge. A miserable, but penitent sinner. I have committed a great crime, but I have abjured the realm, and all I do is seek a ship to take me away.'

'What was your crime?' Baldwin pressed.

'I killed a man.'

'Who, and why?'

Hamund sighed, and told the story: how his master was killed in the war, and Flok arrived with his little cavalcade to demand the manor for himself. 'I was very angry. I struck Flok down with my knife and killed him, and then struck Guy de Bouville down too. De Bouville was his guard and man-at-arms. Because of these offences I'm being sent away. I arrived here today, and this kind sailor has offered me a place with his crew.'

'You found him here, Gil?' Simon asked.

'Yes. And he's already walked into the sea in proof of his ambition to leave.'

'See to it that he does,' Simon grunted. He had not seen the man about the town before, it was true, and he looked an unlikely murderer of a fellow so much taller than him.

There was a sudden stillness in the room. The door had opened, and now a tall, slim, fair man walked in, stooping under the lintel, and remaining just inside the doorway, eyeing the men in the room for a few minutes. He pulled off his fine gloves and slapped them on his forearm before crossing the floor to the innkeeper.

'A jug of your best wine, landlord.'

'Sir.'

The man turned from the bar and addressed the men in the room. 'I have money for those who would aid the King.'

As he spoke, he rested his left hand on his purse and hefted it a couple of times. The leather bag rattled with the weight of coins, and Simon could almost hear every head in the room swivel to that magical sound.

'There is gold and silver here for those who would help me find a traitor, a foul Frenchman who is guilty of raping an English lady. I will pay well for any information.'

Moses swept the floor to clear the old rushes. There were few things in life that would always make him feel more comfortable in himself, but one was the smell of fresh reeds on the floor, and he reasoned that what made him feel better might work for his master too; so he swept enthusiastically, while the dust rose in clouds and danced in the light streaming in through the great barred window.

He pushed the mess out through the door and into the street, where he would pay a scavenger later to clear it up, and returned with a couple of bundles of new reeds. He cut the ties with his knife and began to strew them about the place.

'Please, Moses, come and sit,' Pyckard called faintly.

Moses hurried to his master's couch.

He looked worse than ever, Moses thought. There were lines of anguish on his brow, but although his eyes were bright and feverish, when he looked at Moses he was clearly rational. The pain was surely all but unbearable, yet his mind still functioned as efficiently as it ever had.

'Moses, you have been like a son to me. Of all that I have enjoyed in this world, it is you I shall find most grief in leaving.'

'Perhaps . . .'

'You know I'm almost dead, Moses. I could see it in your eyes, even if I didn't feel it already myself. Ach! It burns me from within! I shall die happy to know I will meet my Amandine again. It will be a delight to find her in heaven.'

Moses nodded tearfully.

'I would have you protect this Frenchman,' Pyckard went on. 'He is dear to me. He is so like her, in so many ways. The same face, the same accent . . . Serve him as you may.'

'I will, master.'

'That is good,' Pyckard gasped, and his head fell back onto the pillow with a grunt of pain. 'Oh, God. Take me to Your bosom soon!'

Baldwin and Simon left the tavern as soon as they had finished their drinks, and made their way up the street to Simon's house, only to find that Sir Richard de Welles was already awake and sitting in Simon's favourite chair in the hall, drinking from a large cup of wine.

'Where have you two been?' he rumbled. 'You look like conspirators.'

Baldwin explained what he was doing here in Dartmouth, ending his story with his suspicion about the identity of the corpse in the road.

'So you understand,' he finished, 'that this Frenchman must escape so that we don't give the French king a pretext for further action. Last time a French sergeant died, it cost us Gascony. If a French knight from the household of the sister of the French king was taken and punished for rape, it would have dire consequences.'

'You think so, hey? Right. I'll have a messenger sent to Exeter to have a full description of the man and see whether there are any distinguishing features. Let's hope it's not the Stapledon lad, though. It's always a bad business to have a famous stiff. No, I'd be happier if he was an unknown cleric or something. So, sir, you have been concealing things from a Coroner who's trying to do his best to uncover a murderer, is that it?' He waved aside Baldwin's protestations with an easy gesture. 'A joke, Sir Baldwin. If you kept something from me, I'm sure you had good reason. Suggesting that there was a foreign rapist in town who was killing people would not be the best way to keep the peace, I daresay? The question is, what do we do about it now?'

'For my part,' Baldwin said, 'I would like to investigate both dead bodies. First I think we need to speak to this strange fellow Cynegils and see what he has to say. Then I'd like to go and meet John Hawley and ask him about the body found on the ship, and question the master of the ship too.'

'The one that matters surely is the fellow in the roadway? The sailor's death was at sea, so it's hardly our affair,' Sir Richard pointed out. A Coroner's duties only extended to deaths on land or within sight of land.

'I hope so, and yet my heart tells me otherwise. In your experience, Coroner, how many murders are actually concealed efficiently?'

'Next to none! You know that yourself. Whether there's an ancient feud between them, or one or other has given offence for some reason, or a man dislikes the look of another's face. The fools tend to pull out a sword and whop anyone who takes their fancy. I never find that murder has been covered up.'

Baldwin reflected that this could simply mean that the Coroner had failed to notice efficiently concealed murders in the past. However, he replied politely, 'In the main, I have found that too. A murder that seems planned and suspicious is a rarity. And yet here you appear to have two such murders. One planned and most efficiently put into force at night in the roadway; the second planned and executed, if you will pardon the word, on board a ship.'

'You realise what you are suggesting,' Simon said. 'The man on the ship – if he was killed in port *before* the loading of the cargo, he would have been seen by the stevedores.'

Sir Richard shrugged. 'So? He was killed at sea, then.'

'If so, the killer knew that the body would be discovered at sea or when the ship docked. If he was on board the ship, he would have been at risk of discovery.'

'It was a risk, I suppose. But he could have run as soon as the ship arrived.'

'No. The ship's master would have all the crew remain on board until the cargo had been unloaded, and when the body was found, I daresay any master would want to see who was responsible. But if the murderer knew that there was going to be an attack on the ship, he wouldn't have had to worry.'

'You mean that there was a pirate spy on the ship?' Baldwin demanded.

'More likely that a man killed this sailor and dumped his body in the ship before it sailed,' the Coroner grunted. 'If he was killed *on* the ship, someone would have heard something.'

'Perhaps. Yet if the rest of the crew thought his death justified . . .' Simon began.

The Coroner shook his head with certainty. 'They'd have thrown him overboard. Sailors who think one of their number is bad luck, or is putting them in danger some other way, generally give him short shrift. The fastest way to be rid of him would be over the side, not knifed and thrown in the hold.'

'True. I had not considered the ways of sailors,' Baldwin mused. 'I wonder if that could help us?'

'I doubt it. Sounds like a marvellous excuse for running about the town like headless chickens and missing the point entirely. No, Bailiff, I think that there is *one* murder that matters here, and that is the death of the nephew of the Bishop of Exeter. The other fellow was a mere sailor. He can be mourned by his wife, but he needn't concern us. Now, are you two going to come and see this disreputable and so-called "spy" Cynegils?'

Baldwin glanced at Simon and nodded. However, his mind was not on the 'spy', but on the fair-haired man in the tavern.

When Walter Stapledon had been so determined to keep all news of the rape secret, Baldwin was curious to know how it was that, within a few days, a man could be here in Dartmouth bruiting news of it abroad.

The best thing, he determined, was to find the man and make sure that he escaped as quickly as possible, no matter how repellent the concept.

* * *

Bill and Alred had been hard at work in their hole. The gravel was laid and tamped down as best they could, and now, as the two stood up on the road, Law was down in the hole spreading the damp and heavy sand about the place.

'Looks like something's going on over there,' Alred said, watching the comings and goings from the inn.

'There're more folks there than I've seen this last week,' Bill agreed. 'Should we go and see what's going on?'

Law looked up and peered between their legs. 'I'll go. You two'll just get thirsty as soon as you get inside there.'

'Meaning you wouldn't?' Alred scoffed. 'You finish the work in there, Law. *I'll* go and see what it's about.'

Ignoring the comments hurled at his back by his disrespectful apprentice, the paver set off for the tavern, determined to have at least one pint of ale in peace.

Law would have to learn that he was still an apprentice. He wasn't a full, equal partner in business, just as Bill wasn't. The pair of them were as much use as a chalk chisel. Hopeless. If only they had kept their traps shut, they would have avoided those two men questioning them. He had nothing against the Bailiff, he'd seen enough of Simon Puttock to know he was a decent fellow, but this Keeper was a stranger, and Alred didn't know what to make of him. The paver had a healthy contempt for most men involved with the law, whether they were lawyers, bailiffs, Keepers or Coroners. All of them were in it for their own benefit, and that would rarely, if ever, accord with the common man's interests.

The inn was full, and as he tried to squint over the shoulders of the men in front, he could see little but a multitude of backs. Even when he managed to get a glance inside the tavern, it was so dark compared with the bright sunshine outside that he could make out nothing.

Remembering the night they had rescued the foreigner, Alred made a quick decision. Leaving the gathering crowd, he made his way round to the back lane behind the inn. At the break in the wall, he quickly clambered into the garden beyond, a noisome place that reeked of piss. A rat scuttled away as he strode past a compost heap, and he aimed a desultory kick at it, disgruntled with the world.

The back door was open, and he entered the corridor, walking past the sleeping chamber and out into the inn itself.

'What's all this about?' he demanded of a man leaning against the wall.

'This man says he's been sent by the King,' he was informed. 'There's a Frenchman here abouts, he says, who raped a noble lord's woman. He wants to hear from anyone who knows where this rapist is. There's a reward in it for someone.'

Alred's face wore the fixed smile of a man who has paid top price for a horse only to hear it bray. 'You say they think he's French?' he asked, recalling that heavy accent.

'Someone saw him in here, apparently. They say he would have been caught if some idiots hadn't knocked down the man who was trying to catch him.'

Alred nodded and turned back to the door. His eyes unblinking as he went, he kept the smile fitted to his lips as he left the inn, strolled across the garden, and climbed out over the wall. Only when he was in the back lane again did he close his eyes tightly, clench his fists, and offer up curses to all those who sought to confuse the poor, honest pavers of England.

'Lads, lads, I've got an idea,' he said as he reached the hole in the roadway again. 'I think we have to find that man we saved the other day. Um.'

The street to which they had been directed would have been a foul alley in Exeter, full of excrement and garbage, waiting until the autumn rains would wash all away down into the Shitebrook. In some areas there were scavengers who would come along with heavy brooms to clear the worst of the mess, but even in the most sanitary of cities, the heavy accumulation outside stables and barns in poorer areas would lead to drains being blocked.

Here in Dartmouth, though, people appeared to have more pride in their street. The kennel in the middle of the road was clean, with only a very few deposits that did not merit investigation, and Baldwin was impressed. Even the dogs appeared to be healthier than he would have expected. Perhaps it was the ready availability of food. Fish were abundant in the seas all about here, and their harvesting was a source of great benefit to the local population.

They had been directed here to the alley in Hardness by Simon's clerk, who had to consult Simon's servant Rob. The fellow seemed to have some interest in the mariners, as though he might one day choose to throw off his servile duties and offer himself to one of the shipmasters. Many youngsters dreamed of leaving England and finding adventure abroad, and Baldwin could understand that very easily. It was what he himself had done when little more than a boy, after all, when he joined the defence of Acre in 1291.

'This it?' Sir Richard boomed.

'Stephen said it was where there was a green door,' Simon agreed. He rapped loudly on it.

There was a moment of silence, and then the latch lifted and the door opened slowly to show a young girl of perhaps eleven, thin from malnutrition, her cheekbones prominent in her pale face. Her hair was caught up neatly under a coif, but her clothing was ragged and threadbare, her feet unshod. She clutched the door as a drowning man might cling to a timber, peering around it at the three men.

Sir Richard smiled in what he fondly considered to be a kindly manner, and bent down to her, saying, 'Where's your father, girl?'

His voice, although muted in comparison to his usual bellow, was enough to bring panic to her eyes. She shrank back, and for a moment it appeared that the door was about to be slammed in their faces.

As Sir Richard bared his teeth again, Baldwin quickly drew the Coroner away and squatted before the child. 'Is Master Cynegils here? We would like to speak with him.'

'Who wants him?'

This was from an older girl, perhaps of fifteen, who appeared now from the darkness, a child of two or so on her hip. She had similar looks to the first girl, and Baldwin was persuaded that the two must be sisters, with similar slanted brown eyes that were sunken and over-bright. It was the same look Baldwin had seen so often before, in the faces of those who were perpetually hungry. All too often children and women held that look, as though to be young and female was itself a cause of starvation. As it was. He knew full well that there were peasant women on his lands who would intentionally eat less than they needed when money or food was scarce, so that their husbands could go to their work with full bellies. When a family depended on a man's labour, others must go hungry so that he could work.

From behind her there came a cracking sound and a loud wailing started, while a fresh young voice shouted angrily. The girl at the door showed some tension, bawling at them all to, 'Shut up!' before turning back to Baldwin with a questioning look.

'I am the Keeper of the King's Peace, this is Sir Richard de Welles, the King's Coroner, and this is Simon Puttock, Keeper of this Port under the Abbey of Tavistock. We are learning all we can about the man who was killed.'

'What's my father got to do with him?'

'I think we should discuss that with *him*, maid,' Simon said.

She looked at him measuringly, then at Baldwin again. 'I'll take you to him.'

Chapter Fifteen

Telling her sister to keep an eye on the other children, and not to open the door in case they ran into the lane, the older girl passed the smallest child to her sister and pulled the door to behind her, eyeing Baldwin and the others suspiciously all the while.

She led them along the alley and the river, until the road curved sharply westwards again, up the hill to Tunstal. Here there was a grassy lane that led to a little beach. Here they found him.

'Thank you, maid,' Simon said grimly.

Cynegils was lying in a broken boat, one leg cocked over the thwarts, the other over the side of the craft. Near it lay a leather wineskin, and from the heavy snoring that made the timbers of the boat shake, it had only recently been emptied.

'Father is a good man,' the girl said defensively. 'He was a good sailor, too, with his own boat – until it was wrecked in a storm. He was on shore, but the winds caught it and pulled it free of the anchor. Now he does what he can, but how is a man to earn enough for all his children when his trade's gone?'

'He could find a new master and work for him.' Simon was unsympathetic. From the look of the man he had a strong conviction that the anchor was loose because the drunk hadn't taken time to tie it off securely.

'What do you think he's been doing?' she snapped. 'How many round here will pay a man to fish for them when they can fish themselves?'

Sir Richard was unconcerned by the troubles of others. He stood beside the boat staring down at the slack-mouthed figure snoring in the foul water at the bottom of the rotten craft, then kicked the side heavily. The boat rocked under the buffet, a timber cracking, and the man inside jerked awake. He tried to spring up with his alarm, but the leg dangling outside the boat prevented him. It flapped and waved, and the man rose to the height of his knee, his face red with wine and exertion, eyes popping as he took in the sight of the three men, before giving a loud gurgle and belch, and falling back with an audible crunch as his head struck the timbers. He wailed.

'Get up, man!' Sir Richard called, and reaching down to grasp Cynegil's shirt, he hauled him up and over the boat's side, then let him drop. 'This boat's rotten. Someone should burn the damned thing.'

'It's all we have left!' the girl retorted. 'Some day, perhaps, we'll be able to mend it and start fishing again.'

'Child, that boat will never sail again,' Simon said as gently as he could.

'What do you know!' she flared.

Sir Richard listened to none of this. He was shaking his head at the sight of the man on the ground before him. 'You are Cynegils? I should ask you why you didn't appear before me at the inquest, man, but looking at you I can only feel a sense of relief. Christ's ballocks, you cretin, will you stop that moaning?'

'Don't hit him!'

Simon turned to the girl again. 'What is your name?'

'Edith,' she replied after a moment's hesitation.

'That's a good name,' he said. 'I named my own daughter Edith. Listen, now. Your father may be able to help us to learn more about a man who was murdered. We aren't here to hurt him in any way, but we have to talk to him, so if you can persuade him to sit up and stop that infernal whining, the sooner we can leave you both. Is that clear enough?'

She stared at him. 'Father, please, just listen to them and help them,' she said.

Cynegils, who appeared to have persuaded himself that the three were angels or demons (his precise conviction was hard to establish), had tried to burrow himself under the boat with his bare hands, whimpering like a whipped cur all the while.

Sir Richard had been aiming his boot at Cynegils's posterior, but on hearing Edith's words, he pulled his foot away again innocently.

'Father?'

'Leave me alone! What are you doing here, Edie? Get back away home. What'll the childers do with you here?'

'Millie can look after them,' Edith said, walking to her father and sitting beside him, taking his hand in hers. 'I think you need me more than they do just now.'

He stopped his attempts at tunnelling and sat back, blinking warily. 'Who're all these?' he slurred.

'I am the Coroner, man!' Sir Richard boomed. 'And we want to learn all about the man you trailed inside the inn. Who told you to go there, why, and how much were you paid to find him?'

Cynegils's face fell. 'All I did was watch a fellow, like the man told me. He said he'd pay me three shillings if I'd go inside and keep an eye on him. That was all. The man stood up and went out to the back, and I went to make sure he was there . . .'

'What did you do first?' Baldwin asked. 'Did you go straight out?'

'Well, I had an ale, if that's what you mean. And then I went out front to talk to the man who told me to go there, to tell him. He said to make sure where the fellow was, so I went out and listened at the door, and while I was there, someone clobbered me. I woke up in the yard behind the inn with a sick headache and a lump the size of a duck's egg. Look, it's still here. And it's giving me grief.'

'Shut up!' Sir Richard said unsympathetically. 'Who was this patron? Did he tell you why he was following the man?'

'He said he was from the Bishop of Exeter and that the man he followed was a traitor to the King. That's what he said. And he promised to pay me three shillings if I found a stranger arriving here. Told me to follow him and let him know. He was staying in the Dolphin, I could find him there. Three shillings, Edie. It would've been enough to keep you lot in food for a month or more.'

'He didn't pay you?' Simon asked.

'I was going to be paid when I was done. But I was knocked out cold. Don't know what happened to him, but I never got a penny.'

'Describe the man you followed,' Baldwin said.

'Tall, well made, with rich clothes, all crimson and blue, really expensive-looking. He had a French sort of face – dark and swarthy, you know? Eyes close together, too. I wouldn't trust a man like him.'

'What of the man who told you to trail him?'

'He was younger, and a pleasant-sounding gentleman. Perhaps twenty-two or -three, with dark hair and a bit of a nervous manner. I think he was unused to this sort of work.'

'Did he say what he intended to do?' Baldwin asked.

'No. I thought he'd be off to call the Hue and Cry, but he didn't while I was there. He was just watching to see what the man did.'

'I wonder why?' Baldwin said.

'What?' Sir Richard demanded.

'I should have expected him to call the Watch and have the man arrested if he thought that this was the French traitor whom he was seeking. Why leave him in a tavern and wait?'

'Because he wanted to make sure it was the right man?' Simon hazarded.

'Or he wished to see who the fellow would meet with?' Sir Richard said.

'That is perhaps more likely,' Baldwin agreed, wondering whether the bishop could have held back some detail which could be useful now. He gazed out at the river, his brow lined with thought. 'But why should he care who the man was going to meet here, if all he intended was to leave the country and get to France?' he added in a low voice to himself.

Yet he already knew the answer. If this Frenchman *was* meeting someone here, then that someone could well be a traitor to the King . . . and any spy watching the Frenchman would soon learn the identity of that man.

Baldwin felt a sinking sensation in his belly as he realised that he was being hurled into a quagmire of political intrigue against his will.

* * *

The sun began to sink behind the hills, throwing Clifton and Hardness into that early twilight that lasted so long each day. Pierre had been left up here in the hayloft for the whole day without any more food or drink, and the tedium was making him fretful. When he heard footsteps approach, and the gate squeaking open as Moses pulled it wide, he slipped quickly down the ladder.

'My friend, you are most welcome,' he said.

'I have some more bread and meat, and a little wine. I hope it will be enough for you,' Moses said.

'It is better than I could have hoped.'

'There is a ship which will be finishing victualling tomorrow. Perhaps tomorrow night, or the day after, I can get you to her. The ship's one of my master's, so you will be given a safe passage.'

'That is marvellous! I am most grateful.'

'There are men looking for you all over the town, though, you know?' Moses continued. 'The man you killed in the road was found, and now people are talking about you and the fact you killed him. They don't know your name yet, but they soon will. If you are found you will be arrested and hanged, and so will I, probably.'

Pierre was quiet. 'What man? I know of no dead man! I was being followed when I tried to find my way to Master Pyckard's house, but I attacked no one.'

'Let's hope you don't have to explain that to the Coroner. He's looking for the murderer.'

'You must tell your master that I had nothing to do with this. I am no murderer!'

Moses had been emptying his basket. Now he stopped for a moment, not meeting Pierre's eyes. 'I wish I could,' he said quietly. 'My master died this afternoon.'

'What else do you know, I wonder?' Baldwin said aloud.

'I know nothing, lord. What can I know? I was told to watch a man, and I did, that's all.'

'You are a poor man, Cynegils,' Baldwin said.

'He's a good man!' his daughter exclaimed.

'And you are a loyal child, but you are scarcely able to judge him,' Baldwin said coldly. He approached Cynegils. 'Churl, you reek. If we pricked you with a sword, you would bleed ale!'

'What of it?' Cynegils mumbled. 'Can't you leave me alone?'

'I do not think so,' Baldwin said. Then he snapped, 'What did you do when you came to?'

'I was cold for a long time.'

'He was hit by that madman! His poor head was hurt!' Edith spat, and threw her arms around her father. 'He's been taken for a fool, but that's no reason to keep on at him.'

Baldwin ignored her outburst. 'I didn't ask that. What did you do after you had recovered from your knock?'

'I went home.'

'Which way did you go?'

Edith shouted, 'Leave him alone!' but none of the men were listening.

Cynegils hung his head. 'Down the hill straight homewards. I live over at Hardness.'

'We know,' Baldwin said unsmilingly. 'So you would have passed right by the hole in the road where this man was found, wouldn't you? Did you notice a body there?'

'I was rolling drunk by then,' Cynegils said, spreading his hands in a sign of honesty.

Baldwin peered down distastefully at the filth encrusted in his palms, and Cynegils hastily closed them again.

'No, I don't think I am inclined to trust you,' Baldwin said after a moment's sad contemplation. 'I think that you are habituated to lying, and that you find it hard to confess to what you found there in the road. *How much did you steal from him?*'

'I stole nothing!'

'I think you found this man, struck him, left him for dead, and stole all you could from his purse.'

'I would hardly do that and stay here in poverty!'

'Because there was much in it?'

'Eh?'

'Who here has mentioned how much was in his purse, my friend?'

'No one!'

'No, and yet you think it was enough for you to find a new life? You have betrayed yourself.'

'I've done nothing!'

'You have enough money to be drunk today. Is ale free at Hardness?'

'My daughter works a little. I took it from her.'

'You can do better than that!' Sir Richard said.

'It's true! She helps nurse children . . .'

'Good for her!' Sir Richard said with a chuckle, glancing at the girl.

If Cynegils felt a momentary relief at the expression of amusement in Sir Richard's eyes, it was gone when he noticed his daughter's face. Edith never looked so much like his wife as when he had let her down again. And now he had. He'd lied about the body, about the money – about everything. And now he had demeaned her in front of these men.

Instinctively he turned towards the man whose face he trusted the most. 'I'll tell you all.'

Hamund was happier than he had been for an age as he sat and listened to the stranger calling to the men there for information.

He was, so he said, Sir Andrew de Limpsfield, the master of the cog, *Gudyer*, which had just sailed into the haven. This Frenchman had raped a gentlewoman in the north, and was fleeing justice. If any man knew of the felon's whereabouts, he should say so now, because there was a good reward.

'I wish I'd seen him,' Hamund said, and burped. 'Could do with some silver.'

'When was the last time you had ale?' Gil asked.

'Oh, about three weeks or so,' Hamund declared lightly. The world felt so much better now that he had found this excellent friend.

'Leave off that, then. You're pissed.'

Hamund was going to furiously deny the accusation, but Gil had already drained his cup and stood. Rather than be left behind, he trailed after his new companion, out into the road. The sudden cool made his head whirl, and he was forced to cling to a post for a moment.

'God's teeth!'

Muttering curses against all land-dwellers and especially the morons who committed murder and got themselves discovered, Gil took Hamund's hand, ducked his head under his arm, and supported the abject abjuror as he walked down the hill.

Hamund was in no position to observe the route they took, but he noticed after a while that they were travelling sharply down the hill towards the water again. They passed along the mixed houses until they reached a place that was, even in Hamund's befuddled state, considerably better decorated than the others.

'In here,' Gil said, and propped Hamund against a post while he banged on the door. In a moment or two it opened, and light spilled out into the darkening street.

'Moses, I've got one man for the journey. We're still light three good sailors, though. God only knows what we'll do about that. Is the master here?'

'Gil, I am sorry.'

Hamund watched with bemusement as Gil gaped, and then pelted along the corridor to the hall's entrance. Touching the wall all the way, he followed behind Moses and Gil, leaning on the doorway as Gil ran to the far end of the hall and out through a small door. He could hear steps above him, and muttering, and a while afterwards Gil came back downstairs. He clung to the rope that had been set by the stairs to ease Pyckard's way, head hanging, and he wiped at his eyes several times as he stood before them.

'He was a good master to us all,' Moses said.

'It's hard to believe he's gone.'

Hamund listened as the two spoke in low voices. It was clear enough that they had lost a man whom they esteemed highly, and it was no great intellectual leap to guess that the man they mourned was the owner of the ship he was hoping to sail in.

'What now?' Gil said.

'We'll have to wait until his body is set in the ground and the Will read out, and then we'll have to see what happens. Hopefully we'll be looked after.'

'Sweet Jesus! And here I was, trying to see to the last shipments. The *Saint John*'s already lost, and there's no point trying to break my cods filling another cog with crew.'

'Why do you say that? You must set sail as planned.'

'Set sail? When there's no master to pay me and the men? What chance do I have of persuading men to join me when the merchant behind the sailing is cold in his coffin?'

'It was his last wish, Gil.'

'What was? That we should make money for his executors? He has no children, no wife!'

'But she leaves relatives,' Moses said. 'And one of them is nearby.'

Gil frowned at him. 'You're saying he wanted his money to go to her family?'

'One half, I think, will be disposed in favour of all those who worked for him, for the Church and for the poor. The other will go to his lady's family.'

'And so the ship will sail?'

'With a new member of the crew,' Moses nodded. 'So you will only be two men short.'

He left the room, and Hamund heard him walking along the corridor to the back of the house. There was a long pause, and then steps approached from outside. Hamund looked up to see a tall, swarthy-skinned man with eyes set too close in a narrow face staring at him. A man in parti-coloured hosen and tunic.

'The *rapist*,' he hissed to himself.

Chapter Sixteen

Cynegils spoke for some while. For the most part his story was laboured, repetitive and self-pitying, but the men gained a good feeling for his tale.

He had come to with a sore head, soaked with water from a bucket which the host of the tavern had thrown over him. Walking home, he almost fell into the hole in the road, and then, horrified, saw that another had already fallen in there. He recognised the man who had asked him to follow the Frenchman. Rather than see all profit lost, he went down into the hole and rifled his purse, taking his three shillings and another twelve pennies as payment for his trouble. He thought that was fair. Not being a thief, he left the rest in his purse. Some men came past, singing, and he ducked down, scurrying away later when all was quiet.

Edith helped her father to his feet, and sighed as Baldwin watched him closely. 'Isn't it enough you've shown him to be a drunken oaf who cares more about filling his gullet with ale than feeding his children?' she asked. There were tears in her eyes.

'Child, I am sorry, but I do need to know a few more details,' Baldwin said gently. Then, with a more harsh tone, 'Cynegils, how did this man find you? Was he a local?'

'I was in the tavern at the top of Smiths' Street, when he came in. He was looking for someone who had knowledge of the town and the people who lived in it, and came to me.'

Baldwin glanced at Edith, then back at Cynegils. 'So he knew of you? How can that be? Was he a friend of yours?'

'No! I don't know how he'd heard of me. Could have been anything.'

'Hardly!' Coroner Richard said derisively. 'A spy should be someone unremarkable, who can blend into a crowd. Not a drunken sailor with shit for brains!'

Baldwin eyed Cynegils reflectively. 'You have spied before, have you not? And this man had heard of you because of that.'

'I'm no spy! But a man will do what he must for some money.' This with a sidelong glance at his daughter.

'So you *have* done work like this before?'

'I suppose. Only a couple of times. When there has been reason.'

'For whom?'

Cynegils shrugged. 'I was paid by the last Keeper of the Port to watch the fisheries and keep an eye on foreigners in the town.'

Baldwin called, 'Simon, who was the last Keeper of the Port?'

'It was poor Sir Nicholas until his death, I think.'

Cynegils was nodding. 'That was him.'

'Who did *he* work for?' Baldwin asked.

'Sir Nicholas was always the King's own man,' Sir Richard said. 'I never heard a word against his loyalty.'

'I see,' Baldwin said. 'Well, then, spy: what have you heard about the destruction of the ship? And the men who've disappeared?'

'Nothing! I was here – how can I tell what was going on out to sea?'

'Do you know of anyone who might have wanted the sailor Danny dead?' Baldwin asked. 'It seems curious that he alone was left behind.'

'Danny had no enemies! He was a pleasant lad, kindly and good-hearted,' Edith declared.

'I've heard of no one hating him enough to do that,' Cynegils acknowledged.

'Yet he was murdered.'

'In the tavern they're saying that it was the devil came and took the crew.'

'Why not Danny too?' Simon asked, trying to conceal the shiver that ran up his spine at those words.

'Because Danny wasn't a foul sinner like the others. Vincent and

Odo were hard men, you understand me? They'd slit your throat soon as look at you. Adam was known for a good fighter, and the others, well they were . . .'

'Adam?' Simon asked, remembering the name Pyckard had mentioned.

'Yes. He was Pyckard's right-hand man. They'd been together since the first sailing Pyckard had made.'

'The others were foreigners, weren't they?' Baldwin said.

'Yes. Kena managed to bribe some of Master Pyckard's crew to leave him and join his ship. They're always trying to stuff each other, those merchants.'

'Would Kena have tried to buy in a man like Adam too?' Simon guessed.

'I expect so,' Cynegils belched, 'but Adam would never accept. He had a good berth with Pyckard. Danny wouldn't either: he'd remember how well his master had treated him from the moment his father died. A man doesn't turn traitor to someone who's protected them, does he? No, Adam and Danny wouldn't be bought. Master Pyckard had no choice but to hire some strangers.'

'Who would naturally have been evil souls whom the devil would wish as company,' Baldwin said dismissively. 'No. These deaths were conducted by some human agency, of that I am assured.'

Yes, he thought inwardly – and if the Frenchman has killed Bishop Walter's nephew, I must take some sort of action, surely. No matter how troublesome, wouldn't Walter want him brought to justice?

He realised the others were watching him, and he pulled a smile to his face. 'I am grateful for your patience, maid. And sorry to have taken so much of your time.'

'That's all right,' Edith said, but ungraciously. He leaned towards her and she was about to move away, when she felt something in her hand.

'I hope your family is fortunate,' he said, his dark eyes serious, and then he was gone, striding back to his companions.

She said nothing, but helped her father over the rough ground until they reached the street. Only there did she open her hand and see the pennies resting there. It was enough to make her heart pound with gratitude, and she kept her booty hidden from her father as they made their way up the street.

Usually at twilight there would be people busy clearing up after the day's work, stray dogs barking, and children screaming, women shouting, men bellowing. Tonight there was an odd calm, and Edith wondered whether a new ship had entered the port. Sometimes when a rich vessel arrived, the people would go to gawp at it.

Sure enough, when they could peer along the street, she could see a great cog in the harbour. Even in the dull light it was plainly a beautiful craft, with richly painted hull and gold gleaming.

'I should go for a job with one of them. Get some money in,' her father said. 'I'm sorry, Edie. God, I'm so sorry!'

'Shut up, Father. You've had too much to drink again,' she said impatiently. It was always the same when he'd got drunk at lunchtime. When he woke he'd be maudlin and apologetic. Later he'd be foul-tempered and threaten her and the others. At least for now he was still docile.

'If I had a job on her, I'd be able to put food on the table.'

'You don't, though,' she said. And he wouldn't. He was too well known as a drunkard for any shipmaster to want to take him on.

They were at their door. Edith pushed it wide and stumbled over the threshold with her father's arm over her shoulders, and then, as her eyes grew accustomed to the light, she began organising her brother and sisters. Millie helped as usual, and at least today they had some bread and a small piece of salted cod which Millie had earned helping the men down by the shore. Edith had been given an egg, too, so she carefully mixed it with the fish and some dried bread to make a thick gruel. For once she did not give the larger proportion to her father. She was still smarting that he could have taken so much money – four whole shillings! – and used it to drink himself to oblivion instead of looking after them.

All the hard months she and the children suffered pangs of hunger and went without to make sure that *he* had a full belly so that he could work – but he didn't. It was they who laboured always, and he took advantage of their efforts to subsidise his drinking. Never again! This time she would ensure that her brother and sisters had enough to eat.

'A good meal, child,' Cynegils said as he used the last of his bread to mop up the juices.

'It's all there is.'

'The Church will provide a little, and there are wealthy houses who will pass out their scraps. We won't starve.'

'For how much longer, though? We've got little enough to live on, and when you do earn something, it goes into your bladder and you piss it all away!'

'Come now, Edie, that's not right.'

'Isn't it? Ach, what do I know. Why should I care? I ought to find a man to marry and leave you to this pit. Take the others with me and leave you to drink yourself to your grave.'

'Edie, it's not like that. I would get work if I could, you know that.'

'But you *can't*, can you? You can't take a job and keep it because no one will trust you on their ship.'

'Don't talk to me like that, Daughter. I won't have it,' Cynegils said, and now his face was growing darker with anger.

'Oh, so you'll beat me now, will you? Then go ahead, Father. You are so brave, indeed, to beat me when I show you the truth. If you don't do something soon, we'll all be dead anyway, so beat away. You want a rope to beat me with?' She stood and went to an old rope at the wall, where it had hung for as long as she could remember. There was a knot wrought into one end which was heavy enough to hurt a man when it hit him.

Before she had reached it, Cynegils had stood. His face was flushed, his eyes bloodshot. 'Leave it, Edie.'

'No, no, Father. I have offended you, and I must be chastised. Here – take it. Beat me! As you used to beat Mother!'

Cynegils stared at her for a long moment, but he couldn't hold her angry gaze, and he turned away and opened the door.

'Where do you go now? To the tavern to drown your sorrows in sour ale?' she sneered.

Cynegils stood in the doorway, his back to her. 'I loved your mother,' he said gruffly. 'I still miss her like life itself. I know I've failed you all. Perhaps you'd be better without me.'

'Where are you going, Father? It's nearly dark.'

'Just out, Edie. Just out,' Cynegils said, and he left the house and walked slowly away, with the quiet desperation of a man with no direction and no hope.

Just then, someone blocked his path. Cynegils looked up to see a smiling man with a club in his hand.

'Are you Cynegils?' he asked.

'What if I am?'

'There's a knight wants to talk to you,' the man said as two others grabbed his arms.

Back in their storage shed, Alred faced his two employees and told them all he had heard at the inn. 'So, if it comes to light that we helped the rapist who killed the man in our pit . . .'

Law spat at the ground. 'Don't see it's our concern.'

Alred looked at him, but it was Bill who grunted, 'Then you ought to keep your mouth shut till you've got something useful to say. If they're saying this man's a felon and we helped protect him from capture, what'll that do to us?'

Crestfallen, Law slumped down on a sack of tools. 'But all we did was try to help a poor sod who was going to be attacked!'

'And who'll believe three strangers?' Alred snapped. 'We have to get away from here or find the rapist. If he's caught by someone else, and he tells how we saved him, we're sunk. At the least we'll get a huge fine.'

'What makes you think he's still here?' Bill asked.

Alred stared at him. 'How's he going to get away from here? Back inland? If he's being sought by men like the fellow at the inn, he won't have a chance of getting away. No, he's a stranger, he doesn't know where to hide outside town, so he's got to be here, waiting until he can get aboard a ship.'

'He'll be seen, won't he?' Law asked.

Bill shook his head thoughtfully. 'Nah. If he's bright, he'll pay a matelot to get him on board somehow. Those buggers have ways of doing things you wouldn't believe.'

'That's what I thought,' Alred agreed with relief. 'After all, he's here at the coast now. He'll stay put until he can get a passage.'

'But you said he was new here?' Law said musingly. 'If so, how come he can find somewhere to hide?'

'He has a friend, obviously,' Alred said, and then he stopped with a gleam in his eye. 'So he must know someone around here, someone with a large house where he could be hidden . . .'

'Why large?'

'A smaller place would be too hard to conceal a man in. All the folk here live on top of each other,' Alred said with the contempt of a city-dweller for one of the country's fastest-growing sea ports. 'No, it'd be a large house. And there aren't too many of them round here, are there?'

Peter Strete was in the counting-room when he heard the thundering on the front door and the loud bellow that followed. He sat back in his seat, expecting to be called out to the hall at any moment, his mind going guiltily to his hidden crimes.

The first time he had stolen from his master, the sum had been minuscule: just enough to cover a drinking session with some sailors. Later on, they suggested a game of their invention, called 'straws'. As soon as he heard it was a gambling game, Peter politely refused to join in. The idea of gambling was repugnant to him: if God wished a man to be financially rewarded here on earth, He would give the fellow money. Trying to fleece other men out of their own meagre wages seemed little better than usury, and he hated usury as much as any.

But the game did seem refreshingly simple. The men took up straws from the floor, and stood with their hands behind their backs. At a call, all would bring a fist in front of their breasts, and they might be holding anything from none to three straws. All a man had to do was guess how many straws were held in total, and he was knocked out of the ring. Then the remaining group continued until one man remained who had wrongly guessed each preceding round, and he would buy the others a drink each. Very simple. And enormously amusing.

Peter had won the first three rounds without difficulty, and he was just beginning to think that it was a typical sailors' game, in which there was little skill or ingenuity required, when he lost a game. The next, he was out early on again, and then he lost another round. There was much comment of beginner's misfortune, and he had taken their words at face value, for while he was in their company, it would have been rude to depart, but at the end of the evening, when the reckoning was due, he realised he had not enough money on him. Nor, when he searched his chamber, did he find sufficient there either.

That first little removal of his master's cash was enough to make him realise how easy theft might be to a weaker man, and he had swiftly repaid it, selling a tunic which he did not need any more. It was a relief to place the coins back in Master Hawley's strongbox.

Three nights later, the same crew of sailors entered his tavern, and he found himself sitting with them once more, a handful of reeds in his fist, laughing uproariously at his own witticisms, glad of the company of men who appreciated his own so much.

At the end of that evening he was shocked to learn how often he had lost. His meagre remaining profit from the sale of the tunic was scarcely enough to cover his debts. And then he tried to recoup his losses with gambling, and suddenly there were several marks from John Hawley's chest that he must replace. Master John was forgiving about most things, but not his money being taken without his approval.

It was that which had led Strete to begin to trade information about his master's enterprises. Information like that could be valuable, especially the prices Hawley was paying for goods, where he got them from, the names of his best contacts. All that was worth money to Hawley's competitors.

All Strete had wanted to do was make enough to pay back the hole in Hawley's cash, and then he'd stop. That was all. He was a loyal man, and he didn't want to harm his master . . . but the amount he owed kept *increasing*. He could only sell information when he had something new to give away, and just now there was little enough. And all the time, when he went out, he met with the same sailors and locals who would call to him to join them in a game or two, and when that happened, he felt bound to sit with them. It would only take one gamble to repay all he owed without a problem, and he was just looking for his luck to return. But for some reason it never did. Whenever he tried his luck, he found it had fled.

The men were in the hall now, and Master Hawley entered to join them.

'Lordings, how may I serve you?' He looked about the room, then motioned to Strete. 'Peter, fetch some wine, man. Our guests must be thirsty.'

Strete jumped up from his seat and hurried out. The bottler was in his little chamber, and Strete told him what was needed, then returned to the room.

'These men are looking into the deaths of those two victims,' Hawley explained to him.

'To be fair, we do not have jurisdiction over the death of a man at sea,' Baldwin smiled.

'Of course not,' Hawley responded. His bottler had entered, and Hawley gestured to the guests first before taking a goblet himself. He continued, 'If you had to investigate everybody washed up on the beach, you'd have a hard time of it, not knowing which ship he fell from, when, where, or why. Often you can't even tell who these poor lost souls are anyway, when half of their face has been eaten away by crabs!'

'You have seen such corpses?' Sir Richard asked.

'Who has not? Every winter the wrecks are washed up and the bodies pile up, eh, Bailiff? You will have seen them too. They always repel my clerk here, but I tell him not to be so squeamish. If you live by the sea, you will see such sights.'

Coroner Richard shrugged. 'For my part, I'm happy not to have any more deaths to investigate.'

'What? Even if it's shown that wandering pirates have attacked and killed an entire ship's crew?' Hawley snapped.

Baldwin eyed him narrowly. 'You feel strongly about this, shipmaster?'

'Of course I do! I depend for my life on the sea and on trade. If there are pirates, all are at risk. The men who killed the crew on Pyckard's ship are as likely to attack one of mine next. And in any case, the life of a sailor is hard enough already without the additional threat of misbegotten whoresons who seek to rob us of our cargoes and kill us as well.'

'But how would someone learn of a ship's passage?' Simon wondered. 'By having a man on the hill up at Tunstal watching to see who was sailing? If so, how would they get the information relayed to their own ship at sea, to alert them to their prey?'

'I don't care how they do it,' Hawley said dismissively. 'All that matters is that they have done so in this matter. It is disgraceful if the King's officers will refuse to aid sailors from Hardness and Clifton who need protection.' He glared aggressively at the Coroner and Baldwin.

'The men of the town are used to protecting themselves, from all I have heard,' Baldwin murmured idly, studying the wine in his mazer.

'We will fight and defend ourselves when we can,' Hawley said firmly. 'A man who robs me will learn I have a long arm and an infinite capacity for hatred.'

'Of course,' Baldwin said comfortingly. He saw Strete shoot his master a look, and the expression on his face fleetingly sparked his interest, but then Hawley was speaking again and Baldwin turned his attention back to the shipmaster.

'The King benefits from our cogs and men whenever he has a war to fight and men to take over the water. Yet when we need aid, there is nothing in return. Is that just? If the rumours are true and this *is* another attack from the men of Lyme, we should be able to expect some support from the King.'

'I could advise him that you and the men of Dartmouth are keen to have him take more interest in all your trade,' Simon said sweetly. 'He would be happy to do that, I'm sure.'

The threat worked. Hawley scowled and shook his head. Simon knew only too well that many transactions were never declared to him or Stephen, and the shipowners made much more money than was declared. It was the reason why shipmasters tended to be more wealthy than their trade should permit. The customs of the port were never quite so high as they should be.

'Do *you* think the men of Lyme were involved?' Baldwin asked.

'Who else?' Hawley said, but slightly too glibly, as though he had expected to be asked just that.

'Of course, this case *could* be different. We could perhaps argue that we do have jurisdiction even over this dead sailor,' Baldwin said softly.

'How so?' Hawley frowned.

'If he can be shown to have died within sight of the shore, for instance,' Baldwin murmured. 'Or even *on* shore, before the sailing.'

'That is likely enough, isn't it?'

Baldwin's eyes hardened. 'Why?'

'I agree with what you said at the inquest, Sir Baldwin. One wound like that: he was plainly not killed in an attack. If he had been, he'd have had wounds all over – stabs and slashes, and probably more than one blow from a cudgel to break his head. And there's another thing, too. When he was dead, he'd not have been left behind on the ship. If pirates threw the rest overboard, they'd have done the same with him. Wouldn't they?'

Baldwin watched as Hawley crossed the floor, stood at his sideboard, drained his goblet, and refilled it. He was a strangely precise man, Baldwin thought. His movements were definite. In all he did he looked a very *exact* man. He had an economy of movement, a fluidity, that Baldwin had only ever observed in warriors of the highest quality before. And his eyes were not dim-witted like so many fighters and sailors. They were intelligent and thoughtful as he turned to face the three again.

'Would you care to explain that?' the Coroner rumbled.

'The ship was attacked, wasn't it? And taken. The crew would have defended themselves, and many, if not all, fought hard. Some would have died. So where were they? Where were their limbs? All were gathered and thrown overboard, surely. As would this man have been, were he alive when the ship was taken.'

'That would make sense,' Sir Richard commented. His brows dropped as his eyes narrowed intimidatingly. 'Do you know anything of this?'

'No.' Hawley waved his drink towards Baldwin. 'In truth, I am not completely sure that this was something to do with Lyme. Why should they burn Pyckard's vessel? The *Saint John* was worth good money, as was her cargo. If they'd taken her, they'd have thieved all they could. Instead, they tried to fire her and left her burning.'

Baldwin nodded. 'Your conclusion?'

'Obviously, they didn't mean to destroy the cog. It wasn't a seamanlike effort. If they'd really wanted her sunk, they'd have made a better job of it. And no pirate nor privateer would have done that. So, if it wasn't someone after a ship and her cargo: what else could they have wanted?'

'Well?' the Coroner rasped.

'I think they attacked the ship to stop her arriving in port. *And that was because there was a man they wanted on board.*'

And Baldwin felt those unsettlingly shrewd eyes on him again.

Chapter Seventeen

Cynegils was feeling terrible. His head seemed swollen, and his mouth hardly worked. There was a dryness when he tried to speak, and the wrong words would keep coming out. If only these bastards wouldn't hurry so much. He needed a moment to pause and take his breath, but already they were hurrying him up the hill towards Higher Street. Even when he stumbled, the men didn't seem to care. They continued hustling him along with his knees scraping the cobbles until he found his pace again and could march with them.

'Where are you taking me?' he gasped.

'Shut it. You'll learn soon enough.'

'Oh come, now. What am I supposed to have done? Who wants me? I've told all I can to the Coroner and his friends. Can't do more . . . tell more.'

If the sergeant wanted someone brought to him, he'd order the nearest watchmen to go and grab him, but these two weren't watchmen. In fact, Cynegils didn't think he'd seen either of them before. They were too well fed and well clothed to be locals, and they didn't look like seamen, either. They had more the appearance of henchmen to a wealthy lord. Suddenly Cynegils felt sick. The nausea seemed to permeate his entire body.

The inn appeared, and to his astonishment, he was bustled through the narrow doorway and allowed to drop to the floor just over the threshold. When he remained on all fours, he was kicked roughly up the backside, and he fell forward onto his face, where he lay panting, trying to keep the vomit at bay.

'Oh, good. I've heard so much about you,' said a voice.

At a bench there sat an amiable-looking man, perhaps ten years younger than him, who held a large horn of ale and slab of meat skewered on a long dagger, from which he alternately gulped or took a sharp bite.

'Master?'

'You may call me that,' the man said affably. 'And now I should like to know all you can tell me about the night when you tried to follow a man in here.'

Baldwin took more wine and listened as the Coroner questioned Hawley again about all he had seen on the day he found the cog, but there was little he could add to what they already knew.

'The convoy never happened, really. Pyckard's ship went off first, and then Beauley's, and we were third.' He sat and frowned as he relived that day. 'There was a thin mist all over the sea when we set off, and I ordered the men to reef the sails to slow her. Didn't want to run straight into another ship. I wasn't too bothered, because my ship is much faster than either of the others', and I thought that I'd catch them in one good day's sailing.'

'You set sail in the early morning?' Simon asked.

'Yes. The other two had left the day before – Pyckard's ship in the early morning, Beauley's late morning. We missed the wind and had to wait. When the fog cleared, we put up all the canvas and ran as fast as we could. Late in the afternoon we saw one ship, which must have been Beauley's. Only a little later, close on evening, we saw the smoke on the horizon and ran Pyckard's ship down.'

'So Beauley could have been responsible for this?' Baldwin mused.

'Why would he do this? The ship was left with cargo and ship intact. It makes no sense! And if you're worried, you can check his ship for the crew. I'd bet you'd find no sign of bodies or blood.'

'He is a seamanlike fellow,' Simon agreed. 'Did you see no other ship at all?'

'No, I saw no sign of another out there. All we saw was the smoke, then the cog came into view.'

'If there was another ship in the area, wouldn't you have missed it anyway?' Baldwin asked reasonably. 'I would imagine all eyes would be on the stricken cog.'

'You imagine wrong, then,' Hawley said sharply. 'What, if you find a woman screaming, tied to a tree, do you go straight to her? No! You stand back and watch to see where is the man who bound her there. Otherwise you'd be walking into a trap. It's the same at sea. If you find a ship like the *Saint John* which has been attacked, you look all about the horizon with care before approaching her. And my men are good. No, there was no ship in the area when we caught her.'

'So the assumption that the attacking ship fled before they could steal the cargo . . .?' Baldwin said.

'Is so much garbage. They may have seen another ship, but not mine.'

'Which means that the ship was boarded and attacked earlier.'

'Maybe, but not much earlier. That part of the sea is quite busy. There are plenty of fishermen who ply their trade about there, and many ships make the crossing to Normandy or Guyenne. If she'd been there for more than a few hours, she'd have been seen. No, I think she was boarded and attacked late in the afternoon, and drifted a while until we found her.'

'If these shipping lanes are so well used,' the Coroner said slowly, 'the men who left her must have known that there was a good chance she'd be found, and didn't care whether she was or not.'

He shot a look at Baldwin as he spoke, and Baldwin found himself nodding. This Coroner was no fool. 'Yes. Which means that they didn't care whether the *crime* was discovered or not.'

'No. Because they consider themselves safe from the law,' Hawley said. 'And that is not a happy conclusion.'

Sir Andrew de Limpsfield smiled affably down at Cynegils. He could afford to be affable, for he was sure that this little sailor-peasant was going to make him a moderate sum of money. 'So you know nothing more from the moment that you were knocked down until you found yourself with a drenching to waken you?'

'Yes, sir. Someone threw a bucket of water over me, and that brought me round.'

'But by then, both men were gone,' Sir Andrew said. 'And one was dead that we know of. Where did the one go who owed you money?'

'I haven't seen him again.'

'Did you see the body they found in the town? It is said he might be the man who you watched or who told you to watch.'

'I didn't see him.'

'Even though he could be the man who hit you, or the man who caused you to be struck, and owed you money?' Sir Andrew enquired silkily. 'What restraint!'

'It's the truth, sir.'

'No. It is utter ox-shit. You are incapable of telling the truth even when it is in your interests to do so. I think that I shall have you arrested and held until you confess the truth to me.'

Cynegils had already suffered enough from Sir Baldwin and the Coroner, and now he bent his head again. 'Sir, I did see him, I think . . . but he owed me money.'

'Tell me all, man, if you don't want to feel the point of my sword at your throat.'

'Have we learned anything from that man that we didn't know already?' Coroner Richard muttered as they left Hawley's house and began to wander homewards to Simon's lodgings.

'I am comfortable that Hawley himself is probably innocent. I think he fears another attack.'

'If he had piratically attacked Pyckard's ship, he would declare himself innocent like that, wouldn't he?' the Coroner said.

'Yes, but Hawley was talking of asking the King to become more involved in the protection of ships. A man who depends for his livelihood on the freedom to behave exactly as he wants at all times is the last who would express those views.'

'But even if he is not guilty of attacking the ship at sea, he could be the man who killed Danny before the ship sailed – if you are right,' Simon put in.

'Why should he kill a sailor?' Baldwin said.

'Jealous of a woman? Or Danny was jealous of his money and attacked him?' the Coroner suggested.

'Possibly, but I should prefer to have a little evidence to suggest those motives,' Baldwin said.

'At least we've learned how the body was thrown into the pit,' Simon said musingly.

Sir Richard gave a grunt. 'Yes. There is not much I would trust from the mouth of that tatty drunkard Cynegils, but I believed his fear at confessing to finding a body and robbing it of four shillings.' He sniggered. 'Astonishing that he should bend to taking one extra shilling as payment.'

Baldwin grinned too. 'In a way, it was only fair. If he hadn't been following the Frenchman as instructed, he wouldn't have received that blow. If he was less honest, he would have taken the whole purse.'

'More fool him,' Sir Richard scoffed. 'I would have taken it, and without shame. It was insane to leave the purse there for any other man to take.'

'But no one did,' Baldwin pointed out. 'Which proves that the man who killed him did not do so for personal gain.'

'At least we know his identity now. Stapledon's nephew,' Sir Richard said. He looked up at the twilight. 'And now, gentles, I think it is time that we considered the work of the day to be past. There are taverns in this little town which would grace a much larger place. Master Bailiff, have you ever been to the Crossed Keys up on the road to the gallows? It used to be an exciting little haunt, with some of the best ale in the area . . . not that the alewife would still be alive, I expect. Good women with a talent for brewing tend to die young, sadly.'

'I think an ale would be an excellent idea, Sir Richard,' Baldwin said cruelly, then, seeing the expression on his old friend's face, he relented. 'But I fear that I am very fatigued after my journey. If you do not mind, I would ask Simon to walk me back to his house.'

'If you must, you must. It's a shame, though. When I was younger, men were better able to hold their drink. Aha, but Bailiff, you can come and join me when this fellow's resting his bones, can't you?'

It was plain enough that the man was drunk, but Pierre would not normally have concerned himself with that. Everyone occasionally drank too much. No, it was the expression in his eyes as he took in the sight of Pierre, as though something clicked in his mind. There was recognition there. *Merde!* His description must be all over the town by now!

'Master, you'll go with these two men,' Moses was saying, but Pierre was struck by a chilly concern.

'Who are they?'

'This is Gilbert, one of my dead master's best shipmen. You can trust your life to him.'

'And this?'

'I am called Hamund. I too am travelling to France,' Hamund managed, and belched.

'He is to help sail the vessel,' Moses explained. 'There are not enough men in the town, and since the last ship was taken and burned, many fear pirates.'

'You do not?'

Moses smiled thinly. 'I do not sail. It is better that you go with these men. They can tell you all you need to know. In the meantime, I wish you well. Go with God, master.'

'Why must I leave now? Is the boat ready to leave?'

'The *Saint Denis* is a *ship*,' Gil said testily. 'She will be ready soon, but just now it seems you'll be safer hidden away on board than out here in the town where someone could clap eyes on you at any moment. If you come with us now, we can hide you.'

'Men still seek me?'

'Is it true you raped a woman?' Hamund burst out.

There was a ringing sound, and Hamund felt his bowels turn to water as a grey steel flash ended with a cold, deadly sensation at his throat. He scarcely dared look down the length of the sword's blade to the man's staring, furious eyes.

'Who accuses me of this?' the Frenchman hissed.

'It was s-said at the inn,' Hamund stuttered.

'He's telling the truth,' Gil said. 'A man, a tall fair knight called Sir Andrew de Limpsfield, came in and said he sought a Frenchmen who'd raped a gentlewoman.'

'He lies,' Pierre said through clenched teeth. 'He accuses me of this? This *Andrew* dares to say that I, *I*, would do such a thing, when his master . . .'

'Who is his master?' Gil asked.

Pierre gave him a look that was a mixture of dread, and pure, ferocious hatred. He seemed to be about to answer, but then he snapped his mouth closed as he reconsidered. Then he withdrew his sword and sheathed it again. 'My apologies. I thought you sought to insult me, my friend. It is not you who is responsible for this.'

Hamund said nothing. It was enough that he dared breathe again. He was grateful for the sensation of blood pounding in his veins.

'You'll be safer aboard with us,' Gil said.

'Very well. Good. Farewell,' Pierre said, bowing to Moses, but keeping his eyes on Hamund. As the other two left, he followed them out along the passage to the garden behind the house, and thence to a gate in the wall which led out to the shoreline.

Their path took them north, following the Dart's shore towards Hardness, until they reached a group of beached boats. Gil motioned to Hamund, and the pair pulled one down to the water's edge, thrusting it bobbing and swaying into the water. Once there, Hamund held it steady while Gil climbed in and grabbed an oar, beckoning to Pierre. The Frenchman splashed through the water, cursing the ruination of his fine clothing, and clambered in alongside him, and finally Gil helped Hamund up into the boat. The abjurer was shivering miserably already, and as the boat rocked and jolted, his face became green in tinge.

'If you want to throw up, do it that side,' Gil said gruffly.

Pierre was scarcely aware of Hamund's suffering. All the way, he was considering the men who had sought him. To lie about him in so foul a manner was . . . was repellent! He had never raped a woman, and never would. His life was devoted to the service of his love, no one else. He would do all in his power to honour her with his acts of selfless courage.

'Why did he want to help you so much?'

Pierre had not been listening, but now he looked at Gil as he rocked back and forth rhythmically. 'What?'

'I said, why did my master want to help you? There must be a reason.'

'Did you ever meet his wife?' the Frenchman asked.

'She died long ago, when I was a child, but yes, I knew her. A lovely woman. Everyone liked her.'

'Amandine was my sister, God rest her beautiful soul.'

Law watched as the little boat bobbed its way out into the river and from there up to the great cog standing out in the middle of the channel.

It had been Alred's idea to stay on the quay here in case the man turned up. He had reasoned that if someone wanted to escape from Dartmouth, the best way to do so would be to take a ship. Bill had gone to Hardness to take a look at the fishing boats up there, and speak to the men who worked them, hoping to learn something of strange movements of ships, or even, if they were lucky, hearing of a sailor who was trying to win a passage to France. Law hadn't reckoned much to the idea. If he was a Frenchie hoping to get away from the country, he'd have just hopped onto a ship and hidden away, wouldn't he?

He was just thinking of leaving the riverside to go and find himself an ale or two, when he heard the voices.

All in all, it had been easier to find the man than even Alred had thought.

Chapter Eighteen

Sir Andrew smiled when the innkeeper told him that there were others already staying at the inn. He nodded understandingly, and asked who was intending to stay in the room with him and his men. Suddenly the inn was full of men contemplating their drinks and avoiding involvement in the discussion.

'I think you will find that the room is now empty,' he said to the innkeeper. 'I will use it with my men for the night.'

Cynegils was already secured. Sir Andrew had checked on where the town's gaol was, and the old sailor was presently enjoying the hospitality provided by the cell by the market square.

'Stealing from a dead man's purse,' he murmured to himself. 'Some will stick to nothing in their greed.'

'What now, Sir Andrew?' asked one of his henchmen.

'For now, we shall rest. The *Gudyer* is to be victualled in the morning, and then we can consider what we shall do. The man will not be so difficult to find, I think; not with the whole town looking for the mad foreign rapist. I am sure that soon we shall be able to announce that we have the culprit, and then we can take him to the ship and leave for home.'

'If you are sure.'

'Oh, I am. I am.'

Sir Andrew sipped his wine and sighed. It was infinitely better to be here, sitting on a comfortable stool which wouldn't rock and slide away every few moments. The ship was a fine creature, it was true, but Sir Andrew was not so convinced of the life of a sailor. He preferred the gait of a horse under his rump to the unpredictable rolling of a cog's hull. Since he could not swim, every sailing was a source of some concern, if not alarm.

It was some years since he had managed to win his present position, and he was content with his life since then. Beforehand he had been a squire in the service of Bartholomew Badlesmere, working hard as squires often did, teaching others younger than himself how to handle weapons, showing them how to master a horse, and the more delicate points of serving good cuts of meat or loaves. It had been a good position for advancement, but he knew only too well that while he could have a position there for life, he would never himself become wealthy. Badlesmere had so many on which to lavish his largesse, the chances of Andrew growing rich in his service were low. And he wanted to be rich.

At the time it seemed a miserable circumstance when his lord was killed. Andrew had thought his prospects were completely ruined – but then matters took a turn for the better, and he began to climb the mountain of social prestige and honour which had brought him here.

It was – Christ's pain, was it really only three years since Badlesmere's downfall? So much had happened since then. In the Year of Our Lord 1321, the Queen had been travelling in Kent, and late one night in October, on the thirteenth, she asked for hospitality at the gates of Bartholomew Badlesmere's castle at Leeds. Badlesmere himself wasn't there, but his wife was, and she, knowing that the King detested her husband, suspected a ruse to gain entry with an armed force. Not surprisingly, she refused entry, pointing out that in the absence of her husband she couldn't let others in. In a rage, the Queen stormed off to a neigbouring priory, but commanded her household to force the castle's gates. In the ensuing fight, six of her men were killed, and their deaths sealed the fate of Badlesmere.

The King had called upon the posse of the county to assist him in laying siege to the castle. Meanwhile, Andrew was inside, wondering how best to turn matters to his advantage. The castle fell in a week. Lady Badlesmere was sent to Dover Castle to be imprisoned; her kinsman, Burghersh, was sent to the Tower; and thirteen men from the garrison were hanged. Andrew had been held in chains for another week, convinced at every moment that he would be taken outside to join the rotting bodies at the gibbet, but then, thank Christ, he had been released. The bloodshed was over for a while.

War was coming. It was clear even then, and when rumours of the muster reached Andrew's ears, he was keen to join the King's host. Soon he was marching west, and he won his spurs after Tutbury, when he was one of those who mortally wounded and caught Damory, one of King Edward II's enemies. His fighting with Harclay against the Lancastrians a short while later won him more praise, and he was noticed by Despenser, who began to take an interest in him.

There was no concealing the avarice and determination of Hugh Despenser the Younger. He had sold his soul in order to win ever greater prizes, so some said, but Andrew, or now *Sir* Andrew as he had become, was happy to be clinging to Hugh Despenser's belt as the man rose to become the wealthiest lord in the country after the King himself. On the way, Despenser's followers were themselves rewarded richly.

Now he was here in this God-forgotten hole.

It was one of the most curious missions which Sir Andrew had been asked to conduct. A man had left the Queen's entourage and fled. Many suspected her and her household, but there were none more suspected than the men who had come to England to serve her from France. Not that it was a surprise that she sought her protectors from so far afield. Since her husband the King had slaughtered the most noble men of the country in the last few years in retribution for the Lords Marcher war, there were few whom she could trust in this country. And her brother, the King of France, was ever willing to foment trouble between her and her husband.

The French were always gazing at Britain with greedy eyes. Their king wanted Britain as a vassal state, just as he wanted the British possessions on the continent for his own, and he would stop at nothing in his intrigues. That was why, when the traitor Mortimer escaped from the Tower, he was welcomed with open arms in Paris. The French could scarcely conceal their glee. And in retaliation, the Queen of England was beginning to have her wings clipped. Soon the

King would have to act if he wanted to protect himself. That much was plain to all who knew the real state of affairs. There was no love lost between the couple anyway. Not any longer.

A shame, really. She was a lovely thing, the Queen. If Sir Andrew had been brave enough, he could have been tempted to try his luck with her himself. Perhaps that was why he was here? Perhaps this impecunious French knight had attempted to storm the citadel of her heart. If he had done that, he would suffer the most painful death King Edward II could contrive. Ironic, too, since it was Isabella who had warned her own father of the adultery of her sisters-in-law, and who had thus seen to the destruction of the two men who had dared become their lovers. What a race the French were!

There was no possibility that the man would escape Sir Andrew now, though. Not with all the men he had aboard his ship the *Gudyer*.

Alred gazed at his apprentice with consternation. 'On the bloody ship? How're we going to catch him if he's out there in the river?'

'Perhaps he's just visiting it,' Law said.

Bill looked at him. 'He's safe aboard a cog and you reckon he's likely to come back to shore to take a last look around?'

'It's possible!'

Alred and Bill exchanged a look. 'If you say so, Law,' Alred sighed. 'Me, I'll put my money on him staying there and waiting until it's time for him to sail. And I'd bet the ship's not there in the morning.'

Law scowled at the ground. He'd been sure that the others would be as pleased as him to see the man getting onto the cog, and to be receiving their contempt was worse than annoying. 'I did better than you, anyway. At least I found him.'

'Never did find out where he was hiding. He must have some friend here in the town,' Bill said. He frowned. 'Maybe we could use that? Like setting a trap for birds, when you flush them from a tree into the nets. I wonder . . .'

'What?' Alred demanded.

'Ach – nothing. We've lost him. And probably not a bad thing. If he escapes, *we're* safe.'

'So long as no one figures out it was us knocked his man down. If that fool from the inn says something about paviours, we're right in the stuff,' Alred said grimly.

'He won't know himself, will he? He was out as soon as you tapped him. So if anyone was going to say something, it'd be the innkeeper or his fellows, and we're here, so none of them has,' Bill pointed out.

'Let's hope it stays that way.'

Stephen closed his rolls, stored them safely in the thick leather cylinders, and walked out from the main room.

He was lucky here, he knew. He had a good master in the Bailiff, a warm room to sleep in, and a plentiful supply of ale and bread. No man could ask for more. And yet of an evening, sometimes he wished to have a little company. Not women – he took his vows too seriously for that – but just occasionally, it was good to have a drink with other men. And tonight, looking out at the fellows walking past, he decided that he needed to join them.

Locking the door behind him carefully, he walked up the alley opposite until he reached the Porpoise. It was not the sort of tavern which his abbot would have appreciated his entering, but he felt justified today. He had been working hard on various reports and figures, and even a clerk needed relaxation occasionally. So he pushed the door open and cautiously stepped inside.

There was a mass of faces within, all lighted by the candles that sat in the holders about the room. He smiled at some, nodded recognition at others, and walked over to the tavern-keeper to ask about an ale. It arrived in a cheap jug, and he drank it gratefully, eyes all but closed. At the rear of the room, he knew, was the gaming room, and as he stood there, he saw Peter Strete leave it, an expression of anguish on his face. Well, it was no more than he had heard rumoured about the town. Strete was regularly fleeced by the men in there. Stephen shrugged. It was none of his concern.

But Strete saw him, and with an inward sigh, Stephen made space beside himself. Strete soon began to talk to him about a shipment of cargo he was overseeing for Master Hawley, but then he stopped. Following his gaze, Stephen saw a heavy-set, very drunk man leaving the gaming room.

'Is there something wrong?' he asked.

'That man . . . I am sure he is familiar.'

'So? It's only a small town.'

'Yes, but I thought he had left port . . . Ach, it's just my memory playing tricks.'

Stephen privately thought it was more likely to be something connected with his gambling, but that would have been discourteous. Tactfully, he changed the subject.

Hamund lay on his back on the deck and stared up at the stars, a heavy cloak over his legs. Every time he moved, the nausea returned, but for all his feelings of sickness, there was a sense of relief that he must soon leave these shores and escape to France. There, perhaps, he could make a new life, and forget all about the past.

He glanced at the Frenchman's shape over near the mast. He was a strange one, too. Desperate to be out of the country, and the man at the inn had said it was because he had raped a woman. He didn't seem the sort to do something like that, though, from the little Hamund had seen of him, and he wondered whether the accusation had been made maliciously. The fact that Pierre was here on the ship was proof that he believed his life to be in danger if he was caught.

'There are too many of us in the same boat,' Hamund reflected, and winced at the pun even as he closed his eyes once more.

'That man will be the end of me,' Simon growled as he rose slowly from his bench.

'He was only trying to be friendly,' Baldwin countered. 'And you didn't have to accept.'

'I thought if I drank one cup with him, he would grow weary and seek his own bed,' Simon protested, scowling at his friend from eyes narrowed in pain. 'Instead the damned fellow kept refilling our cups.'

'I did not witness him holding you down and forcing the drink down your throat,' Baldwin pointed out.

'It would have been churlish to refuse his generosity,' Simon attempted loftily. 'Christ's ballocks, but some rat's left shite and piss in my mouth.'

'Stop your complaining and dress yourself,' Baldwin said, eyeing his flabby naked body without enthusiasm. 'Simon, you should rise earlier and exercise. For a man so young as you, your body is growing too rounded.'

'It's all this sitting around doing nothing except agreeing with Stephen's adding,' Simon admitted.

'Hah! It's too much knocking back ale and wine, I'd guess!' boomed a new voice, that of Sir Richard, as he entered the room. 'Morning, Bailiff, Keeper. Sleep well? I was out like a snuffed candle. Wonderful place this, and you have a good bed, Master Bailiff.'

'I am so glad to hear it,' Simon said, bearing his teeth in a mockery of a smile.

When Simon rose and had dressed, he leaned on the doorpost and gazed into his parlour in amazement. Rob had already been in, he saw, and there was a fire already crackling brightly! His sour feelings towards the Coroner took on a more mellow aspect.

'Today, then, we should go and see if there is anything to learn about this lad found dead on the ship.' Baldwin was sitting at the table, studying his fingernails. He rubbed his index finger nail against his tooth, grimaced, and took out his little knife, using it to pare away a fragment. 'After that, I suppose we should take the nephew of Stapledon and have his body sent to the bishop. Dear God! I hate to think of that. His brother will be so distressed to learn that his son has been murdered.'

Sir Richard clumped into the room with his thumbs in his belt. 'Good idea. Don't need stiffs lying about the place if we can help it. I'd have buried him here if you hadn't told me who he was.'

'I still cannot make sense of the man on the ship, though,' Baldwin said. 'It is curious that two murders should take place so near to each other, and the ship be so devastated, and yet none of the three incidents to have any connection.'

'I have known such occurrences,' Sir Richard said easily. He sat on a stool and bellowed suddenly for Rob, making Baldwin wince almost as much as Simon. 'Boy, take these pennies and see what you can find for our breakfast. And fetch us a little ale, too. You can finish what we don't, so make the most of the money. Understand?'

Rob took the coins and stared at them as though he had never in his life held so many – which, Simon reflected, was probably no more than the truth. In an instant he had darted from the room, and the three men heard his feet slapping down the lane.

'He's not too bad, that lad. Needs a strong hand to guide him, though,' Sir Richard said approvingly.

When the three heard a light step, a little later on, they thought it must be the boy returning. There was a tentative knock, as though Rob was leaning a heavy basket against the door as he sought to lift the latch. Baldwin stood and crossed the room, pulling the door wide.

Outside stood a hooded figure, and even as he opened his mouth to speak he saw the flash of steel.

Sir Baldwin de Furnshill had been trained well. The blade was thrust at his heart, but he fell to his right, grabbed the wrist with his right hand and slammed it across his torso and into the open door. The wrist caught the edge of the door itself, and he felt the shudder as the hand released the knife. He swiftly kicked it aside, pulled the figure in bodily, and booted the door shut.

'Now, Edith, that is the least gratitude I have ever experienced after attempting to aid someone. I assume you have some reason to want to harm me?'

'You think you can forget your actions by buying his family?' she spat.

Simon had joined Baldwin, and stood behind his shoulder. 'What is all this?'

Edith saw the knife on the floor near the door. She made a move as though to dart to it, but Baldwin did not release her wrist. Instead he hauled her with him further into the room, leaving the knife where it had fallen. 'Sit, child, and tell me why you tried that.'

'What can we do if you have him killed? It's bad enough paying for his keep while he's out, but at least he can help mend nets and earn a few ha'pennies here and there. But now? You've condemned us all to death!'

'I have not the faintest idea what you are talking about.'

'My father! He's in the gaol for stealing some silver from the dead man's purse, and you made out you weren't going to do anything about it! You deceived us, and now he's—'

'Wait!' Baldwin snapped. 'I know nothing of this. Coroner?'

'What?' Sir Richard growled.

'Is this your doing?'

'Why me?' Sir Richard asked with a baffled lifting of his eyebrows.

Baldwin nodded. 'Edith, it is none of us here. Where is the gaol?'

'At the market house.'

'Come with us now, and we shall have him released if we may.'

She stared at him warily. 'Why should I believe you? You'll have me arrested too!'

'Edith,' Baldwin said with some asperity, 'it was *I* who gave you money to help the family. Would I then order your father to be arrested? You have drawn steel against me, but I have not killed you as I might. I have no intention of hurting you or your father. Now come and help us.'

Her expression remained suspicious, but when he released her hand, she walked to the door. Standing by her knife, she looked back at Baldwin. He nodded, and she picked it up, concealing it in a sheath under her cloak, and led the way outside just as Rob appeared, whistling. His whistle became low and appreciative as he leered at her, and Baldwin was tempted to cuff him as he passed. Instead he heard Sir Richard take a pie.

'Good choice, lad,' he bellowed as he munched. 'Keep them hot by the fire at the Custom House. We won't be too long.'

Chapter Nineteen

When Rob arrived at the Bailiff's place of work, Stephen was already sitting at his desk and eyeing a set of new figures with a dubious expression on his face. The numbers were very precise, and he distrusted any figures from sailors which were precise. To his mind, that spoke of dishonesty.

'Bailiff's off questioning. Says you're to get on with things,' Rob said as he placed the pies carefully about the hearth.

'Good. I shall. And *you* should return to your home and clear it up. I have heard that you leave it in a terrible state. Do you never do any work?'

'Me?' Rob demanded indignantly. 'I'm always working. Look at my hands, almost completely worn away, they are. And all this for next to nothing. I tell you, if I could get on a ship, I'd sail away tomorrow. Any berth would do. I'd be better than most in climbing aloft, you know. And I can—'

'Clear off home, boy. Get on with your work and leave me to get on with mine!'

'You? Don't know what work is, you don't,' the boy called derisively as he slipped quickly from the door, leaving it open.

A small gust blew in, lifting the corner of Stephen's roll, and he irritably set a pebble on top before rushing to the door and staring down the road at the disappearing back of the servant. 'Little monster!' he muttered, and turned back to the chamber.

As he did so, he caught sight of a face in the alley, and felt his heart quicken. It was the man from the gaming room who had made Strete stop. An unremarkable man, short, almost squat, with the complexion and the rolling gait of a sailor, but with a shaven jaw that looked odd.

It was as he peered at the man that he was noticed. The sailor glared at him aggressively as though about to demand what the clerk was so interested in him for, but then he spun on his heel and hurried away.

The clerk slowly closed the door, wondering what had been so odd about the man, and then he realised that the fellow must only recently have been shaved. The flesh of his jaw was pale and smooth.

With that little conundrum settled, he returned to his desk.

Cynegils had passed a miserable night. The floor was damp, unyielding rock, and he had huddled shivering in the corner, wondering what latest misfortune could visit itself upon him.

When the trapdoor above him opened, the light flooding the cell all but blinded him, and he had to cover his face with a hand. There was a rattle and thump, and he saw that the gaoler had let the ladder down into the chamber.

'Come on up. Apparently you're free.'

Cynegils remained where he was for some heartbeats. The idea that he could be sprung loose had been so far from his mind that he found it hard to accommodate it. 'Me?'

'GET UP HERE, MAN!'

The raucous tones of the Coroner were not to be ignored. Cynegils groaned as he eased himself upright and hauled himself up the ladder to the chamber above.

'Father!' His daughter was there; she had been weeping.

'I wouldn't get too close, Edie,' he said. The stench of the prison was on him, a foul miasma of decay, fear and excrement.

'Who ordered you here?' Simon demanded.

'A knight – Sir Andrew, he called himself, off that ship, the *Gudyer*, in the haven.'

'Where is he?'

'He was at the inn last night. They took me in the street at Hardness, and dragged me to the inn, and when he was done he had me brought here.'

'By what right?' Simon asked in a low voice.

Cynegils shrugged. He had no idea. A man of his low status was fodder for any powerful man who chose to snare him. They needed no reason.

Baldwin glanced at Simon. 'This man needs to be away from here. He's a sailor. If there were a ship with a master who swore to keep him from ale while he was at sea, he should be safer.'

'You want me to find him a place on a ship?' Simon asked with some disbelief, staring at the noisome figure before him.

Edith was about to fall to her knees and beg, when she saw the Keeper shoot her a look.

'I feel sure that he needs all the protection he can find,' Baldwin said. 'So do his children. Find him a berth on a ship and pay all the money to this excellent girl. Oh, come on, Simon! There must be a ship somewhere that needs another hand.'

'Come with us, then,' Simon said. 'You can bathe and change your clothes, and then we will ask Stephen what he would recommend.'

'And *then*,' Baldwin said grimly, 'I think we ought to go to this Sir Andrew and enquire by what right he seeks to arrest men here in Clifton and Hardness.'

'Why are you here?'

The soft voice cut into Hamund's thoughts as he sat with his back to the *Saint Denis*'s planks. He looked up at the Frenchman's dark features and sighed. 'I killed a man who has powerful friends.'

'All men seem to have powerful *enemies* in this country now.'

'I fear you are right.'

'How did it happen?'

Hamund looked away, and his gaze was attracted to the sky. Even there she haunted his thoughts: he could see her sweet face in the clouds. 'My master died, serving his lord, and that same lord now covets his lands. So, he has ordered my master's widow to go. He will have her evicted so that he can take possession. The man sent to tell us was a foul, cruel brute, and I was disgusted. So I went to the inn where he was staying, and I killed him.'

'In an inn?'

'Yes.'

'My friend, you have inherited your English race's talent for subtlety.'

Hamund frowned. 'You would have stabbed him in the back on the open road, I suppose?'

'With a man who could do that to the widow of a comrade, I would have challenged him on the road, and I would have killed him,' Pierre said, but then he grinned. 'Or perhaps I should have paid another to do it . . . Footpads are so cheap, I believe, since so many have lost their homes. It would be good to give one of them some real employment.'

Hamund was not inclined to trust this foreigner, and he didn't know whether the man was speaking with genuine sincerity or was being flippant. 'Rapists are not usually considered so subtle.'

'Rapists?' Pierre's face hardened in an instant. 'If I ever meet a man who accuses me of that, I shall castrate him!'

'You didn't rape a lady?'

'On the Gospels, I swear it,' Pierre said.

'Then why do they hunt you down?'

'I loved a lady who was as far above my station as the moon is above the earth!' Pierre exclaimed, and then his voice dropped. 'You have loved. You know what it is to love and leave the object of your desire. My lady was honourable, and would not consider leaving her household for fear of the shame. And I would not torture so sweet a creature by remaining. So I thought to leave the country and return to my native land where I may find some peace.'

'I am sorry. You are in the same position as me, then.'

'Yes.'

Hamund shook his head slowly and sadly, but then his eyes narrowed. 'But why are they chasing you? Did they realise you were in love with this lady? You didn't—'

'Neither of us committed adultery,' Pierre said flatly. 'I would have, but she would not. She is honourable. No, they chase me because I am French, my friend. I think that all Frenchmen will be pursued from the realm before too many weeks have passed.'

'Our Queen is French.'

'And that is why the King harries all her countrymen. He despises her, and would see her shamed. He is a cruel man, this King of yours.'

'Not of mine,' Hamund said sadly. 'I have no liege now. I am outlaw.'

Pierre glanced at him, and saw to his surprise that the fellow was weeping with silent despair, the tears trickling steadily down his cheeks. It was an odd sight. Pierre had seen many men cry with pain, or heard them sob with sorrow, but never to his knowledge had he seen a man give himself up to hopelessness in such a manner. For a while he stared, and he became prey to a sudden whirl of thoughts. First loathing and disgust that a man could display such weakness at all, let alone in front of a stranger; then plain contempt. And yet even as he sought to look away he seemed to hear his own lover's sweet voice and see her thick brown tresses, and he felt the prickling at his own eyes to think that he would never see her again either.

He knew what it was to have lost, just as had Hamund. And as he thought again of his lady, he understood what Hamund must feel. Except Hamund had lost his woman, his livelihood, his property and his King. He was outlawed and alone in the world.

'My friend,' he said quietly, 'you are alive. Much may still happen. Do not lose heart. There is always the hope that you and I will again meet our loves, if not here, then perhaps in heaven.'

Hamund blinked and wiped at his eyes, then nodded.

Pierre patted his shoulder. 'When we arrive in France, my friend, you will come with me. You will be safe with my protection.'

Hamund could say nothing. These were the first words of genuine compassion he had heard since leaving his lady and fleeing to the church's sanctuary. All he knew was, as Pierre stood and stalked away on his long legs, that Hamund could follow him to the ends of the earth and back for those words.

There was a shout from the stern and Gil appeared clad in his best tunic and cote-hardie, his head decorously covered with a cowl. He stood near Hamund and gave a command. Three of the sailors joined him then climbed over the side down to a small rowboat that wallowed in the lee of the cog. It had rowed out to them a short while earlier, and the rower, a cleanshaven, older man, sat in it waiting.

'What's this? Where do you go?' Pierre asked Gil as he cocked his leg to follow them over the side.

'My master's body has to be taken to the church. His servants will carry him to the funeral.'

The house of the dead sailor was out at the fringe of Hardness, on the road up to Tunstal.

Simon thought that it was a typical cottage of a reasonably well-paid sailor. All the timbers were limewashed to preserve them from the worst the sea could throw at them, the walls were patched, but not haphazardly. All the daubed areas were themselves coated by limewash, and the thatch was renewed where necessary. It was a house whose owner had lavished attention upon it.

The front was given up entirely to a neat, well-laid out garden, with leeks and cabbages growing well in the sunshine. There was a profusion of leaves of all kinds: alexanders, parsley, and salads, while the first crop of peas hung from the rafters of the little log-shed at the cottage's side. They would dry there on the vine and be threshed from the pods in the winter. Onions and garlic grew in ordered ranks, and Simon was reminded of the little vegetable patch he had at his home at Lydford. The sight of the plants here, so mundane, brought home to him how far he was from his wife, and he felt a momentary pang at the separation.

But his separation was nothing compared to that which afflicted this house. There was a turf bench built into the garden on their left as they entered. From there the seated woman would have a fine view of the river and the hills opposite. Near her was a small herber, surrounded by fragrant flowers, in which a small child rolled and gurgled in the sun while she sewed.

In her middle twenties, the woman was sun-burned to the colour of a nut, but her brown eyes still stood out clearly in comparison. They were startlingly distinct, as though they belonged to another face, and when they lighted on the men walking up her path, they showed no recognition, only stolid resignation. 'What did he owe you?' she said.

'Nothing, madam, I assure you,' Baldwin said.

'You may call me Alice. You'll be the first, then. Everyone else has come demanding money for tools or drinks.' She set aside her work listlessly. 'May I serve you some ale? With my man dead, there isn't much else I can give you.'

'That sounds very . . .' Sir Richard began.

Baldwin glared at him. 'We wouldn't dream of taking what little you have.'

'What do you want, then?'

'We wondered about the cause of your husband's death. Of course it is likely that he died during a fight for the ship, but—'

'Yes? *But*?' she asked coolly.

'There is no apparent reason why he should have been left aboard the ship. All the other men were removed.'

'They were slaughtered, you mean,' she said, and there was a break in her voice. 'Oh, God in heaven, why have You done this? All those men . . . good men. And me with three children! What will I do now?'

'You knew many of the men on the ship?' Baldwin asked.

'One was my brother, Adam. I have lost husband and brother in the same night!' Her tone was growing wilder. 'What can a woman do without a husband? If he is gone, there's nothing!'

'He had been with Master Pyckard for some years, I heard?' Simon said.

'Yes. Danny learned all about the sea on Master Pyckard's ships.'

'So he began with Master Pyckard early on?'

'When he was orphaned, the master took him in. Danny started as a cabin-boy, and gradually worked up to being a trusted sailor. He was lucky, too, and the men liked to have him sail with them.'

'Why lucky?' Baldwin asked.

'He was in dreadful storms once or twice. He used to say that he was like a cat: he had many lives.'

'Was he shipwrecked on Pyckard's ships?' Baldwin frowned.

'Yes, the once. And he was in terrible squalls a few times. The storm that killed Master Pyckard's wife, he was there then.'

'What happened?' Simon said.

'There was a sudden storm, and the ship was blown onto rocks. It was mere luck that they didn't all die. He never spoke of it afterwards, and I think the memory was terrible. He was floating about for days holding on to a lump of timber. The others never thought he'd survive. Sailors are often like that, they don't want to talk about the worst weathers.'

'How long ago was that?'

She went blank for a moment. 'A long time – may be fifteen years.'

'What can you tell us about this last sailing?' Simon asked.

'Nothing! I know nothing about it.'

'When did he leave you here?'

She looked at him, a depth of despair in her eyes. 'I didn't even know he was going. He always used to tell me when he was about to sail, but this time there was nothing. I hadn't even known he'd been asked to join the ship!'

Baldwin's head snapped up. 'Are you quite sure? You say you had no idea he was going anywhere . . . Did he usually take anything special with him when he went on ship?'

She shrugged. 'Just odds and sods. You know what sailors are like. He always had his lucky charm about his neck – it was a lead badge of St Christopher – and a spoon. He was so proud of that spoon. He bought it ages ago in France from a metalsmith. Nothing else much, just a spare shirt and . . .'

'Is his spoon here? Have you noticed whether it has gone?' Baldwin asked urgently.

'I haven't had time to worry about that!'

'Look for it, mistress, please. It could be important.'

She stared at him, huffed a deep sigh, and rose. 'Wait there.'

Disappearing inside, she left Simon with the impression that she thought Baldwin had lost his mind. He glanced at Baldwin. 'What in God's name?'

'Well considered, Sir Baldwin,' Sir Richard muttered in an uncharacteristically quiet tone. 'I hadn't thought that through.'

She was back a few moments later with a confused expression on her face. 'You are right,' she said, and opened her fist. In it lay a long, thin-handled spoon with a broad bowl, and a lead badge like the pilgrims wore, set on a thin chain. 'Why did he leave these behind?'

'Madam, I am sorry that you have lost him, but I think we may be able to explain more later. Do you know whether your brother was expecting to sail?'

'Oh, yes. I know he was. I had thought Danny might have been asked to join the ship because they were short-handed, but he always *told* me when he was sailing! And he would never have sailed without these. Oh, God, what does this mean?'

Her sudden wail caught Baldwin by surprise, and as she slipped down to her seat again, he heard a sound at the door. Startled by her cry and the suddenness of the noise, he automatically reached for his sword as he snapped round seeking danger, but all he saw was a girl of maybe five or six and a little boy. The children stared fixedly at Baldwin as though expecting him to launch an attack on their mother.

'Look at them!' she added. 'They think everyone coming here is trying to steal a few more pennies from my husband just because he's gone. We can trust no one! No one!'

As she began to sob, the three children began to cry as well. It was for Baldwin one of the most appalling scenes he had ever witnessed. The distraught weeping youngsters, and their mother, bent over, arms cradling her belly, racked with deep sobs that wouldn't go away.

Chapter Twenty

Moses was only just able to keep himself calm as he walked with the priest to the church, his master's body behind him, carried by six sturdy sailors and servants. People came from their doors to peer at the small cortège as it passed. It was rare enough that a man would have such a fine procession in the town, and all wanted to take a peek at it as Pyckard's body passed by.

After his death, Moses had insisted that he himself should clean his master's body and prepare him for his coffin. He was as near as any, Pyckard's son, and he jealously guarded his right to perform this last service for the man who had saved him and his brother from penury and probably death. With one of the stable-boys he stripped the corpse and washed away the mess from voided bowels and bladder, before clothing the dead man in a shift. A bolt of linen had been ordered days before by his foresighted master, and he took it up with a sob in his throat. As he and the boy unrolled it by his master's cooling body, he could scarcely concentrate, his mind was so taken up with thoughts of all the kindnesses Paul Pyckard had shown him.

He could hardly remember Mistress Pyckard, she had died so many years before. A terrible day that. Moses had thought he had lost his brother too, but luckily Danny had survived the shipwreck. At least it meant that Moses had a family to watch over. He would do all in his power to protect his nieces and nephew. And Danny's widow.

By all accounts, Master Pyckard had loved his wife dearly. Amandine had been a rare beauty, with her flashing, dark eyes, her long tresses of blue-black hair and pale complexion. Her calm disposition and gentleness had won the hearts of all the household, and her husband had been utterly devoted. Certainly in all the years that Moses had lived with Pyckard, he had never seen another woman with him, although there were plenty hereabouts who would have been happy to earn a few shillings while their husbands were at sea. No, Paul Pyckard had remained loyal to the memory of his wife. Even as he breathed his last, Moses could have sworn he had heard a whispered, 'Amandine!'

It was only fitting that he should be buried next to his beloved wife. Her body had been found washed upon the shore with some sailor's body after the wreck. Only her clothing identified her after the scavenging sea-creatures had ravaged her, but Moses knew Pyckard was content just to be able to give her a funeral.

The priest had arrived a little before noon, giving them plenty of time to roll the body in the long shroud and bind it at head and feet. Moses had ordered the coffin a week or more before, and it was brought as soon as news spread of the death. He had an elderly ex-sailor help him heft Pyckard's corpse into it, and he stood with his hand on his master's breast for a few minutes before he could bring himself to place the lid atop. With a sigh, he finally submitted to the sailor's persistence, and stood back as the cover was placed over Paul Pyckard, shutting off the light from his face for the last time.

Formed of seamen from Pyckard's household and business, the procession moved off now to the churchyard. The six coffin-bearers wore mourning black, but their appearance and manner, although solemn, gave the impression of stern restraint, as though at any moment they might break into a sailor-like song. At the front walked the priest, taking care to show proper respect, as well he might. Moses knew how much money Pyckard had promised the church for the funeral and prayers afterwards. The bell tolled in the hands of the fossor, who paced slowly in front of the priest and set the speed for them all.

There had been nothing like this for Danny. When *his* body had been carted off to the church, there had been only Moses, Annie, Alice and the children, with the fossor and a priest.

Gil and some of the men from the cog had arrived, Moses saw, and he was warmed to think that they had not yet set sail, but came here to witness Pyckard's funeral. With the loss of the *Saint John*, so many who should have been here were missing, and it was good to see the household's numbers swollen. If Gil and his men had already left port it might have looked as though Pyckard had few friends, no companions or servants. In reality he had many who depended upon his patronage, from widows whose men had died in Pyckard's service to waifs and strays like Moses himself, and the foreigner – the Frenchman. Well, at least he'd carried out his master's last wish regarding *him*.

They carried on along the street, down to the mill pool and over the two-arched bridge that connected Clifton with Hardness, past the mill itself with the wheel sitting almost stationary as the tide lay idle at its lowest point, and on up the hill towards St Clement's Church at Tunstal. Here, there were more seamen and fishermen standing. Pyckard had given so many of them chances of earning money, and they wished to show their respect for the man who had helped them.

As they passed by one group, Moses saw a tall, fair-haired man eyeing the procession with a condescending air. The expression made Moses set his jaw. The stranger couldn't be expected to understand how important Master Pyckard had been, and yet to display such disdain was foul when any man was being carried to his last resting-place. Moses could see that others nearby had noticed his attitude and were giving him black looks.

And then his eyes met those of a man who stood hooded only a short distance from the fair man, and he felt a shock run through his frame. This was the man he had tried to save, the one he'd put on the ship to ensure he was protected: *the Frenchman*. What was *he* doing here?

Peter Strete wiped his metal pen on his sleeve, pushed it gently into his leather penner, thrust the cork into his inkhorn, and leaned back, yawning. There had been much to do today, and he was content that he had achieved a lot already. Most of the details of the last cargoes were recorded now, as well as the goods which had been rescued aboard the *Saint John*, and he felt it was time to find some lunch.

He tended to avoid eating lunch within the house. The other servants could be uncouth. There was one man who insisted on picking his nose and flicking the contents away, often speckling other men's clothing; another could not help but spit and dribble as he chewed, as his mouth had been hit by a sword in a battle protecting Master Hawley's ship some years ago. All in all, it was less stressful to eat something in the tavern. Today he desired a good capon, he decided, and was about to leave when John Hawley strode into the room.

'I have to be off,' he announced. 'Everyone's going to Pyckard's funeral. Quickly: where are the accounts?'

Peter brought out his rolls again. He set to quickly, explaining what he had done, and then ran through the calculations of the values of the items again.

'All good,' Hawley said. 'What of the money?'

He always kept tight control of the cash in the house. Any merchant had to be careful about the total amount he held at any time, but Hawley was more cautious than most. When he needed it, he must have money to buy in goods. There were always deals to be struck with the cloth-makers in Totnes, and if Hawley didn't buy their goods, others would. There had to be enough ready coin to pay for surprise purchases.

'We have plenty,' Strete chuckled. 'There will soon be even more, too. The salvage of Pyckard's ship will be very profitable.'

'Good. Now, how much do we have presently?'

Alred felt the guilt of it. Bill could see that, and although he tried not to condemn his friend of so many years, it was hard not to.

'I didn't have any choice,' Alred said again. 'What else could I do?'

Law nodded. 'I'd have done it if you hadn't.'

'He probably killed the man in our hole,' Bill admitted. 'So I suppose he deserved to be captured.'

'Yes. We made a mistake when we knocked that fool on the head and saved him last time. We couldn't do anything else.'

Bill took a long pull at his horn of ale. It was the sort of thing Alred would worry at for ages, like a hound with a tree-root, trying to pull it loose in vain, because the tree was too large. Alred felt guilt about his action because he knew too well that the man he had betrayed would die if found by Sir Andrew. There was no doubt in their minds of that.

'He didn't look like a rapist,' Law said judiciously.

'How can you tell what a rapist looks like?' Alred snapped. 'Any man can let himself fall foul of his humours and attack a lady. You don't have to be a churl to fancy a tumble with a pretty wench and push your luck.'

'He deserves to be caught, anyway,' Law said, ignoring his bitter tone.

'I wonder what they'll do,' Bill said.

'What do you mean?' Alred asked suspiciously. He could tell Bill was not convinced that his actions were justified, but then Bill had always been against anyone in authority. Bill had had one or two run-ins with the law, and both times he'd lost a lot of money, which was why he was working for Alred now and not a paviour on his own. No, he just didn't trust the law or the men involved in administering justice.

'Only that he's on the ship now, so will they storm it and take him from it, or will they try to catch him by getting him back on shore?'

Law gaped delightedly. 'You think they'll try to take him on the ship? Let's go and watch!'

'Oh, Christ's pains! Will you shut up!' Alred snapped with a burst of frustration.

He stood and strode from the room irritably, and Law turned to Bill. 'What's his problem?'

'Can't you see what he's done?' Bill said with asperity. 'He's sent that Frenchman to be hanged. He'll die now.'

'So? If he hadn't raped the woman, he wouldn't have anything to fear, would he?'

'If he *did* rape someone. How do you know he's guilty? All we have is the word of this knight. Even when a man's taken to a court, you can't trust the witnesses,' Bill said bitterly. 'A rich man can bribe anyone he wants to get the result he desires. So all Alred's done is send that man to be hanged to save our skins – even though he doesn't know if the Frenchie was guilty or not. How do you think that makes him feel?'

'Who gives a rat's cods? I reckon he's guilty,' Law said.

'And you're so wise you can read his guilt?'

'I can see what's before my nose as clearly as any.'

Bill's jaw jutted. 'Sometimes, boy, people make mistakes and the wrong man is convicted.'

'If he had nothing to fear, he wouldn't have run away to here. Only a man with something to hide does a runner.'

'Maybe he just knew that if he didn't run, hotheads would assume he was guilty and kill him?'

Law curled his upper lip back from his teeth, his brow creased. 'What are you on about? Look, that French scrote tried to get his hand up a lady's skirt, it's as simple as that. If he was innocent, he wouldn't have run, would he? Come on!'

'Come on, *ballocks*! Don't you ever wonder why I'm here? Why I don't have my own business? I was hunted once, boy. Yes, me! Another woman was raped, and because I was on the spot, they tried to blame me for it. And I had to flee for my life because the man who'd actually done it said he'd seen me. He was rich, so I couldn't stay to tell the truth. No one would have believed me. No, so I had to run, and all my property was taken.'

'What are you doing here now, then?'

'I'm safe now. I abjured the realm, and I only came back when I was given a full pardon. But a pardon doesn't mean you can recover all the property you had to give up. Yes, I am safe, but I lost everything. So don't tell me that justice is fair, boy. It sure as hell isn't.'

'Just because you ran off doesn't mean this one's innocent, does it? If you'd stayed, you'd still have all your property,' Law said cockily.

'If I'd stayed, I'd have been hanged.'

'Yeah, sure.'

His open amusement, his smile of disbelief, made Bill's face redden with anger. 'You think I am lying, you little turd?'

Bill couldn't help himself. He lashed out with his fist. It caught Law on the nose, and the lad was flung over backwards, crashing against a table and knocking the jugs and horns higgledy-piggledy as he went, arms flailing.

'You mad bastard!' Law said, shaking his head like a wetted hound. His fingers gingerly went to his nose and he wiped it with the back of his hand. 'What did you do that for?'

Bill slumped back in his chair. 'Just don't judge men. Don't judge me, don't judge the Frenchie. You don't know what he's done. You don't know what I've done. You have no idea!'

'Go and swyve your mother!' Law spat, standing. The blood was trickling from his nose, and he sniffed, his head tilted back slightly as he tried to stem the flow with his sleeve. 'Sweet son of God, you're mad today, just like Alred. I don't have to stay here and have you punch at me, you old prickle!'

'Where are you going?'

'Out! I'll go watch that foreign sod getting taken on the ship. I expect they'll have him already. Maybe he's hanging from a mast, eh? Probably dancing his last right now, and I'll be glad if he is. You may not trust people, but I'd trust an Englishman over one of them Frenchies any day. You're just weak because you're old, Bill. You're *too* old!'

'Come back, lad,' Bill said tiredly. 'Look, I shouldn't have hit you. I'm sorry about that. It was just frustration. I'm sorry, all right? Now sit down, and we'll wait for Alred to come back.'

'No – *you* wait. And when he gets back you can tell him why I didn't want to stay with you. Christ's cods! There's a bad smell about the place while you're in here!'

Law pushed past Bill, left the tavern and walked down an alley to the water's edge, where he sat on a log and stared out at the ships in the haven.

'Sod them both, stupid old gits,' he muttered, and threw a stone spinning into the water.

Chapter Twenty-One

Hawley ran his finger down the roll and checked off the figures. Then he slapped his purse. 'Where's the strongbox? I need more money. I'm off to the funeral of poor Pyckard today, and have to make a decent donation.'

Peter nodded and took his key, opening the great chest behind his desk. It was solid ship's oak, built by Henry Pyket from old planks from a ship he'd repaired, the bands of iron beaten by Hawley's own smith, the locks cut and filed to size by an expert in Exeter. Lifting the heavy lid, Peter took up a leather sack filled with coin from the pile within.

Hawley took it and glanced into the chest. He turned, but then hesitated and slowly went back to it, his face betraying a certain doubt. 'I thought there would be two more sacks?'

Strete felt sweat break out on his back. 'I don't think so, master. Do you forget the two which went to the men victualling the cog ready to sail? It's all in the account.'

'Oh, I see. That's good, then,' Hawley said. 'Right, I'd best be preparing myself for the funeral. Don't forget to lock up.'

He walked out, and Strete drew a long sigh of relief. When his master had seen that the sacks were gone, he had thought he was about to be discovered. As soon as he could, he would put the money back in the chest. It would only take one more win . . .

Only a short while ago he had been close to winning enough to repay the whole debt. He had enjoyed a near-miraculous run of good luck at the gaming, and it was only when fortune turned against him that he realised he'd lost almost all his profit again. Thinking that his luck was on the turn, he had borrowed another sack. One more game or two, and with some heavy betting he'd recover the lot, and hopefully no one would ever know that he had stolen from Master Hawley.

But the clerk's relief was short-lived.

'I'm early still. Before I go, shall we check the contents of the chest?' Hawley said.

Peter sat bolt upright. His master had returned and stood in the doorway watching him. 'What – all of it?' he gulped.

'Yes. Why don't we start adding up the coins?' Hawley said with a thin smile, and Strete looked out at the sunlight in the street, giving a nervous grin.

'There isn't really time, is there, master? Not if you're going to the funeral.'

'I think I can make the time.'

Strete heard a sound at the door and glancing up, saw two sailors standing and staring at him with grim expressions. He felt a terrible sinking sensation in his belly. It grew worse as Hawley glanced at his belt. 'By the way, Strete, that is a good new purse. Have you found some money to buy that?'

Pierre watched the procession slowly walk past, the bell tolling mournfully as they all went, and he bowed his head respectfully, remembering the man who had saved his life.

'For God's sake, let's get back to the ship!'

'Hamund, be calm. There is no need to hurry anywhere,' Pierre said. With his hood over his face he felt invisible, and perfectly secure.

'Oh yes, there is! I am an abjurer, and if I'm found here on the land I'll be hanged. I don't need to die, do I, to satisfy your curiosity about this master of yours?'

Pierre was about to reply with a stern reminder that the deceased had saved both their skins, when he saw a face he recognised. 'Hamund,' he hissed, 'do you see the man behind me, he with the fair hair and the smile? You see him – with three men about him?'

Hamund shot a look over his shoulder. From here the four men were in plain view, and he could see the fair man in their midst. 'He looks like a nasty piece of work.'

'He is! His name is Sir Andrew de Limpsfield. He has no heart, and is only interested in that which can advance him. If he heard you had swallowed a ring, he would paunch you to see whether it was really there,' Pierre said with a chill certainty. He was torn now. He was keen to go with Master Pyckard's body to the church to pray for the soul of that good and kind man, but he also wanted to see where Sir Andrew was going and what he was up to.

'You're making a joke, aren't you? Do you really know him?'

'He is the most evil man I have ever met.' And Pierre took Hamund's shoulder and led him away from the crowds.

Hamo the cooper had finished making and mending the last of the barrels for the cog, and now he was rowing them out to the *Saint Denis*, ready for her sailing.

'Ahoy! Anyone up there?'

He sat on the thwarts gripping his oars and staring up at the stern of the ship towering above him, waiting. It was a long while before a face appeared above him and a thin, tremulous voice called down to him. 'Who's that? Oh, it's you, Hamo.'

'Having a nice sleep, were you? Where is everyone?'

'Didn't you hear that Master Pyckard died? Most everyone from his crews will be with him now in the church. He was much liked, was Master Pyckard,' the man said and burped.

Hamo vaguely recognised him. 'You're Dicken, aren't you? Look, is there anyone else aboard? These barrels are full of fresh water. Gil asked for them. They'll be the devil's own job to pull up without a bit of help.'

'There are some men up at the prow. Wait there.'

Hamo grimaced, muttering, '*Wait there!*' to himself in a falsetto imitation of the man's whine, adding in his normal voice, 'Where else am I going to go, you blasted moon-struck fool?'

As he waited, he gazed idly about him. From here the two towns that had united to form Dartmouth were clearly visible and distinct. Each climbed the hills on either side of the cleave that was the mill pool, the white houses a series of rectangles. He could see the mill and the mill's wheel, and could just make out the line of dark-clad men walking slowly up the hill to Tunstal from Hardness. Bowing his head reverently, he crossed himself as he thought of Master Pyckard.

The men should have appeared by now. He had a sudden suspicion that the fellows on board were drinking the health of their dead master again, and he was about to shout up at them when he saw some boats – three long-oared vessels moving quickly through the water towards him.

Of course there were boats all over the haven. There was nothing unusual in that, but Hamo saw something glinting from them as they came, and he frowned, uncertain. It was odd for lighters to be moving so swiftly in such a busy haven, and although they all looked low in the water, it seemed to be more because they were full of men, than because there was a heavy load of goods aboard them. And then, as he watched, he saw a man in the prow of the first boat draw a sword and point it towards him, and he felt his stomach churn . . . and then rage filled him as he realised these men were about to board and attack the cog.

'Dicken! HOY, DICKEN! Look out! You're going to be boarded!' he roared at the top of his voice, thrusting with his oar at the steep clinker wall of oak and pushing himself off. He measured the distance: the boats would be here in a few moments. Making a swift decision, he set his oars ready and pulled himself away, back to his store on the Clifton side of the mill pool, watching as the men snagged anchor chains with grappling hooks and hurled grapnels before scrambling up into the ship herself.

Strete sat huddled in the corner of the room and stared as his master's men went through his belongings.

'You see, Peter, I think it's a lot of responsibility looking after my money. It could tempt some men. Are you a strong man, Peter?'

Strete looked from him to the men at the doorway. 'You can't think any money's gone missing, Master Hawley. I would have noticed if it had.'

'Yes, you would, wouldn't you?' Hawley said with a cold tone. He waited while another sailor came in with a clerk. The two of them began to empty the chest, logging the items against Strete's own rolls.

There was a relentlessness about the way that the two men lifted out the leathern sacks, one counting the coin inside aloud, and the clerk nodding and ticking off each against the notes. Neither of them looked at Strete. That was the prerogative of Hawley and the two guards at the door. All three watched him closely.

'Master, surely you trust me? If you have any suspicions, you should tell me so that I can explain . . .' Strete started, before he saw one man at the door pull a small cudgel from his belt and slap it into his hand rhythmically.

'I dare say you could try,' Hawley said with a short baring of his teeth. 'But whether or not I'd choose to believe you is a different matter, isn't it? All I can see right now is that you have robbed me, Peter. I don't like that.'

'I haven't robbed you!'

And his voice carried his conviction. He hadn't. How could he rob his master? No, he had made a foolish error and tried to make good that error by borrowing to replace the money lost, but he would return it. As he had.

'I have heard before now how you enjoy the gaming at the Blue Boar and Porpoise, but I was too trusting. I never thought you'd actually steal from me to finance your fun. You've been well looked after here, Peter. Very well. I pay my men well to keep their loyalty, and if I was seen to let a man like you escape after taking my treasure, what would others think? They'd think I was soft, wouldn't they?'

Hawley stood and marched to the chest. The great box was almost emptied now, and the two men at its side were ticking off the last coins and making a total of the full sum. The clerk glanced at the sailor, who nodded, and then both looked up at their master, the clerk holding up the amended roll. Hawley took it, ran his eye down the columns, and scowled. 'Sweet Jesus!'

Strete felt as though his bowels were about to open. Perhaps if he'd been standing, they would have done. As it was, all he could do was swallow and wipe his forehead with his sleeve. How his master had come to suspect him like this was beyond him – he'd been so careful.

'It looks as though I owe you an apology,' Hawley said gruffly. He passed the parchment back to Strete. 'The accounts are wrong by exactly three pennies. I don't know where they came from, but your accounting is out by that much.'

'I am sorry, master, I—'

'Shut up, Strete. I'm in *credit* three pennies, not debit. Take the money as an apology for the way I spoke about you just now,' Hawley said. He shook his head. 'It's this matter of the *Saint John*. It's making everyone nervous. Hmm. Yes.'

Strete watched as he turned abruptly on his heel and marched from the room, irritably beckoning the three sailors to follow him.

'Who's a lucky boy, then?' the other clerk said quietly.

'What do you mean?' Strete demanded.

'You must have made a killing last night to pay back all you owed. I've seen you gaming and I've heard how much you've had to pay out. You're the laughing stock of the inn, you are. Everyone wants to play with you.' He grinned. 'Best not try it again, mind. Our master will have his eye on you from now on!' Touching a finger to his cheek under his eye, he laughed aloud as he walked from the room.

Strete fell back on his seat, and suddenly began to shiver uncontrollably. If he hadn't received that money from Paul Pyckard just before the merchant died, he would have had a hole of seven marks in the accounts. As it was, he was five shillings short until he'd found the body in the pavers' hole and took the purse. That had been a real stroke of luck! And that would have been enough for Hawley to have him dragged from his door all the way to the gaol under the market house. No man robbed Hawley with impunity, and if he had learned that his own clerk had fleeced him, his rage would have been uncontrollable.

Thank God he had made good the money with his payment from Pyckard and what he found in the dead man's purse.

Hamo arrived back at his cooperage and grabbed for an axe. Already, when he looked back over the water, he could see that the crew of the cog had been overwhelmed; the cries of the attacked suddenly grew silent, as did the ringing clashes of iron and steel, and now all that could be heard was an occasional bellow to disturb the normal noise of slapping water at his feet.

He set off at a fast pace to Hawley's house in Upper Street, and beat on the door with his axe's haft. 'Master Hawley? Master Hawley!'

'Who is that?' An elderly sailor appeared in the doorway and glared at him. 'What do you want?'

'It's me, the cooper, Hamo,' he panted. 'The cog in the haven – three boats have just overtaken her. Don't know what's happening, but tell your master urgently.'

Without waiting for a reply, he turned and fled along the road and down to the mill's dam. He hurtled along the path, past the silent wheel, over the sluice gates, and up into Hardness. Here he saw Ivo le Bel.

'Ivo! You have to raise the men of the town!' he gasped. 'Someone's just attacked Master Pyckard's cog the *Saint Denis*. Three boats, full of armed men.'

The sergeant sneered. 'You been drinking? What boats!' Then he looked past Hamo's shoulder towards the haven, and suddenly his smile left his face. 'Christ's cods!'

Baldwin stood watching the slow progress of the funeral party up the hill. 'Who died?' he asked.

'One of the merchants here – a man called Pyckard.' Then Simon reverted to their former conversation. 'First, how did you guess Danny wasn't supposed to be sailing?'

'His wife said so. Sailors don't normally just up and leave their wives without saying their goodbyes, in my experience. A man will rarely go to sea without taking a sentimental leave of his woman. That may mean that Danny was killed on shore and thrown onto the ship as we had thought. It's a small detail, but important. Now, this merchant, Pyckard – he died naturally?'

Simon nodded. 'Aye. He was a good enough man, I think, and successful generally.'

'Why "generally"?'

'Well, Pyckard was the owner of that cog, the *Saint John*. He owns other ships too, but that was one of his best, and it's partly lost in salvage now.'

'You said it was this fellow Hawley who found the vessel?' Baldwin asked. 'Do you think that he could have . . .'

'Taken it, slaughtered the crew, chucked 'em overboard, bar our Danny, and brought the ship back to port? It's possible. The two of them were rivals in business, so perhaps there was enmity between them – although to be fair I never saw much sign of it. There are some I'd not put past business like that, but Hawley seems to be an honourable man.'

Baldwin pulled a face. 'Ah, well. It was worth a try!'

The Coroner was standing a short distance from them, watching over the town with a proprietorial eye. 'A good place that. I had fun there when I was a lad. So! What do you two think of all this?'

'I think that there is a vessel out there which tried to burn the cog, but it wasn't the work of pirates,' Baldwin said. 'Nor was it a foolish attack by a different town. The burning was to conceal the crime of killing all aboard. But the sailor, Danny, he was not killed in that attack. If I had to guess, I'd say he died here in the town while the ship was moored.'

'And we can't speak to the men who worked with him because they've all disappeared,' Simon noted.

'Their bodies will turn up eventually,' Baldwin said with sad confidence.

The Coroner scratched his head. 'You don't think that they have been taken as hostages, then, or as slaves?'

'If this was all about making money, the attacker would have taken the whole ship, not a few crew members,' Baldwin pronounced. 'No, I believe that all the men were removed from the cog to be questioned as their ship burned, and now they'll have been killed.'

'Why, though?'

'They sought something or someone,' Baldwin said.

'This Frenchman you mentioned?' Simon prompted.

'If I had to guess, yes. Someone thinks he is dangerous and must be stopped from reaching French shores, and that someone is prepared to kill many men in order to do so.'

'Who could it be, though?' Simon wondered aloud.

Baldwin smiled. 'Well, I do wonder about this Sir Andrew. He is seeking the Frenchman, and he has a ship in the haven.'

Sir Richard harrumphed. 'I know the man. He's a toady of the worst sort. If you have money and power, he'll clean your boots with his tongue. Or your arse. No sense and no breeding. Reminds me of an alaunt I had once. Had to kill the thing in the end. Mad as a baiting mastiff, he was, and just as vicious. Some alaunts can be loyal creatures, good at hunting, good at holding at bay. I've known many which have been ideal for boar . . . but this one, he was mad. He'd go for anything at all.'

'It hardly sounds as if Sir Andrew is like that,' Baldwin observed mildly.

'You don't think so? This alaunt, he'd stay with me, then when I wasn't looking, he'd go and kill the neighbour's cat or attack some churl's hog. And when the crime was recognised, he'd come back to me, wagging his tail, and grinning like an innocent. He'd lick my hand as gentle as a lamb, and then go off and kill something else. It was when he tried to have a go at my steward's little boy that I thought enough was enough, and had his head taken off. Shame, though. Damn good hunter, he was.'

Simon looked over at Baldwin, shaking his head in disbelief.

The knight was smiling faintly. 'So you consider that this man Sir Andrew could have attacked the cog?'

'You mentioned that this Frenchie wanted to get away and he was being watched. Someone wanted him stopped. Sir Andrew was sent down here to flush the man out, or kill him. He found the ship, fired it, killed the crew in the hope of finding the man, and when he didn't, he came here to look again, with some cock-and-bull story about a rape. I think that about explains the whole matter,' the Coroner stated with calm satisfaction.

'Apart from Danny,' Simon noted.

Baldwin was about to respond when he saw a small dustcloud up at the top of the hill. 'Aha! Who can this be?'

A short while later, the three saw a man on horseback appear at the crest of the hill. He pointed the horse down the hillside and was soon scattering people on either side as he cantered down towards the mill's dam. When he drew nearer, Baldwin called, 'Whom do you seek?'

'Sir Baldwin de Furnshill, sir. Is that you?'

Baldwin nodded. He vaguely recognised the man from Bishop Walter's household. 'You have a message for me?' he asked.

It was always hard to be the bearer of sad or evil tidings, and Baldwin had no doubt that when his messenger had reached Bishop Walter, the poor man would have been appalled to learn that his rash decision to send his own nephew to spy on this Frenchman could have brought about his death.

Baldwin was just putting his mind to the manner of transport of the coffin back to the bishop's household when the messenger grinned at him.

'Yes, sir. My lord Bishop sends his greetings, and offers you his best wishes for your journey, as well as his apologies for wasting your time. The man whom you sought? His nephew is back at home. Bishop Walter hopes and trusts that you have not been seriously inconvenienced by your journey down here, and wishes me to tell you that you may consider your mission at an end.'

Baldwin felt a sense of shock, followed by several other emotions. Then he voiced the question uppermost in his mind. 'In that case, who was the dead man?' he muttered.

Chapter Twenty-Two

Cynegils had spent the morning in a state of bemusement. First he'd been rescued from the stinking gaol, then taken up to Stephen's chamber, where he was given clean clothes and some food and water (to his disgust) and then he was led to Master Pyckard's house. He was seated while the others discussed what to do with him, Stephen arguing that he should be taken aboard ship as soon as possible.

'You can sail with Gil,' the clerk said. 'He can do with all the help he can get.'

Cynegils shivered. 'What, and be killed by the devil like the crew of the *Saint John*?'

'You have to make up your own mind, it's true. Still, the risk of a possible attack at sea is one thing; dying here at the hands of this Sir Andrew could be far worse, I'd have thought.'

'What of money?'

'You think I'm foolish enough to give you some? You'd spend it on ale in an instant, wouldn't you?' Stephen laughed. 'No, friend, you'll have to wait until you return for that. I've given orders that you're not to have any drink on board, and when you land in France, if you go ashore to drink ale, the ship will leave you there. It would be a terrible shame if you were left behind on a foreign coast, but that's what will happen if you fail to obey.'

'What now?' Cynegils said sulkily.

'I should go and make your way to the *Saint Denis*. There's nothing to keep you here. There'll be a wake, I expect, and I don't want you to be here for that. The Bailiff has done all he can for you. Whether you take advantage of his kindness is up to you.'

Cynegils was determined just now to take advantage of anything and anyone who could save him from the cold-eyed blond man. 'I will, I swear. I'll go now and make my way to the ship.'

'Good. You do that. In the meantime, I have work to be getting on with,' the clerk said. He left Cynegils and trotted hurriedly towards the alley that would take him back down to Lower street, where he worked.

Cynegils hunched his shoulders, for it seemed to him that the sun was chilly today, and set off towards the lower town. He had made it down past the main thoroughfare, when he suddenly thought that his daughter would be wondering what had happened to him. In order to prevent her and the other children from worrying, it might be best to tell them he was going on board ship again. Edith would be pleased to learn that he was employed again.

It was with a spring in his step that he moved on. On the way, he passed a tavern and looked longingly at it, thinking of the ales inside waiting to be bought. But he had no money and they would lend him none. No one would believe him if he said he was to be sailing again.

Once back at the house, he found the door open, and he peered in, a little wary of his reception. He hoped that the wind was blowing from the right quarter in his daughter's disposition. Women!

'Edith? I'm home.'

There was no answer, and he walked through the house to the little yard at the rear; no sign of the children. They were probably out helping mend nets, he told himself, and he walked back to the front of the house, standing in the roadway while he considered what to do. Perhaps one of the neighbours would help? He knocked at the house next door and spoke to the mistress. From her he learned that all the men locally had been called to repel a force attacking a cog, and he stared out to sea, wondering if this was yet another attempt by Sir Andrew on his life.

He thanked his neighbour, left a message to explain that he had a job again, and wandered away.

It would put Edith in her place, to hear that he had won a sailor's work again. She'd said some hurtful things yesterday – for instance, that no one could trust him – but he'd soon show her. There wasn't much he could be taught about sailing. He had a wealth of experience, unlike some of those little arseholes who were half his age and who refused to listen to a man like him who had been sailing these waters for many years. They thought they knew it all, the fools!

Striding back across the dam again, he was almost at the far side when he caught sight of a young man, and nodded at him civilly. Continuing, he suddenly stopped, turned and stared after the man, and then he shivered with alarm.

'No! He's dead!' he said. He set off again, and this time there was no desire to drop into the tavern. He walked straight past and didn't stop until he had reached the jetty and could sit and wait for a rowing boat to take him out to the *Saint Denis*. His thirst had completely left him.

Simon saw his friend gape and enjoyed the sight for a good few moments before bursting out in laughter.

'What, may I ask, is so amusing?' Baldwin demanded coldly.

'Your face, old friend! There you were, fully anticipating a dreadful scene, when you learn that the dead man is nothing at all to do with Bishop Walter!'

The Coroner too could see the funny side, and he slapped his thigh with delight at the thought that lumbered into his mind. 'Ha! A good thing you didn't jump into action and have the man's body sent straight back to the bishop, eh? What then? He would have been alarmed to learn that you were collecting stiffs for him in case one suited him, eh?'

'Most droll,' Baldwin said coolly as he slipped a coin into the messenger's hand and gave him directions to a stable. 'Wait in the Bailiff's hall until we return,' he instructed him. 'Rest and prepare to return, but I'll have a message to take back, I expect.' Then he turned to face Simon.

'It's good news that the nephew's alive,' Simon said.

'Yes, but it does not help us. The man on the ship was killed here on shore, I am fairly certain of that. But he died *before* the fellow in the street. The ship sailed the day before our unknown died, surely. If only we knew who he was.'

'No one recognised him at the inquest,' Coroner de Welles shrugged. 'I had thought that it was because the fellow was the bishop's man, but of course if he wasn't . . .'

'Precisely.'

'Could there have been a second man watching this Frenchman?' Simon asked. 'Perhaps the Frenchman noticed him and killed him, just as we thought had happened with Stapledon's nephew?'

'Perhaps,' Baldwin muttered, unconvinced.

Coroner Richard put in shrewdly, 'There's one man who is bound to have more news on this – that wily little sodomite, Sir Andrew de Limpsfield.'

Baldwin nodded slowly. 'Yes, that would make sense. He seems to have an unhealthy interest in the town.'

'And he could well have had something to do with the capture of the cog,' Simon mused. His eyes turned to the haven and the wreckage, and then he frowned. 'What's going on there?'

Baldwin and the Coroner followed his finger and took in the sight of the boats clustering about the cog.

'Isn't that the *Saint Denis* ship which was about to sail?' Baldwin asked.

Simon's face was darkening, and now he shifted his belt about his waist and glowered as he set off towards the shoreline. 'Some bastard's been trying to capture a ship at anchor in my harbour! I'll have his balls for that!'

Pierre de Caen watched surreptitiously as Hamund sidled away, trailing after Sir Andrew and his henchmen. The abjurer looked like any other bystander in the crowd, just a scruffy churl clad in salt-stained woollen tunic with holed and patched hosen that flapped rather loosely about his thin legs, and Pierre was confident that he would be all but invisible in the throng. It would be interesting to know what Sir Andrew was doing here. How he knew that Pierre had come this way was a mystery to him. And it was a shock to learn that

Sir Andrew had spread malicious rumours about him: to think that the man could accuse him of rape! It was an outrage!

There was no time for righteous indignation just now, though. Pierre joined the tail-end of the procession, head down, and made his way up the hill to the chapel at the top. He must pay his last respects to Paul Pyckard, the man who had saved his life.

'Lads! Lads! Someone's tried to catch the *Saint Denis*!'

Pierre heard the shouts, and was in time to see the last of the men scrambling up the ropes on board the great ship in the haven. He saw blades flash in the sun, and then the spray of blood from a man's throat, and heard the angry growling from the men all about him.

'It's the men from Lyme again!'

'Pirates!'

'Murderers!

'They're taking Pyckard's ship when he's not even cold!'

The procession was diminished as men began to leave, hurrying down the hill, some men darting off down alleyways, returning a few moments later with a heavy-bladed sword, or an axe, or a long-bladed knife. Sailors were hastening along the shore towards the larger rowing boats, while others made for smaller ones, and soon there was a whole naval force making its way over the water towards the cog.

Up in front, Pierre saw Moses waver. The servant clearly wanted to go with the others, but he had a duty to see his master buried decently. Then Moses made a decision. He snapped an order to the pall-bearers and pushed the boy with the bell onwards, before running at full pelt down the hill to the shore. Pierre desperately wanted to join him. It would be so good to draw steel again, especially in the defence of the property of his brother-in-law, but he dared not. He couldn't risk exposure, not now that everyone believed he was a rapist.

Instead, he thought to take advantage of the departure of the others. It would give him time to light a candle and pray for Paul in peace.

* * *

Hamo clouted Ivo over the shoulder, and in a few moments, his horn was sounding, and with it, men began to gather. Hamo explained what he had seen, and the sailors immediately grasped the seriousness of the situation. Axes, knives, cudgels and hammers appeared, and there was a general movement down towards the water's edge.

Every boat in the area was grabbed and thrust into the river, and men tumbled into them, oars being shoved out and lustily pulled. In a few minutes there were almost fifty men in the river, pulling strongly for the cog.

On the *Saint Denis* there was a cry, then a couple of snapped orders. Hamo could hear them distinctly over the rush and hiss of water at the boat's keel. He had his axe ready, and as the boats approached the three which were already tethered to the cog, he prepared himself to leap. His boat thudded heavily into one of them, and he sprang out and into it. There was a stout line running up the side of the ship, and he grasped it a few moments after another man, who shinned up it with natural agility, as though running across flat, level ground, Hamo holding it taut as the man went. Then he shoved his axe into his belt and climbed.

'Hey, who are you!'

He heard shouting and then a scream, cut short, and then he was over the sheer and on the deck. Over to his left, he saw Dicken, who lay with his throat cut, rolling in the scuppers. Another man was sitting beside his body, his arm savagely wounded with a slash that began near his shoulder and finished a scant two inches above his elbow. He was trying to hold this immense flap of ruined flesh in place with his left hand, glaring balefully at the men before him, while beside him Cynegils stood with an expression of hatred twisting his features.

There were twenty or more of the intruders about the ship, and it looked as though they were searching for something or someone. None of them noticed Hamo or the first four others to arrive. Then a man stumbled and fell, dropping his sword with a clatter, and they were seen.

Their leader, a heavyset man in mail coat and wearing a steel cap, bellowed an order. Immediately eight of the men took up their swords and approached Hamo, one wearing a fixed, sneering grin, the others eyeing Hamo and the men with wary expressions. These changed to surprise, then alarm, as more and more men piled over the ship's side to defend it.

Another order, and now the men rushed forward to drive Hamo and the townspeople over the side, swords waving wildly as though they could intimidate free-born Dartmouth sailors. As the first reached Hamo, he swung his axe, the heavy blade shearing through the man's cheap mail at his shoulder, and burying itself in his neck and collar bone, and Hamo grabbed his wrist, snatching the sword from him as the dying man sank to his knees. Hamo placed his foot on his chest and pushed him away, keeping the sword in his left, the axe in his right.

'Remember the *Saint John*!' he bellowed, and the cry was taken up by the others as they reached the deck. '*Saint John*! *Saint John*!'

There was another order, and the enemy began to withdraw into a huddle about the mast in the face of this terrible threat. As the Dartmouth men approached, weighing their weapons in their hands, Hamo stood determinedly in front of them, his axe bloody, tapping the head against the sword's blade.

As though aware that they were to blame for the bloodshed and could expect no mercy, the attackers looked nervous. Pirates could only expect the rope. At least they were not contesting the recapture of the *Saint Denis*. Hamo was glad to see that all fight seemed to have left them.

By the time Ivo arrived, they were thoroughly chastened. The sergeant pointed at them. 'You – put down your weapons. You're all arrested for trying to take this ship.'

It was the sneering man who spoke now. 'We were only obeying our orders. We are here on the command of the King.' He was scowling, as though wondering whether to run for the ship's side and leap over. His neck was so short his chin seemed to rest on his chest, and Hamo told himself that if he fell headfirst onto one of the boats that lay bound to the cog, it could hardly make his neck shorter.

'You tried to capture a vessel here in the haven of Dartmouth. That's piracy,' Ivo said nastily. 'Drop your weapons, or we'll take them from you and you'll join your dead friends.'

'We're only here to arrest the felon. The Frenchman.'

'What Frenchman?'

There was a pause.

'He doesn't seem to be here,' the man admitted at last.

'Doesn't seem to be here?' Ivo bawled. 'And you've committed murder to learn that, eh? You're all arrested. Put up your weapons.'

There was a short discussion among the men, then the first weapon rattled to the deck. Soon there was a low pile of knives and heavy-bladed swords at their feet. As Ivo ordered them all to be collected and the men to be bound at the wrist, Hamo gazed about him and pondered on the spokesman's words. If they didn't find him here, where *was* the Frenchman? he asked himself.

Chapter Twenty-Three

Simon was glad to find a boat in short order. 'Take me to the ship,' he commanded to the old fisherman who sat on it, a bone needle in hand as he mended a net. He was short, with a round face as brown as the boat's timbers he sat on, and his beard was a thick, grizzled mass that spread from ear to ear and entirely obscured his mouth.

'What?'

'You heard me! Take me to that ship.'

The sailor looked him up and down, lingering on his smart new boots. 'Go piss yourself. I take orders from no one.'

'You'll bloody take this one, man,' Simon spat, and put his hand to his sword.

Instantly the old fisherman whipped out a short, ugly knife and flicked it up. It stayed in his hand, poised to throw. 'You try it, you'll be marked right where it hurts.'

Baldwin already had his hand near his hilt, and the old man shot him a look and said, 'I can hit you too, just as easy.'

'Perhaps. But I was reaching for this,' Baldwin said, opening the draw-strings of his purse. He withdrew a penny. 'For your trouble, Master Fisherman.'

'Ah. That's different!' the old man said and spat. 'Give it me. Jump in, then. Look lively!'

The three men stepped in, Baldwin with alacrity, Sir Richard with a stern look about him as though gauging the quality of both boat and shipmaster, and Simon with a wary expression. He had been sick too often in ships of all sizes to be enthusiastic about setting off in so small a craft.

To his surprise, the journey was easier than he had expected. The little boat's mast was soon stepped, and the old sailor fitted a sail to a rope, pulled on one end, and the little spread of canvas rose, snapped taut as the wind caught it, and in a few moments they were moving through the water, the river hissing and sucking at the boat's planking as they went. As the craft rose and fell, Simon felt none of the usual queasiness, and he could even think to himself at one point that this was quite an enjoyable method of travelling. They were at the cog in a few minutes, and it was only as they approached to within a few yards that Simon began to take notice of the men up on the *Saint Denis* deck. There was a group talking animatedly at the prow, their faces turned to the approaching boat.

Simon grabbed at the side as the boat thumped the others already tied up, and then he swallowed unhappily as he felt the boat sway and wobble. The sail was soon down, and the fisherman leaped about his craft like a great hound, completely at ease and unconcerned by any fears about his safety. Meanwhile the thing bobbed about until Simon felt like a demented frog on a lilypad that was too small for his weight. With that thought came an urgent desire to be off it, and he hurriedly rose to follow Baldwin and Sir Richard.

'Dear God in heaven, man! Stop wobbling or you'll have the boat over,' the Coroner snarled as he grabbed Simon's wrist from the safety of the next boat.

Simon felt himself half pulled, half toppling into the boat with them, and took a deep breath. At least he would be safe once he was aboard the cog, he told himself, and began to clamber into the next vessel. It was deeply unpleasant, but soon he was at the side of the cog and staring at the hull towering above him. He grabbed a rope and a few moments later he was up on her deck, blowing out his cheeks with relief as he took in the mess.

'Who is in charge here?' he called as Baldwin and Sir Richard climbed over the ship's sheer. He took in the sight of the men who had attacked this boat, then saw the bodies and his mood hardened. 'Who is responsible for this slaughter?'

'Bailiff, these men attacked the ship and we had to take her back,' Ivo said. He was standing leaning on a sword which he had liberated from the men at the mast. 'They say they were acting on the King's orders, but I can't see him here. Apparently they were looking for a Frenchman, but he's not here either. I reckon they're mazed. Either that or they're pirates and saw this as another easy target, like the *Saint John*. Bastards!'

'We're not pirates!'

'Where are the crew of the *Saint John*, then?' Simon demanded.

'The . . .'

'You are arrested for the murder of the crew of the *Saint John*, for piracy, and for breaking the King's Peace. You will be held in the town's gaol until you can be tried in the court.'

'I swear you'll see us released before that, Bailiff,' the spokesman said with a curl of his lip.

'And *I* swear you will be put on trial for your lives for all the men who've died as a result of your piracy!' Simon said with vigour. 'Ivo, bind them and take them back to shore. I want them off this ship and out of my sight!'

Sir Richard was prodding at the corpses with a toe. 'Here was I, thinking my work was all but done here, and now I've another parcel of bodies to sort through and hold inquest on. This town is good for a Coroner, Simon. You do me proud down here.'

'I am glad you are grateful,' Simon said sharply and without humour. He could see four dead from where he stood, and he didn't find the sight amusing in the slightest. 'You! Cynegils! Bring all the weapons over to the boat down there. I don't want anything left behind.'

'You can help collect the bodies too,' Sir Richard said. He was walking from one to another, and now he called Baldwin. 'Please remember how all these men are lying, Sir Baldwin. Walk about them with me. I can't get the jury to come out here to the ship, so best we witness the scene and then have the bodies carried back to shore for an inquest there, don't you agree?'

'Quite so,' Baldwin nodded.

Cynegils moved among the men, gathering all the swords and knives together, and despositing them behind the Bailiff. It took three attempts.

'Now,' Simon said. 'What is all this about?'

'They arrived here and killed poor Dicken as soon as he asked what they were doing.'

'You're sober?' Baldwin asked not unkindly.

Cynegils shuddered. 'Oh, yes.'

'What's wrong?' Simon said.

'You know some men can see what's not there if they drink too much? I knew a man saw spiders crawling up his arms. Hundreds and hundreds of pink spiders. He tried to beat them off, screaming all the while. It was horrible! I felt like that myself today, because – well, I saw a ghost. Yes, you can laugh if you want, but on my way here today I did, I saw a ghost. It was young Ed, who died on the *Saint John*. I don't care what you think, I saw him, and I'm sure he was warning me from going to sea again. He was a good lad, was Ed.'

Baldwin leaned nearer and sniffed. 'He hasn't been drinking, Simon.'

'Bailiff!' The spokesman was addressing him, but Simon ignored him. He was mulling over Cynegils's story. He *had* heard of ghosts returning to warn men of danger. Simon had more faith in the truth of the inexplicable than Baldwin did.

Reluctantly, he faced the leader of the attackers, who stood now at the sheer, wearing a sarcastic smile. 'What?'

'Oh, Master Bailiff, I would be grateful if you could speak to our master in the town. He is Sir Andrew de Limpsfield, and he is staying at—'

'I know him and where he stays,' Simon snapped. 'Do you hope he will release you? I tell you now, man, that is not going to happen. You've caused the deaths of many men here today, and you will pay the full price for that.'

'This lot? Most of the injured are Sir Andrew's men. I'd be cautious, Bailiff, lest he demands payment from *you* for the harm done to his ship's company.'

Simon swore under his breath as the man was led over the side. 'I'll speak to him, all right. And I'll learn what the murdering bastard thinks he's doing here.'

* * *

Pierre was still crouched on his knees in the wide space of the chapel as he prayed.

Not all had fled to the shore to save the cog. Some of the older men and some children were still here, and Pierre felt less conspicuous than he might. It would be hard, though, to remain here when the other men all began to return. Better by far that he should leave the place and get back to his ship, where he should be safe.

With that thought in his mind, he rose to his feet, bowing and genuflecting to the cross, and remaining there for a moment or two as he honoured his brother-in-law's memory. Then he turned sharply on his heel and made his way to the entrance.

Outside, the bright sunlight was blinding, and he stood a few moments, his cowl shielding his eyes as he took his bearings. He spotted the shabby figure of Hamund a short way down the hill, and moved off towards him.

'Did you see where he went?' Pierre asked.

'Yes. I heard what he said, too.' It was odd, now Hamund reflected on it, just how easy it had been to listen. In the past, perhaps he too would have been the same – ignoring some tattily dressed churl as though he was deaf and irrelevant. Certainly that appeared to be the attitude of Sir Andrew. Hamund was nearby, and yet the knight had spoken without any attempt to lower his voice.

'What was that?'

In answer, Hamund pointed down to the haven. 'See the ship there? That man told his men to search it from stem to stern to find "the Frenchman". He didn't care about anything else, just finding you.'

'As I thought,' Pierre said. It was a blow, but not a surprise. He had expected Sir Andrew to be looking for him, as soon as he had realised the Frenchman was here. Well, so be it. Pierre might not be able to escape on this ship now, but he would find another, with luck. A ship to take him away from his love.

'I don't think he'll like what's happened now,' Hamund continued.

'Hmm?' Pierre was deep in thoughts of his beloved as Hamund spoke, and for an instant he was disorientated.

'Haven't you seen? He's been humiliated.'

Pierre stared at him, baffled, and then out to the haven again. He could see men down the side of the ship once more, the little boats bobbing and moving as they landed in them. One was pushed too forcefully, and Pierre saw him tumble down into the boat's interior, while sailors from Dartmouth laughed at the sight. 'Those are Sir Andrew's men?'

'Yes. And now they're being sent back, from the look of them,' Hamund said with satisfaction. 'I saw them take the ship, because there was a cooper down there who started bellowing about pirates, and then it seemed as though the whole population of Dartmouth took to their boats and rescued her! Isn't it wonderful?'

Pierre licked his lips. 'If it means that Sir Andrew is to be held here without a crew, then it is, as you say, good news.'

'Of course they'll hold him here. He tried to steal a ship, didn't he? That's what all the people here will think and say, anyway. And since it is just after that other ship, the *Saint John*, was taken and her crew killed, that will be all the more reason for the men here to hate the murderers. They'll do all they can to frustrate him and help our cog to sail.'

He was right. Of course he was right. And yet, Sir Andrew was capable of inventing a lie just to have Pierre held there and prevent him from escaping to France.

It was impossible to know what to do for the best!

'Can you show me the place where he is staying?'

Simon had always liked the cooper, and trusted his judgement. Now, as the disgruntled crew of Sir Andrew's ship were led away, he beckoned Hamo to him, drawing him a short distance from the rest.

'What really happened, Hamo? Ivo is such a fool he can usually only see as far as the ground at his feet. He never confuses himself by looking up at what's happening in the world about him. You were here, you must have seen what went on.'

'I was up at the ship in my boat, gone to deliver some barrels they'd asked me to repair, and while I was there, I saw the vessels coming up fast. Well, I wasn't going to hang around to be knocked on the head. My first thought was, these must be they pirates as took the *Saint John*, so I shouted up to the deck to warn Dicken and the others, and put my head about. While I was going, I saw the ship took, so I raised the Hue and Cry ashore.'

'Is it true what he said about looking for a man?' Simon asked, indicating the leader of the men in the boats far below.

'When I got up here, that was what it looked like. Who did they mean?'

'There's a Frenchman about here, apparently. The man they all work for said he's wanted for raping a woman, but I don't believe them.'

'Why?'

Simon looked back at the burned wreck of the *Saint John*. 'Whoever heard of men committing that many murders because of a rape? If they were the ones who killed the crew of that ship, they are entirely evil, and they deserve to be gaoled until they can be hanged.'

While the two had been talking, Baldwin and Sir Richard had completed their initial view of the bodies. Now Sir Richard stood at Simon's shoulder. 'We are all done here, I think, Bailiff. Could you arrange for someone to have these bodies brought back to the market hall? We can hold the inquest there. Right – I'd best speak to that fool of a sergeant and see when he can call the juries together. I'd like to get it all finished as soon as possible, though. How about this time tomorrow? Could he cope with that, do you think?'

Simon looked at Hamo, who shrugged. 'Ivo isn't good at doing things in a hurry,' he said.

'He'd best learn, then,' Sir Richard growled. 'I'll tell him so, if he doesn't believe it. I find that men often discover new talents when I tell them to get something done!'

'And now,' Baldwin said, 'I think we should go and speak to Sir Andrew and ask what he means by committing piracy. The man is a damned fool if he thought he could get away when his hands were covered in the blood of innocents!'

As he cocked a leg over the wale, ready to descend, he glanced back at the ship and caught sight of the figure of Cynegils. He frowned. The man *was* sober, but he had spent his life pickling his brain in ale. The dead sailor, Ed, was more than likely a product of his imagination than anything else. Cynegils was simply petrified of dying at sea, as were most sailors, as few or none of them could swim.

There was nothing more to his story than that.

Simon and Baldwin arrived back at the inn with the Coroner just as Sir Andrew was about to leave.

'Good morrow, lordings,' he said courteously, bowing to them all.

Simon was impressed. The man possessed all the trappings of prosperity, and had impeccable manners. Not that wealth was any indicator of a man's personal value, for Simon tended to hold to the Devon attitude that a man's worth was more in how he behaved than in his purse. A successful thief could, after all, appear prosperous.

Baldwin's own instinctive reaction was: 'Beware! This fellow has the look of a killer.'

'Sir Andrew?' the Coroner boomed. 'Remember me? Saw you at the last Parlement at York.'

'Ah, yes, of course. You are Sir Richard de Welles? I am glad to make your acquaintance again,' Sir Andrew said with apparent pleasure. 'And your friends are?'

'I am Sir Baldwin de Furnshill, the Keeper of the King's Peace. This is my friend Simon Puttock. I am afraid I have some news for you.'

'News concerning me? Intriguing. However, I am in a hurry, gentles.'

'First: the man you had arrested and thrown into the gaol is released on my orders,' Baldwin said flatly.

'May I ask why?'

'Perhaps you could explain why he was arrested in the first place?'

'He robbed a corpse.'

'No – I think he took some money which was owed to him.'

'If you say so, my friend.' Sir Andrew's eyes glittered as though with merriment. 'I hope he doesn't try robbing a live man next time, though.'

'I am sure he will attempt no such thing. He had already confessed this offence to me, and I would not have him believe that I would betray that trust by having another arrest and punish him.'

'Hmm. You have a curious attitude for a man who is supposed to be maintaining the law. Justice demands that a man who admits to guilt should be punished.'

'Perhaps. And now I would like to ask you what *you* are doing here.'

'Me? I am here to find a rapist.'

'What is his name?'

'Pierre de Caen. He is a very dangerous man, Sir Baldwin. He raped a lady in Queen Isabella's household. Can you imagine such effrontery? To actually violate a woman in the Queen's entourage! And then he hurried here to escape the justice that pursues him. But perhaps you think that he too should go free?'

'A rapist?' Baldwin refused to rise to the bait. 'Whom did he attack?'

'I do not think that she would like her name to be bruited about. It will be enough to catch him and take him back to the household where she rests, so that she can see him punished for his crime.'

'If you wish to arrest him here, you will need to give me more evidence than the word of a lady whom you refuse to name,' Baldwin said with quiet conviction.

'I think I may arrest him whether you wish it or not,' Sir Andrew said with a broad smile.

Baldwin studied him. 'Have you heard of the attack on a ship? Just recently, a great cog, the *Saint John*, was attacked at sea and her crew taken, the vessel burned.'

'Should I know of this?'

'You would if you had seen anything of the attack.'

'But of course,' Sir Andrew said. Now he yawned and looked about him. 'This is most fascinating, Sir Baldwin, but I fear I should leave you and get on with my work. It was good of you to advise me that the scruffy fellow has been released from gaol. I shall have to keep an eye open for him.'

'I will not have you walking about the town taking whomsoever you wish,' Baldwin said. 'If you have evidence against a man, let me know, or the Bailiff here.'

'You are most kind to offer your help,' Sir Andrew said with a short bow.

'Perhaps you would like to explain what you were doing, seeking the Frenchman on the *Saint Denis* in the haven?' Baldwin continued.

'I do not think I need trouble you with this matter any further,' Sir Andrew smiled.

'Then your men shall remain in the gaol until you decide to explain,' Baldwin said blandly, picking his tone of voice carefully. There was no threat in it, only a flat certainty.

'What men, Sir Knight?'

'Those whom you sent to take the cog this day. They are all in custody and shall remain there until I hear a satisfactory explanation of their behaviour.'

Sir Andrew's manner stiffened noticeably. 'Those men are mine. I wish them released immediately.'

'And *I* wish to know what they were doing on the *Saint Denis*.'

'That is my business, not yours,' Sir Andrew said, with steel in his tone.

'You have no authority in this town.'

'Do I not?' Sir Andrew considered Baldwin for a long moment, and then he pulled a parchment from inside his cote-hardie. He opened it and passed it to the knight. 'Here is my authority, Keeper. Do you agree I have the power to stop ships and arrest any whom I suspect?'

Baldwin read with a frown, holding the writing near to his nose and up to the light as he made sense of it. 'It would seem so.'

'Then you will please leave me alone while I continue to carry out the wishes of our King?'

'I will be happy to leave you alone. In the meantime, your men caused an affray on the cog in this haven. This order does not exempt your men from penalty of law when they break the King's Peace here in Dartmouth. They will be held until I deem that they pose no more threat to the peace of this town.'

'You will release them now!' Sir Andrew snarled. He took a half-step forward as though to attack Baldwin, but when the older knight stood his ground, he hissed: 'This will be brought to the attention of Lord Hugh Despenser! I shall personally demand your punishment, Keeper.'

Baldwin shrugged, but felt anger rising in his breast. Here he was, despite all his best intentions, thrown headlong into a dispute with a man who was a loyal supporter of Despenser.

'Rural knights like you are more danger to the work of the realm than all the outlaws in the land,' Sir Andrew said with cold certainty. 'We try to keep the country working, and it is men like you – old men – who prevent us. England is in danger, and you would have us ignore it because it upsets your sensibilities.'

'What is the danger from a rapist?' Simon interrupted sneeringly. 'There is more danger from arrogant fools who throw whole towns into disarray by attacking the ancient rights and privileges. Trying to take a British ship by force was lunacy! You killed one man and wounded several more – to catch a rapist, you say? Well, *I* say you are unconvincing, sir. And until I hear the truth, I will certainly not sanction the release of any of your men.'

'That parchment allows me to demand—'

'You can demand all you want,' Baldwin said firmly. 'I would never willingly thwart the King's wishes, but my duty is to the King's Peace, and I will *not* see you pointlessly discard all semblance of peace here without an explanation.'

'I, Sir Richard de Welles, Coroner, witness these two statements and I have to say, Sir Andrew, that I find their arguments convincing. If you cannot bring forth evidence that compels them to release your men, why the hell should they? At present I have six or more bodies being brought ashore as a result of your escapade on the cog today. These same men, I assume, took the *Saint John* and killed all the crew. Why, in God's holy name, do you expect these honourable officers to allow those same men to be free to attack more shipping?'

Sir Andrew drew his lips up into a dry smile. He glanced from one to another, and then said, 'Gentlemen, if you would care to propose a house where we can speak without being overheard, I think I can explain this story to you all.'

Chapter Twenty-Four

Pierre was there just as the men walked from the inn, and he quickly darted into a doorway, shoving Hamund before him.

'What d'you—'

'Shut up!' Pierre snarled, peeping around the wall and watching as the four men, followed by two of Sir Andrew's men-at-arms, walked briskly up the road towards the paver's road works. They strode on until they came to a smaller private house, where Simon opened the door for Sir Andrew, and waved his guests inside.

'Why are they there?' Hamund wondered.

'They want to talk in secret, without interruptions and spies listening,' Pierre said. He gnawed at his inner cheek. The strain was beginning to tell on him. In the past he had always been cool and comfortable even in battle, but now he was prey to doubts. He knew that he must be doing the right thing in setting off for France again, but he wondered now whether he was really helping *her* or not. The idea that his action could lead to more distress was appalling, but his only alternative was to kill Sir Andrew. Surely he must kill or be killed.

'What can they talk about that's so important?' Hamund wanted to know.

Pierre could not answer that. He was too anxious already. If these men decided to pool their resources, it would be impossible to escape. They could stop the ship from sailing until all the crew had been questioned and tested, they could hold all vessels in the haven. Perhaps he could persuade Gil to collect him farther down the coast? Pierre could make his way to another town, or maybe just a small fishing village, and take a boat out to meet Gil from there? But no.

What would Gil want with that? It would be a nuisance, and even if his old master had wanted him to help Pierre, now Paul Pyckard was dead, there was little incentive for him to ensure that Pierre was safe. Better for him if he never saw Pierre again.

'Master, don't be downhearted,' Hamund said. 'Look, we'll soon be on the ship again, and then we can sail for France and start afresh like you said.'

'I hope so, friend. I sincerely hope so,' Pierre said.

'What was it, Baldwin?' Simon asked in an undertone as soon as he had closed the door. Sir Andrew was inside with his two men, and Simon warily observed them as he thrust the bar home to stop intrusion.

'A written authority from Lord Despenser, giving him powers of arrest and judgment, in the name of the King,' Baldwin said equally quietly. His voice was cool, betraying none of the rage he felt at his treatment by that arrogant puppy.

'What's he got that for?' the Coroner mused less quietly. 'It's more than I have. It's more than *you* have as Keeper.'

'I was sent here to keep an eye on a man who was supposed to have offended some lady in the Queen's entourage,' Baldwin said. 'I think that this Andrew is here for the same reason. He has been sent here to try to capture that man.'

'But Bishop Walter said . . .' Simon began.

'Mistakes have been made before now,' Baldwin reminded him.

'The bishop's nephew is home and safe.'

'So who is the man who was killed?' Coroner Richard wondered. 'The man we thought was the victim has reappeared safely.'

'We still have two dead men – Danny and this fellow we haven't identified yet,' Baldwin said. 'Let alone the eleven others from the *Saint John*.'

'You still seek to blame me for that?' Sir Andrew asked.

Baldwin crossed the room to stand before him, his arms folded. 'You have the ship, you have the men. Who else would have wanted to stop a ship that might have harboured a man whom you hate? You took the vessel, but the crew was determined to defend her to the last, perhaps, and you were forced to kill them all. It would be understandable when a man with a royal warrant like yours felt that he had an urgent mission to fulfil.'

'You think I would forget all reason and attack without a qualm?'

'You did today,' Simon reminded him.

'I had good information that the man was aboard her,' Sir Andrew said with an unpleasant glint in his eye. 'I paid good money for that information.'

'Information can be sold in good faith and still be wrong,' Simon suggested. 'Much of the crew was ashore to witness the funeral of their master.'

'It can also be sold knowing it is false,' Sir Andrew said uncompromisingly.

'What do you want from us?' Baldwin asked.

'The tale I had told of this man . . . it is not the entire truth.'

'We had guessed that,' Simon said.

'He is French,' Sir Andrew said. 'And just now, perhaps you know that relations between the French king and our own sit upon a knife's edge. The French demand that King Edward go to them to swear fealty for the lands he still possesses there; the King fears for his life, if he were to go. It is a terrible situation. And in the meantime there is a great household in the heart of the nation, which is full of scheming Frenchmen. One of them has disappeared, and he had hurried down this way, we believe.'

'What of it?' Baldwin demanded. 'He is of the Queen's household, you say? He should have safe passage, surely?'

'The Queen is corresponding with her brother in France without the King's permission. He has no idea what she is writing, just as we are slipping towards war in Gascony once more. No king could tolerate that! The dangers – well, they cannot be exaggerated. There is a lot of information that could be passed to the French that might be deleterious to our prospects in Gascony.'

'It may also be that there are no letters,' Baldwin said.

'There are. We know that.'

'Even if there are, you hurried here in your great ship in order to catch the Frenchman, not knowing whether he was here or no. And then you took the cog *Saint John* and slaughtered all the men aboard her, even though you had no proof that he was on her?'

'I had good intelligence from some . . .'

'Like your damned intelligence today?' Baldwin snapped. 'You murdered eleven men on board the *Saint John* because of a man who may have lied to you for money?'

'If you had allowed me to finish my sentence, Sir Baldwin, I was about to say that I had good intelligence that he was here, so I hurried here to the town. I never said I had attacked that ship. I suggest you be careful about the allegations you level against me.'

There was a firmness in his tone and a set to his shoulders that showed the suggestion had annoyed him, and perhaps even worried him slightly. Baldwin considered him for a few moments, assessing the danger this fair-haired man posed.

Meanwhile, Simon was frowning. 'What would bring him here, though? His path would have been safer, were he to go to London or some other port, surely. What would make him come here?'

'His brother-in-law,' Sir Andrew said, and now his face grew black with disappointment and frustration. 'I had hoped to catch them both together, but when I got here, I learned that his brother-in-law was dead.'

'Pyckard?' Baldwin asked.

'Yes. He married Amandine de Caen, the sister to Pierre de Caen. It is him I seek. If we catch him, we may well stop a dangerous spy from communicating secrets to the French king.'

'And you will be richly rewarded, no doubt,' Baldwin said.

Coroner Richard shook his head. 'Don't you have enough money already?'

'Can a man ever have enough?' Sir Andrew asked with a cynical smile.

'You have a rich craft there,' Simon pointed out. 'What is she, sixty? Eighty tuns?'

'The *Gudyer*? She's not mine,' Sir Andrew shrugged. 'She is owned by my lord Despenser. He told me to take her, in order to reach here all the faster.'

Baldwin's eyes narrowed. 'Is that the ship he used when he was in exile?'

There was a sudden silence in the room as all the men considered his words. The henchmen behind Sir Andrew caught the atmosphere belatedly, and one stepped forward, his hand on his sword-hilt. Sir Andrew blandly raised a hand without looking at him, and the man let his hand slowly fall away to rest on his belt buckle as though prepared to grab for steel at the earliest opportunity.

'I wouldn't know whether it was the same ship, Sir Baldwin. I had no part in that adventure.'

'Lord Despenser lived as a sea-wolf, didn't he, while he was exiled,' Baldwin said quietly. 'He turned pirate, and robbed English and French shipping at will.'

'Do you say so? How interesting.'

Baldwin saw the sly grin return to the other's face and knew that he should be silent if he wished to be safe. The Lord Despenser was a dangerous enemy, and now here was Baldwin, making allegations of a serious nature in front of one of the Despensers' own household, and yet he could not help himself. The connection was too clear and apparent.

'It is curious, is it not, that only a short while after the *Saint John* was attacked and her crew murdered, you should appear in your nice ship with a crew that has been trained in capturing other vessels.'

'That is an extremely serious accusation – and naturally I deny it utterly,' Sir Andrew said. 'And I think that bearing in mind the importance of catching this mad Frenchman, you would be better served to help me discover where he is now.'

'How do you know he was not on the ship?' Coroner Richard grated.

'Because, my dear Coroner, the man was here in the town after the *Saint John* sailed, was he not? The man I held in gaol, who stole from the body in the road, was watching him.'

Baldwin nodded. 'And the man who was dead in the road – I suppose you are not missing a spy in the town, are you?'

Sir Andrew smiled and looked away. 'I do not suppose a simple denial would suffice, would it? But no, I had no one here.'

'You expect us to believe that?' Simon snarled.

'I do not care whether you do or not. I have no one here. Someone else may seek the same man, though, and may have been killed.'

'You mean another man from Despenser?' Coroner Richard rumbled.

'It is possible.'

'You will come with me now, then. I don't like the idea of a man being buried unnamed when someone is perfectly capable of giving his details to the Coroner. If he is from your master, you may recognise him.'

'When I have time,' Sir Andrew said.

'I think you have time right now. Come.'

Law was sitting at the far end of the hole, his face carefully averted, when Alred returned with a pie.

'Oh, in God's name, boy, will you not forgive him?'

'Leave it, Al,' Bill said.

'Why should I leave it? The longer you two sit there sulking, the longer it'll take to get the hole fixed, and that means the longer I'm losing money!' Alred hissed sharply. 'Christ's blood, how can I get it into your thick skulls that this is important? We're only being paid for the whole job, so the longer we take, the—'

'The less we can earn elsewhere,' said Bill. 'I know.'

'Then act like you do! Talk to him! I've done all I can,' Alred said. 'Look, Law, why won't you just come here and shake his hand and make things good again? Eh? There's no point sitting there like a . . .'

'Leave me alone. If you want to keep in with a felon who likes to punch people, you do that. I don't see I need to talk to him, though.'

'Oh, in God's name, I give up!' Alred said, throwing his hands in the air with despair. 'What is the point of trying to keep the peace when you two just want to bicker. Well, all I can say is, I don't have to listen to you both. You get on with this hole while I go and speak to the town's reeve to see about our pay. Not that he'll give us anything if he's any sense, looking at you both. Still, we've nothing left. You understand? We've no more money, and if we want to get some, we'll need to get moving. Yes?'

'All right, Al,' Bill said. He took up the pick as Alred made his way down the road, still muttering bitterly to himself as he went.

Bill started scraping away at the surface in a desultory attempt to look busy, but as he worked, he could not help but glance at Law. That was fine, until he caught sight of Law shooting a look at him too, and the pair instantly turned away from each other and carried on as though nothing had happened.

The shadows were moving and growing longer by the time that Bill finally let his pick rest against the side of the hole. He stood with his head still bent. 'Law, I am sorry. I shouldn't have hit you, all right?'

There was no response, but Bill could tell from the fact that there was no sound of shovelling sand that Law was listening.

'When I was telling you about what happened to me, I lied, you see. That's why I was so upset.'

'What do you mean?'

'Look, she was the fuller's daughter in my home town. I was there one afternoon after harvest, and I saw her in the river. God, I can see her now . . . There are some women, Law, who glow, you know? They are so lovely that they're just like a candle-flame to a moth – a man can't help but go and be scorched. Well, I saw her that day, and the sight of her in her shirt at the river just . . . *I had to have her*. I suppose I'd had a bellyful of ale, and seeing her there was just the last . . . No, that's not it. I'd always wanted her, I think.'

'So you *did* rape her?' Law said breathlessly.

'Dear God, yes,' Bill whispered. 'I thought I loved her, and I thought that if she was taken by me, she'd agree to marry me. That was all I wanted, really. She had a boy she liked, one of the cottars from the vill, but that didn't worry me. I thought she'd accept me rather than go to another man as damaged goods. So I went to her and had her there on the river bank. And she didn't want me, Law. Didn't want me at all. I had to silence her screams and pleading. Kept telling her I loved her, and not to worry. Christ's bones! I told her that!

'The rest of the day went by in a blur. It wasn't until next morning I remembered what I'd done, and I had a qualm, thinking she might denounce me and accuse me of rape, but then I reckoned if she did, it wouldn't matter. I'd say she'd asked for it. Say I'd wed her. Damn, if she refused me, I'd say she'd always flaunted herself before me, and she'd been experienced. No, I wouldn't accept all the blame. You see, I was feeling guilty, and the guilt made me want to put the blame somewhere else. Anywhere else. If there was no one else I could blame, I'd blame her. It's what men do, Law, when they're weak and stupid. Christ knows, I was both.'

'What did she do, then? Accuse you?'

'I wish she had. You don't know how often I've prayed that she had. But she didn't, no,' Bill sighed. He slumped down to sit on the road's edge. 'No, instead she stayed there by the river that evening. Some time that night she took her little knife and opened both her wrists. I've seen some women and men commit self-murder, you know, and always they try to kill themselves several times.' He held up his wrists. 'Both wrists will have parallel lines of cuts from slashes, as though they need to test their resolve before they can cut deep enough. Not her. She cut both wrists to the bone. She must have died quite quickly. God, I hope so.'

'So you weren't found?'

Bill swallowed. 'Someone had seen her with her lover, Law. It wasn't me, I swear, but the lad was accused of raping her. She loved him, and I think he loved her. If he'd taken her, she'd not have argued. Instead, *I* took her and she killed herself. I might as well have killed her with my own knife.'

'What happened to him?'

'He was a poor cottar. What could he do? He ran to the church and claimed sanctuary, and when the Coroner arrived he abjured the realm. Me? I stayed there like an innocent, until sour self-loathing forced me to leave. I've never been back again.

'So when you hear someone say that a man is plainly innocent or guilty, Law, you remember that. The man here – *me* – is guilty. The man who bolted and I hope who's alive now in a better land, he was innocent. But he's the one who could have been hanged, because of the way he had been seen with the girl. And I was safe.'

'Bill, I'm sorry. I didn't know, though, did I?'

'No. You couldn't have known,' Bill agreed. And then he put his hands to his face and sat very still until the need to sob had subsided.

Law wanted to go to him and show him some compassion, but Law was only half Bill's age, if that. He didn't know how to help. Instead he took the next best alternative to a show of sympathy, and carefully looked everywhere but at his friend.

Then: 'Sweet Jesus, Bill! Look over there!' he hissed.

Chapter Twenty-Five

'Come, we should return to the ship, or at the least find Gil and he'll tell us when we can,' Pierre said.

There was nothing to be learned from the house. The two had loitered cautiously outside, but from the street there was nothing to be heard, and when they tried to wander down the alley at the side, there was no access to the house from there either, or at least, none that appeared to help them.

He led the way back up the street, and the two of them were in time to see the Coroner and Sir Andrew leave Simon's house and make their way along the street down towards the mill.

'Should we follow them?' Hamund asked as Pierre stopped and stared after them.

It was tempting; in God's name, it was tempting. To see Sir Andrew swaggering happily away in the company of the Coroner – it was *intolerable*! The man deserved to have his mouth silenced for ever for what he had said about Pierre, dishonouring him just when he was trying to re-establish some modicum of honour. He wanted to draw steel and stab the liar and traitor in the back for what he had done.

But if he did, it would cost him his life, and it would mean the messages must become known, and that must itself harm his lady. Dear God, what a man must do to remain loyal!

He said quietly, swallowing his pride, 'For what purpose? If we go across that bridge and they hear us, they may see us. You have been behind that man almost half day, and if he sees me, he will remember me, I am sure. No, I think we should forget them and get back to safety. At least I achieved what I needed to this day: I paid my respects to Master Pyckard.'

'I wonder where Gil will be now?'

'In the tavern if he is not already at the ship,' Pierre guessed. He stared over towards the haven. 'I only hope he hasn't decided to leave without us.'

'He can't without more sailors,' Hamund said with confidence he didn't feel. 'He needs us.'

Pierre did not respond to that. So far as he was concerned, the shipmaster would be happy to leave without embarrassing supercargo like them, and now that the reason for Pierre's berth had been removed, because surely it was only Pyckard's insistence which had persuaded Gil to take him in the first place, Pierre was uncertain of his reception at the ship.

He led the way hurriedly after Sir Andrew as soon as he and the Coroner had disappeared at the bottom of the hill and had started to cross the mill's dam. From here he could see the ship still sitting out in the haven, which was some relief, but he and Hamund still had to find a means of reaching it, and although he could see several small boats at the shore, he could not simply take one. That would bring yet more attention to him, and it was bad enough, so he felt, to be walking about in broad daylight like this. No, better by far that he should find a man who would be prepared to row them to the cog and then . . .

His ruminations were interrupted by a cheery call at his side. When he looked down at the scruffy man there, the first thing that caught his notice was the short dagger poised near his belly.

'Now, Sir Whoever you are, me and my friend here would appreciate a few moments of your time.'

Pierre was within a twitch of pulling his sword from its scabbard, but as he stood momentarily stunned, he was astonished to see the blade taken away and sheathed.

'We saved you once, friend. Now we'd like to know whether we were right to do so.'

Master Hawley had watched as the men from the *Gudyer* were brought back slowly in the boats, their guards watching over them all the way. When they reached the shore, he went down and eyed them suspiciously as they were pushed from the boats. Several stumbled, three fell, one at his feet, and when the man was grabbed by the arm and pulled up, there was a blotch of blood on the ground where stones had mashed his nose and lips. He still looked dazed as he was taken, lurching away.

Hawley felt no sympathy for them. Why should he? The fools had tried to overrun a private ship. Christ's bones, if he'd been on the *Saint Denis* he'd have had every one of the bastards strung up from his mainmast as soon as blink. They were filth! Felons every one of them, they deserved to be killed for trying to steal a ship.

Cynric was with him, and as his master stood staring down at the blood, Cynric tentatively said, 'What do you think about Strete?'

'You saw him in the tavern, didn't you? I don't think you're a liar, Cyn. You've been with me as long as I can remember. No, it was him who lied. In truth, if he hasn't lost me money, it doesn't matter if he plays at gaming. What he does with his own cash is his concern. It's only if he takes mine that I worry. And if you're right and he is a laughing stock for his losses, I don't see how he can afford to pay his debts on his own. So either he took my money and hid the theft, or . . .'

'He replaced it.'

'How could he do that?' Hawley took his mind back to the hall. In there was his sideboard, with a profusion of plate on display. 'No, if he'd stolen from me and pawned a plate or two, I'd notice. It can't be that. How else could he hope to gain money, though?'

Cynric grunted. He wasn't a great creative thinker. That sort of business he left to Hawley himself.

And with good reason. Hawley's wrinkled brow suddenly cleared. 'The bastard could have been telling someone else about the business. Except who would pay for untested information? That would be mad. I can't see Kena or Beauley coughing up. Pyckard would have done if it was juicy enough, but what information could Strete have sold him about me? There's nothing that would have interested the old goat.'

While he considered the matter further, he sent Cynric to see whether anything was known of the reason for the attack on the cog.

'They came from the new ship up there, the *Gudyer*,' his man said when he'd asked on Hawley's behalf.

'Really? What would they be doing, trying to steal a ship like this in harbour?'

'They said they were seeking this Frenchman who had raped a kinswoman of the Queen. He wasn't there, though. They've been pulled off the ship with their tails between their legs.'

Hawley nodded absently, but his eyes were thoughtful. 'Could they have taken the *Saint John*, do you think?'

'There's enough of them, that's certain. But who'd know?'

'Yeah,' Hawley murmured. It was an interesting idea, though. 'So they say that they're here for the Frenchie. If he'd raped someone, though . . . they sent a ship that size just for one man?'

Cynric pulled a face and shrugged. 'Hardly likely.'

'No, not at all. Unless he'd raped the Queen herself.' His face darkened and he stood silent for a long moment.

'You don't think he'd dare do that, master?'

Hawley made an attempt to shake his head, but could not quite manage it convincingly. 'Anything is possible, but surely the Queen would have enough men-at-arms about her at all times to protect her from that.'

'If she wanted to be.'

'You can't believe that the Queen would succumb to lusts like some draggle-tail from Sutton harbour,' Hawley scoffed, but the thought did linger. A man who had dared to bed the Queen, willingly or no, was someone to be respected. 'No, that's hardly likely. It must be something else.'

'If he was from her household,' Cynric said slowly, 'he could have tried to take one of her ladies-in-waiting?'

'Shit! Yes, that's more like it! And when his offence became known, this knight Andrew was sent to cut his balls off. That makes more sense.' He shook his head. 'Or it's nothing to do with rape and we're completely wrong. Maybe he's a spy? Who cares? There is probably money on his head. Right! You make sure that all the fellows under our control are aware: if they see this fellow, or any other man who looks like a Frenchie, I want to know. If they can, they should take him and bring him to me. Clear?'

'Sir.'

As Cynric trotted off to do his bidding, John Hawley made his way back to his hall. The Frenchman, the great ship in the haven and the curious matter of Strete's money exercised his mind all the way up the hill to his front door, and when he reached it, he stood a moment, his hand on the latch, head to one side, considering.

'What could he have sold about me?' he wondered again. Or was it information about *someone else* that his clerk had been selling?

'He gamed at the tavern,' he whispered. 'The sailors all drink there.'

And he had a sudden intuition. He knew what information Pyckard would pay for, and suddenly he felt sick to think of what his man must have done.

It was quiet in the storeroom, and Pierre stood in the darkness, from where he could keep an eye on the doorway. 'What do you want with me?'

'Just to know that you shouldn't be in gaol and we sprang you to safety would be good,' Bill said. 'Ach, I'm not used to this shite. Where's Alred when you need him, eh, Law?'

'Law? It is a curious name.'

'It's just short for Lawrence.'

Pierre inclined his head. 'You English – you have to give a nickname to all, do you not? What is wrong with your full name, my friend? Surely it would be easier for all if you stuck to that?'

'I like it shorter.'

Hamund was frowning. 'Look, we have to get off to the ship, right? If they sail without us, we're dead.'

'If you had been on Pyckard's boat today you'd be dead. Come to that, if you were on his last ship, you would be too,' Bill said. 'Looks like you're a very lucky fellow.'

Pierre set his jaw, but his reserves were beginning to fail him. 'I was not here to catch the earlier ship,' he said. 'I only arrived in this town after the ship had sailed.'

'Still makes you pretty fortunate, though,' Bill said.

'Yeah, I'd say he was lucky,' Law said. 'Look at him! Rich clothes, fine sword . . . and he's still alive and breathing.'

'You think this is lucky? Being held here by two fools who think they can guess my style of life just by looking at my clothing?'

'You reckon you're so high above us, that it?' Law spat.

'Who broke your nose?' Pierre asked. 'Perhaps I should treat with him instead of you, heh?'

'You prefer we should call the Watch to talk to you?' Bill threatened.

'You look at me,' Pierre said, his frustration overwhelming his limited patience. 'You see a knight, yes? A noble knight, with power and men at his command? But all I am is a man like you, boy. Just like you. Except I have no household to serve, as my mistress cannot allow me to return to her. My friends have deserted me, except for one down here in this town, and he is dead. I had a passage on a ship, that one out there, but you are delaying me so I may miss her. If I do not miss her, I may be captured here by an enemy who wished to harm my lady, and he will torture me to get any information he can! You call me lucky? I am without friends, without hope, in a foreign land where all seek to kill me. This is lucky? I wish you much luck of the same sort!'

Bill sucked at his tooth. There was a hole in it that hurt like the devil every so often, and especially when cold air got to it. He eyed the Frenchman speculatively. 'How do we know you're not lying to us?'

'All this talk about me raping a woman – it is a lie! I have not molested a woman in my life. And as for a noblewoman – I could not. I fell in love with a lady, it is true, and I now travel to France to return to my home because I could not touch her. That is all.'

'What if you did rape some woman?' Law said with suspicion unabated. He wasn't at all sure about this foreigner.

'Oh, if you believe I did, then call the Watch and have done with me. But let my companion here go to the ship. He is paying for his crime already.' He slumped down by the wall. After losing woman, master and ship, there was nothing else for him. There was an English expression – 'fed up'. Well, he was *fed up* with this land, its people, and with life on the run.

'Law, trust me on this,' Bill said at last. 'All right, friend. I reckon you deserve a little better fortune. How about we help you down to the shore and take you to the ship. What then?'

'You'd let him go?'

Pierre ignored the lad's strangled cry. 'You mean this? If you take me to the ship, I swear I will—'

'No – on second thoughts, no promises,' Bill winced. 'Let's just say I'll feel better in myself if I don't judge another man's guilt or innocence. It'd make me feel I've done something useful with my life. All right?'

In the church the body of the dead man from the roadway was still lying next to the coffin of Paul Pyckard. Danny had been buried as soon as the inquest was done with him.

In stark contrast to the fresh-planed boards of the coffin for the merchant, the unknown man's corpse was loosely wrapped in a linen winding sheet, through which noisome fluids leaked. The priest was already setting fresh herbs about it to conceal the worst of the odours before it was installed in its own coffin.

'Oh, good, Coroner. I was planning to get this body put away this afternoon. We heard it wasn't the man Sir Baldwin thought, so my fossor's been over the cemetery, and he should have a grave ready. It's a shame, I know, to set a man down in an unmarked grave, but there are times when you can do no more, eh?'

'And I am glad to say that there are times when you *can* do more, eh, Sir Andrew?' the Coroner boomed as he nudged the knight at his side.

'Quite,' Sir Andrew said. He sniffed, then motioned to one of his men, who began to unwrap the head of the corpse. 'Ah, yes. I know him.'

'Who is he?'

'His name is Guy de Bouville. He was a man-at-arms in the service of my lord Despenser. I knew him quite well.' Sir Andrew frowned. 'He was with one of my lord Despenser's bailiffs, a man called Flok. A bookish, studious knight, he was competent to help with accounts and affairs of law, so he was very useful to my lord. What he was doing here, I do not know. He ought to be up north of the moors, I believe.'

'Well, I am glad. So you are a friend of his?' the priest asked.

'No. I knew him.'

Coroner Richard smiled broadly, his beard moving alarmingly. 'And the good knight here who "knew him" quite well will be delighted to pay for the burial of the body, I am sure. Otherwise Lord Despenser may wish to learn why it was that one of his men-at-arms was not properly treated after death when one of his own servants was here in the area and perfectly ready to do so. Isn't that so, Sir Andrew?'

'I have better things to be doing with my time, you understand?' Sir Andrew said stiffly as he pulled some coins from his purse.

'So have I, Sir Andrew. Just now I think I ought to be searching for the bodies from that cog, don't you?'

'They were all killed far from shore, Coroner. You have no authority in that, do you?'

'Strange how many people keep saying that to me. Reminds me of a joke I once heard. About a terrible story being told in a church in a sermon, and the whole congregation listening burst into weeping and lamentations. All that sort of nonsense. But there was one fellow who was untouched, and the priest turned to him, and said, "Aren't you affected by this terrible tale of woe?" and the churl responded, "Bless you, Father, no." "And why not?" the priest thundered. "Well, sir, I'm not from this parish," the man replied. As though it matters whether you're from the same parish or not to be saddened by a story of despair and misery.'

'What does that have to do with all this?' Sir Andrew asked.

'I am not from this parish either, you see. I grow anxious when I learn that a ship's complement is taken and slaughtered, whether it's legally my jurisdiction or not.' The Coroner smiled, his teeth showing brightly amongst the thatch of his beard. And he leaned towards Sir Andrew slightly as he added, 'In fact, Sir Andrew, I can grow more than simply anxious, I can grow downright choleric. And when I tend to hot, dry humours like that, I don't give up. Not when threatened, not even when ordered.'

'You would do well to remember that my master is Lord Hugh Despenser,' Sir Andrew hissed. 'He would not like to hear that a rural knight has taken it into his head to command one of his own knights, let alone that this knight dared to threaten a man of his household.'

Sir Richard looked down at that, suitably chastened. Or so Sir Andrew thought at first. When he looked up again and met Sir Andrew's gaze, there was no fear. His eyes were fixed and unwavering, unblinking in their conviction. 'I say to you, Sir Andrew, that I am a King's Officer and cannot be made to turn aside because of your threats. I believe that there has been evil work here in this town and on the seas about it, and I will find the men guilty and bring them to justice. If you do not like my statement, so much the worse for you. But be you the Despenser's man or the devil himself's, I care not a whit. I serve the King. You would do well to remember that.'

'Oh, I shall, Sir Richard,' Sir Andrew said smoothly. 'I promise you I shall not forget that in a hurry.'

Chapter Twenty-Six

Bill peeped around the wall and stared cautiously down the lane towards the haven. In the distance he could still see the cog at anchor, but there was no sign of anyone else. He beckoned with his hand urgently, and the other three slipped down the cobbles towards him.

He had already been to three taverns trying to find the man whom Pierre called Gilbert, hoping that the seaman would be drinking his dead master's health still, but there was no sign of him. Pierre prayed that Gil was on the ship already, and hadn't disappeared somewhere else.

'There's no one about,' Bill said with a frown. 'I suppose many must be in the gaol watching the captured sailors, while others are in the taverns praising their courage in catching such a prize. Others will still be at Pyckard's wake. So, maybe you'll find it easier than you thought to get away.'

'I am very grateful to you, my friend,' Pierre said earnestly. 'I am sorry that you have been given so much trouble at my account.'

'Just make sure you escape and that'll be enough for me,' Bill said gruffly.

'I will do my best,' Pierre smiled, but not without anxiety. He kept throwing looks at the ship, hoping that there was not a trap there. It would be all too easy for a man to sit up there and wait for him. And then they were moving down the hill as swiftly as they may. There was a short interlude when Bill ran into a low shaft that projected from a wall, and had to stop, hugging his shin in silent anguish, but then they were off again, and soon they were at the end of the alley. From here Bill could glance in both directions up and down Lower Street, and he saw nothing to give him concern. There was no one about.

'Come with me,' he said, and set off for the shore. His plan was to borrow a boat, row the two out to the ship, and then bring the boat back. No one would be harmed by the loan, and hopefully it would not be noticed as missing. Down on the shingle they went, and soon selected a fair-sized craft. Law helped Bill to turn the thing right way up, and then they all carried it to the water. Here they put it in, and all clambered in, only to realise that it was resting on the stones with all their weight inside. Grumbling, Bill and Law climbed out again, and this time they pushed the little vessel into deeper water, standing up to their shins, and tried to climb in again. Law hopped up and tumbled in headfirst, and Pierre had a job turning him upright again. Bill attempted a more elegant entry, but almost caused the boat to tip over. At last he was in, and then, as the boat began to drift, the men smiled at each other for a moment before their smiles froze. There were no oars.

Swearing low and mean, Bill jumped back into the water. It was almost to his armpits now, and he grabbed the painter and pulled the thing back towards the shingle. When he was far enough in, Law jumped out with a great splash and missed his footing, disappearing from view. He bobbed back up, spluttering, and hastily made his way to dry land, drenched and shivering. Soon he was back with two large oars, and at last the four were on their way to the ship.

It was harder than Law had realised to steer a little vessel like this one. He had thought the things must be easy, because no sailors ever had trouble, and it wasn't as though sailors were particularly bright, by and large. For some reason, though, as Bill pulled his oar, the boat bobbed and dodged, and then seemed to go its own way.

'There is a small group of men at the shore watching us,' Pierre said with restrained anxiety. They were pointing at the four, and one man was all but hopping from foot to foot. 'I think one is the man who owns this boat.'

'What do you expect us to do about it?' Bill panted.

Gradually the thing began to come under control. It was

much like a small pony in many ways. It would go its own way, but after having its head a while, it would obey them. Slowly but surely they were approaching the great *Saint Denis*, and at last an enormous shadow fell over them all, and they were in the lee of the huge hull.

Pierre grabbed at the rope ladder, clambering up the side of the ship. At the top he risked a quick glance all about him in case of ambush, but there was nothing he could see that indicated danger. That in itself should have been warning enough.

He swung himself over the sheerstrake and landed inelegantly on the deck, his ankle twisting slightly, and his attention was distracted as Hamund pulled himself over and sprawled at his feet. The Frenchman reached down and took his wrist, helping him up.

'Ah, ain't that sweet?'

Pierre turned. Three sailors he didn't recognise were standing at either side of the mast. Thoughts of springing to the ladder and escaping were quashed as he saw the rowing boat already returning to the shore. He spun back, reaching for his sword, determined to sell his life as hard as he may, but as he moved he heard Hamund shriek, and grew aware of more men rushing towards him from his left. He pulled his sword free, but as he did so, a rope whipped about his legs, weighted with lead that whirled and cracked into his shin. It was tugged, and even as he tried to maintain his balance, he felt himself topple, and must throw his arms out to break his fall.

A man stepped on his sword; he saw Hamund try to pull the leg away, but Hamund was knocked aside with contemptuous ease, his face running with blood. Then Pierre rolled to his back, reaching for the dagger at his belt, even as he was hauled along the deck by main force, and another fellow gripped his wrist firmly.

'Evening, Frenchie!' he heard, and then a cudgel slammed into his head and Pierre felt the decking open up and swallow him into a pitch blackness.

Strete was already at the tavern at the time when Hamund and Pierre were captured. The little chamber behind the main hall was small and noisome, but the fug of sweat, damp wool and sour ale was to him the very epitome of hope and possible fortune.

'You want more?' the dealer said. He held up the knuckles with a questioning eyebrow.

'No, no. I'm only here to repay my debts,' Strete said with a comfortable smile.

He could feel nothing but satisfaction as he took out his new brown purse and withdrew a handful of coins. The eyes of the sailors in the room were avariciously fixed on his hand. They knew how much strong ale that handful of coins represented, and he could almost hear their minds considering his good luck in possessing so much.

As they should. These men were really contemptible. They thought they were so clever because they could sail, and they thought that the fact that they could brawl and lift heavy weights made them better than a man like him. Well, they were mad if they believed that. They called him 'only a pissy clerk'. He'd heard them! Yes, he'd heard them. When he was unlucky and lost a little money, they were all scathing about him, as though the fact that a man made a small loss once in a while made him inferior. But at least he knew that soon his luck must change, while they only gambled because they thought they must always win. More fool them!

'It's enough?'

'Yes, that covers your debt,' the man with the knuckles declared. 'So, you want to play again?'

'I have work to do,' Strete said easily. He thrust the spare coin back into his purse and, smiling, set it back dangling from his belt. 'You carry on.'

It was in this bar that he had learned what had happened on the ship all those years ago. Danny and he had been here, and Vincent and Odo were drinking hard, back from a sailing to Guyenne for wine, when a short fight broke out. Amongst others, Vincent and Odo were ejected from the tavern. It was a regular enough event, just an average afternoon's squabbling.

It meant nothing to Strete, and he continued drinking, watching the gambling in the corner, thinking he ought to join in, when he saw Danny's face. 'What is it?'

'That noise! It's terrible!' The lad was petrified – literally! He was fixed there as though nailed to the floor, his face appalled.

'What *is* that?'

As Strete asked, there was laughter from the roadway outside, and Vincent's voice came loud and clear. 'Ripe like a French whore, eh?' and then there was a scuffle, a resounding crash, a sudden sharp scream and the noise of bare feet running. Madam Kena had been attacked by the two in the street, and it was only when Adam saw Vincent and Odo trying to hustle her into an alley that he realised what was happening. He called to some of Kena's men who were also in the tavern, and they ran after the two, who left her and pelted away.

'That noise,' Danny said, white-faced. 'They had her mouth covered!'

'Wouldn't want her screaming in the road, I suppose,' Strete agreed.

'That moaning – it sounded like the ship . . .' Danny's voice halted. It had not taken long for Strete to understand his fear. And then he had been able to capitalise on Danny's anxiety by asking him to remain quiet until he, Strete, could speak to his master. Calling her a 'French whore' indeed! They shouldn't have said that.

The man shook the knuckle bones in his hand, setting them rattling, and then threw them across the floor, and all in the room peered forward to see the score. It was a game of raffle, in which three knuckles were thrown, and if they all landed the same, or if there was a pair, the next player must throw a higher pair or trio.

'This is ridiculous!' Strete said to himself. He shook his head and began to leave the room, but even as he did so, he was itching to know what the man had thrown. Common sense told him to leave and return to Hawley's house, but it surely couldn't hurt to drink one ale with these men. They were such fools, all staring down at the knuckles. And the score was useless. The man must lose, no matter who went against him. No, it would be silly, when he'd just covered the amount he'd borrowed from his master's chest, to run the risk of losing more. He watched as another man threw. This time the knuckles were unlucky. They did not even equal the first throw.

'Let me show you how it's done!' he shouted at last.

'Bailiff, I am happy to present you with the man you've been hoping to meet,' Hawley said. His men brought in the body and set it on the floor, not gently. 'Why it took you and that fool Sir Andrew so long to find him, I don't know. I laid a trap and caught him. Oh, and two of the paviours who've been in a fight on the shore, too. They may need help.'

Simon's brows dropped as he heard this. 'You attacked them?'

'No. The owner of the boat they stole to deliver these two men to the ship attacked them,' Hawley said easily. He cocked a leg over a stool and rested his backside on the table. 'All we did was stop the fight when the two were already still on the ground.'

'How did you get him?' Baldwin asked, walking around the figure lying on his back on the floor.

'I paid the master of the ship to let my men wait there. Cynric stayed on board with them, and when this disreputable-looking fellow appeared, Cynric knocked him down and brought him to me.'

'That easy?'

'If you know the man to bribe, life is always that easy,' Hawley said comfortably. 'Do you have a pail of water?'

Simon bellowed for Rob, who soon returned carrying a leather bucket. At a nod from Simon, he up-ended it over the snoring man's face.

There was a spluttering, and then Pierre started to roll over. He lifted himself on all fours, shaking his head and moaning softly.

The room was dark, and he could scarcely hold his head level, but where he expected the planks to move with the ship's rolling, these felt firm. Not that it helped his head. He felt as though he had been drinking ale all evening, and his belly was unsettled.

He could be sick at any moment, and then his head ached abominably too, and his eyes felt swollen and gritty, as though he had been awake too long. 'Who has done this to a poor traveller?' he attempted at last.

'What is your name?' Baldwin asked.

'I am Sieur Pierre de Caen.'

'What are you doing here in Dartmouth?' Simon said.

'I am returning home. Is it illegal for a man to go to his homeland?'

'It is said that you have raped a woman.'

'That,' Pierre said, slowly turning until he was seated on the floor, 'is a lie. Ask my mistress.'

'Who is she?' Baldwin asked.

'You don't know?' Pierre smiled drily. 'I had thought that the dishonourable Sir Andrew would have told you. She is the Queen. My lady is Queen Isabella.'

Hawley stared at him. It was one thing to upset a local magnate, but he had probably offended the Queen herself, if this man was telling the truth. 'Oh, shit!'

Alred left the tavern feeling considerably happier than he had on his way in. Those blasted fools! Bill should know better than to upset Law. The lad was only young. It served no useful purpose to get him all annoyed. Sweet heaven, if they didn't keep sensible they'd never complete this damned roadway, and then where would they be? He needed the money in his pocket as soon as possible so he could go and leave this forsaken collection of hovels.

He didn't know why, but sailors made him nervous, and living here for so long amongst so many was making him even more twitchy than the lateness of the project. The threat of violence, which had seemed merely latent when he first arrived here, appeared now to be all too specific: everyone hated him.

Perhaps he was just superstitious, but he didn't think so. The paver was a mild-mannered man, and the idea that he might be living in a place where violence was part of daily living, was appalling. The sailors of this place cared only for other sailors. They didn't give a damn for other men. Hah! They'd soon notice if there weren't paviours about the place, though. Without his roads, they'd be stuck. They might be able to sail off around the coast, but they'd not be able to get fish and cargoes loaded on carts. Not that many did, he told himself. They were lucky to have a packhorse to carry their wares to the local community. Oh, the devil take it. He was wasting his time here. They didn't care, and they didn't need him.

He was just reaching this grim conclusion when he heard a door open, grating on the rough ground, and a man walked past him to the rough bar set in the corner of the room, and asked for a strong ale.

Alred had seen him before. This was the man who had been in this same tavern only a few days ago, talking and laughing with his companions. It was just before Alred and the other two had gone out and saved the man from the fellow who'd meant to knock him down. Only they'd apparently hit the wrong bloke. You just couldn't do right for doing wrong in this life.

The man drained a horn of ale while Alred watched, and then walked slowly from the inn. For some reason, his attitude spoke to Alred entirely of despair. It quite destroyed any remaining pleasure in being there in the tavern, and Alred stood and made his way to the twilight outside. There were the smells of suppertime now: fish stews and pottages lending their wholesome scents to the evening air, and he snuffed them for a moment or two before making his way back to the storage shed he shared with the others, wondering how much longer they must all remain here. Tomorrow he would make sure that they got that section of road finished so that they could get away from here.

He set off up the lane, and as he walked he passed by the pale-featured man from the gambling room. 'Evening,' he called.

The man leaped as though shot by a sling.

Alred eyed him askance and said no more. Someone that jumpy was plainly not in his right mind, and he didn't wish to be attacked by a lunatic.

* * *

'Sir, please, tell us your tale,' Baldwin requested.

'My story is not long,' Pierre said. He had been passed a towel by Simon, and he dabbed gingerly at the bruise on his skull. 'Who did this? I have grown a goose-egg on my brow!'

Hawley smiled. It was not his concern if a felon was knocked down. 'My apologies. My men were perhaps over-keen to obey my command, friend. They sought to restrain someone we had felt was a wild and uncontrollable criminal, driven by his humours to attack and ravish a lady.'

'Well, I am no such thing. I am Pierre de Caen, as I say. I was the son of Philippe de Caen, and a loyal servant of the French king. I came to the notice of my Lady Isabella when she visited her father in France, and I was not loath to come and see this country.

'My Lady Isabella is a lovely lady. She is honourable and devoted to her husband,' he said, his eyes on the ground before him. 'She wishes only to serve him. I was in her service for nine years. However, in that time I began to grow enamoured of a lady. It hurts me to tell you this, but I was so stricken with desire for this lady that I began to pine for love, and to cut my tale short, I decided that I could not remain at the side of my Lady Isabella. My health must suffer and my joy in service must fade. So I asked her if I could serve her in some other capacity, and she graciously permitted me to leave her household in England and travel to France once more.'

'What will you do there?' Baldwin asked.

'Remember the woman I loved, and hope to be deserving of honour. I shall seek trials of combat at every opportunity and hope that my example may serve to inspire others. I will not be able to marry. I have lost the only woman who could ever have filled the hole in my heart.'

'Did you murder a man here when you arrived?'

'You mean the man in the hole in the road? No. When I reached this town, I found myself lost. I sought my brother-in-law's house, but it was so long ago that I was last here, that it was impossible. Instead I went to an inn for the night, deeming it better that I should seek his home in the morning. As it happened, while I was in this place, I realised I was being watched. There was a dullard there, a short, grizzled, rather foolish old sailor, who sought to keep me watched. It was plain what was on his mind. So I slipped out to the back, pretending to seek a bed for the night, and when he followed me, I was determined to strike him down.'

'Kill him?' Simon asked.

'No. Just break his head to keep him away from me while I decided what to do.'

'What happened then?'

'Some friends had seen this man follow me, and they believed he was about to murder me for my purse. They knocked him down for me and let me escape.'

'Who were these charitable men?' Baldwin enquired.

'I will not name them. They were kind to a stranger. What good would it serve me to have them punished for saving me?'

Simon grunted, 'It might just save you from arrest and a period in gaol.'

'It is a risk I can afford. So I ran from the inn, and went up to the top roadway, where I came upon the hole in the road. There I was accosted by a man with a knife. I thought I was about to die, but it was not my enemy from earlier, but my brother-in-law himself.'

Simon looked up and peered at Pierre keenly. 'You say Master Pyckard was out in the roadway?'

'Yes. I had sent a message to him when I arrived in Dartmouth, and he was looking for me.'

Simon shot a look at Baldwin. 'This sounds unlikely. Master Pyckard is dead, as you know, and the day after Pierre's arrival, I saw him. He looked dreadful. I'd be surprised if he could have made it to the inn – he found it hard enough to get to his own door when I visited him.'

'I swear it is true. You may ask his servant, Moses. He was there, and he saw me with his master.'

Baldwin nodded slowly, his chin cupped in his hand. 'I have known men to have the most appalling illnesses or wounds, and yet be able to go and fight. The reaction hits them all the harder afterwards, but they do not know that at the time. Perhaps, Simon, this man Pyckard did go to the tavern as our friend here asserts, but was then brought down severely as a result. I should enquire of his servant, certainly. Please, continue.'

'There is not much more to relate,' Pierre said. He described how he had returned to Pyckard's house, how Moses had fed him and then taken him to the old stable and hayloft, where he stayed until told of his passage on the next ship of Pyckard's to set sail. 'I would have left on that ship this morning, but when the crew heard of their master's death, all wished to drink his health and attend his funeral. They all came to the shore, and it took little money to persuade a man to bring me and my companion to visit the church.'

'You are being sought by this knight Sir Andrew de Limpsfield,' Baldwin said. 'Who is he to you?'

Pierre's face paled, but not from fear. 'He is my most mortal enemy! He seeks my destruction.'

'He asserts that you . . .'

'I know the lies he has spread about me. They are all untrue. I am no felon, and I would like to force him to take back his foul allegation at the point of my sword!'

'No doubt. In the meantime, he accuses you of spying and taking letters to France to aid our enemies,' Baldwin pressed.

'It is a lie. Who are these letters from, hey?'

'He does have authority on his side. He can force us to give you to him, if he commands it,' Baldwin said.

'Do not give me to him! He is a vassal of Lord Despenser!'

Simon and Baldwin glanced at each other. There was no need for them to speak: each knew the other's mind. While Baldwin detested the man for the stories which were circulating about Despenser's brutality and avariciousness, he was not yet a traitor, and no matter what a man said about Despenser, he was still the King's advisor. Baldwin's sense of honour would not allow him to openly flout the King's will. He had a family to think of.

Simon had a subtly different view. In his world, Lord Hugh de

Courtenay was his liege-lord. It was that simple. Lord Hugh had not broken from Despenser and the King, so Simon was unwilling to risk supporting any man against the King.

'If you are against my Lord Despenser . . .' Simon began, but Pierre cut him off.

'I am a loyal servant of my Lady Isabella, your Queen. And she is being sorely tried by this man Despenser. He has refused to pay her the money he owes her for the farm of Bristol, for example, and denies owing arrears. They have taken her castles and brought her to low poverty. If you give me to him, you will see me dead, and my lady the Queen brought lower. Can you do thus to your Queen?'

'If she's in such a terrible state, why isn't her husband doing anything about it?' Simon asked cynically.

'He can do nothing against the Despenser,' Pierre stated. It was true. The King was so infatuated with his lover, he could see nothing wrong in any action the man took. Despenser stole, ransomed and tortured at will; he was Edward's favourite and could do no wrong.

Pierre looked about him at the faces in the room. The knight Baldwin sat studying him from dark and serious eyes; his companion the Bailiff was less analytical and more sympathetic to his position; the shipmaster was scowling with concentration, making sure that no snippet of potentially useful information passed him by.

Baldwin sniffed, sitting back at last. 'Well, my friend, I feel anxious for you, but I'm equally convinced that we have to do our duty. I am afraid that you must be held until we hear from Sir Andrew about what he would have us do.'

'If you give me to him, you will give me over to my execution,' Pierre said with finality.

'If we don't, we may be signing our own death warrants,' Hawley pointed out. He stood. 'You want me to take him to the gaol now?'

'No. He will be safe here,' Baldwin said. 'We have servants and guards enough.'

'If you are sure.'

'Wait, Master Hawley,' Baldwin said. 'Perhaps you could just ease my mind on a couple of other points? I believe you were not alone in being at sea on the day you found the cog burning. Is that correct?'

'Yes. I think all the ships were at sea. Mine, Kena's and Beauley's. Why?'

'I am merely trying to understand what may have happened to the unfortunate crew on that ship.'

'Do you think one of them killed the crew and fired the ship?' Hawley demanded, and chuckled to himself. 'I promise you, any of us would have made a more seamanlike end to the *Saint John*.'

'Yes. That is fine. I know that,' Baldwin said.

'So why ask about them, then?'

'Because it interests me. The idea that the cog could be taken and all her men killed with such ease, that seems most odd. The fact that the men all disappeared is also strange, as is the matter of the cargo.'

'It was all there.'

'Precisely.'

Hawley eyed him for a few moments, and then shrugged. He turned to Simon. 'I'll take my leave, Keeper. Let me know if there's anything more you need from me.'

Chapter Twenty-Seven

Gil stood on the *Saint Denis* with his legs braced and took a long swig from a jug of wine. 'We will set sails in the morning,' he declared. 'If we hang about any longer, we'll miss the market.'

'Good,' Moses said. 'It's for the best.'

'What of the Frenchman?' Hamund asked.

Moses turned to the abjuror and looked him up and down with slow deliberation. 'You are a sailor for this trip, friend. Do not test our patience, or you will remain here. Do you want that?'

'No, but our master wanted him taken to France, didn't he? Wasn't it one of his dying wishes? And now you're proposing to leave him here.'

'He has been arrested. What do you expect us to do?'

'The men took him from this ship with someone's agreement! Who allowed them aboard?'

Gil controlled his temper with difficulty. 'I would shut up now while you still have your teeth, sailor. Now get off my deck!'

Hamund sniffed, wiped his nose, and walked away. There was no point in continuing this argument, but as he stood and glanced about him, he was reminded of the story of the death ship's arrival in the haven. Others had spoken of it at length in the tavern while Gil was trying to find more crew-members, and the tale of the poor man who'd been grasped by the cold, dead hand of the corpse in the hold had mesmerised all who heard it. The man had all but died of terror, apparently, and his hair had turned white on the spot. True!

Less inclined to believe the stories of ghosts than most of the others, Hamund was sure of one thing as he stood there on the deck, and that was that there were plenty of opportunities for a new sailor like himself to fall overboard on the voyage to France. Perhaps he should be silent. The man Pierre was not worth dying for.

He found a quiet corner near an immense coil of thick rope, and settled dejectedly beside it. In all the time since he had left Mistress Sarra and come down here, only one man, Pierre himself, had spoken to him kindly. Gil had been generous enough while he wanted sailors, but now Hamund was gaining the impression that his kindness and courtesy would last only as long as the shore was visible from his deck. No, it was only Pierre who had been good to him for his own sake. Perhaps it was because the two of them were all alone and despised by everyone else, one because he was a confessed murderer and abjurer, the other because he was thought to be a rapist. Despite knowing of his crime, the Frenchman had offered to help Hamund start a new life. That counted for a lot.

'What can I do to help *him*?' Hamund muttered dismally. He gazed back towards the shore. Torches flickered, and the water reflected the pin-pricks of yellow light. The cooper was working still, his braziers lighting the front of his shop.

An idea began to come to Hamund, gradually at first, but then with more force.

'Leave us,' Baldwin said to the man at the door. The latter looked to Simon for confirmation, and the Bailiff nodded.

'We are in no danger from this fellow.'

When they were alone, Baldwin drew up a stool in front of Pierre. 'Now tell us the truth, fellow. If you do, it may help me to see how to aid you as well.'

'What, you would deny me to the Despenser? You would stand in his way when his man Sir Andrew came to demand me?' Pierre said doubtfully.

'For my part I have no wish to see another man destroyed in Lord Despenser's search for personal aggrandisement. What of you, Simon?'

Simon stood and leaned against the wall near the window. 'I am a servant of the King, but I despise all I've heard of Despenser. If you tell us the truth, we may be able to find a means of evading him.'

'What do you wish to know?'

'First, I want your assurance that you are not seeking to aid the French king against our nation.'

'How could I?'

'A spy can help in many ways. You are as aware of that as I am,' Baldwin said sternly. 'Now: do you seek to bring about the end of the realm?'

Pierre gazed at him unwaveringly. The knight had intense, dark eyes, and Pierre found them unsettling. It was as though he could pierce a man's breast and read what was written on his heart. Pierre considered for a long moment, then nodded. 'I will tell the truth. I have nothing to lose. If you sell me to Despenser, I am dead. There is nothing I can do to save myself. I do not seek the end of England. I serve my lady, your Queen. All I can do to protect and serve her, I will.'

'That does not mean you will protect the King,' Simon observed.

'No. Nor Despenser. You know he demanded that Queen Isabella should swear to live or die with him? He wanted her to swear this!'

'I believe there is no friendship between the two,' Baldwin said diplomatically.

'None! She hates him . . .' Pierre was quiet for a short while, then, 'It is said in the court that he and the King . . .'

'That is rumoured through the whole country,' Simon said shortly.

'It is also said that Despenser has raped her,' Pierre said.

Baldwin and Simon were instantly still.

The knight was first to recover. 'Are you sure? It is a very serious charge to lay against any.'

Pierre shrugged, but his mouth was tight. 'If you had seen how she reacts to the man, how she recoils when he draws near her, you would not doubt my word. I have no proof, sir, but I think that she was attacked by this man, and that her husband did not care and did not stop it. I am sad to have to say this, because it is a shameful thing to confess that I could know such a thing had happened to my mistress and be unable to prevent it or protect her, but what can one man like me do against a magnate like Despenser? There is nothing!'

'I am shocked,' Baldwin whispered. 'Surely even Despenser would not dare to lay hands on her . . .'

'She says that someone has come between her and her husband, trying to separate them by every possible means. She means Lord Hugh Despenser.'

Simon shook his head. 'This is too much for me. What can we do against a man who'd dare that, Baldwin?'

'Little enough,' Baldwin said. 'Sir, you have not answered: do you swear you do not intend to go to France to aid the French king?'

Pierre closed his eyes and swallowed, considering. It was hard to keep calm as he thought back to that time, but after so long being mistrustful of all, to unburden himself would be to remove an intolerable weight from his soul. His inclination was to remain secretive, but he didn't dare. Not now. If he remained in possession of this last confidence, it might cost him his life. It could do no harm to speak now, surely.

'Masters, I was forced to leave my native land. I did not come here to England just because of love for my mistress. I *had* to leave. I would never do a thing that might aid the French king.'

'Why?' Baldwin asked quietly. He was struck by the man's manner. It was as though a strengthening beam within him had been removed, and the Frenchman suddenly sagged. Exhaustion and defeat could do that to a man. He had seen it all too often before. Pierre looked like a man who had been stripped bare not of his clothing, but of every little deceit which had made up his character over time.

'There was a dreadful matter. A terrible, awful stain on my family. You must know that I come from an area near Caen. I had two older brothers. I was the younger, and more foolish, but I always revered my brothers Philippe and Gautier.'

Baldwin started. 'You were their brother?'

'Who?' Simon asked, bemused.

'My brothers were not evil,' Pierre said, his hands held palms up in a show of openness. 'They were young, vigorous men, and their hearts were ready for love always. Who is not when he is young? They had no thoughts for their danger, or the danger they would put others to.'

'I don't understand any of this,' Simon said pointedly. 'Come to the point, sir.'

Baldwin answered, his eyes fixed on the French knight with a certain sadness. 'The Queen gave some silk purses to her sisters-in-law when she was in France on a diplomatic mission, Simon. And then she saw them being worn on the belts of two brothers.'

'She had embroidered them herself,' Pierre said. 'She recognised them immediately she saw them. Of course, many men would be granted favours of such a type by the lady they serve, and it is not proof of anything, but it alarmed her, and she was persuaded that there was something wrong. So she told her father the King, and he had Philippe and Gautier watched, and then tortured until they confessed.'

'They'd been committing adultery?' Simon breathed, shocked. 'I had never heard of that.'

'It rocked the foundations of the House of Capet,' Baldwin said quietly. 'My friend, I am sorry.'

'They had committed the crime,' Pierre said dully. 'They confessed.'

'Under the torture,' Baldwin said. He recalled the discussion with Stapledon before setting off for Dartmouth. 'And they died most horribly.'

'Flayed alive, castrated, their limbs broken, and finally decapitated,' Pierre whispered.

'And the Queen who did all this welcomed *you* to her household?' Simon asked with suspicion.

'There was no suggestion that I had had anything to do with the affair,' Pierre said. 'And I could not blame her for noticing the crime and telling her father. She mentioned a strange thing, simply that her gifts had been spurned and given to knights in his household, no more. It was King Philippe who had my brothers watched and followed, and who had evidence collected.'

'Philippe is dead,' Baldwin observed.

'Yes!' Pierre said with a cynical laugh. 'You think his son would trust me more? King Charles hates all my line. He would be suspicious of anything I could say to him. My family is marked with the same foul suspicion as my poor dead brothers. More! King Charles would think me keen for revenge. For me to go to him with news . . . it would do little good, I think. I would be distrusted and perhaps killed. It is because of me that his wife is still incarcerated in Château Gaillard. He cannot remarry until she dies or the Pope annuls their marriage. He has no reason to love my family.'

'You deny taking information to France to succour King Charles, then?' Simon said.

'Absolutely!'

Simon turned to Baldwin. 'I don't know what to do with this. I wonder whether we ought to keep him here and seek advice from someone else. Could we write to Bishop Stapledon and ask him to intervene on this fellow's behalf?'

He had mentioned the idea as it entered his head, thinking that at least Bishop Walter would be able to provide support at a high level, taking a little of the responsibility for this decision away from them, and acting as a buffer and protection from Lord Despenser. The vehement response of the Frenchman startled him.

'No! No! You would throw me to the dogs? You inveigled my story so you could destroy me? Do not send me to that evil man Stapledon! It would be giving me to my murderer!'

Chapter Twenty-Eight

Hawley reached his house late, after a detour past a tavern. He had needed time to think after all he had heard about the rapist at the Port Keeper's house, and now he stood at his door with a frown marring his features.

If he was getting himself into deep water without a sail, he would need to make sure that he had a degree of protection. Just now he felt very exposed.

From all he had learned from the Frenchman, Despenser wanted him. Clearly that was why that poxed whoreson Sir Andrew had demanded the arrest of the man. And Hawley had only handed him over to the knight and Bailiff because he had thought they would keep him until Despenser might come and take him. That was all well and good, provided no one forgot who it was who had sent men to catch the fellow in the first place. If there was to be a good reward, Hawley didn't want it frittered away in the direction of Sir Baldwin or Simon Puttock. That was all too often the way that officers behaved. The last Keeper of the Port here had been as corrupt as a Cinque Port sailor.

However, there were other considerations to keep in mind. It wasn't only a matter of the money which should come to him from one reward: there was the matter of the men on the ship. If Sir Andrew and his merry men *had* killed all the sailors on the *Saint John*, they should be forced to pay. Hawley was utterly devoted to the rights of men at sea, especially insofar as they affected him personally. If some captain of a warship decided to come and take a Dartmouth merchantman, that was a very serious interference in the maritime trade of the port. He would not have that happen.

He thought how much he would like to go to Sir Andrew's ship with a force of Dartmouth sailors, and put the vessel to the torch – after relieving her of any useful little dainties, of course – but it was not a part of Hawley's plan to die young after provoking the most important man in the country after the King himself.

Yet . . . he had no proof of any criminal actions by Sir Andrew. More likely was his earlier suspicion. Beauley was a desperately ambitious man, and with Pyckard out of the way, it would be easier for him. Yes, Hawley had a feeling that this was nearer the truth.

It was at this stage in his mental consideration that he opened his door and entered his home.

He made no concession to those who might already be asleep, for which man does in his own house? As soon as the door slammed, kicked closed by his boot, he noticed the flickering light from the doorway to his hall. Instantly the light was extinguished, and Hawley stood silently, listening. He crossed the screens slowly, shuffling like a man whose brain was fuddled, and entered his hall. The fire was out, and he stood by it a moment, considering. The light had not come from here, because there was only a slight residual heat from the stones of the hearth. He shambled over to the box on the wall where some candles lay, and took one up. Striking flint and steel, he made some burned cloth catch, and used it to light his little candle. This he set in a holder by his chair, and then he drew his sword and sat down, the blade across his lap as he waited, watching the doorway to his little counting-room.

'I can wait as long as you want,' he said conversationally. 'What? You don't wish to come out and talk? That seems discourteous in one who is happy to rifle through my chest.'

There was no sound, and he grinned wolfishly. 'There's no way out, except past me. But you know that, don't you, Peter? How much were you going to take tonight? I knew I was right. You can't keep gaming in a shit-hole like the Porpoise without being flayed. Only you never had enough money to afford that, did you, so you had to be getting it from somewhere else. Where did it come from, eh? Did you steal it?'

'I am sorry . . . so sorry.'

Hawley smiled broadly. 'I expect you are, yes.'

Strete had appeared at the doorway now, and he stood, rubbing his hands together as though washing them. 'I didn't mean to . . .'

'To steal from me?'

'I didn't! I wouldn't! I paid everything back, master. You know that!'

'How much?'

'Now? Four marks.'

'In how much time?'

'Just this evening . . . but it all started so well, that's what I don't understand! It's not *fair*! I should have won, but the dice went against me.'

'Much like life, dice,' Hawley said, rising. 'As soon as you think they're in your favour, that's when the damned things turn against you. Where's my money?'

'I've taken nothing, master. I was just—'

'About to take what you could,' Hawley completed for him. 'But I got here too soon. Did you think you'd be able to hide it from me?'

'I was going to repay you, like last time.'

'How many times, Strete? How many times have you robbed me?' Hawley asked sweetly.

'I haven't robbed, sir, only borrowed. And then I gave more than I'd taken, in compensation for the loan.'

'A loan is normally agreed between both parties, Strete,' Hawley said. He was still grinning widely, even as he swung his sword and brought the heavy pommel swinging round to Strete's head. The unfortunate clerk tried to block the blow, but the pommel struck him behind his ear, and his raised hand merely caught the blade and lost a flap of skin as he tumbled to the ground.

Hawley kicked him, hard, in the cods. 'You'll never work for me or anyone in Dartmouth again, you stupid *shit*. Jesus!'

'What on earth is wrong with Stapledon?' Simon demanded. 'He is a friend of ours. A more decent, honourable cleric would be hard to imagine.'

'You are allies of his? I am lost then!'

Baldwin watched the man clench and unclench his fists, gazing about him distractedly as though seeking a means of escape. 'Please, my friend, just explain to us what you fear. I swear we will not unnecessarily endanger your life.'

'You swear? On your oath as a knight? On the Gospel?'

'I do so swear.'

Pierre glanced up at Simon, who had moved to stand nearer Baldwin, and the Bailiff nodded silently in agreement.

'Believe me, I am no spy,' Pierre said passionately. 'But my poor lady, the Queen, is assailed on all sides. I told you of the shocking way in which the Despenser has treated her. He is a monster! Vile and rapacious! And his willing ally is this Bishop of Exeter. He is as evil as Despenser!'

Baldwin shook his head. 'No, my friend. You are wrong there. Bishop Walter is a devoted servant of the King, and he is in no way evil, I assure you.'

'Do you say so? But I have seen his words written to the Queen. He has threatened her. He hates her because she is French, and he thinks she will betray her husband just because of that! As if she would behave in such a dishonourable manner!'

'It is true that the bishop seeks ever to protect the King and the nation from danger,' Baldwin said, 'but he is not so made that he could consider harming the lady. He is fair and reasonable, I promise you. I know the good bishop well.'

'If you give me to him, you thrust a dagger into my heart,' Pierre said dramatically. He rent his shirt, bearing a hairless breast. 'Do it now, and do it quickly. I would not be tortured like my brothers. At least spare me that!'

'It will not come to that,' Baldwin declared quickly. He had lost his friends and companions to the tortures, and could not inflict that on another man. 'Bishop Stapledon is but one man we could ask for advice. I think he is the best, but there are others. Calm yourself, my friend. You are safe here with us.'

'I am in the land of my enemies,' Pierre said sadly. He huddled down again, his hands pulling his shirt together. 'I am hated for my nationality, for my family, for my loyalty to my mistress . . . I cannot be safe until I escape from England. And you two, who declare yourselves my friends, will try to save me by delivering me to my worst enemies!'

As the clouds passed over the sickle moon, there was a sudden darkening of the world. The silver light, which had seemed so bright, was extinguished, and a deeper blackness was all that remained.

The ship was silent, apart from the slow tramp of a solitary sailor who yawned and scratched as he moved about the ship, desperate to remain awake. Those who failed in their duty of guarding were flogged, so Hamund had heard. Gil was a hard taskmaster, albeit considerate to those who demonstrated obedience. If he had wanted, Hamund could have remained here on board, become part of the crew and settled here in Dartmouth. Others had done so. When abjurers were released to make their way to the coast, many slipped off the roads and became outlaws or merely walked to a distant town and began a new life. So long as he never returned to where he had been convicted, he should be secure enough.

The ship would set sail in the morning, and he could then travel over the sea with this crew and find himself a new home in France. *But without his friend.*

Although he had only known Pierre for a short time, a matter of some hours, he felt sure that the Frenchman would desert him, were the tables turned. He knew it, and yet in the depths of his heart, he also knew that this man had meant to help him when he had been desperate for a word of comfort. What's more, Pierre had promised to look after Hamund when they arrived in France.

Slipping over the side of the ship, Hamund let himself down the rope slowly. From the ship here to the shore was only a matter of some tens of yards, no more than that. The pond at home used to be wider, and he swam that from side to side every summer.

The chill of the river caught his breath. He clung to the rope for a moment, growing used to the cold and staring up at the sheer of the hull, considering the safety that it represented, the promise of a new life . . . and then he let go and started swimming for the shore.

He didn't know where Pierre was, nor did he know what he could do to save the man, but he knew he had to try.

Will the gaoler was irritated to be on duty tonight. Normally he'd be snuggled up to his wife, not here in this godforsaken dump.

'Shut up!' he bellowed as someone underneath him shouted again, demanding to be allowed to see his master, and warning Will that he'd suffer for this later, sticking servants of the King's Advisor in gaol without reason. 'You murdered eleven of our men at sea, you did, and we don't let murderers go without trial down here. Don't know what you do up north, boy, but here we stick to the law.'

'We did nothing of the—'

'My daughter Annie was keen on one of the lads you murdered, so if you think I'm going to let you out so you can go and cut the throats of others, you're mistaken! Now pipe down and let a body sleep!'

It still rankled. Little Annie had been sweet on that brawny young matelot Ed, who'd died on the *Saint John*. God's teeth, since the ship appeared, she'd near had conniptions, poor maid. The weeping and wailing in the house . . . Well, that was one attraction of remaining out here, he supposed.

'Open this door, gaoler!'

This command, given in the tone of a man who was used to issuing orders and having them acted upon, worked on Will like a small bolt of lightning. He shot up from his chair and peered suspiciously at the barred and latched door to the street. 'Who is it?'

'Sir Andrew de Limpsfield, acting on the King's warrant. I want to have this door opened now.'

'I was told to leave the door locked, Sir Knight,' Will whined, and chewed his lip. The orders had been quite definite: he was to keep these men down in the cell until Master Hawley said they could be freed. This Sir Andrew sounded a powerful, dangerous man, but Will knew he must obey Master Hawley.

There was a loud crash from the door, and the timbers shuddered.

It was barred with a large piece of oak, and the latch was pegged shut, but just now neither appeared to offer a great deal of security. A fine cloud of soot and dust fell from the loose timbers of the roof.

'Don't do that, the roof'll fall in!' Will shouted in alarm, choking on the thick air.

'Open the door, or I'll have it off its hinges,' Sir Andrew stated implacably.

Will waited until there was one more crash, but that was enough. There was no possibility of the door surviving the onslaught, and even if the door had survived, he reckoned the roof would have fallen about his ears. 'I'm opening it, master, just give me a moment,' he declared, and started to pull the peg from the latch, lifting the heavy timber from the locking slots.

As soon as it was opened, the door was thrust wide, and a powerful sailor pushed him aside. A second marched in after him and held a knife to Will's belly, forcing him against the wall. Only then did Sir Andrew cross the threshold, glancing about him distastefully as he did so.

'What a repellent hovel! Release the men.'

The knife was moved at Will's belly, and he took the hint. He lifted the keys from his belt, and the sailor threw them to his companion. He caught them and bent to the trap door, unlocking the great padlock and lifting the door up and over.

'Good,' Sir Andrew said as the ladder was dropped down into the hole. He waited, tapping his feet as the prisoners began to climb up and stood about the room disconsolately, one or two throwing looks at Will that made him anxious.

'I do *not* expect to have to rescue you and your men from a gaol again, Jan,' Sir Andrew said to the leader. 'None of you. You may be able to redeem a little honour, if you can capture this traitor and spy. He is currently at the home of Bailiff Puttock, the Keeper of the Port. You have your orders. Go and bring him to me. I shall be back at the ship. We sail first thing in the morning.'

'What of the Bailiff?'

'What of him?'

'If he refuses to hand over the man, what do we do then?'

'You have your orders. You know under whose authority we work. Any man who wilfully obstructs the King's men will suffer the consequences. I trust that is clear?'

'What about this old fart?' asked the man guarding Will.

Sir Andrew walked over the floor and eyed Will contemplatively. 'He kept my men here, and then would have prevented my entering, wouldn't he?' he said, and all of a sudden took hold of the sailor's forearm and thrust his knife forward, placing his other hand over Will's mouth.

He watched dispassionately as Will jerked and tried to pull away, his eyes wide and maddened. Unable even to scream, his body wrenched and lurched as Sir Andrew pulled the blade slowly upwards, opening Will's belly to the breastbone. When the gaoler began to slip down the wall, Sir Andrew let go of his sailor's arm and took his hand away from Will's face, eyeing the saliva-sodden palm disdainfully. Will slumped at the floor, trying to hold his belly together, shivering with shock, unable now to make more than a whimper.

Sir Andrew turned and found all his men staring. 'What are you all waiting for? Get going!'

When he reached the shore, Hamund was shivering badly, his teeth chattering. There was a stone jetty, at which some rowing boats were tied, and he had to clamber up the rough stones to reach Lower Street. Here he huddled for a moment, trying to quell the spasms that rattled through his body, his arms wrapped about his upper torso. Dripping, he was frozen to his core, and desperate for a fire to warm himself.

As he stood there, he saw a glow from the northernmost tip of the street. As soon as he had begun to swim, he realised how powerful the current was just here, because he could see from the few lights at the shore that he was being swept out towards the mouth of the river and the open sea. One light in particular attracted his attention: a large open brazier near the mill. It took all his strength to keep to a more or less straight course towards South Town. Desperate for heat, he forced himself to his feet and hurried along the street towards the fire.

Blessed heaven! The coals glowed with a fierce heat that began to scorch him almost before he could feel it. He sighed with relief, holding hands out to it reverently, wondering what he could do next. Hamund had no idea of the town's layout, but most small towns had a holding gaol somewhere, probably near the market square itself. He would go there.

'You all right?'

'I . . .'

Hamo eyed the dripping figure with alarm in his eyes. 'You fallen off a ship, mate? You're drenched.'

'I am fine, I thank you, but I have some business to attend to.'

'Business, eh? At night? Only felons go about in the dark, friend.'

'I am no thief!' Hamund exclaimed indignantly, and then he could have laughed at the thought that no, he was no *thief*, he was merely a murderer. How he had fallen!

'Come in here, then, and dry yourself off. Whatever your business, it'll be easier to conduct if you've warm clothes on instead of soaking wet ones,' Hamo said kindly. 'Come on. I've cloths in here. You can get dry and then the brazier will do more good.'

With a feeling of great good fortune, Hamund followed his benefactor the cooper inside.

Chapter Twenty-Nine

'What did you think, Simon?' Baldwin asked when they had left Pierre in the lower storeroom at the back of Simon's house. It was impossible to hold him in the gaol when the crew who wanted to kill him were all there. Safer by far to keep him here.

'Entirely convincing, I thought. It's rubbish, of course, but he does seem to believe it.'

'Yes,' Baldwin said. He was struck by Pierre's sincerity, and yet why should anyone think that the good Bishop of Exeter would behave in such a fashion? He and Simon knew Walter Stapledon personally, and the idea that he could be working to destroy the Queen would be laughable, were it not for the unaffected earnestness of Pierre's manner.

'He was determined not to have his name given to Walter,' Simon said.

'For the moment we can indulge that, I suppose,' Baldwin said. 'But we do have to decide what to do with the men in the gaol. They will be clamouring for release, I expect. And when they are out, what then?'

'I'd be all for telling them to weigh anchor and bugger off,' Simon said, 'but I suppose you'll tell me not to be so mad.'

'I agree with you that the best course would be to be well rid of them,' Baldwin admitted, then added more quietly, 'but if you behave in too high-handed a fashion, all that will happen is that you'll antagonise them. And if you don't fear Sir Andrew himself, you know what Despenser is like.'

Simon nodded. All knew how ruthless he could be. Force was not a last resort for him, but rather an everyday means of achieving whichever ambition he possessed at the time. 'What shall we do, then?'

'I wish I knew. Where is the Coroner?'

Simon shrugged. 'Probably in a tavern somewhere insulting the locals, if I know him at all.'

'Send your boy to find him. I think we would benefit from his experience and knowledge. I have to confess, Simon, I find this situation very worrying.'

He sat for some while after Rob had been roused and sent to seek Sir Richard. Simon fetched them both wine and poured liberal measures into two mazers. For once Baldwin did not remonstrate about the quantity. Although he was usually abstemious, this was one occasion when he felt the need of a stimulant.

The country was falling into despair, and the fault lay with the King. Edward II had been weakly and foolish for so long, people had grown used to his manner. But now he had shown himself to be pitiless and brutal in his pursuit of his enemies. It was incredible to many that he should seek to destroy his cousin, Earl Thomas of Lancaster, but it was his callous behaviour to all Thomas's allies and friends, not least his own widow, that shocked and terrified many in the country. Yes, some praised the King for his determined actions and first military success, but Baldwin feared that there was a destruction of the trust between ruler and ruled. It scared him.

Perhaps he should go to Parliament as Stapledon had suggested. There he might be able to show his peers how damaging the King's actions were. It was a subject's duty to show where the King was failing, surely.

He rubbed his temples. If only he could be back at Furnshill with his pregnant wife and their child. He was not made for great political intrigues and dealing with matters of such danger and importance.

'Baldwin, it's late. Perhaps you should go and rest,' Simon said gently, sensing his mood.

Baldwin grinned quickly. 'Do I look decrepit? No. I am fine.

But this issue of the Frenchman is a problem. How can we resolve it, I wonder?'

His question was answered by a sudden pounding at the door.

The Coroner had left Sir Andrew shortly after identifying the corpse in the church, determined on an investigation of the little tavern out by the Tunstal road. As a lad, he had been there, he recalled, and got into a glorious fist-fight, during which he had knocked down two opponents. Now, standing in the little space, it was hard to imagine that he had truly been able to throw the first to the floor and pound the second three times in the nose before kicking his legs away and dropping onto his chest, driving out the air from his lungs in an almighty 'whoosh' that could be heard, so they said, at the other side of the road. Aye, happy days.

Now it looked too cramped to hold a cock-fight in. Sad how a man's memory could play him false. He left that place and wandered on up the hill to look in at the Porpoise. Here he only had three pints of strong ale, on the basis that he ought to save a little room for some of the Bailiff's wine. Simon was a generous man with his drink, even if he did suffer for his generosity afterwards. Still, that was hardly Sir Richard's fault.

It was at the Porpoise that Rob found him.

'Looking for me, eh? Fine. You want a drink while you're here?'

Rob was well used to the drinks from this place, and he took a quart of their stronger ale. The Coroner watched him over the rim of his horn as the lad closed his eyes and tipped the jug back, slowly drinking the quart in one long draught.

'You enjoy your ale.'

'Always, sir.'

'You'll go far. A lad who drinks so firmly,' Sir Richard said, standing and making his way to the door, 'is a fellow of substance and determination. You must have both in life, lad. Remember that.'

'Yes, sir.'

'And when you're Sheriff in charge of this whole county,

remember me in your prayers for having told you how to make your fortune, eh?'

'Yes, sir.'

'And . . .' Coroner Richard stopped. Along the street there were shouts and curses, while a small mob swung a bench at a door. 'Good God in heaven, that's the Bailiff's door!'

The first battering had made Simon and Baldwin leap to their feet. They listened to the angry shouting and the clattering of weapons against the door, and then with one accord, they sprang out into the small passage that led to the front of the house. There they could see the door shaking, a timber working loose from its nail.

Simon had ordered that the door should be locked so that there was little chance of Pierre escaping by that route, and when Rob had left, the door had been firmly closed and barred behind him. Now it rattled under the determined pounding of weapons. A more solid crash declared that the men had found something substantial amongst the rubbish that littered the street, and Baldwin watched in silent dismay.

'It must be Sir Andrew and his mob. We cannot hold the place against them,' he murmured.

'I am reluctant to free the Frenchman,' Simon countered. 'If Despenser heard, we'd have our necks stretched. Baldwin, I don't like it, but for the sake of the King's Peace and commonsense, preventing bloodshed, we'll have to give him up to them.'

'If we do, those fools will tear him apart,' Baldwin said, grabbing Simon's arm. 'Listen to them! These are madmen baying like hounds. Think of the *Saint John*. These men may have killed the crew; they would have done the same in the haven today. In God's name, I wouldn't leave a ravening wolf in their company.'

'Well, there's no way out through the garden,' Simon said. 'And any escape simply means his capture is deferred. There is nowhere for him to hide, not if Despenser's men are all over the town. If we mean to save him, it'll be at the sword's point.'

Baldwin nodded. He motioned to the guard at the door, and then drew his sword. Glancing at his friend, he hesitated, and then put his arm about Simon's shoulder and clapped it.

'Open the door,' he said quietly to the guard, and the man leaned forward and pulled the bar free. Immediately the door swung open, and three men almost fell inside, gaping at the swords held open in Simon and Baldwin's fists.

'Who are you, and what do you mean by this intrusion?' Baldwin demanded loudly. As he spoke, he stepped forward, his peacock-blue blade flashing wickedly in the light. Now that he could see the men in the street, he realised they were the ones from the ship. 'Who released you?'

'Our master. You had no right to hold us. We want the traitor!'

'And what is his name?'

'Eh?'

'I said, "What is his name?" If you expect a man to be thrown to you, you can at least dignify him by title and name.'

'The Frenchman. That's the one!'

'A Frenchman?' Baldwin enquired. 'Which one would that be?'

'Don't play games with us! We want him now. Fetch him out or we'll get him ourselves. We have the King's warrant.'

'GOOD! LET'S SEE IT, THEN!'

Baldwin felt as though the weight that had formed on his shoulders was suddenly fallen away. The man in front of him was peering up the road with consternation on his face. 'Who're you?'

'My name is Sir Richard de Welles, my fellow,' the Coroner boomed as he approached, the sword in his hand a glistening, grey wraith in the darkness. 'But "Sir" will do. What are you doing here? I believe that waking a poor Keeper of the King's Peace is probably an offence. What say you, Sir Baldwin?'

'I would say it is definitely an infringement of the law,' Sir Baldwin said. 'Any man who tried to break into a Keeper's residence without permission should be publicly castrated, I'd have thought.'

As he spoke, his sword's point dropped until it was aimed in a painful direction. The sailor opposite him swallowed noticeably, his Adam's apple bobbing. 'We've been told to fetch the traitor.'

'Which traitor?' the Coroner demanded. He was at the man's side now, and the fellow's companions retreated some little distance, away from the swords of Baldwin and Simon with their guard at the door, and the Coroner's own blade at their flank.

'The one who's been searched for. The one from the ship. It's on the order of Lord Hugh Despenser. He's the King's advisor now, and he's given us written orders to fetch the Frenchman. He's a spy and felon.'

Baldwin muttered something, and the Coroner glanced at him. 'Eh?'

Happily, Simon was able to elucidate. 'He said: "My arse".'

Sir Richard nodded. 'Quite right, too. Now, I think you ought to come back in the morning for this French fellow. We may give him to you then. If we deem it right.'

'We have orders. We have the right!'

Baldwin set his jaw. It was tempting to ignore the parchment Sir Andrew had shown him, but that would be to invite serious risks. 'It's no good, Sir Richard. I think we shall have to let the fellow go with these fine men.'

At his side, Simon nodded. 'We have no choice.'

'Very well,' Sir Richard agreed. 'In that case, before anything else, I want a full list of your names right now, and then I'll personally deliver him to your hands.'

With much reluctance, the men waited while Rob was sent to knock up Stephen. The tousled cleric appeared some minutes later, and he set to immediately with a reed and ink, scrawling the names of the sailors onto a sheet. As soon as he was done, Simon took the parchment and passed it to the Coroner, who grunted agreement. 'Fine. Master Jan? You may take him, I suppose.'

Disconsolately Simon walked back along his screens passage to the room where the Frenchman had been installed.

'Baldwin! Get here, quickly!' he bawled back along the screens as he took in the sight of the fallen figure by the door. He ran to the man's side and felt for wounds, and breathed a sigh of relief when he saw the man's breast rise and fall. Then he spotted the bloody lump on his head. '*Shit!*'

* * *

Hamo was no fool, and he could feel danger when it was sitting in front of him and drinking a cup of his warm spiced ale, but the mere fact of a man being a danger to others was not reason necessarily to throw him out. In his time, Hamo had traded with men who had killed many others, especially at sea. He never found them a risk, although some had flexible concepts about paying on time for a contract.

This one was clearly no immediate threat to Hamo. If anything, he was an embarrassment, sitting there so skinny and white, with his clothes steaming near the brazier, while he shivered in a heavy rug. 'So you can't tell me what you're doing here?'

'I was on that ship, but a friend of mine was caught earlier, and I wanted to learn why.'

'The Frenchman?'

'You know of him?'

'News doesn't have far to travel, does it?' Hamo said sarcastically. 'He was arrested on that ship of yours, wasn't he?'

'Do you know where he is now?'

'Surely he must be in the gaol.'

'I just want to see if my friend is all right.'

'I'd cool your ardour, friend. If he's banged up in the gaol, he'll stay there until the Bailiff reckons he can go.'

'I can do nothing to save him?'

Hamo eyed him. Hamund sat with his head bowed in misery. 'Why not tell me about this friend of yours. I may be able to help.'

'You can't help. No one can,' Hamund declared miserably.

'Not if you don't try them, no,' Hamo agreed affably. 'However, I'm told I've a good ear for listening, and since we're both here, we may as well humour each other, eh?'

Hamund began to tell his story: how he had killed Flok, taken sanctuary, abjured at the church in front of the Coroner, and came directly here to Dartmouth as he had been commanded, and now hoped to flee with the man who alone had helped him.

'You should return to your ship,' Hamo said. 'This is no refuge for you, is it? If you're found, you could be executed on the spot for not remaining on the ship.'

'But what of my friend?'

Hamo considered a fresh strake of oak. He weighed it in his hand, thinking. 'If he's been taken by the men from that ship *Gudyer*, you can kiss his arse goodbye. I could go and see whether he's in the gaol, I suppose. If he's not, he's probably been taken by the pirate bastards to their flashy cog.' Hamo had strong opinions about men who tried to storm and take a Dartmouth ship.

'Let me come with you! I want to speak to him. Please!'

'All right.' Hamo looked at him. 'But no silly attempts to spring him. I won't have my old friend Will hurt just because you want to save some fool who deserves all he's got. Word is, he's a spy and traitor.'

'I cannot believe that!' Hamund said, shivering as he pulled his still-damp clothes back on.

'Hmm. You'd best follow me,' Hamo said. 'It wouldn't be good for you to be found wandering about the town, you being abjured and all.'

He walked away from the river, through his works, and to his small chamber behind. His simple palliasse lay on the floor, and Hamund stumbled over the blanket laid overtop. Hamo gave him a cold stare, but took him out through the door to the tiny yard behind. From here he led Hamund through a small gate to an alleyway which opened on to Upper Street.

They hurried up here and turned to the marketplace and the gaol.

'Will? Will – are you there?'

Hamund felt a thrill of fear as they took in the broken door and mess inside. The trapdoor was wide open, and Hamo set his jaw. 'This isn't right,' he said.

It was Hamund who heard the rattling breath at the wall. 'What . . . ?'

'Will, you poor old bugger,' Hamo said chokingly as he rushed to the grandfather's side. 'Who did this?'

'It was the bastards from that shiny new cog, Hamund,' Will

managed. There was a burning pain in his belly, and although he tried to keep his hands over the mess to hold his guts in, the fire was spreading. 'They've killed me.'

'Confess to me,' Hamo said quickly. 'Let me hear your confession, old friend.'

It took little time. Will knew of few crimes he had committed that merited serious confession. When he was done, and had breathed his last, Hamo stood and ran to the door. Hanging on a hook behind it was Will's own horn, and now Hamo took it and blew three mighty blasts. 'You, Hamund, wait here and tell people what's happened. I'm going to fetch the Bailiff. This is simple murder, damn them. I won't have them slay a friend of mine unavenged!'

The first man arrived in moments, a scruffy fellow with a leather jerkin pulled hurriedly over a linen shirt, and boots without hosen. 'What's all this?'

Hamo explained briefly about the murder. 'Don't let anyone hurt my friend there,' he added in an undertone. 'He's with me – right?'

Hamund felt deserted as Hamo punched his shoulder, before turning to fly up the roadway. 'No! Let me come with you. This man can stay here and guard Will.'

Hamo nodded, but did not speak, and Hamund caught a glimpse of the thick trails of tears on the cooper's sunburned cheeks.

Chapter Thirty

'He knocked the poor bastard out, then ran,' Simon summed up to the others. The sailors had followed him, and Baldwin and Richard stood near the body while the sailors stood muttering to themselves in the corridor.

Jan sneered, 'You'll have to answer to Lord Despenser for this. You've let one of the country's worst traitors escape. I doubt whether the lord will be pleased with you for that!'

'Right now I don't give a shit what he likes or dislikes,' Simon snapped. 'The main thing is, finding him again!'

'I for one am not convinced that this man was not struck down by your confederates,' Sir Richard rasped. 'You may be entering dangerous territory, Jan, if you had anything to do with this. Breaking and entering at night to assault a guard doing his duty, and capturing a man who was already under the protection of the Keeper is a serious matter.'

'I was out in the hall with you!'

'If you were found to have instigated or incited this crime,' Coroner Richard continued, shaking his head menacingly, 'you would be as guilty as the man who committed the offence in law.'

Baldwin was at the rear door. There were marks on the floor, and he lit a candle to study them. Shielding it from the wind, he stood at the doorway for some while, his eyes on the outer wall of the house. He then stopped and picked up a straw, Simon saw. Then he hurried outside as fast as the candle would permit, and traced the Frenchman's steps all the way down the path, over some recently turned soil, past a puddle, and finally to the garden's wall. It was there that his candle flickered and died, and he moved back to the doorway and the light.

'He clearly left by the wall there. I can see where his feet went. See, Simon?' he walked back with Simon and pointed. Simon and Sir Richard went to join him, and Jan and the other sailors trailed after them, glowering suspiciously at the dirt on the ground, as though Simon and Baldwin might conceal something from them. Turning back and seeing them, Baldwin rolled his eyes bitterly. 'I congratulate you all! You have now effectively hidden any further signs he may have left! You poor examples of marine life! Do you have no understanding of hunting a man on the soil? His tracks were all over here, but you've hidden them all.'

Simon was surprised at his vehemence, but left him to it. While Baldwin berated them, he peered over the wall. From his own garden, the wall backed onto the small lane with another garden and house at the other side. The back lane here was narrow, and he remembered the locked gate at the southernmost end, the northern entrance which was open.

'He must have gone that way, running out of the town,' he said, pointing southwards.

The sailors needed no more urging. Their leader bit his thumb at Baldwin. 'You say we're foolish? We'll catch this man now, without your help, Sir Knight. And we'll do it faster because *we* understand *real* people. Signs in the mud? Pah!'

Bellowing and roaring at his comrades as though vying with a powerful gale, he led them, their horny feet slapping on the hard ground, up through the garden and out along the screens. Soon the place was quiet again.

Baldwin and Simon exchanged a glance, and then Baldwin looked up at the house. 'You can come down now,' he called softly.

To Simon's surprise, there came a rustling from his roof, and soon a dishevelled Pierre was at their side. He looked at Baldwin ruefully. 'You have remarkable powers, Sir Knight. How did you know I was up there?'

'You stepped in a puddle there, but there was no moisture on the wall, only back there near the house. Clearly you ran to the wall, thought better of it, and darted to the house and up. Besides, if you want to clamber up a roof and remain hidden, you'd be best served not to pull handfuls of straw out and leave them scattered for all to see. Not that you need fear if you leave it for a man like that sailor. He couldn't find his arse with both hands.'

'They've gone towards South Town,' Simon said. 'But they'll realise soon enough that they can't get you down there.'

'You told them I had gone there,' Pierre said.

'Yes,' Simon said, irritated by his own actions at trying to aid this man. He felt no need to explain that he had guessed Pierre wouldn't be able to escape that way and must have headed in the opposite direction.

Hamund and Hamo reached the watchman's house and banged heavily on the door, shouting for Ivo.

'What is it?' he said, appearing at the door. 'What's going on?'

'Ivo, you have to come quickly! The sailors from the *Gudyer* in the haven have murdered Will. He's dead in the gaol now!'

'You don't . . . *Shit!*'

Ivo disappeared and they heard shouting, a woman's voice petulantly arguing, and then the rattle of a sword in a cheap scabbard and the thump of boots on stairs. Soon he was back, gripping a staff in his hand with the look of a man who wanted to use it.

'You sure about who did this?' he growled.

'He was still alive when we found him, and he told us it was the fair-haired knight from that ship.'

Ivo stopped. 'I thought you said it was a sailor, not a bleeding knight!'

'What difference does it make?' Hamo demanded. 'He killed our Will.'

'Aye, and he may kill us next, you fool,' Ivo pointed out. 'How many men do you think he has on that ship of his?'

'Could be forty or fifty, I suppose.'

'And he's got the Lord Despenser's papers. All he does, he does in Despenser's name.'

Hamund frowned disbelievingly. 'You mean you'll do nothing about it? The man's got papers, and that means he can murder who he wants?'

'No, of course not. Not unless he's got good reason.'

'You reckon Will would have given him good reason?' Hamo choked. 'Gentle old Widecombe Will?'

Ivo gestured peevishly as he struggled to think what to do. 'I can't just jump on a ship and arrest a knight. He'd have us all taken off and hanged.'

'He might be dead before he could do that,' Hamo said.

'You think so?' Ivo said icily. 'Look – the bloke's a friend of Despenser. Haven't you heard anything about him? He'll just sign a paper releasing his friend, and then we'll be hanged. The Sheriff won't dare to do anything to help us. Who're we to him?'

'Right. If you won't come, I'll get help elsewhere.'

'Tell me where, and I'll come too,' Ivo said.

'The Keeper of the King's Peace – he's staying with the Port's Keeper.'

'Another knight . . .' Ivo mused.

Hamund was keen to see the Keeper for his own reasons. 'Shall we go and see him, then?'

Ivo chewed at his lip uncertainly, then without speaking led the way up the road to Simon's house, where the three found the door standing wide. 'Bailiff?' Ivo called. 'Bailiff?'

There were voices in the hall, and he entered slowly, fearing what he might find. No man left his door gaping in the middle of the night unless there had been some disaster. He peered round the doorway into the hall. 'Sir?'

'Get in here, man,' Simon snapped. 'What do you want at this time of night?'

Hamund followed him inside and saw his friend. 'Pierre! Thank God, you're all right!' he cried in delight.

'I am so at present,' Pierre smiled, glad to see Hamund again.

'What is all this about?' Baldwin demanded.

'The gaoler, a good man called Will, is murdered,' Hamo said, bowing his head respectfully to the knight. 'There were sailors held there, but their master, the knight Sir Andrew, freed them and killed Will because he took too long to open the door. That's what he thought, anyway. He died a little while after telling me this.'

Baldwin and Simon exchanged a look, but it was Sir Richard who snorted, shifted his sword, and hooked his thumbs on his belt.

'Keeper,' he said, 'I know that this is a dangerous affair, and we don't know where it might end, but this man Will has to be avenged. It is our duty to catch the murderer.'

Simon said nothing, but took up his sword and buckled it about his waist. 'Take us to the gaol first,' he said to Ivo.

Hawley had spent some time going through his chest with his second clerk, who spent much of his time when he thought his master wasn't looking, staring at the bound and gagged figure on the floor rather than keeping tabs on the money.

A small sack of coins had been found in Strete's tunic, hidden at his breast, and at last, when Hawley had the tally, he sat back on his heels and nodded to himself. He put the sack back in his chest and locked the lid. The key he weighed in his hand a moment, then he reopened the lid, took out three pennies, and locked it again.

'These are for him. Stick them in his purse,' he said to the clerk.

It was tempting to hang the bastard or, more sensibly, to stab him and leave him in the woods over the town where he wouldn't be found until his bones had been picked clean. Or take him to sea and dump him there. The man had been as treacherous as any could be, and he deserved to die for that. Any sailor found stealing at sea could be summarily dealt with, and a man who stole from his master here on land deserved the same fate. That was Hawley's view, and he held to it rigidly.

However, he *was* on land – and killing men willy-nilly in Dartmouth would be sure to be frowned upon. God damn it.

'Get Cynric and bring him to me,' he said to the clerk. 'You can go back to your bed.'

The man scuttled away, relieved to be free of his stern-faced master. Before long Cynric appeared in the doorway, saying laconically, 'He told me what's happened. You want me to string him up?'

'No. I've a better idea. Take him to the Porpoise and leave him in there by the gaming room.'

'They'll not like him being unable to repay his debts,' Cynric smiled, seeing how Strete was shaking his head in shock and horror, moaning through the gag.

'He has three pennies – perhaps they'll help him a little.'

'Yes. It'll make them keep him to entertain themselves that bit longer,' Cynric chuckled, and grabbed Strete by his ropes. He swung the body up and over his shoulder with arms that had muscles standing out like cables. Then he turned and left the house.

The gaoler remained on the floor, the blood slick on the ground all about him. Baldwin felt his anger rise as he took in the sight. 'This is a disgrace,' he muttered coldly. 'He was only doing his job.'

'They released all the men, and then Sir Andrew just pushed the knife into him and ripped it up to kill him,' Hamo said.

'I will not let a damned butcher like this escape,' Coroner Richard grated.

Baldwin glanced at Pierre. The squire and he had both seen such killings before.

'It's a slow way to kill an enemy,' Pierre said. His face was twisted with disgust. 'The slowest, perhaps.'

'And the most cruel. This was the act of a man without honour or compassion. He must be caught.'

Simon, who always had qualms about viewing the more unpleasant corpses, stood at the door with his arm at his nostrils to keep the smell of opened bowels and blood at bay. The thought of a knife slicing through the belly and intestines of this old chap Will was appalling, and he felt himself filled with a righteous fury.

'RIGHT!' Sir Richard said, speaking slowly and precisely. 'Sergeant, I want you to gather some men and go to the inn. If Sir Andrew is there, arrest him. If he attempts to escape or refuses to go with you, you have my authority to use all force necessary. *Is that clear?*'

'Yes, sir.'

Baldwin added, 'If he is not there, come straight back here at once. You – Hamo, isn't it? You must go to the houses of Master Hawley, Master Kena and Master Beauley. Tell them that the *Gudyer*'s crew has attacked and murdered this man, and that we need a force to protect the town against them.'

'I will, sir.'

'What of us?' Hamund said.

Baldwin glanced at him, then at Pierre. 'It is for you to decide what you wish to do. I would ask you to help us, but if you feel you cannot, I will understand.'

Pierre nodded. 'I thank you for that. I would like to help you against this man.'

They had only a short wait before Ivo came hurrying along the street with a couple of extra men at his side.

'He's not there, Sir Baldwin. They reckon he must be on his ship.'

'Then we shall arrest him there,' Baldwin said.

The man at Hawley's door was a scrawny sailor Hamo had seen about the town often enough, usually drunk. Hamo pushed past him and marched into the hall.

'What do *you* want?' Hawley asked, surprised and annoyed.

'The Keeper has asked you to come and see him, master.'

'Why?'

'There's been a murder. There are some sailors abroad in the town, and he wants to catch them – quietly.'

Hawley nodded as he pulled his baldric over his head, settling his sword at his hip. Then he followed the lad out into the street and up the road. At the gaol he found Kena and Beauley waiting for him, and Baldwin explained what he intended.

'The men we seek have run off to the south. We may be able to catch a number of them. If so, all well and good. They can be held in the gaol again. The one I want, though, is their master, Sir Andrew de Limpsfield. He it is who incited murder, and he killed the poor gaoler here as well. He's on his ship. I want him arrested for this killing.'

'I will come too in my capacity as Coroner,' boomed Sir Richard.

'It's a large ship,' Kena commented, eyeing the big man doubtfully. He was wondering whether such a bearlike fellow could climb her sides.

'We can take it,' Beauley said. 'We've done it before, haven't we, Master Hawley?'

Hawley nodded, but gave Beauley a hard look. Capturing ships was a part of their job, should they come across an enemy vessel, but it wasn't something that was spoken of too much, especially in front of men like a Keeper. He wondered whether Beauley had intended to make him sound like the attacker of the death ship.

'Do you go and prepare, then,' Baldwin said. 'I want that man arrested by dawn.'

'Very well,' Hawley said. 'Beauley, I'll see you at the shore with the men.'

He strode off from the marketplace and hurried to his house. There he roused his steward and told him to gather as many of his crew as could be found quickly, before taking a long draught of wine. Cynric was already back from his mission to the Porpoise, and grinned wolfishly at the thought of the fight to come. Hawley's belly felt as though he had swallowed liquid fire as the wine hit it, but then a warmth spread through him.

When he had finished the wine, he went out into the street. The steward had done well. There were five-and-twenty of his stoutest men gathered there, all equipped with their favourite weapons. He beckoned them to follow and set off, explaining what they must do.

The ship stood out clearly from here. Lights sparkled over her deck and two on her mast, and Hawley mused on the best means of attack as he went. The shore was empty: the others weren't here yet, and he studied the vessel while he waited for them. Before long the Coroner himself arrived, and he and Hawley spoke in low tones, trying to make sense of the defences and plan the assault. As if they needed any warning, they heard a guffaw from the ship, and a man speaking to another, causing a loud explosion of laughter. Sound travelled well over the still water, much better than over land. They spoke in careful whispers.

By the time Kena and Beauley had arrived, the two had made their choice. The *Gudyer* was lying with her bow pointing up river. If they rowed straight to the ship, their vessels would be shown clearly against the lights of the town behind them. All the flickering torches and lamps would make glittering reflections on the soft waves of the river; their oars would leave a fine phosphorescence, and even if the men crouched low, a half-awake watchman must see them clearly. In preference, making use of the darkness that lay on the opposite, eastern shore, they would be almost entirely hidden.

Kena and Beauley agreed with the outlined plan. Hawley and Beauley would circle about the ship. They were the younger and more vigorous men (a comment with which Kena was content to agree) and would mount the main attack with the fifty men at their disposal. Kena's team of a further twenty-two would wait until the main attack was underway, and then race for the ship themselves, arriving as a mobile reinforcement. Using their boats they could aim straight for the part of the ship where Hawley and Beauley needed them, ideally.

'We'll go down the coast until we're level with Kingswear, and then cross over,' Beauley said quietly. 'Then make our way upriver.'

Hawley shook his head. 'Go upriver from here. It'll be slower and harder work, but when we go down towards the ship, we'll have the river with us, making the approach faster. As soon as we reach the ship, it's grapnels out and all aboard as quickly as may be.'

Ordering their men to keep all their weapons quiet and prevent them knocking or rattling, the commanders led them to the water's edge. There were many small rowing boats here, hauled up on the shingle, and the men made a great effort to enter them silently. Even when one man slid under the water, his feet losing their grip on the slippery stones, he held his tongue. All Hawley could see were two anguished eyes gazing at him before they disappeared. Instantly Coroner Richard pulled him up again, and the man stood, mouth clamped shut, shivering with the cold and his shock.

Then they were in the boats. Sir Richard joined Hawley in his, sitting a little ahead of the merchant, who took the steering oar at the back.

At a signal from Hawley, his men began to row slowly upstream, pulling away firmly in time to his fist's pounding on his thigh. Other boats followed in the darkness, one overhauling another and making the oars tangle, but they were soon sorted again, and continuing up the river.

Hawley watched the ship from narrowed eyes as they went, convinced that someone must realise the danger, but the watch on the ship appeared to be unaware of them, or, if he had seen them, thought nothing of a group of small rowing boats making off up river towards a fishery on a poaching expedition. They carried on until Hawley considered that they were safe from view. Unless they had a watch in the prow itself, it was unlikely that a sentry would notice them. The man on the main deck would have his view of the river obscured by the jutting castle at the front.

'*Now!*' he hissed, and the boats turned swiftly and began the race to the *Gudyer*. Hawley crouched down, the steering oar gripped firmly in his left fist while his right played with the hilt of his sword. The ship was a small, black shape in the distance, a curious round-sided lump with a projecting spike that looked as though it reached up to the clouds that fleeted by. Horn lanterns glowed at the mast and on the deck, making the prow stand out in relief against the blackness beyond.

When Hawley saw that they were nearly at the ship, he hissed a low command and the oars were raised and shipped. The vessel now was a growing mass of wood and spars, ropes thrilling to the wind.

Hawley risked a quick look over his shoulder and saw the boats catching up with him, and the *Gudyer* was near enough now to see the separate strakes of her clinker hull. He let the boat move on until it reached the rear of the ship, and only then did he nod to the man in the prow.

He stood easily, balancing on the balls of his bare feet, a rope with a grapnel in his hand; swinging it, he eyed the ship and then hurled it upwards. There was a clatter, a rasp of metal on wood, and he had it firm. Another man grabbed hold of a dangling rope and pulled, and then others had their own handholds and were swarming up the sheer side of the ship like so many spiders.

A face appeared, frowning with disbelief that turned to horror. It was whipped away and a high, screaming noise came to Hawley's ears. He went up at a run, his sword a clattering encumbrance at his hip, until he was at the top and could throw a leg over. A bell rang once, twice, and then there was a shrill cry, and silence. Hawley sprang down on to the hard wooden deck and drew his sword.

Coroner Richard was already running over the slippery planks towards the cabin under the stern deck. As he passed the mast, a man jumped at him, and Hawley saw the Coroner whip his sword about. There was a wet, sucking noise, and the man's arm was parted from his body. It fell to the ground, twitching like a worm cut in half, and the huge man lumbered on his way as though nothing had happened. Hawley ran to join him, finishing off the wounded sailor on the way. At sea there were no prisoners: it was kill or be killed.

The door was barred, and Sir Richard pounded on it to no avail. When Hawley reached his side, he too battered the timbers, and then whistled. His carpenter, a man with oak for arms, ran to his side, then took a hatchet from his belt and swung it at the panel beside the door. Three blows and a great crack opened as he turned the hatchet and levered the panel away. Another swing, and the panel fell inside. He hacked at the morticed plank beneath, then kicked the bottom panel, and there was an opening.

'Come out now, master,' Hawley called through the hole. 'If you come out, you'll live.'

'You will pay for this *piracy*, man!' shouted Sir Andrew. 'You'll be flayed alive for the damage done to Lord Despenser's ship, and I'll be delighted to witness your dying agonies!'

'You'll see nothing at all if you don't come out now!' the Coroner roared at his side. 'I have the authority and duty to arrest you, and if you don't come out at once, I will have your body dragged out.'

Even as he bellowed, Hawley heard the shouting from the other end of the ship. The sailors who'd been woken by the bell were appearing, and a ferocious fight had broken out. Steel rang on steel, and men's voices, hoarse with rage or fear or both, bellowed defiance or hatred. Hawley turned to see that his men were winning. The crew were already so depleted, with half of them still wandering about the town, that the outcome was inevitable.

'Your men cannot win. Come out and you may live,' the Coroner declared.

'So you say. How do I know you will hold to your word?'

'YOU DARE ACCUSE ME OF BAD FAITH? It was *you* who murdered a man from this town, Sir Andrew! You won't leave here alive while there's a man in Dartmouth to stop you, and you only have a small crew. If you come out now, you can save some of your men and perhaps save yourself from disaster too. But if you make me go in there to get you, I'll make damn sure you die.'

Hawley stepped back as a burly figure ran at him. He had already stabbed the man in the breast when he realised the body was headless, and he withdrew his sword distastefully, kicking the corpse towards the ship's side, where it toppled into the water.

'You have no crew, Sir Knight. You are going nowhere.'

The bar at the door slid back, and the door opened to show Sir Andrew, clad in tunic and gipon, sword at his side, that sneering expression on his face still.

'What now? Will you bind me?'

The Coroner stepped forward and clenched his fist, holding it underneath Sir Andrew's nose. 'You contemptible little shite. If you tempt me, yes, I may have you put in chains. Or I may pass you over to the mob here in Dartmouth for them to deal with you. So *don't* tempt me, Sir Andrew.'

Chapter Thirty-One

Alice, Danny's widow, was sitting on her stool at the table, trying to sew by the light of a flickering candle. She could barely see to thread her needle, but with the children having no father, and with her losing her husband, there was no money. She must pull herself together and set to, to mend all their clothing, and perhaps take in other people's mending too.

There would be work when the ships came in. The fishermen always needed help in gutting and salting down the hauls, while sailors would always be glad of extra hands to repair torn sails or nets. Yes, there would be work – and the older children must look after the younger. In God's name, it would be hard, though. The church would offer alms, and the food would be useful, but she would have to spread herself to survive.

Her eyes suddenly misted. God, how she missed her gentle Danny. Wiping her eyes with the back of her hand, she then closed them in defeat. She could do no more tonight. Glancing at the children asleep on the floor, she forced the tears away. There was no time for sorrow. She must plan the next day's work so that she might collect some money.

At the knock on the door, her heart pounded in fear. No one came visiting this late: whoever it was must have some evil purpose.

Taking hold of her knife from the table, she rose and went to the door, peering through the gap at the side to see who was there. As she did so, a shiver tore through her frame with the speed of a plummeting hawk.

She dropped to her knees and gasped with horror. One of the children snuffled in her sleep, and Alice went to her on all fours, even as the door rattled. If she could, the terrified woman would have recited the *Paternoster*, but she wasn't educated enough to have learned such recitations. She simply called on God to save her, to protect her children, and meanwhile the door thudded as a fist struck it.

'Go away!' she cried. The children were all stirring now, and the youngest began to sob.

A whisper reached her, like the soughing of wind through the branches.

'Adam! You're dead,' she sobbed, averting her face. 'Go back to the hell you came from!'

Baldwin and Simon had a fair-sized force when they left to seek the sailors. It did not take long to guess where they might be. Screams and shouting were coming from over towards South Town, and the two of them waved to the others to join them as they hurried on.

The town of Clifton had grown to join South Town, but where the two had originally met there were some rough areas of land. Beyond these were the beginnings of the old town that had once been separate. Simon knew it moderately well, although he tended to keep to the Clifton end of town, for that was where the bulk of his work was. He was aware that there were brothels down here, and several taverns that catered for other tastes, with cock-fighting pits, dog-baiting, and gaming rooms where a man might sit and lose his month's income in one game of chance.

The crew from Sir Andrew's ship were involved in an altercation with the owner of a small alehouse, with the slatternly drab who tried to ply her trade there standing before the door screeching at the sailors who were trying to gain admittance.

'Keep off, I say! Ow! You think you can barge in here and do what you want? I say you can . . .

Simon chose this moment to exercise his authority. 'Good evening, Malkin! I think you have no more to fear. As for you lot, you were to be held in the gaol, I think?'

'Piss on you! We're trying to find the Frenchie,' the leader of the sailors shouted.

From his complexion and speech, it was clear that Jan and the others had drunk a quantity of liquid bellicosity since leaving his house, and Simon smiled with relief that this was one opponent he need not fear. 'Him? Oh, he's here with us,' he said glibly.

'We'll take him, then,' the man declared loudly, stepping forward.

'First we'll escort you back to the gaol. Not only have you attempted to take a ship in the haven here, but you have also helped in the murder of a man who was guarding you on behalf of the King. You are all arrested. Drop your weapons!'

The ringleader stood in front of him, befuddled and bleary. He eyed Simon with a frown, then looked down at his sword, swaying slightly before spitting at Simon's feet and rushing forward at Pierre with a yell. Three others lifted their weapons and followed him, and Simon was buffeted from the path of the first two, before coming to blows with the third, who gripped a long knife in one hand, an axe in the other.

He swung his axe at Simon's head, and the two-headed weapon clashed from the Baliff's sword, missing his shoulder by less than an inch. The long knife slipped towards his belly, and he had to reverse his blade's movement to knock it aside, but as soon as he had recovered, the axe was moving again, first up at his neck, then round in a flashing arc and swooping down towards his knee. He leaped back, feeling foolish after his initial confidence about Jan.

The trouble was, sailors always started fighting when they were drunk: they were worse even than the miners on the moors for grabbing for a knife or dagger. The slightest insult to a man's wife, sister, mother, ancestry or even his methods of choosing his plots for digging, were all fine incentives for a fellow to reach for the nearest piece of steel and try to spit his opponent, even if the opponent had yesterday been his best friend.

The axe returned with a punch towards his face, and he had to duck. Quickly, he slipped his sword across to his right, opening the man's breast and slashing at his fist. A finger fell away, and the knife was dropped, and then Simon held his sword's point at the man's throat, and hissed, 'Yield, fool!'

There was a loud clash as the axe fell to the cobbles, and Simon breathed a moment's sigh of relief before looking about him. Baldwin had three men kneeling on the ground under his sword's blade while he gazed around with genial interest as though measuring the competition. Beyond him, Simon saw Pierre with one of the sailors, and as he watched, the frenchman snapped his sword back-handed and stepped away. There was a gout of blood and his opponent fell, his head rolling over the cobbles. Hamund was behind him with a dagger smeared with blood, looking dazed at the sudden eruption of violence, while other members of the posse stood about with their weapons dangling.

Simon heard a cry, and turned in time to see a man with a steel war-hammer in his fist running towards him.

A war-hammer was a fearsome weapon. On one side was the inch-square hammer head, while on the reverse was a vicious spike that projected four inches from the haft. A spear-tip at the top that could stab or slash shone wickedly in the occasional silvery moonbeams, and the whole was set atop a three-feet-long haft of wood strengthened with tangs of steel.

The man held it like a spear and he ran at Simon as if determined to gut him. Simon could only smash at the weapon with his sword and whirl from his path, but the fellow was quick on his feet and immediately tried to club Simon with the butt, which was weighted with a large ball of iron. It found its target, and Simon cried out as his elbow felt as though it was smashed to pieces. His hand was suddenly nerveless, and his sword dropped clattering to the ground.

'Baldwin!' he screamed.

Missing finger or no, the axeman was already grinning ferociously, and had gathered up his weapons again. He blocked the path of the others as the man with the hammer prodded it forward at Simon, forcing him away from his companions.

Holding his dead right arm with his left, desperate, Simon could only watch as the spear-tip waved before him, close to his face, at his throat, at his belly or groin. It moved, regular as a pebble on a string, and Simon was utterly engrossed at the sight as he moved back. Then something hit at the back of his knees, and he toppled into a carved moorstone horse-trough. The jarring sensation made him cry out with pain, but before he could attempt to regain his feet, the hammer was at his head, and it caught him a glancing blow over his eye. Simon felt sick with pain, and then he saw the hammer rise again, and begin to fall. He made a quick prayer . . .

And it stopped. There was a blade beneath it, blocking it – Pierre's blade – and Simon couldn't breathe as he watched the duel in fascination. The heavy blade swung around sharply, and the hammer was flicked away, only to stab out at Pierre, nearly nicking his thigh. Pierre leaped back, and the hammer was aimed at Simon again, but then Pierre returned and stopped it with a ringing crash that shook the hammer away, and now the hammer-fighter turned his full attention on to Pierre, leaving Simon to roll out of the trough, carefully protecting his arms as he landed on the ground again. He stayed there on all fours, panting, exhausted, as he watched his saviour.

Pierre handled his blade like a man who had been possessed by a fighting demon. He thrust, parried, blocked a great crashing blow that would have knocked Simon to his knees, and then began to move more swiftly, pressing his enemy with speed and determination, forcing him back farther and farther. The axeman was keeping the others away, but seeing his friend being pushed back, he lost concentration for a moment, and Simon saw Baldwin and Hamund attack together, Baldwin's sword cleaving through his arm near the shoulder, and while the man screamed in rage and hatred, Hamund's knife thrust in through his back, the point appearing in his breast. He shook Hamund away, and tried to reach the hilt of the knife with his remaining hand, but panic made him mad even as the blood pumped from his shoulder and he weakened. Soon he fell to his knees, and he flailed at his back ineffectually for a little longer, before keeling over and screaming once as the stump of his arm crashed into the cobbles. Then he was silent at last, and Hamund and Baldwin rushed to Pierre.

The hammer man knew that he was lost, but he wouldn't give up. He snarled at the men, even as they surrounded him. It was only a matter of time now, and he gazed at them all, eyes running from one to another. Pierre and Baldwin exchanged a look, and both sprang forward at the same moment. The hammer man shifted his weight and flung his point out, trying to spit one of them, but too late. Pierre's blade slapped into and through his thigh, while Baldwin's stabbed upwards, piercing his throat and running on until Baldwin's fist was below his chin, the knight's other hand gripping the wrist of the hand that held the hammer.

The man went over backwards like a sack of flour, and thrashed desperately as he drowned in his own blood, the fluid jetting from his nostrils and erupting from his mouth. Baldwin withdrew as the man gradually eased, and wiped his blade on his tunic.

'Simon? Are you all right?'

The expression of concern on his face was the last thing Simon saw as he felt himself fall into the great emptiness that appeared to open in the street in front of him.

It was broad sunshine the next morning when he woke, and his first thought was to condemn the loudly shouting fool. 'The great slubberdegullion cretin!' he said, wondering who it was. Then he remembered the name – Sir Richard de Welles – and with that, the sickness and headache were both fully explained. Simon burped and winced with the taste of acrid gas. At least this time he had made it to his own bed. Sir Richard hadn't taken it last night.

But then he had a recollection of the flash of a sword, the point of a war-hammer, and his eyes snapped wide as he remembered the desperate fight. It was enough to make him start to roll over to climb up from his bed, but even as he did so, his arm gave a sharp twinge, and he hissed with the pain.

'It's not broken,' Baldwin called quietly.

Simon carefully turned. Behind him, at the wall, Baldwin was standing easily, an anxious smile on his face, while Rob knelt beside him, rinsing a cloth in a bowl of warmed water scented with fresh lavender. 'I'm relieved to hear it, but it feels as though it may disagree with you.'

'We had you looked at last night as soon as you collapsed,' Baldwin explained, walking up and standing beside the bed, gazing down at him sympathetically. 'I know what it's like to wake with a head like yours. I would remain there and wait until the sickness passes. It is the best way to recuperate, old friend.'

'Perhaps,' Simon said, pushing himself up to a sitting position, 'but it wouldn't do anything for my determination to see that druggle Sir Andrew pay for his actions! To murder that gaoler because the man got in his path – that was the action of a coward!'

'I cannot disagree.'

'Where is Pierre and his companion? Are they safe?'

'They are here, in your hayloft. I thought it better that they should remain there than that they should be seen wandering the town.'

'He saved my life. I would not wish to see him harmed by some political liar and bully,' Simon mused.

'We can protect him, I think.'

'From the damned cur Andrew?'

'He is in your hall even now, being questioned by the Coroner. I left him to it.'

'Have you been here all night?'

Baldwin tilted his head slightly. 'Not all the night, no.'

'No. He went to wake the Coroner at dawn,' Rob said, stepping forward to wipe Simon's face with the cloth.

'Ouch! Be careful, fool!'

'You've been beat about the head and the arm, and you call *me* the fool?' Rob said insolently.

'Why do I only ever find servants who consider it their duty to bait me?' Simon grumbled, pushing Rob away and swinging round to set his feet on the ground. He took the cloth and placed it gently over his head, breathing in the fumes, and in a short while he did feel improved. He threw the bunched cloth at Rob and stood. 'Come, old friend. Let's go and see what this lying cretin has been telling the good Coroner.'

Simon had been sleeping in his back parlour, for the men could not have carried him up the steep stairs to his bedchamber, so all he need do was walk the short distance to his hall, but even that felt like a great trial, and he slumped onto a stool as soon as he arrived, glowering ferociously at the fair-haired knight.

'Ah, Bailiff. You appear to have slept late – but well, I trust?'

'You are clever, Sir Andrew. A most witty guest,' Simon said. 'I hope you shall be as witty when they place the hemp about your throat. They have an interesting variation on killing people here – had you heard? Sometimes they'll take a man out to the river, and hang him from a yard in sight of the town. They'll release him to fall into the water, so that his first gasps will start his drowning, and then they'll lift him up again. If they are careful, a murderer like you can be forced to struggle four or five times before he dies. It is good sport, I hear, for the watchers.'

'This is brave talk, but you should know that the ship in the haven is the property of my lord Despenser, and I am his trusted vassal. Any harm you do to me, you do to him, and my lord Despenser does not suffer people to insult him in this manner. If you further embarrass him by treating me in such a manner, he will visit vengeance on you. Be in no doubt of that!'

'He would protect even one such as you?' Baldwin enquired. 'A murderer, pirate, and ravisher of women?'

'I am no ravisher,' Sir Andrew spat.

'But you are pirate and murderer,' Simon declared. 'You killed all the men on the good ship *Saint John*.'

'You have stated so before, and I have denied it before. This is an untrue statement. It is a vile calumny.'

'You persist in this denial?' Coroner Richard rumbled.

'Of course I do! If I and my men had attacked the ship, as you say, would the crew not have defended themselves? Where are the damaged sails, the arrow-marks in the timbers? That ship of mine has been at sea only a short while, and it has no damage so far as I know.'

'Damage can be mended,' Simon said. 'Sailors are most adept at making repairs.'

'Sailors are also determined thieves. Didn't I hear that the ship was not despoiled? The whole cargo remained? You have seen my crew at work. Can you believe that they would have allowed me to sail away without taking all they wanted? It is ridiculous to suggest that I could have persuaded such a gathering of doddi-poll joltheads into obeying such a command. They would have emptied her, then fired her, and they would have fired her properly, not leaving a partial wreck to float about – and if I tried to stop them, they would have thrown me on it as it burned!'

That argument held force, Simon knew. He glanced up at the Coroner and Baldwin, and saw that they too were doubtful. 'Then who could have committed such a crime?'

Baldwin responded, 'If this is true, and seamen would not leave such a profit to go to waste, then surely we have to assume that someone other than a sailor is responsible.'

'How could that be?' Sir Richard scoffed. 'Only sailors go to sea.'

'A sailor would have taken the profit, though,' Simon said. 'As Sir Andrew said, a sailor wouldn't have let the cargo be wasted. He would have . . .'

He stopped, his mouth fallen wide.

'Simon?' Baldwin asked apprehensively. 'Is it your head again? Are you all right?'

The Bailiff waved his hand in denial. 'Coroner, let's have this worthless jolt-head returned to the gaol where he belongs. We need time to consider this anew.'

Chapter Thirty-Two

Rob had heated more water over his little fire, and the scent of lavender was filling the room with its delicious odour as the men sipped warm, spiced wine.

'What occurred to you when we were talking?' Baldwin demanded. 'It must have been a good thought, for you looked like the man who'd married a crone, only to learn she was a young virgin under an evil spell!'

Simon smiled at the idea. 'We know that the ship was not burned severely, do we not?'

'Of course.'

'And we agree that sailors would invariably have ransacked the ship – yet there was no need for them to have rushed away, because so far as we can tell, there was no threat to them. If they were near the ship when Hawley appeared, pirates would prefer to attack him as well, rather than flee after setting the ship on fire.'

'We have been over this,' Baldwin said. 'If they were on board, why should they flee and not remain and protect their prize?'

'Exactly!' Simon smiled. 'And the final point is, why on earth would they remove the bodies?'

Coroner Richard looked from one to the other. 'What are you two on about? Surely a pirate would happily throw all the victims overboard. Pirates are not fastidious about a soul's protection – they wouldn't bring a corpse back to land for burial, would they? Hey?'

'What is your point, Simon?' Baldwin asked.

'Just this: what if the whole reason for the ship's destruction was in order *to conceal something else*?'

The Coroner looked at Baldwin and tapped at his head with

consternation. He made to move towards Simon, but Baldwin held up his hand. 'Explain!'

'What if the crew were not all killed . . . Sweet Jesus! That is it!'

'What?' Sir Richard snapped.

'Only a few of the crew were killed . . .' His face suddenly beamed with understanding. 'Baldwin! You were right! The young virgin! Pyckard's wife!'

'That's it!' Sir Richard said, and sprang on Simon. 'Sir Baldwin, he's babbling. Best get a physician and tie him down. Seen it before. Bad bash on the head, brain gets scrambled. Poor fellow, but can't do anything for him.'

'Get this scurvy lobcock off me!'

'Sir Richard, Sir Richard, please,' Baldwin said soothingly. 'Let us just hear him out.'

After continued persuasion, the Coroner removed himself from the Bailiff's prostrate figure, although he stood nearby with a doubtful scowl on his face as Simon clambered grunting from the ground.

Holding his damaged elbow carefully, Simon addressed both men. 'What if the whole affair was made up? The attack on the ship, the death of the crew – all was invented. The cargo wasn't stolen by pirates because there *were* none!'

'Who attacked the ship, then?'

'Pyckard.'

Sir Richard moved imperceptibly towards Simon.

'Listen to me, Sir Richard, before you try leaping on me again!'

'Why should Pyckard invent this assault?' Baldwin asked.

'His wife! You remember she died in a squall? I heard that some of the men who died on the *Saint John* were also on that ship, the *Saint Rumon*, with Mistress Pyckard when she was on her last sailing. What if Pyckard had learned that there was something wrong about that sailing? How can I have been so dim!'

There was a loud knocking at the door, and the three men remained silent as Rob went to open it. He was soon back, a muddy, sweat-stained man behind him, clad in a tunic of red and green with a shield on the breast. It meant nothing to Simon, but Baldwin and Sir Richard recognised it at once.

'Quarterly Argent and Gules, in the second and third a fret Or, overall a bend Sable,' Sir Richard muttered. 'Blast!'

'Eh?' said Simon.

'Despenser,' Baldwin explained quietly.

Simon swallowed, but stood and beckoned the man. 'I am the Bailiff, Representative of the Keeper of the Port. How can I serve you?'

'I am sent by the lord Despenser, Bailiff. I have a communication which is being delivered to all towns throughout the realm.' The man handed Simon a rolled parchment, and he took it warily. He unrolled it and glanced down the flowing script. Modern writing he found rather hard to read. It was so often like this: rounded, each letter rather like the next. Still, first he looked at the huge seal as though he recognised it, and then he absorbed the message itself.

'This is . . . astonishing.'

'What does it say?' Baldwin demanded.

'It says that since the hostilities with the French king, and the loss of Gascony, the realm must take care with all threats to the nation's security. I must immediately hold any French subjects who might pose such a threat and deliver them to the Lord Despenser's representative, Sir Andrew de Limpsfield.'

'Aha,' Sir Richard said without humour.

Simon re-rolled the parchment and tapped it against his palm. 'You have travelled far. Can we offer you ale? Wine? Some food?'

When the messenger had been seated, and Rob sent to fetch a good meat pie and some more spiced wine, Simon looked at him seriously. 'You will have more news, I am sure. Come, I am the King's man in the port here, this knight is the King's Coroner from the King's own estate, and this is the Keeper of the King's Peace. We are all his loyal subjects. Can you tell us more news of what is happening in the country?'

'Gladly. All the Queen's estates have been sequestered by the King. I have messages for her stewards in Cornwall from Bishop Stapledon.'

'The good bishop?' Baldwin said sharply. 'He is involved in this?'

'I heard it was all on his own advice. The bishop is anxious about the nation's security, and recommended to the King that he take actions to protect himself. After all, the Queen is sister to the French king.'

As Simon spoke to the man, Coroner Richard adding some words of his own, Baldwin heard little of it all. He was too stunned at what he had learned.

In all the years since his return to Devon, he had trusted the integrity and honour of the bishop. He had believed the man when he had said that he was interested in this Frenchman in case he was a spy, and had been reluctant to believe Pierre when he asserted that the bishop was hand-in-glove with Despenser. But now it seemed it was all true, and his friend, Bishop Walter, was on the side of the man who would despoil the nation.

He was cold suddenly. In this room with the fire flickering merrily, he felt as though his soul had been encased in ice. It was a terrible sensation. To lose a friend like Stapledon was appalling, but he was sure now that he could not trust the bishop. Perhaps that was why Stapledon had asked him to pray with him, just to reinforce the bond that lay between them – to make it easier to pull the wool over his eyes.

'It's rumoured that all the Queen's household will be reviewed. All the French subjects in it will have to be arrested and held away. We don't want potential spies within the royal household, and it'd be too easy for her to write messages to her brother,' the man was saying.

Arrests without evidence, without trial. This was not the behaviour of a monarch who had respect for the law and the people: it was the action of a despot. Baldwin felt a sour nausea rising from his stomach. The Queen was being persecuted, unfairly and unreasonably, and he was revolted by it.

What sort of country was this to live in, to raise children in, when a reckless and malevolent King could on a whim deprive his own wife of all her friends and protectors? Isabella's closest companions were all French, so these were the people King Edward II was bound to arrest. But they were not spies, they were merely her circle of friends, those on whom she depended. If the rumours were true, she'd seen little enough of her own husband recently. He reflected on the relationship between Despenser and the King. Only a cruel and implacable enemy would put this idea into the King's mind.

'I need to walk to clear my head,' he blurted out, and stood.

The messenger looked bemused, not realising how his words might have affected the knight, but Simon saw his alarm and would have gone with him, but his feet stumbled even as he stood.

Baldwin shook his head. 'No, Simon. You remain here with our guest. I shall go for a short walk. I won't be long.'

'Where are you going?' Simon murmured.

'I don't know. Anywhere away from him and Sir Andrew,' he said harshly.

Leaving Simon's house, Sir Baldwin walked out through the weed-infested garden to the small barn, which he entered; he then climbed the ladder. Up in the hayloft, he saw Pierre sitting in the far corner, a thick blanket over his shoulders, watching him with a smile. Hamund lay near his feet, curled up in a nest of hay like a dormouse.

'You have some news, I think?' Pierre asked, studying his expression.

'Pierre, we have received orders to have you captured and give you to Sir Andrew. We can delay his release from prison for a short while, perhaps, but the orders are explicit. All Frenchmen are to be watched and arrested.'

'This order comes from . . . ?'

'It was signed by the King – but the messenger comes from Despenser.'

Pierre stood. 'Then you have no choice. I would not expect you to hold me safe when that monster makes his demands. You have to give me up.'

'*No*. At present no one knows where you are. Last night you saved the life of my friend Simon. We must help you as we may. I will not send you back to be tortured or murdered.'

'This is a very different song from the one you sang only yesterday,' Pierre said. 'What has changed your mind?'

'I have heard that Queen Isabella's estates are to be sequestered, at the suggestion of Bishop Stapledon. If I was wrong about him, I was wrong about much. I cannot save you if you fall into Despenser's clutches, but I can at least help you escape to France from here. The ship is still in the haven. Let us go to it now. Once you are aboard, it should be easy enough to set sail and you will be secure, I hope.'

Pierre knelt and took Baldwin's hand. 'I am your servant, Sir Knight. You risk much to save me.'

'In the Queen's name, I believe it is only right,' Baldwin said.

As the messenger left the chamber Coroner Richard walked to Simon's bench and sat heavily. 'I am sorry about this. I would prefer to have Sir Andrew kept in gaol and tried for murder, but what can we do?'

'There is nothing we can do when a fellow like him has such powerful friends,' Simon said flatly. 'He has escaped us, Coroner.'

The idea that the arrogant prickle could escape all justice was sickening, and Simon felt a wave of revulsion. Sir Andrew would continue with his bullying and threatening. No one would be safe from him. No one at all. Anyone who dared to stand in his path would be removed. As would Pierre.

'What can we do to protect the Frenchman?' he asked.

'He is naturally at risk all the while he remains here,' the Coroner said slowly. 'Once he is aboard a ship bound for a foreign port, he could be followed by another ship, but only if the ship is ready to let her sails fall and has provisions . . .'

Simon shouted for Rob. 'Get over to my place of work and tell Stephen to come here at once!'

'You do that, and I'll just go and make sure that the men in the gaol are all well enough,' Sir Richard said. 'We wouldn't want any of them to be held up because of a minor scratch or two after the fighting last night. And I may drop into the Porpoise on the way, to order a barrel of ale for them all. Perhaps they would appreciate some refreshment before I tell them they are free to sail.'

'An excellent idea. Don't hurry yourself,' Simon smiled.

'I didn't intend to,' the Coroner admitted. 'This reminds me of the old joke about a recruiting sergeant. He was sent to fetch some men for the coming battle, and in he marched, ready to pay any man he found to come and fight with him. "Men, are there any among you here who'd join his lordship's host and protect our lands from the dreadful invasion of the enemy? I have a shilling here for every man who will come with me and fight." Well, there were twenty men in there, and they all put up their hands and joined him. And before they left the tavern, all wanted to buy a drink. Now the sergeant, he was a dedicated man, but he saw that if he turned down their offers, it wouldn't serve his master well, for most of them would decide not to join a force with such a miserable sergeant. So he drank all they gave him, and woke up the next afternoon with a headache and no coins. "Where are the men?" he asked the tavern-keeper. "Oh, they all left last night, master. They said to thank you for the ale, though." Well, the sergeant didn't hurry back to his camp, and when he got there, he found it ransacked. The enemy had arrived in the night and taken the place. He walked disconsolately about until he came across one of the men from the tavern. "You all got here, then? That's good, anyway." "Oh, yes," the man replied. "It was a bugger taking this place, though. Took us ages!" You see, they'd gone back to the wrong side!'

'I see,' Simon said. It was not sufficient to make him laugh uproariously, but he could manage a small grin at the joke.

However, the Coroner didn't appear to expect laughter. 'I wonder which side Sir Andrew will fall on, if his master should ever quarrel with the King.'

Stephen was at his desk when Rob came to summon him. He rolled up the great parchments and stored them in the waxed leather cylinders, and eyed the lad disdainfully.

'What are you looking at?' Rob asked pugnaciously.

'It is good to be reminded that even boys are part of God's plan,' the clerk replied loftily, 'although in your case you're more a part of His mystery, it should be said.'

In truth, though, he was reflecting that Rob had changed much in recent days. His demeanour was as truculent as ever, but now he had the appearance of a lad who was trying to help. He had cleaner clothes on – not *absolutely* clean, of course, but much better than usual – and if Stephen was correct, his face had been washed in the last day. Even his hands appeared less grubby than usual.

'I don't know what you're on about,' Rob said, and was gone.

Smiling to himself, Stephen packed his penner and locked the door securely behind him. He took the alley west up the hill, and when he came to the top, he saw Danny's widow. He was about to go over and sympathise, when he saw that her manner was not that of a recently bereaved woman. Yes, there was sadness in her, but also a look of great relief.

'A good morning to you,' Stephen said politely.

'And you, sir,' she smiled back.

He eyed her. Perhaps the loss of her brother Adam and husband Danny had unhinged her mind? 'Are you well? Is there aught you need?' he asked cautiously.

'No, no. I am well, master.'

'You have money?' he questioned doubtfully.

'We have a little put by. I think we'll survive.'

There was a brightness in her eyes that seemed to demonstrate the onset of fever – or perhaps it was merely the result of having slept little. What with worrying about her future and that of her children, it would be little surprise if she was restless in her bed at night.

He bade her farewell then hurried on to Simon's house, but as he went, he could not help but throw a glance over his shoulder. She was still there, lips slightly parted, eager as a woman waiting for a lover. The thought sent dread into his soul.

Entering Simon's house, he could not help but feel a vague sense of dissatisfaction. It made him irritable, and when he found the Bailiff was not concentrating on him, but instead was staring at the wall deep in thought, he snapped, 'What is all this about, Bailiff? I thought our work was more or less done for the week.'

'I need to know which ship is most likely to be ready to sail, and what the level of preparedness is on the great cog of Sir Andrew's.'

'What business is that of ours?'

'Stephen, I apologise,' Simon said wearily, and explained about the last night's events.

Too late, Stephen spotted the large bruise and scratches on his master's forehead. Earlier, in his less sympathetic mood, he had assumed that the unwonted paleness of his face and the slight tremor in his hands were all signs of excesses of wine the night before. Now he realised he had been uncharitable, and sought to make amends.

'Sir Andrew's ship, the *Gudyer*, is being victualled, and made ready to sail. The only ship in better condition is Master Pyckard's, the *Saint Denis*. She is ready. Should have gone this morning, but the master felt uncomfortable since he lost a crew-member or two.'

'Right, tell him that he'll have his man back shortly. In the meantime, use any means you can think of to delay provisioning Sir Andrew's ship. I have a feeling that they'll want to sail as soon as they may, and I'd like them to be stopped in that ambition.'

'I don't see how they can go anywhere when you have half the ship's company in the gaol,' Stephen said tartly.

'They'll need to be released soon,' Simon said, and explained about the message.

'I see,' Stephen said. He stared into the middle distance for a little while, and then declared, 'Right, I can arrange for that. Leave it with me.'

When Baldwin reentered the hall a few minutes later, Simon was alone again. 'Coroner gone?'

Simon nodded. 'He'll delay matters a while, but we will have to set Sir Andrew free, even if the thought chokes me! Still, we need not be hasty about it. If we can keep him and his men in gaol for a little longer . . . You spoke with Pierre?'

'Was it that obvious?'

'To me, yes. I have arranged for the ship to wait for him and

Hamund. Hopefully they can set sail as soon as they both arrive on board.'

'Good! With luck they will be on the ship by midday,' Baldwin said.

'Let us pray, then,' Simon said fervently, 'that he reaches it.'

Chapter Thirty-Three

'Weather has changed, hasn't it, Law?' Alred called. He had set up a brazier near their hole so that he could heat a pot of water ready for a cup of hot mint drink, and was watching the pot with his hands held to the warmth.

The lad grunted in response. 'When you spend all night in an alehouse, I suppose you feel the cold more.'

Alred sniffed, but couldn't be bothered to deny it. His hands were shaking, and his eyes felt like someone had scuffed sawdust into them. It wasn't his fault, though. He hadn't been intending to go to the tavern. It was only because that baggage of pus and wind had been arguing with Bill that he'd gone. He'd have stayed out here else. Still, while his belly was rumbling like the lid on a heavy cooking pot, he was in no position to argue.

Arguments were the bane of his life. Now, no doubt, these two would be at each other's throats all day, too. Or worse, they'd not be talking. He hated it when they got like that. Working steadily at either side of a trench, as though the man three paces away didn't exist.

'How was Bill last night?' he asked tentatively.

Law was still for a moment. 'He was all right. We both were.'

It was not quite true. When they returned to shore, they had a brief battle with the owner of the boat and his friends. The fact that they'd brought the thing back had saved them more of a pounding, but as it was they had been struck down, and the menace in the boat-owner's voice had been unmistakable when he explained what he would do to any 'thieving landlubberly sons of whores', and Law and Bill hurried away from the river as quickly as they could. Alred was still in his tavern when they got there, and the two of them wrapped themselves in their blankets with many a grunt of pain from bruises and scratches. When he stumbled in, burping, humming merrily, and tripped over a pile of tools to fall on his face in the hay, giggling inanely until he started to snore, neither spoke.

'Good. Good,' Alred said. 'He's taking his time, though.'

Law shrugged. It was all one to him. Bill had only been sent to fetch some pies. No doubt he'd be back when he had them.

Alred threw him a look that mixed offence with loathing, before turning back to his drink. The water was boiling well, so he wrapped a strip of cloth about his hand and drew the pot from the heat, pouring a liberal measure over the crushed mint leaves. The smell made his mouth water. Good and pungent, just as he liked it.

'Gaming's a fool's errand,' he said, blowing to cool the drink. 'You know, I saw a man yesterday, must have been playing dice or something, because when he came out into the road, he was like a man with his brain cut out. No sense at all in him.'

'Can't imagine anyone like that,' Law said sarcastically.

'Law, what is the problem?' Alred demanded with despair.

'Oh, it's nothing. Look – here's Bill.'

Bill was trotting up the lane, pies in his hand, and as he passed them around, he looked at Law, who shook his head. 'You've told him nothing?'

Alred was instantly listening. 'About what?'

'Last night we took the Frenchie back to his ship to let him escape,' Bill said bluntly.

'You . . . you did *what*?'

'Aye, but then we didn't know he was going to be caught as soon as he put his feet on the deck.'

Law gaped. 'You don't say!'

'I bleeding do. And he was taken to the Bailiff's house, but then a mob broke in and tried to catch him. Didn't manage it. Still, Sir Andrew, rot his soul, is in gaol with most of his crew, and Pierre is safe.'

'Who caught him?'

'What I heard, this man Hawley took over the ship in the dark with some of his crewmen, and they knocked the poor devil down as soon as his head was over the rail.'

'Will he be safe now?' Law asked, goggle-eyed.

Alred felt the need to interpose at this point. 'We have this roadway to finish.'

'He should be safe enough, so long as he gets back to the ship . . . and there's no one else trying to catch him there.'

'I *said*: this hole here has to be filled, Bill.'

Law frowned. 'Do you know where he is, then? If he's found in town without any help, he could be taken again.'

'Ivo won't do that. Poor sod's acting gaoler now, since old Widdecombe Will got killed last night. Sir Andrew did that himself, so they say.'

'No!'

Bill nodded dourly. 'Stabbed him slowly. He likes killing, that bastard.'

'So is Pierre still at the house?'

'I reckon he's hiding somewhere.'

Alred smiled brightly. 'Good. So in that case, there's nothing more to be said. The man's safe enough for now, and while he's in his sanctuary, wherever it is, we can finish the road here.'

Bill nodded. Law scowled.

'What are we?' Alred asked.

'Paviours,' Law muttered. Bill was silent.

'What are we?' Alred repeated, turning his ear as though deaf.

'Paviours,' Law said. Bill murmured the word condescendingly.

'I said, *What are we*?'

'Bloody paviours, you arse,' Bill snapped. 'Now stop this daftness and let's get to work, eh?'

Stephen hurried back to his place of work, still feeling guilty for snapping at the Bailiff. The poor man must have been in quite some pain from the look of his brow. Terrible business. And the gaoler dead! Poor Will didn't deserve that.

He was scarcely heeding where he was going, when he saw her

again. There at the end of the alley was Danny's widow, talking to a man. Oh yes, there were lines of worry and sadness on her face, but for all that she was as animated as a maid with her first lover as she expostulated with this man.

His back was to Stephen, but then the clerk felt a devil tempt him, and he turned back to the alley, pushing past her with a muttered apology. The man stood aside, and for an instant Stephen saw him. It was the same man who had made Peter Strete stop and frown the other evening. His face was as square as he recalled, and the line of his jaw was prominent, uncovered as it was by any beard. It had a pale look, as though it was only recently shaved after a long time.

Stephen nodded to him and continued on his way. The man was familiar, but *why*?

Hamund and Pierre left the little garden by springing over the wall into the foul lane beyond, and thence hurried northwards towards the alley that led down to the waterside.

Pierre suddenly tugged Hamund back, and for a second the older man thought he was pulling rank on him, as though a lowly abjuror and peasant was not significant enough to be permitted to lead the way before a noble knight . . . but then he saw Pierre put his finger to his lips and peer cautiously around the corner.

'Two men down near the shore,' he whispered. 'We cannot get past them without raising the alarm.'

Hamund nodded. They could not to fight their way through this. If they did, they must be captured when the Hue and Cry was raised against them.

Pierre eyed him, then breathed, '*Viens, mon ami*! With me, friend, quickly!'

Hamund saw him dart out and lean against the wall of a house as though overcome with tiredness. Hamund joined him, and Pierre put his arm about the other man's shoulder, singing a saucy tavern-song in a deep voice. Hamund joined in with the chorus about the tapster's daughter, and the two sang their way up the alleyway, staggering from side to side and out into the lane.

Once there, Pierre stopped singing, and peered back along the alley. 'We are safe, I think. They were too dull-witted to consider that we could be the men they seek. Now we must go this way, perhaps. The ship is there? Yes.'

It looked so near. Yet it was such a distance out in the river. Hamund felt his hopes failing. 'Can we swim to her?'

'I cannot swim,' Pierre confessed. 'I never had the skill.'

Hamund frowned. 'Then what can we do?'

'I have an idea!' Pierre was staring down at where the paviours were shovelling gravel into a hole. 'Come!'

Pattering along, Hamund had the feeling that he was being led on an adventure. He felt like a squire to a great knight who was showing his quality by hunting a dragon or rescuing a woman from unimaginable dangers. At any moment he might be confronted by a great beast . . . No. This was enough of an adventure without thinking of mysterious animals. For the first time in his life, he was truly living, and it was all thanks to this man with him, Sieur Pierre de Caen. He hurried to catch up as the Frenchman reached the paviours at their task.

'My friends. You helped me yesterday, and I am most grateful to you for that.'

'What are you doing here?' Law demanded.

Bill gave a wry smile. 'Thought you were safe.'

'We would be, except . . .'

'We heard,' Bill acknowledged.

'No! I will not have this!' Alred expostulated. 'We cannot risk ourselves on your behalf, sir. No! You must go before someone sees you here.'

'I would be very grateful if you could help us again.'

'Didn't you hear me?'

'What do you want?' Law asked.

'Law, I said—'

'Al, shut up, all right?' Bill said wearily. 'You know what I did before. This helps me feel that I'm making some sort of compensation for that man. If you don't like it, you don't have to join in, but if I can save this man's life, it's worth it.'

'Go ahead, then!' Alred exclaimed, throwing his hands in the air. 'Don't worry about me or this contract, will you? You don't know this man, nor what he's done – nothing! But you'll drop me in it, won't you. Fine. Just go, then!'

'Sorry, Al,' Bill muttered.

He and Law clambered from the hole, and strode to where Pierre stood.

'Wait!'

Flushed and angry, Alred followed them. He stood before the Frenchman and stared angrily at him, hands on his hips, head jutting truculently. 'I hope you're proud of yourself, that's all I can say. Just for you, the people of Dartmouth are going to have to wait longer for their road to be mended. Hah! Well? What are you waiting for?'

Baldwin poured himself some wine. 'So the crew will soon be released?'

'Yes. But their ship will have some problems being prepared for sea, I think.'

'Let us hope that it will be enough. I would not have the man arrested and then executed. I think I was misled about him. By Walter.'

'For my part, I know he saved my life. I do not care what another says of him, I would not see him harmed. I don't understand Walter's part in all this, though.'

'Nor I,' Baldwin said. He looked up as a knock came at the door.

Simon shouted, 'Yes!'

Stephen pushed the door wide, and entered anxiously. 'Bailiff, the men in the gaol . . . they are gone!'

Even as he asked, 'How can they be?' Simon was rising and grabbing for his sword.

'I heard that they had a messenger, a man with the Despenser's shield on his breast. He asked where the gaol was, and went straight there. He showed Ivo a parchment that demanded their immediate freedom, and the sergeant let them loose. He had no choice!'

Baldwin clenched his jaw. 'Come, Simon. We have to make sure that our friends are not molested.'

The way to the shingle was barred. Law went first, on his own. He had tried an alleyway, and could get to the shore itself, but once there he found his way blocked by sailors. They looked him up and down and decided he was not worth their bother, but everywhere he looked, he saw more men lounging, watching the roads with care.

'I can see no way past them,' he reported back to the other four.

'Even if we could slip past, they would soon catch us on the shore,' Hamund said. He had a vague memory of the beach in his mind. 'How is the tide, Master Lawrence?'

'It's out just now, so to reach the boats you have to run along the mud.'

'We cannot manage this,' Hamund said. This was less an adventure, more of a nightmare.

'There must be a way,' Pierre said.

Hamund tentatively murmured, 'Perhaps, if we crossed to Hardness and took a boat from there . . . we could row to the ship and avoid all the men waiting here.' In his mind's eye he saw the line of buildings as he rowed the ship over the smooth waters towards the *Saint Denis*. The mill's great wheel, the line of little workshops and tradesmen's sheds, the drying and salting trestles set out for the day's catch . . . and then back.

Bill was saying, 'If we try to cross over that bridge, they'll see us for certain!'

'Hamo the cooper showed me a way,' Hamund said suddenly. 'If we can get in there, we'll be safe enough.'

Hamund led them along the street until he found the last alley. Taking them down this, he told them to wait for him. 'I'll have to get Hamo to open up the way and let us through.'

'How do you know he'll help?' Alred demanded suspiciously. 'If he's got half a brain, he'll turn us in and collect any bounty.'

'His friend was the gaoler, Will. When I tell him that the gaoler's murderer is the man who seeks Pierre's death, he'll help us.'

Hamund was convincing, but Bill pulled him aside before he left them.

'In case they recognise you, friend, take this,' he said, and pulled off his cowl and hood, setting them on Hamund's shoulders. With that drawn over his head, he looked very different.

Once back down the alley to the shoreline, he made for the cooper's works. Groups of sailors stared at him as he passed, but none recognised him, apparently, with his simple disguise.

'Master?'

The cooper was tapping rings of steel down about the staves of a barrel, and he scarcely looked up as Hamund appeared.

'Do you remember me from last night?'

Hamo peered under his hood and laughed. 'The drowned rat, eh? What're you doing back here?'

'You know your friend who died?'

'Will, aye. Poor sod.'

'It was the man who killed him who seeks my death also, and that of my companion. Will you help us?'

'It sounds like a dangerous sport, aiding you. What should I do that for?'

Quickly Hamund explained what he needed, and the cooper nodded slowly, but grimly. 'If that's all you want, I don't see why I shouldn't let you through to open up the yard's gate. I could give you a lift too, if you wish. My boat is down below us.'

Hamund gasped out his thanks. This was more than he had hoped for – he'd imagined he would have to borrow a boat from a fisherman, but this would be much safer. After expressing his gratitude, he hurried through the cooperage, through the chamber at the rear, and into the yard. Throwing the gate wide, he looked up and down the alley. Seeing Alred at the corner, he whistled and beckoned, and soon the others were with him. They slipped through the gate, then made their way to the workshop.

Hamo was still knocking the hoop down over the barrel, but he looked up and nodded briefly as he saw the men.

'Master Cooper, we owe you our thanks,' Pierre said stiffly.

'That's good. Any enemy of the man who killed Will can't be all bad.' Hamo set down his hammer, pulled his leather apron from his neck, and jerked his head towards the waiting ship. 'Reckon you want to be going, eh? I'd best help you.'

They set off to the flat pavement before his shop, then went down the slippery ladder to the shingle. Here Alred and his men left them as they trod, squelching, towards the boat. It was some way, and they must avoid the thicker pools of mud which oozed glutinously as they stepped in it. Suddenly, they heard a cry, then a long-drawn-out call, and Hamund threw a fearful look over his shoulder as he wondered what this meant. It was clear enough in a moment.

Alred, Law and Bill had been encircled by a group of sailors, and now Bill roared at the top of his voice: 'Go! Run!' before he was knocked to his knees.

Pierre grasped his sword and would have turned back, and while he stood undecided, Hamund felt as though his belly had fallen from his body, leaving only a terrible emptiness. All at once he could see Pierre running back, fighting alone against the host of sailors, falling under their knives and swords. And he would be alone again, without even this companion.

But then Hamo took Pierre's arm. 'Seems to me that if you go back there, you'll die, friend. And that would make anything that happens to them pointless, wouldn't it? I think you should come with me and get to safety.'

'They are being taken! It is wrong for me to escape and leave them to be blamed for my offences!'

'They're taken already,' Hamo said. 'Won't help much for them to be watching you get killed, will it?'

Pierre gave a short nod, and turned back to face the river. He began to trudge onwards.

Hamund blew out a breath of relief, feeling like a felon who'd been given a reprieve even as the rope tightened about his neck. The three dragged Hamo's boat to the water and pushed it in a short way. Pierre stepped in, then Hamund, and finally Hamo pushed and climbed in at the same time. He took the oars, and was about to sit and begin rowing, when he stopped and stared over Hamund's shoulder.

Looking in the same direction, Hamund felt as though his bowels would melt. 'No!'

From near the great mill-wheel, two larger rowing boats were pushing off. In the front of the first Hamund could clearly see the long, flowing fair hair of Sir Andrew. He had a drawn sword in his hand, and he was waving it about his head like a hunter urging on his steed.

Chapter Thirty-Four

Stephen ran along behind them as Baldwin and Simon hurried down the hill. They reached the gaol in time to see Ivo closing the door after him.

'What have you done, you fool?' Baldwin roared, grasping the unfortunate man by the throat and forcing him back against the door he had just locked.

'What? What do you mean?'

'All the seamen, where are they?'

'A man came, a man with the Despenser shield on his breast – he had orders for me to release them. What could I do against a letter like his? I'm only a sergeant, I'm not a man-of-law or anything. If I'm given an order from someone with authority, what else can I do?'

Baldwin threw him back, releasing him with disdain. 'You repel me! Which way did they go?'

'To the shore, I think.'

'They've gone to head Pierre away from the ship,' Simon breathed.

'Yes. And now we must hurry there ourselves,' Baldwin said. 'You, Ivo le Bel, and you, Stephen, search the Porpoise and the other taverns and see whether you can find Coroner Sir Richard de Welles. Is that clear? Tell him what has happened here, and that we are to go to the shore instantly. We would be grateful for his support.'

'I will tell him.'

'Do so. And now, Simon, are you well enough to trot?'

Simon gave a twisted grin. His head was still enormously painful, but the sickness was retreating. He tested his blade in the scabbard, and the two ran over the cobbles to the first alley. Here Baldwin ducked under a line of drying clothes, and the two skidded and slid down a path made slick. There was no kennel here, and the wastes from all the houses were thrown straight into the lane itself, to lie there until the next storm washed the mess away. Simon was only aware of a desire to keep from falling.

At the bottom, they immediately saw that something was wrong. There was a small group of men held back by a pair of grinning sailors. Two others were whistling and making lewd suggestions to a flush-faced young woman of perhaps sixteen years.

Baldwin saw beyond them a group of men ringing some others. There was a flash or two of steel in the sunlight, and he cursed. Yet he would not leave the girl to suffer the indignity of the men's words. He put his hand to his sword, and even as he did so, there was a hoarse bellow of rage at his side as the Bailiff drew his sword and, lifting it high, roared abuse at all four sailors, running in to close with them.

'Simon!' Baldwin groaned, and then dragged his own blade from its scabbard, and ran to catch his friend.

There was little need. Perhaps the sight of the Bailiff filled with righteous anger was enough to terrify the sailors, or perhaps it was the realisation that if two men attacked from their side, there was little they could do to subdue the men before them too, but whatever the reason, the four suddenly took to their heels.

Baldwin was about to stop and tell the men huddled with the girl to go and find some help, when he realised that Simon had not paused like him. Rolling his eyes heavenwards, he cried, 'Murder! Out! Out! Out! Fetch weapons, come and help!' and took off after him at a sprint. His booted feet slapped on the hard moorstone of the way, and his ankle was jarred at one point, but he forced himself onwards, until he had almost caught up with Simon. The sailors were a short distance ahead, and now they shouted for help, and instantly two more of their companions ran back to meet them.

Baldwin bellowed, 'For the King!' and kept on running. His sword was ready to stab, his left hand forward, when he met the first of them. He flicked his sword up and right, knocking aside a long knife, and then he slammed his fist forward, the full weight of the sword in his hand catching the sailor over the temple. The man crumpled to the ground as Baldwin danced to his left, creating space between him and the next man. This one was joined by a fresh man; he had a short knife in each hand, while the other held a stout cudgel.

It was the cudgel he feared most. The daggers looked fearsome, but Baldwin was content that he could protect himself against them; however, the cudgel had a longer reach and could incapacitate him. He retreated a little, glancing this way and that over his shoulders, until he saw a narrow entrance to an alley. Carrying on, he waited until he could dart into it, and when the moment came, he sprang forwards.

Both had expected him to run away, and the change of direction startled them. He slipped quickly right, his sword ready, and as the man with the cudgel turned to meet him, Baldwin thrust once. His sword opened the man's thigh, and he screamed shrilly. Even as he dropped the cudgel to grab at the wound, Baldwin was at the other. Behind him, he could see Simon hacking and stabbing with gusto, still with two men at him, and Baldwin was anxious lest his friend might come to grief. Rather than prolong the fight, he tapped the knife in the man's left hand away, grabbed his right wrist in his own left hand, and pulled him forward, off-balance, his sword at the fellow's throat. 'Surrender, or die.'

'I yield! Please!'

The knives both clattered to the floor, and Baldwin kicked them away. They went over the edge of the quay, and he heard them strike the mud.

Without thinking, he was at the men about Simon. The first he stabbed in the flank, and the man grunted with the shock. The second saw his mate falter, and turned to face Baldwin with a long knife, but Baldwin's expression made him reconsider. In a matter of moments, all three were running away, back to join their comrades, and Simon and Baldwin followed them more slowly.

'There are lots of them,' Simon muttered, eyeing the crowd.

'I don't care,' Baldwin said. 'You! Stand back in the name of the King.'

'King?' the man sneered. 'We work for Lord Despenser. The King is our ally.'

He was suddenly silent as a bloody sword touched his throat. 'I am the King's Officer, and *I* say, "Stand back"!'

Simon used the point of his sword to emphasise Baldwin's words, and in the midst of the parted sailors, he saw Alred and his two assistants. 'What is all this?'

'These three helped the French spy to escape, that's what!'

'I've heard enough about this already,' Simon growled. 'He's no spy.'

'We have been ordered to stop him reaching France with his messages, and that's what we'll do.'

'Look!' Alred shouted, pointing.

Simon and Baldwin could see the two rowing boats overhauling the smaller one. The cooper was pulling as hard as he might, but he could not draw away from the others with four men in each working the oars.

The men whom Baldwin and Simon had rescued from the first four sailors had arrived now, and they pushed the sailors away from the quay as Baldwin and Simon peered out at the desperate chase.

'They'll kill them all, won't they?' Simon said.

'We can't catch up with them now.' Baldwin swore under his breath.

'The knight is almost at them,' Simon said quietly.

He could see the fair man waving his sword about his head, almost on the little rowing boat, and then there was a scream, and a small figure leaped from it at the larger boat. The fair man stumbled backwards, and with his arms outstretched, fell back over the side, making a vast splash, the smaller man at his breast. The two disappeared from view. Meanwhile, Pierre stood in the boat, his sword in one hand, dagger in the other, and waited. A crimson feather appeared in the sea even as the figure of Sir Andrew showed below the water. Of Hamund there was no sign.

Baldwin cupped his hands about his mouth and roared at the top of his voice: 'TURN YOUR BOATS AND COLLECT YOUR MASTER. LEAVE

THAT BOAT ALONE. I ORDER YOU TO LEAVE IT, IN THE NAME OF THE KING!'

There was a moment's pause. It was plain that the sailors were wondering what would be best for them to do, and then a cry came from the further craft, and the two turned their prows about, heading down river to where Sir Andrew's body had floated. As they struggled to gather him up, Baldwin saw the little boat making its way to the *Saint Denis*. Sir Pierre raised his sword in salute, bowing his head, and Baldwin made a bow in return. Then, as Pierre reached the ship and made his way up the rope ladder, Baldwin turned away, suddenly exhausted.

The inquest on this latest body took but little time, and Coroner Richard was pleased to be able to declare that the murderer, the notorious Frenchman called 'Pierre', was responsible. Baldwin looked across at the shipmaster from Sir Andrew's ship, Martin Pyngin, as this was recorded, and the man didn't blink. Well, if it could be said that he had achieved what Lord Despenser had commanded, even if Sir Andrew was dead, that would mean the man would live a little longer. It was no surprise he had chosen to present matters in the best possible light. So had Baldwin.

He had taken the shipmaster to the tavern as soon as Sir Andrew's body had been brought ashore, and indicated that were the murderer of Sir Andrew also dead, partly from being stabbed, partly from drowning, it would be so much the better for everyone. Especially since the man responsible for causing mayhem in the town the night before, murdering a gaoler for no reason, causing the Abbot of Tavistock's Bailiff to be badly hurt, and threatening violence on others, not to mention the piratical attack on another man's ship, had died. The crimes could die with them, Baldwin intimated.

The old shipman didn't comment, but sniffed and took a long pull of his ale. Later Martin left, still without speaking, but now he glanced across at Baldwin and gave a short nod before turning away and shouting at his crew in a voice that could have been heard clearly at Kingswear.

'A satisfactory end to the affair, I think,' the Coroner said with a smile as Stephen began to put away his pens and ink. 'All done that was needful. Now all we need consider is the matter of the other deaths.'

Alred was with his fellows, and he looked up at the Coroner as Sir Richard spoke. 'Perhaps a small reward would be in order, Sir Coroner?'

Richard gazed at him with a beatific smile. 'I have no need of one, but if you insist on it, I would be glad of a quart of ale, good fellow.'

Alred smiled at his joke, but then he realised the man was serious.

Simon and Baldwin between them bought the ales in the end. All walked to the Porpoise and took a bench outside. Baldwin called to the host and demanded ale for all of their company, and soon they were drinking cheerfully enough.

Alred looked about him as he drank, recalling his departure from the tavern the previous evening.

'Something wrong, Master Paviour?' Simon enquired, seeing his distraction.

'No, no. Just wondering what might have happened to a fellow who was here last night. Big lad, but very sad. I think he'd been out at the back in the gaming room.'

'The gaming rooms cost many of the sailors all their money,' Simon said.

'Yes. Daft pursuit,' Alred said with the comfortable knowledge that the last three games he'd played had made him a profit.

'Who was it?'

'I don't know. Some fellow I've seen about the place,' Alred said, adding candidly, 'I often see people walk past me, but they rarely look down at me when I'm in the hole. I've seen him with someone else, though. One of the merchants.'

'Tall? Slim? Short? Fat?' Simon asked.

'Quite tall. Not fat. Not the scrawny one who looks like he's only just out of his apprenticeship, the older one.'

'Hawley,' Simon said. He mused. 'This man, then – could it

be his clerk? A fairly well-fed look to him, round face, wears a blue tunic?'

'Yes, that's him. He was out here last night and when he left, his face was quite tragic, almost like he'd seen a ghost.'

Stephen smiled with the rest of them, but then his smile faded. 'A ghost . . .'

'You all right, clerk?' Simon asked.

'I . . . I think I have seen Adam, Bailiff.'

'Who?' Simon said absently.

'Didn't you say Pyckard told you Adam was on the ship? Adam, Danny's brother-in-law?'

Simon nodded, but his eyes were drawn back to the tavern, and now he stood, staring inside with a thoughtful frown. He turned and peered out at the haven. The *Gudyer* was just moving out into the channel off Kingswear, and he could see the great sails reefed in as she made her way down the river. 'I wonder . . .'

'What?' Baldwin asked sharply.

'In God's name, I think I see it all, Baldwin. I think I see it all.'

Baldwin was confused to hear that his friend wanted to go and speak to Hawley about his man, but he was loath to leave Simon to go on his own. In the back of his mind he wondered whether the Coroner was not in fact right when he suggested that Simon had hurt his head more badly than he had realised, when the sailor's hammer had struck him.

'Master Hawley, we want to speak to you about Strete,' the Bailiff declared. 'Is he here?'

Hawley had been sitting at his fireside when they entered. A clerk was at his side, and the master from his cog, Cynric, stood at the wall. 'I fear my man left my service last night.'

'He ran off, did he? Took his belongings and left your service?' Simon said. 'I suppose that's not surprising.'

'Why?' Hawley demanded.

'We've been struggling to understand this matter of the murders of Danny and Despenser's man here, Guy de Whatever . . . and the matter of the *Saint John* being attacked. And do you know what I wondered? I wondered why the ship should be empty. All I could think of was that someone killed the crew, and didn't bother to steal the cargo because they knew they'd win it all anyway.'

'So you're saying that *I* attacked the ship, put my men aboard, then pretended to fire her, slaughtered her crew and brought her back?'

'Yes. A salvage arrangement is better than nothing, and it runs less risk of a noose. You appear the hero of the hour by bringing the ship back, and win a pleasant salvage.'

'Except I had already agreed to waive my salvage.'

'What?'

'If you ask Pyckard's man of business, you'll learn that I agreed some while ago not to take my share. It seemed ungenerous when Pyckard was dying. I had no desire to hasten his death.'

Simon frowned. 'You have this in writing?'

'Pyckard's man will have it. I gave him a formal note rejecting my salvage. So no, Bailiff, I had nothing to do with it. I found the ship burning and brought her back. That is all.'

'I will check this.'

'Do so. But what made you wonder such a thing?'

Simon shot a look over at Baldwin. 'The ship was not entirely destroyed, and one crew member was dead. Any sailor would know how to destroy a ship, and if he fired it, she would be sunk. So I thought that you must have taken her and then brought her back to port for the salvage.'

Hawley scoffed. 'Just for the money? You think I'd ruin a dying man for profit when I could make more by reaching port before him?'

'I think you are a very capable sailor and master,' Simon said seriously. 'Where is your servant Strete now?'

'I had him deposited at the gaming hall in the Porpoise. He had been taking my money and using it to pay for his gambling.'

'What, taking the money from your chest?' Sir Richard said. 'Didn't you notice?'

'I trusted him,' Hawley said shortly, adding, 'and he replaced it sometimes.'

Simon leaped on that. 'Did he replace money just recently? About the time of this sailing, before Pyckard's ship sailed?'

'Yes,' Hawley said steadily.

'You know what he did, don't you?' Simon pressed him.

'He sold information about people. What he heard in the tavern and gaming rooms, he would sell to whoever wanted it,' Hawley admitted. 'It must have been lucrative.'

'Did he sell something to Pyckard in the weeks before the sailing?'

Hawley was still a moment, but then he gave a short nod. 'Yes. I think so.'

'That's why you chose to forfeit your salvage, wasn't it?'

Hawley didn't reply to that. 'If you want to learn more, you'll need to speak to Strete. He may still be able to talk – but the men in there grow mighty impatient when they think someone may be unable to repay their debts.'

Chapter Thirty-Five

Strete had never known such pain. His skull ached from the buffets it had taken, but that was nothing compared with his cods. He had been kicked so hard, it felt as though they had swollen like pigs' bladders, and all the while his arms were strained behind his back so that he must stand on tiptoes to relieve the agony so far as he could. Naked, he shivered with the cold in this dark chamber. He knew he was still at the tavern, but in a small storage room out behind the gaming hall.

He heard steps approaching, and whimpered to himself. They stopped at the door, and it opened, letting some light into the dim interior. He had to avert his face from the sudden flare of candle-light, but not before he had heard a muttered, 'Sweet Christ in heaven!' and a gasp of horror.

There was a ringing of steel, and he panicked, crying out, 'No more! No more, I beg!'

He felt his wrists being jerked, and he wept. Then the terrible strain on his arms ceased. Without the rope to support him, he collapsed, falling to his knees. There was a sudden shouting, and he heard a clash of weapons, but he was all but incapable of comprehending. His entire concentration was fixed on his shoulders and wrists. The sudden release had led to an anguish so entirely overwhelming that he was left shivering and weeping, unable to speak or even cry out.

'You're safe enough for now, Strete. Come with us,' he heard, but he couldn't respond. He was lifted gently to his feet. Another jerk at his wrists, and the ropes binding them fell away. There was a hand under each armpit, and he was helped to shamble and shuffle his way from the room. A cloak or blanket was pulled over him and wrapped about him, and he shuddered at the touch of another's hands. All night the only contact he had received had been from fists. 'Thank you . . . thank you . . .' he said, over and over again.

Back at Simon's house, they installed poor Strete in the rear parlour by the fire, and Rob, probably for the first time silenced by the sight of a figure in real distress, walked quietly to fetch water, wine and spices to make him a warming posset. Simon saw him staring in horror at the wretch huddled, shivering, on the bench.

Strete had been severely beaten. His hand looked as though it had been crushed or struck with a hammer. Certainly there was blood all over the swollen, ruined fingers. His face was unrecognisable, with his nose broken, lips mashed against teeth, an ear swollen and bleeding, and both eyes puffed and purple. They had almost completely closed, and as the men in the room talked, Strete turned his good ear to them like a permanently deaf man.

The Coroner had witnessed enough judicial beatings to be able to study Strete with a purely professional interest, but Baldwin had none of his objectivity. When he walked into the gaming hall, Baldwin had politely asked to see the clerk, and only when he had gripped a man by the throat and asked again, this time with his dagger drawn, did he begin to display his anger. When he saw the body hanging with its arms bound behind his back, his mood became black, and Simon feared that he might kill the clerk, with his bare hands. However, Baldwin merely slapped him twice about the face and thrust him away, muttering an oath. He had gently taken the terrified, blinded victim and eased him down. The wrath had not left him, though. It remained with him even now. It was in his deep brown eyes as he watched Strete.

'Strete,' Baldwin said, 'I think you know why we want to speak to you.'

'I've done nothing.'

'You have lied and stolen from your master,' Sir Richard commented happily. He had found a chicken leg from somewhere, and was chewing on it. 'That's enough to have a good beating in any house.'

'Not only that, I think,' Simon said.

'What do you mean?' Sir Richard asked.

'The missing purse from the man in the road? Someone took it, and although the churlish old devil Cynegils took what he thought he was owed, he left much behind. Someone else took that. Someone who passed by that way a little later – eh, Strete?'

Strete's head hung disconsolately. 'I didn't think it would matter. *He* didn't need it any more, and it was enough to save me a beating from my master, so I thought.'

'So you took his purse and took the money?'

Strete's silence was confirmation enough.

'Very well. And you had information which you could sell for profit too. Who to?' Simon pressed him.

'Master Pyckard. It was about his wife.'

'What did you tell him?'

'It was about the night she died. I heard that she wasn't killed when the ship was wrecked. She was already dead.'

'How do you know that?'

'Do you recall the sailor Hawley found dead in the ship – Danny? He was drunk with me one afternoon, and he told me. He had been on the *Saint Rumon* when she went down, and he told me that he'd seen Mistress Pyckard as the wave broke the ship. The water washed away the master's cabin, and she was dead in there. Blood on her legs and clothes. He just thought it was the water did that to her, but later on he realised it wasn't that. He'd been hearing her moaning.'

'How on earth did he suddenly know that?'

'It was when we heard Philip Kena's wife being attacked. She was gagged – Vincent or Odo put their hands over her mouth to stop her screaming – but we could hear her trying to cry out. It fair put the fear of God into Danny. He knew he had heard that sound somewhere before. That afternoon, he suddenly realised it was the sound of a woman in terror with a man's hand over her mouth.'

'That sounds like a guess,' the Coroner said.

'Except the two of them were talking about her, and said she was just like a "French whore". They'd been the two who killed Madam Pyckard. That's what Danny believed. When the ship sank, it covered up their evil deed.'

'Why didn't he tell his master? He worked for Pyckard, didn't he?'

'Yes. Paul Pyckard saved him and his brother Moses. When it happened, all those years ago, he didn't realise what he'd seen. He was nothing but a boy. It was only much later, quite recently, that he understood what must have happened.'

'What of Adam?'

'Danny thought Adam was innocent; he had done nothing with them. He was never their ally, and Danny saw him about the ship fighting to save her. No, it was only Odo and Vincent who were in the cabin with Mistress Pyckard.'

'What made Danny suddenly tell you all this?' Baldwin snapped.

'I was there when he heard about the woman. I don't know exactly what it was, but I think that later on, Odo was boasting about fondling Mistress Kena, saying how ripe her body was. Danny got all upset, and he shot from the room. Outside, when I saw him and asked him what was wrong, he said that Odo and Vincent had raped Mistress Pyckard. He was in a terrible state – really shaken up.'

'What did you do with this information?'

'I told Danny to keep his mouth shut or Odo would kill him. If he spoke of it to anyone, he'd be killed.'

'He took your word for that?'

The battered man winced. 'I warned him that if he told his master, poor Master Pyckard would die all the sooner from a broken heart. It would be kinder to let him die in ignorance of the truth.'

'Kinder indeed! While *you* went to tell him instead,' Baldwin commented sourly.

'I needed money! I knew what would happen if I didn't replace what I'd borrowed from Hawley. He'd kill me.'

'What did Pyckard say?' Simon pressed.

'He said he was thankful for the information, and that he'd see what he could do.'

'What of Danny?'

'I don't know. I have no idea what happened to him, the poor lad.'

'Who killed all the crew?' Simon asked.

'I don't know! I swear it! I wasn't on the ship. I didn't see what happened any more than you!'

Baldwin and Simon left Peter to the care of Rob, and took the Coroner out to the road.

'It is clear enough who killed the men on the ship, then,' Baldwin said.

'Beauley,' Simon responded.

'His ship was there, yes. He is the only one who could have brought this ghost-like Adam back to shore,' Baldwin said.

'Hold hard!' the Coroner exclaimed as the other two set off for Hardness. 'What is all this?'

'The answer to the whole riddle of the ship lies at Beauley's house,' Baldwin said, but refused to answer more questions until they had reached it.

Here they were directed out to the back of the property, where they found Master Beauley talking to a shipwright about a new vessel.

'You are increasing your shipping?' Baldwin asked, glancing at the wright as he picked up a large scroll detailing expenses and listing requirements.

'Yes. I have some money set by, and I want another craft. Why are you so interested in the daily workings of a mere merchant seaman?'

Baldwin eyed him closely. 'I am not impressed with men who kill for money and then use the money for their own benefit.'

Beauley's smile broadened, but there was an edge to his voice when he said, 'You accuse me of killing?'

'Aye,' the Coroner rumbled. 'Odo and Vincent and their crew.'

'I deny it! On my life, my mother's life, and the Gospels, if you want. I deny I've had any part in killing any man against the law.'

'Who did, then?' Simon asked.

'How would I know?'

'Because it was you who took their bodies and the rest of the crew from Pyckard's ship, naturally,' Baldwin stated.

'What makes you say that?'

'Adam.'

Beauley stared at Simon for some while, trying to guess whether he was bluffing or not. The silence was lengthy, but Simon remembered Baldwin once saying that when questioning a man, it was best to ask once and then wait until the other man gave an answer. It came, at last, in the form of another question. 'He admitted the murder?'

'Tell us what you did. He said you killed the men on your ship, and that you threw them overboard yourself,' Simon grated.

'He said *what*?' Beauley glared. 'The lying shit! They were dead when we came to the ship!'

'Tell us your side of the story, then. Otherwise we may have to arrest you as well,' Baldwin said.

'Very well. I was paid, and paid well, as you can see, to race to catch up with Pyckard's little ship. It would be waiting for us in the sea, so we were told. All we had to do was take on board the crew, and leave the ship looking as though it was scuttled. That was all.'

'This was at Master Pyckard's request?' Simon confirmed.

'Of course. Who else?'

'How many died?'

'Ask Adam – I wasn't there. Certainly we took off eight men, including him.'

'Did you know anything about the men aboard? About what they had done?'

'You don't think I'd have got involved if I hadn't, do you? Of course I knew what they'd done. They raped poor Amandine and told everyone she died in a storm. Odo and Vincent were always prone to violence, especially when they had drunk enough. The fools raped her, killed her, and the ship crashed into the rocks, fortunately for them. It explained her death. Otherwise they would have found that hard to get away with.'

'So you took these eight men from the ship and set it alight?'

'No. It was Adam who burned the ship. Only superficially – Pyckard didn't want the *Saint John* to be too badly damaged.'

'Why all this subterfuge? Why not just have them stabbed in town?' Baldwin demanded. 'All this effort and trouble . . . it seems ridiculous!'

'Ask his steward. Moses will tell you. He knew everything about Pyckard's business.'

The three waited in Pyckard's hall while a young servant went to find Moses. There was a jug of wine on the sideboard, and Simon lifted the lid and sniffed the interior. He poured a mazerful and lifted it in silent toast to the dead master of the house.

Pyckard's mark was all over the place. His body might be in the church, but his soul yet remained here. His chair was still at the fire as though waiting for him to return to it; his cloak and hat sat on top of a chest in the corner of the room as though he had walked out to his privy for a moment before leaving to go and view his ships.

For all that, the room reeked of spilled ale and wine from his wake. From the sour odour near the sideboard, Simon guessed that several of his seamen had participated over-enthusiastically in the celebration of his life and thrown up before returning to the drinking.

'Lordings.'

Moses had entered quietly, like a monk. He was clad in black in memory of his master, Simon thought, and stood surveying them with a sad but confident expression, like a man who knew his position in the world and was content. The only indication that he was not completely at ease was the twitching of his fingers: he picked continuously at the hem of his sleeve. Seeing all their eyes upon him, he crossed the floor noiselessly, to stand before them all beside his master's chair. One hand upon it, he faced them resolutely, or, as Simon guessed, resignedly.

'You know why we're here,' Simon said harshly. He waved his hand about the room, slopping the wine in his mazer. 'Pyckard was a wealthy man, wasn't he? He wouldn't want to lose too much money. He couldn't bear to lose a whole ship and the cargo too, could he?'

'If you say so.'

'So when he decided to punish the two who had killed his wife, he chose to do it in a way that wouldn't damage his business.'

'I don't know. I don't think he cared that much. He planned to give most of it away anyhow.'

'Ah, of course – the salvage for Master Hawley. He'd have been shocked to learn that the good shipman did not want any part of a false salvage. Hawley must have been sickened and angry to be fooled.'

'He was angry,' Moses conceded. 'He came here early today to demand to know what had happened.'

'You told him?'

'I have nothing to conceal.'

'Tell us all, then.'

'My master wanted to punish the two who had tortured and killed his wife. She was ever a kind, generous woman. All spoke of her beauty and calmness. Yet they raped her and planned to throw her overboard at dead of night. When the ship struck rocks, they thought that they had the perfect story to tell. Only two others survived that night – Adam and my brother. All the others perished.'

'So his punishment was to take them to the middle of the sea and kill them there?'

'Afterwards. First they prepared the ship for the sailing, and only when all was ready were they brought back here for a last talk with my master. And then he told them he knew all about their rape and murder.'

'How did they react?' Baldwin asked.

'They denied it like the cowards they were. Adam and some others worked on them, and they knew what would happen to them when they reached a certain place in the sea. There Beauley was to meet the ship and take off the other crew, and put them ashore farther up the coast.'

'So the two were hanged? Stabbed? What?'

Moses looked at Simon coolly. 'They were taken in the ship to a place far from land and thrown into the water with a rope about their necks. They were lifted from the water and then dropped in. I think they lasted several duckings.'

Simon shuddered. Unable to breathe in the water, they must have wished for a friendly hand to pull them up, but the only help they received was from a rope at their neck. A hideous death.

'You think me little better than a murderer?' Moses said. 'I would have seen them die a slower death than that if I could. My brother told me of their crime. They must have realised what he had done, so they killed him too.'

'Your brother?' Coroner Richard said sharply.

'Yes, Daniel was my brother.'

'And the man in the road? What of him?' Simon demanded. He walked to the sideboard. Receiving a stern look from Sir Richard, he poured two mazers and took one to the Coroner.

Moses glanced away. 'My master and I were looking for Sir Pierre, Master Pyckard's brother-in-law, when we saw the stranger in the road. He was accosted by that repellent fellow Cynegils, and we overheard him discuss spying on a stranger.'

'Did you hear him mention Sir Pierre by name?' Baldwin asked.

'No – he only asked about "the foreigner", but that doesn't signify. What of it? There was only one foreigner in town that night. My master was unwell already, and he said he wouldn't see his wife's brother killed by some foul servant of a thieving reptile like Despenser. So he took a rock and knocked the man down. He fell without a sound, and my master hit him again thrice. It was close to the hole in the road, so I removed the trestles at one side and we rolled him in to make it look as though he had come by an unhappy accident.'

'Do you know who he was?' Simon asked.

'I didn't introduce myself before my Master killed him,' Moses said with a touch of scorn.

Coroner Richard drained his mazer. 'He was Guy de Bouville. Sir Andrew knew him. He worked for Despenser.'

'And Despenser wanted Sir Pierre dead because he was French and a friend of the Queen,' Moses said. 'That was what Sir Pierre told us.'

Baldwin frowned. 'Although Sir Andrew denied knowing of a man here already when he arrived in town. Just as he denied piracy with Pyckard's ship.'

'Hah! At least that denial was true,' the Coroner chuckled. 'He told me that this de Bouville chappie was man-at-arms to a fellow called . . . what was it? Flok?'

Baldwin blinked. 'Flok?'

'You've heard of him?'

'Flok was the man whom Hamund Chugge murdered. It was the reason for Hamund being sent here as abjurer,' Baldwin said.

'Good God!' Simon said. Then: 'You said Odo and Vincent killed your brother, but you also say that they were held before sailing. How do you know they killed him?'

'Who else would have done it?' Moses snapped. 'They realised who must have told my master about his wife's murder, and punished him for it.'

'If that was the case, they would have fled, surely,' Baldwin said.

'Eh?'

'If you were guilty of a woman's murder, and heard that her husband, the man whom you worked for, knew of your actions, would you wait to sail on his ship, with his men aboard? Or would you flee instantly?'

'I don't know how evil men like them must think. I don't pretend to understand them. They were condemned from their own mouths, anyway. They said that Madam Kena was just like the French whore, or somesuch.'

Baldwin grunted with disgust. 'They sailed regularly for their master?'

'Of course.'

'How many French whores do you think they will have used in their lives?'

Moses shook his head in confusion. 'What do you mean?'

'I mean, they were not guilty of the murder,' Baldwin said more confidently. 'Your master heard of the story your brother told, but it that was entirely wrong. Just as the murder of the man in the road was wrong.'

'He was asking about a foreigner,' Moses began.

'He was asking about a short fellow by the name of Hamund Chugge, who killed his master. De Bouville was here to avenge him. An abjurer will be told in public by which roads he must go to a port. I think this de Bouville was looking for Hamund to kill him. Instead your master killed *him*.'

'Oh, dear heaven.'

'And in the same way, I do not think your brother died because of Odo and Vincent. Another man killed Danny.'

'Why do you think that?'

'The only man who could tell the truth about Mistress Pyckard's death was your brother. Perhaps if he had noticed one more detail, he would have been aware of another man who could have killed her.'

'Who else was in the crew of the *Saint Rumon*, fifteen years ago? And were any of them on the *Saint John* as well as Odo and Vincent?' Simon urged. His head was hurting again, and he touched the lump where the hammer had struck.

Moses thought about it.

'Most of them were strangers. Master Pyckard wanted as few men as possible from about Dartmouth, because it would be hard to have them reappear when their families had thought them dead, so he hired strangers from another town.'

'But there *were* two men on the *Saint John* from here?' Baldwin insisted.

'Two, yes. Ed and Adam. But Ed was too young to have been working on the *Saint Rumon*.'

'But Adam was on her, wasn't he?' Baldwin demanded.

'Well, yes.'

'And Adam was keen to help torture Odo and Vincent, wasn't he?' the Coroner rumbled. He had returned to the sideboard, and now he waved a full mazer. 'I don't know about these two, but I think you killed the wrong men.'

'No . . . that's not possible,' Moses said, but he had taken a step back as though struck by a physical blow.

Baldwin was pensive. 'I still don't understand. When the *Saint John* sailed, your master had given instructions for her to be fired as though she had been raided?'

'Yes. It was always his plan.'

Baldwin frowned. 'And Adam knew of that?'

'He knew the ship must be afire when Master Beauley arrived, yes. Although he didn't realise that he was only to make a poor job of it. I know that the day they sailed, my master was keen to send me to explain that the ship was *not* to be burned to the waterline.'

'Why?'

'Oh, I think Adam said something to Odo and Vincent about leaving them in the ship to burn to nothing, and my master thought he didn't appreciate that the two were to be thrown into the sea. The ship wasn't to be harmed, after all. Perhaps he thought he was to destroy the whole thing, now I think of it.'

'Where is Adam now?' Baldwin demanded. 'He is the final link in the chain.'

'I'm not sure,' Moses declared. He had paled under the onslaught, but he stood with an attitude of defiance, a hand stroking the wooden chair's back.

'Essay a guess,' Sir Richard said. He drained his mazer, peered into the jug and when he saw it was empty, set it down with a sigh. Taking hold of his sword, he walked over to Moses. 'But be quick, eh?'

Chapter Thirty-Six

The house he directed them to was another not far from Cynegils's own in the street at Hardness. It was a shabby building, much like the other, but there was no sense of misery about the place. This was not a home filled with hunger, but one where the master was regularly employed.

'Think he's in?' Sir Richard asked Baldwin in what he fondly imagined to be a discreet whisper.

Baldwin rolled his eyes at Simon, and then nodded his head once; Simon returned the nod, and then they nodded a second time, a third, and both launched themselves forward.

'I expect he's out, wouldn't—'

Hearing the splintering crunch as the two men hit the door together and burst through it, the Coroner was quiet for a moment. Then he sniffed disdainfully and stepped forward to the doorway. 'Proud of yourselves?'

'He's not here,' Simon declared, coming back from the rear of the house. 'He could have got away over the fence.'

'We shall have to seek him in the town, then,' Baldwin said. 'We could fetch Ivo, I suppose, but he's as much use as a kettle made of ice.'

'You two are so impatient all the time,' the Coroner stated, eyeing them reprovingly. 'Why don't we just go to where he's bound to be?'

'What are you on about?' Simon asked a trifle wearily.

'Good God, man! He was brother to Danny's wife, wasn't he? And he was friend to this man Ed, whom we were told was also saved from the ship. Is this Ed in the town?'

'He lives with Widecombe Will's family,' Simon said.

'Well, I should check both houses. Adam is going to be hiding himself, isn't he? So let's flush him out!'

He had left Ed with his wife. The lad was gormless, thick as the oak of a keel. All he saw was that he was alive. He didn't care about anything else. Even though Adam had tried to persuade him to lie low, remain hidden, disguise himself as Adam had, shaving, washing, changing his hair, wearing different clothes, the fool could think of nothing but dipping his wick in his woman.

Adam was content that he had survived. It hadn't been easy to think of a story to save himself. When the *Saint Rumon* had foundered, he'd thought it was a miracle of good luck when he found a spar and floated away, washing up safely on the sand. Only one or two men could have witnessed what had happened, and he was sure that they were dead. Later, when he'd seen Odo, there had been only praise from the latter for managing to survive, and from Vincent too. No one had spotted him with Pyckard's strumpet.

She'd been good. He had wanted her for months, ever since he first saw her, but he couldn't do anything about it, except take the occasional whore from the stews to slake his desire. Then Pyckard had sent him to escort her over to France. And he had done what he'd wanted for ages.

It'd been easy. She was weak from vomiting, and hardly even noticed when he walked in. He'd thought she might even want him, as when he'd put a hand on her back, she hadn't recoiled or anything, just stayed there, kneeling over the basin. He rubbed her, his hand going lower and lower, and when she finally realised what was happening, she tried to jump up and away. Only his hand clenched over her skirts, and he pulled her back, slapping a hand over her mouth when she tried to break free. He kept his hand there while he lifted her skirts and forced his other hand up. Her eyes widened in horror, and they stayed like that all the time until he had finished. Just staring at him. And all the while there was that moaning, low in her throat, like a dog with a broken back. A keening sound that made him ashamed.

That was when he knew he couldn't let her live. Master Pyckard would see him hang for this. He took his knife and stabbed once, carefully, in her breast. She'd thrashed, her body spasming in death. But still her eyes were on him. Accusing.

He'd been going to throw her over the side when it was dark, but the squall flew up and he'd had to leave her body there and go to help the others. And then the wave came, and the wreck, and that would have been the end of it, had Danny not remembered something crucial, years later.

Pyckard had never suspected Adam. Why should he? Adam was his best sailor. The old skinflint never guessed how much the jealousy tore at him. Adam should have been a merchant. At the least he should have been granted more of the profits from the sailings he made, risking *his* life, *his* health, so that Pyckard could make money. And he made tons of it. Without his wealth, he couldn't have afforded to win Amandine, either. It was only fair that the man who helped Pyckard get the money that won him his bride should share in the spoils. And since Pyckard wouldn't share his money fairly, Adam took his wife. Simple as that.

Danny's tale had made sense to everyone, especially when told by that tub of lard Strete, and Adam had volunteered to look into it. First of all, though, he'd made sure that Strete understood that Pyckard and Adam knew it was Odo and Vincent. Then he went with two others and snatched the pair of them from outside a tavern. It took some effort to make them confess, but first Vincent and then Odo admitted killing her, just to stop the pain. They'd been held for a day and then brought to the ship. Meanwhile, Adam had Danny taken there too, and while he was aboard, Adam sought him out. It was easy to kill him. Danny was the only remaining person who could accuse him. And he died quietly.

The damned fool, Pyckard. He had agreed to let the ship be burned, and Adam thought hiding Daniel there in the hold would be safe enough, but no! His master had to try to save the ship so that his profit wouldn't be lost, didn't he! So the ship returned home under Hawley's crew, and the body was soon discovered. If not for that,

Adam might have been able to return and live happily enough, but now he had only danger at every step.

For the first time, Adam wondered whether he would ever escape. He sipped ale moodily, and tried to smile when his sister returned.

'Still feeling miserable?' Alice said. 'You couldn't do anything to save them. You did your best, Adam.'

'I tried.'

'It's just a miracle that you escaped the pirates and made it back home.'

Adam smiled sadly. She was as stupid as her dead husband.

Simon saw young Humphrey at the street corner, and beckoned to the lad. He came reluctantly, eyeing the Coroner as though he expected to be punched at any moment for molesting another woman. 'I've done nothing!' he said sulkily.

'Right now, I don't care,' Simon said. 'I need you to run a message.' Quickly he explained that he needed Humphrey to run to the gaol, rouse Ivo and have him collect some men, and go to Will's house to see if Ed was there. 'And tell them to be careful. If Adam's there, he may be dangerous. All right?'

'What's in it for me?'

Coroner Richard took two steps forward, and Humphrey turned and fled.

'How do you do that?' Simon asked.

'Years of practice, young Bailiff. Years of practice,' the Coroner asserted smugly.

They took the short cut to Danny's home. Simon strode to the door and struck it with the hilt of his sword.

'Yes?' came a woman's voice from within.

'It's the Bailiff, mistress. Can we speak to you for a moment?'

The door opened, and Alice stepped out warily. There was still that sadness in her that spoke of her loss, but it was moderated now. 'Well?'

'Where is your brother?'

'In the sea, isn't he?' she responded swiftly, but her face blushed with guilt.

'Madam,' Baldwin smiled, 'we know he's alive. He's been seen. And we have heard how he protected his master and had the two sailors shown to be dishonourable and treacherous. May we speak to him?'

'He's not here. I don't know where—'

Simon shook his head. 'Alice, it was he killed your man. *He* murdered Danny.'

She gaped. 'What? You're mad! You tell me my own brother would orphan his nieces and nephew? He'd make me a widow? Why would he do that to us?'

'It is true. The men, Odo and Vincent, were not guilty of the rape of Mistress Amandine. It was Adam did that. He tortured them to make them confess, and then, when all was done, he had to silence the one witness who could denounce him – your brother. Danny saw something that night, that he only recalled very recently. Adam killed him to silence him.'

'No! Tell me it isn't true, in God's name!' The woman's face was deathly white now.

'Danny was killed on the night before the *Saint John* sailed. You saw him earlier that day, didn't you? So he was alive then.'

'Yes,' she sobbed.

'Odo and Vincent had been tortured and were being held in Master Pyckard's house by then, so they couldn't have killed Danny. The man who did it thought the ship was to be destroyed, so he would get away with it, as Danny's body would never be found. Only Adam thought that. *No one else could have murdered your husband, woman.* Now tell us where is he?'

'I . . .'

There was a faint clatter from behind her, and Baldwin saw a figure darting out through the rear of the house – a big man, beardless, and with the rolling gait of a man well used to the sea.

Simon jumped to his feet, but his head thundered with pain, and he swore, suddenly pale and giddy.

Baldwin and the Coroner sprang to the doorway, and Baldwin was marginally faster through the screens, urged on by the screams of Alice. As he came into the daylight again, Baldwin threw a quick look all around. There up at the far side of the garden was Adam, and Baldwin set off in pursuit even as the blundering figure of the Coroner reached him.

'Where is he? Ach! This is work for younger men. Still, never let it be said . . . that a Coroner . . . ever let a mere *Keeper* . . . catch a man when . . . ach, damn it!'

Baldwin grinned to himself, but conserved his energy instead of talking.

The ground here sloped steeply upwards, and all three must labour to climb the hill. They had left the last of the cottages behind them now, and were toiling through scrub and thick grasses, with sprinklings of furze and heather. Baldwin felt his leggings catch on the spikes, and thorns scratched him as he pushed himself onwards. It was ever harder, and as he went, he felt the air searing his lungs; his mouth was dry and his throat sore. But the man would not give up, and Baldwin must follow him until one of them could go no further.

And with that thought, Adam disappeared over a lip in the ground. When Baldwin reached it, he found himself looking down into a natural hollow. There was a rocky mess within, with lank grasses sprouting between each, and low, hunched bushes that looked stunted and crabbed like the trees on Dartmoor.

A loud panting and blowing at his side announced the Coroner's arrival. 'Where is the bastard? He nearly made me throw up that wine from Pyckard's house, and no man – *no man*! – should do that. I'll open his gizzard for him, the pox-ridden cur!'

Baldwin said nothing, but drew his sword and slowly paced along to his right.

'Are you sure he's here?' the Coroner shouted after a few paces. 'Can't see him yet.'

Baldwin did not speak. All his attention was fixed upon the ground nearby and any rocks or bushes that could conceal a man of Adam's size. It was only at the last moment that he realised that there was a tree nearby that was less stunted and hunched than the others. As he did so, he remembered that a sailor could climb like a monkey, and he darted back just as the figure dropped.

Adam was a big man, and his knife looked little more than a toy in his fist, but there was no doubting his skill as a fighter, as he stamped his bare feet on the ground and jumped towards Baldwin.

'Yield, man, or you'll die here,' Baldwin snarled.

The dagger came close, but Baldwin had the range afforded by his sword, and he was not going to allow a dull-witted sailor to get inside his defence.

As he brought the sword around to stab at the man's breast, Adam stepped forward, blocking the movement with his forearm. The blade hit with the flat, and Baldwin knew he was lost unless he was quick. The dagger was already lunging forward. He forced his tired legs to leap, and moved to his right. The dagger missed him – just – and he brought his left hand down onto Adam's wrist. Adam now had his sword-wrist in his own grip, and Baldwin felt, to his horror, that his left hand was moving. He squeezed with his fingers to try to force the man to drop the blade, but there was no joy there. All he saw was a brutal glee in Adam's eyes as the dagger turned in towards Baldwin's chest. Then began the inexorable journey. It was only a matter of six inches or so, but Baldwin fought it with all the strength at his disposal. He could do no more. But his left hand was not so strong as Adam's right, while his own right was locked, his blade up under Adam's armpit. Adam would not allow him to move his hand to attack . . . but then an idea occurred to him. He suddenly yanked his right hand back. Adam was surprised by the simple movement, and Baldwin nearly thrust the weapon into his breast before he felt that astonishing grip tighten again, and saw Adam's teeth shine ferociously. His sword's progress was halted, and the sailor's knife was moving nearer and nearer.

'No harming him. He's the King's man!'

Baldwin looked up to see that Sir Richard's sword was resting on Adam's shoulder. The point was close to Adam's chin, and as he stared down at it, the Coroner angled it and brought it to Adam's throat so that the edge snagged on a lump of leathery skin.

'I said, I won't see him harmed, churl. Let him go and drop that knife before I drop you, eh?'

Adam made as though to drop the knife, but then he suddenly whirled about to stab Sir Richard. As the Coroner stepped sharply backwards, his sword dragged along the back of Adam's neck, and then as Adam span, it ran along the side of the sailor's throat – and Baldwin was drenched in a sudden shower of blood.

It was some days later that Baldwin reached Exeter. He sat on his horse for a long while on the hill overlooking the city, trying to make up his mind whether he should continue as he had planned or ride straight home. Home, where Jeanne his wife would be waiting.

He sighed and kicked his horse into a slow amble down the hill to the bridge.

The Cathedral Close was abustle as usual, with several pack ponies and horses feeding on the last of the grass in the cemetery, and children playing among the tombstones and the tall elms that stood between the cemetery and the streets of the Close. Already drifts of leaves were piling up. He rode over the little bridge that spanned the open ditch, little better than a sewer, that ran from the canons' houses to the city walls and out to the shitebrook.

Piles of filth and rubble lay all around, and the Cathedral itself was still being rebuilt at this, the eastern end. Several bonfires were burning waste from the canons' houses and the building works.

In the past, Baldwin had enjoyed the sight and sounds of all the raucous liveliness about the town – builders shouting and singing, merchants at the fish-market over by Broad Gate calling their wares, while animals wandered about, dropping their dung in the cemetery – but today, from his new perspective, it looked as though this Cathedral was less a place of worship and praise, more a hellish imitation.

'Sir Baldwin.' The steward at the door to the Bishop's Palace smiled in recognition as soon as the knight appeared in the roadway.

'My lord Bishop is holding a Chapter meeting, but he will not be long, I am sure. Will you wait here while I fetch you some food and drink? You look as though you have travelled far today.'

'I would be most grateful, yes,' Baldwin said, dropping tiredly from his horse and pulling off his gloves. Here in the bishop's grounds he had no concerns for the way that his horse would be looked after, and he watched a groom take the rounsey away to be brushed and fed without a second thought, then entered the Palace behind the steward.

In the hall there was one other man – a messenger in the livery of Lord Despenser. He glanced over at Baldwin and bowed respectfully, to which Baldwin responded with a courteous but not fulsome bow of his own, and the steward left them alone while he fetched Baldwin his refreshments.

'Sir Baldwin!' Bishop Walter strode into the hall with a broad smile. He glanced at the messenger as he held out his hand to Baldwin, and the knight bent to kiss the Episcopal ring quickly, but not before he had caught sight of the bishop's short frown.

'My lord Bishop,' the messenger said. 'I have an urgent communication for you. Lord Despenser has persuaded the King to accept your advice. Can you please take these and deal with them?' He held out a handful of warrants.

Bishop Stapledon took them, staring at the seals and pursing his lips. Setting them on his table, he dismissed the man, and turned his attention on Baldwin.

'A successful journey to Dartmouth, I hope? Tell me, how is Simon?'

'Bishop, why did you send me there?' Baldwin asked.

'I told you. We wanted to make sure that the Frenchman left the country, and that Her Majesty could not be harmed by rumours of his actions becoming known.'

'And yet Despenser's man was sent to catch the same Frenchman and bring him back?'

'I cannot speak for him, naturally,' Stapledon said. 'What is this, Baldwin? Are you discontent?'

'I am not discontent, no. I am *angry* to have been your tool without the courtesy of an explanation. You wanted the Frenchman found and captured, didn't you? You sent me after him because you felt sure he would go there, not because your nephew was near the town.'

'Now, Baldwin!' Bishop Stapledon said warningly.

'No! You knew about Pierre's sister being married to a merchant there. You knew when he set off to the coast that he'd go straight there. Where else would a man like him go, if not to his sister's house? He could be sure of aid there. And you wanted him caught and brought back to show how degenerate the Frenchmen are who guard the Queen.'

'Nonsense! I would care for no such thing,' the bishop declared.

'It struck me as curious that Sir Andrew arrived so soon after me. I suppose you thought that I would be able to point to the Frenchman and so save him a search of the town that might cause fights and antagonism. I can imagine that Sir Andrew would have been ruthlessly ferocious in looking for a man – and that you would prefer to have a quieter, calmer investigation. Yet you always intended to have Pierre found and caught. Because it would help you to alienate Queen Isabella from the King.'

Bishop Stapledon was still at the table on which the warrants lay. He put out a finger to touch one. 'Do you know what these contain? If I had to guess, they have orders for me to take over the main resources at the Queen's command in Cornwall, so that they cannot be used to fund her any more. The mines could be at threat of invasion from the French, and she is French herself.'

'She is your Queen!'

'She could be negotiating with her brother, Baldwin. She is not loyal.'

'How dare you!'

'Baldwin, calm yourself. I know her better than you! You did not see her when she went to her father and told him of the affair of the silken purses. A woman who could break her father's heart, telling him that his sons were all – *all* – cuckolds, who could see her sisters-in-law ruined, imprisoned . . . such a one is too self-absorbed to worry about her husband and the realm.'

'That is preposterous! You say that she is wicked because she brought judgement on those who broke the law? That is reason to trust her.'

'No. She could be treacherous to her sisters-in-law, and she could be again to her husband. It is a risk we cannot take. For that reason the King is to take away her dower. She will have a reduced annual budget which he will control through his friends, and all Frenchmen in her household will be removed.'

'She is to be imprisoned?' Baldwin asked, appalled.

'No, not imprisoned. Just held for the safety of the Realm, and perhaps for her own. These are hard times, Baldwin.'

'Very!' Baldwin said, picking up his gloves and beginning to tug them on.

'You are leaving? Will you not remain a little longer? We have much to talk about.'

'No, I do not think we do, Walter. My lord Bishop, you are right to say that there is much danger today. And you have thrown me into the midst of it.'

'Sir Baldwin, I do what I do for the good of the Realm. I am sorry if you think I deceived you, but I assure you, I never had any such intention.'

Baldwin faced him, and bowed. 'I will take my leave, my lord.'

'There is one last point. I suggested that you should be put forward to the next Parliament. I feel sure that you will be chosen.'

Baldwin screwed up his brow. 'But there is no call for Parliament yet, is there? The last was earlier this year.'

'But when the summons comes, your name will be selected. It will be good for you, Sir Baldwin. And you and I can travel to the Parliament together.'

Baldwin nodded, took his leave, and went out to find his horse. The beast had been well cared for, and he had him resaddled and prepared. Mounted, he sat gazing about him at the mayhem all around.

It seemed to him that this rowdy place was like the kingdom. Noisy, messy, in many ways unmanageable: but when those who ran it bickered for power, all in this Close would be forced to choose sides, and then many must die.

He was profoundly sad as he rode out and along the road towards the great bridge. It was a sadness he could not dismiss no matter how hard he tried. He only hoped that his name would not grow too renowned. To be well known would mean being courted by the wealthy and powerful, and no matter to whom he gave his loyalty, the other would be his enemy.

It was impossible to protect a family when the Realm was at war.

Chapter Thirty-Seven

Hamund and Pierre had reached Normandy after some days of travelling, Hamund gazing about him with some trepidation at this, his new land.

Their path would take them beyond Caen and out into the countryside, Pierre told him, and they must continue walking for another two or three days, so they rested in a tavern for an evening before preparing to set off the next morning.

Hamund was astonished by Caen. The bright yellow stones were beautifully carved and created marvellous, airy buildings that seemed to float over the great city. Even the taverns and inns seemed exotic and wonderful. He spent the whole of the first afternoon in France gaping at the architecture.

'You will be happy at my home, I hope,' Pierre said. 'You will need to learn the language of my people, but that should not take long. It is so much easier than your own.'

'I'm glad of it,' Hamund said. He was sipping at a French beer that tasted very bitter to him. He wasn't sure if it was supposed to be like that, but from the way that the Frenchman drank his own off happily, Hamund assumed it was all right. He sipped a little more.

'We are safe now,' Pierre said. He spoke in a soft voice, thinking back to his lovely woman. Living with her would have been more dangerous, but there would have been compensations.

Hamund nodded, but dolefully. 'I can never go back, though. I'm exiled.'

'Hamund Chugge may never return to his home, no. But *you* may,' Pierre said.

'Any man may kill me if I go back.'

'I think you will find that everyone thinks you are dead. When you swam from Andrew's body, everyone assumed you had drowned. They thought that on the ship, and I am sure they will have thought that on the boats, and on shore too.'

'I only dived down so no one would attack me with an arrow or something,' Hamund said.

'Do you not see? You were out of view as you swam about the ship and climbed up the far side. All there will have declared you dead. You are safe now, my friend,' Pierre said.

Hamund blinked. It was not something he had considered. 'Well, no matter. I think I'm safer here. Even if it is sad to think of her I left behind.'

'Yes. I understand your sadness,' Pierre said. He drank some more beer. 'My own life is easier because of your action, though. When you killed my mortal enemy.'

'He was an evil devil. I could not let him take you,' Hamund said stoutly.

'He would have killed me. I think he did not look at you, so he never saw his danger,' Pierre said.

'He must have hated you to chase you to Dartmouth.'

'Yes, he hated me,' Pierre agreed. He said no more, but in his mind's eye he saw her again: Sir Andrew's beautiful wife Jeanne. The woman Pierre had loved for so long. He sighed. 'Come, let us finish our drinks and rest. Tomorrow we set off at first light. It is still a long walk to my home.'

Hawley looked about him on the jetty as he waited for his rowing boat to arrive. It was a grey October morning, and a fine mizzle was blowing straight in from the sea – a thin spray that would make all damp in a short time with this wind behind it.

Hearing steps, he glanced over his shoulder. 'Master Beauley! How goes it?'

'Not bad. I have just ordered a new hull to be laid. I hope before long I shall rise even to your level, master. Perhaps I shall have as many ships as poor Paul Pyckard, but with larger tunnage.'

Hawley smiled without humour. 'Best be careful you don't have any fires aboard ship, then. We wouldn't want any accidents, would we?'

'Don't you worry about me, Master Hawley. I feel sure I'll be safe enough.'

'I do hope so,' Hawley said. 'It would be very sad to know that you had failed to expand as you wished. I am glad to hear you are laying a new hull, though. I was thinking of doing that myself. Perhaps I won't bother. There won't be enough men here in Dartmouth to crew all these ships, will there?'

Beauley bared his teeth in what might have been a smile.

Hawley looked up. 'Ha! Here's my boat.'

The little rowing boat approached from the south, and in the prow stood Hawley's son.

'Father, I've brought him as you asked.'

'Master Pyket! I am glad to see you here,' Hawley said, reaching down to help Henry Pyket up from the boat. 'You know my friend Beauley, I think?'

'Of course we know each other,' Beauley said. 'He's building me a ship.'

'Is he?' John Hawley said innocently. 'Why, Henry, I didn't know you had the capacity for two ships at the same time.'

Pyket frowned. 'I haven't. I've just got the one on the go right now, master.'

'You hadn't forgotten *my* commission?'

'Of course not!' Henry said emphatically, wondering what commission that was. Perhaps Master Hawley wanted an older cog docked and careened. Some of his ships were ancient enough.

'Good. So you can begin to proceed soon?'

Henry shot a look from him to Beauley. 'Ah . . . um.'

'You're building my ship first, aren't you?' Beauley demanded, getting nettled. He shifted his stance to face Hawley more directly, his hands near his belt. 'Henry, you have agreed to build my ship next.'

'I see – there's been some sort of misunderstanding,' Hawley said easily. 'I had asked Henry a while ago to build me a new ship. The plans are agreed. Perhaps he didn't realise that the commission was to begin as soon as possible.'

Henry felt both pairs of eyes on him as he fidgeted uneasily. 'I . . . er.'

'So that's agreed, then,' Hawley said.

'No!' Beauley stated. 'He's building my ship first, *Master* Hawley. I ordered it and he accepted the commission.'

'No, he'll build *my* ship first,' Hawley said. He clicked his fingers, and three of his men appeared from the alley at their side. 'I am the most successful merchant in Dartmouth, and I *will* remain in that position.'

Moses stood at the entrance to his brother's cottage and watched as the children played in the garden. It was cool here in the early October breeze, but the sun gave a spurious feeling of warmth. He was aware of a vague feeling of returning ease. Ever since Danny's death, and then the death of his master, he had been tortured with a sense of loss. He had known nothing like it since first his mother, then his father died and orphaned Danny and him. For many years, the only meaning to his life had come from his service to the man who had saved them both.

He heard steps behind him, and turned as Alice walked to the turf seat in the wall. She sat listlessly, staring past him to the Dart as it flowed down to the sea.

'How are you, Alice?' he asked gently.

'I'm alive,' she said without humour. 'If this is life.'

Moses nodded. He rose and walked inside to warm some ale for her, as he had done every morning at about this hour for the last few days since the Bailiff, Keeper and Coroner had questioned him and killed Adam.

He could still scarcely believe the revelations about Adam. He had been such an easygoing fellow, so far as Moses had known. There were no other accusations of rape in the town that he knew of. Perhaps it was just the act of a man who was desperate and lonely while on ship?

But that was no excuse. The man had known that Mistress Amandine was his own master's woman. The idea that he should take her was obscene, the worst form of treachery. And then he had accused two others of the crime *he* had committed and executed them. And also killed poor Danny to silence him – Danny, his own brother-in-law. It beggared belief. Perhaps if he had needed to, he would have killed Alice too. And her children.

The thought was enough to loosen a man's grip on his sanity.

At least Master Pyckard had not known he was wrong as he died. He had thought he had so arranged matters that the men responsible for the rape and murder of the woman he adored had finally paid for their crimes – when all he actually managed to do was to help protect the guilty man.

He took the pot of ale out to Alice and stood beside her while she sipped the warm brew. She was thin, terribly thin, but he was ensuring that she ate and drank enough to keep body and soul together. He had been well trained in that during the last weeks of his master's life.

She finished the drink and without looking up, passed him the pot. He took it, and as he did so, their fingers touched. Only for a moment, and then the contact was broken, but when he turned to go inside, he heard a sob, and stopped. Her hand grabbed for his belt and she pulled him to her, and for the first time since Adam's death, Moses heard her weep for her brother and husband as she clung to him.

He had the pot in one hand, and the other hovered over her back and head – she was his brother's widow, in Christ's name – and then he crouched at her side and put his arms around her.

And from that day, she began to improve.

Epilogue

Rob was happy enough to go and watch the ships at every opportunity when his master would let him, or when Simon was away and he could spend his time more as he wanted. The sea held a particular fascination for him, and he liked to come to the jetty and watch the lighters rowing out to the great vessels in the haven.

It appealed to him, the idea of floating away from here, the sails filled with the wind, men sitting and lazing in the sun as the boat did all the work. Oh, yes. Rob knew all about sailing. The only hard work was when you arrived in a port and had to get the ship emptied and refilled with all the goods, but apart from that, all the work was easy. You sailed during the day, and when it grew dark, you stopped and slept. A life sailor's was a good one, so far as Rob could see.

Of course there were some, like that old woman Stephen, who tried to warn him that ships were filled with men who had unhealthy interests in young boys, but Rob knew that was rubbish. He had a little knife in a sheath about his neck anyway, and if some matelot tried anything nasty, he'd soon see the filthy sod off. He wasn't scared of anyone. Bailiff Puttock had also told him not to get involved in the sea, but that was just because the big lummock got seasick stepping over a puddle. Hopeless. No, it was the sea for Rob. Without a doubt the best way for him to earn a living.

One morning, he had had enough. He had risen as early as he could, and it wasn't his fault that he was a little late to his master's house. With all the complaints, you'd have thought he never bothered to turn up at all. He lit the fire immediately he got in, anyway, and that was all he was supposed to do. Light the fire, get some water heating, and warm up some food if there was anything. Well, there wasn't that morning. He couldn't help it, he had forgotten to buy anything the night before. He'd been on his way to the baker's shop when an older seaman had offered to buy him an ale in the Porpoise, and he'd left there much later feeling a little wobbly.

But the Bailiff didn't accept any of his reasons for the lateness of his start, and to be honest, Rob didn't give a clipped ha'penny. Not now. He had friends on a ship, and he was going to go out and join them. He'd bet there was a place on a ship for him: all he had to do was ask. He was strong and fit. It'd be a piece of piss.

It took him only a little time to find his friend from the night before. The man was a great barrel-chested, black-haired giant with one eye and a mouth devoid of teeth on one side, where another man had hit him with a stool in a brawl.

'I want to be a sailor,' Rob told him eagerly.

The men with the giant looked rather taken aback. One laughed, but two others eyed him speculatively. The giant bent down and peered at him more closely with his single eye. 'Why?' he asked simply.

'Because I don't want to have to work so hard. I have to get up with the dawn now, and clean the house all day, and cook . . .'

He trailed off as all the men began to laugh.

One asked, 'Do you get to sleep through the night?'

'Do you get thrown out into the rain when the weather's bad?'

'Have you ever been whipped with a leather belt for being slow to run up a rope?'

Rob looked from one to the other, then back to the giant. 'I want to be a sailor,' he repeated.

'You do?' The giant took him by the shoulder. They were not far from the Ropery, a long building in which the hempen strands were twisted and joined to create long cables. Outside was a tall flagpole as advertisement. A long rope dangled from the top, thirty feet overhead. 'Climb that.'

'Me?' Rob squeaked, staring up at the flag fluttering from the top.

'Go on!'

'I can't climb that, it's too high!'

'Come back again when you can,' the man said, and returned to his friends, laughing.

Rob looked up at the flag again. 'No one can do that!'

The oldest, greyest man strolled over and stood beside Rob. He looked down at the lad with a sorrowful expression. Then he sprang up lightly, gripped the wooden pole with his hands, crossed his shins about the wood, and quickly slithered his way up it to the very top. Once there, he kept on rising until he was sitting on the topmost button.

Rob didn't wait to see him return to the ground. He walked homewards, disconsolate. At Simon's house, he looked about him in the small parlour and began to re-lay the fire, throwing a faggot on top and wondering whether he'd ever be able to go to sea.

As luck would have it, that afternoon and evening there was a foul thunderstorm. Rob remained in the house while it raged, and Bailiff Puttock spoke of another storm he had known. He had been off the Islands south and west, when the storm struck, and the ship had almost foundered on rocks. He had been miraculously lucky to survive.

In his mind's eye, Rob had a vivid picture: a ship with shredded sails, rolling and slipping towards rocks. The waves crested over the green/black shapes, exploding upwards as the ship moved towards them. And Rob saw a face at the prow, a face full of terror as he screamed the danger to the crew. It was his own face he saw.

And in that moment Rob decided he would prefer to remain on land.

Of all those who survived the murders of Dartmouth's terrible September 1324, Peter Strete, disgraced clerk to the powerful John Hawley, was the most fortunate.

His injuries were a long while in the mending. However, when he could move again, and his eyes had healed and re-opened, the Bailiff had him taken to the monastery at Buckfast for convalescence. There he gradually healed, under the careful nursing of the Brother Almoner, until at last he could walk unaided.

The Brother Almoner was a quiet, kindly old soul. When Strete gradually came to speak to him, and mentioned his tribulations in the gaming dens of Dartmouth, the old man cackled himself into a coughing fit.

'I suppose they preferred games of chance, like those with dice? Hazard or somesuch?'

'Many dice games, yes,' Strete admitted. 'But they are safe, because they depend upon chance. That is as fair as any man could hope for.'

'Unless the dice were marked, or had a little hole drilled in them so that a bit of quicksilver could be dripped in, and the hole filled. Then you only have to tap the dice once or twice to change the fortune of the thrower. A man can fleece another with ease like that. Dear oh dear. They must have taken all you had!'

Strete pondered that. They had beaten him cruelly for not paying them the debt which they had made him incur because they had used unfair dice. He had never heard of such a thing before. 'They could have killed me for cheating me!' he exclaimed. What a fool he had been.

'Aye. They wouldn't want someone else in town to hear that they'd let a man off too lightly when he owed them money, Peter. No, I think you're much better off away from them. Where will you go now?'

Strete felt a great wash of enthusiasm. 'I shall go to Exeter,' he declared.

In Exeter, he knew, there were manufacturers of dice. With a little advance on his first winnings, he was sure that a man could be persuaded to make a special set for him.

'What are we?'

'No, Al, not again!'

'Come on! What are we?'

'I said no, Al. I'm not having it!'

'What are we?'

'Shit, Al, since you ask, we're cold, we're wet, we're without a job since Dartmouth took so bleeding long, and we're footsore and weary and pissed off. All right?'

There was a moment's silence, and then a new voice: 'Cor! Did you see *her*? She was looking at me, she was! Do you think if I was to go and—'

'Shut up, Law!'

'Once you've got a beard, boy, you can think about girls like that.'

'Just because you couldn't get a girl like that, Bill.'

'What did you say, you young tyke?'

'I said, old man, that you couldn't hope to attract a girl like her. She wants young and fit like me!'

'I think she'd prefer a man with brains, lad. Someone like me.'

'So, come on, boys! We don't mind a little rain, do we? No, because we're bleeding paviours, that's why!'

In unison the other two voices rose:

'Al, will you shut *up*!'

And Alred smiled to himself under his cowl because when the two were bickering like this, all was right in his world. It was only when they sulked quietly that he worried.

For now he had not a worry in the world.